Marion Lennox has written over one hundred romance novels, and is published in over one hundred countries and thirty languages. Her international awards include the prestigious RITA® Award—twice!—and the *RT Book Reviews* Career Achievement Award for 'a body of work which makes us laugh and teaches us about love'. Marion adores her family, her kayak, her dog, and lying on the beach with a book someone else has written. Heaven!

Three-times Golden Heart® Award finalist **Tina Beckett** learned to pack her suitcases almost before she learned to read. Born to a military family, she has lived in the United States, Puerto Rico, Portugal and Brazil. In addition to travelling, Tina loves to cuddle with her pug, Alex, spend time with her family, and hit the trails on her horse. Learn more about Tina from her website, or 'friend' her on Facebook.

Also by Marion Lennox

Finding His Wife, Finding a Son
English Lord on Her Doorstep
The Baby They Longed For
Cinderella and the Billionaire
Second Chance with Her Island Doc
Rescued by the Single Dad Doc

Also by Tina Beckett

One Night to Change Their Lives
The Surgeon's Surprise Baby
A Family to Heal His Heart
A Christmas Kiss with Her Ex-Army Doc
Miracle Baby for the Midwife
One Hot Night with Dr Cardoza

Discover more at millsandboon.co.uk.

PREGNANT MIDWIFE ON HIS DOORSTEP

MARION LENNOX

RISKING IT ALL FOR THE CHILDREN'S DOC

TINA BECKETT

MILLS & BOON

First Published in Great Britain 2020
by Mills & Boon, an imprint of HarperCollins*Publishers*
1 London Bridge Street, London, SE1 9GF

Pregnant Midwife on His Doorstep © 2020 Marion Lennox

Risking It All for the Children's Doc © 2020 Tina Beckett

ISBN: 978-0-263-27977-1

MIX
Paper from
responsible sources
FSC™ C007454

This book is produced from independently certified FSC™ paper
to ensure responsible forest management.
For more information visit www.harpercollins.co.uk/green.

Printed and bound in Spain
by CPI, Barcelona

PREGNANT MIDWIFE
ON HIS DOORSTEP

MARION LENNOX

MILLS & BOON

With thanks to the wonderful Kate Hicks,
who delivered Maisie's puppies with skill and friendship.

CHAPTER ONE

HIS NEIGHBOUR MUST be evacuating her dog—but this late?

Dr Josh O'Connor had been watching the forecast for the last twenty-four hours. Cyclone Alma was supposed to stay well north of Camel Island, but the weather was building to extreme. When the radio broadcaster had said, 'An unpredicted change has the eye of the storm veering south,' Josh had started to have serious qualms. Should he leave?

But he'd looked through his sturdy double-glazed windows and seen the heaving sea, he'd thought of the rickety bridge across to the mainland and he'd decided it'd be safer to hunker down. His house was new, long, low, solid and set on the lee side of the island. Heavy shutters provided protection. He had plenty of provisions. The storm might cut him off from the mainland for a few days but he'd be fine.

But what about the others? He barely knew the residents of the only two other houses on this remote island, but he knew enough to worry. By mid-afternoon, with the change in weather prediction, he'd tried to contact them.

The house on the far side of the island was occupied by a couple of artists and their kids, and his phone call had made him feel like he was overreacting. 'We'll be right, mate,' Mick Forde had told him. 'Skye and me have seen storms like this before. It'll give us something to paint. We're staying.' Josh had thought of their ramshackle cottage with misgivings but there was nothing he could do in the face of their intransigence.

The only other house was on his side of the island, owned by the very elderly Moira Byrne. She was a loner. When Josh had first arrived and introduced himself, she'd been curt to the point of rudeness.

'If you think we're going to play happy neighbours think again. I bought this place because of its isolation and that's the way I like it. Keep out of my way and I'll keep out of yours.'

He had, though her frailty and solitude had him concerned. Once a week she drove her ancient white sedan across the bridge, presumably heading to the town on the mainland for supplies. Occasionally a little red car arrived and someone stayed for a few hours, but whoever it was kept to themselves as well. The driver of the red car seemed to be Miss Byrne's only personal contact, but Josh was the last person to want to encroach on her solitude.

But this afternoon he'd been uneasy enough to intrude. Her phone had rung out so he'd battled his way over there. He'd heard a dog whining inside but there'd been no other response to repeated knocking. The house and garage were locked, curtained, shuttered.

He'd stood on her doorstep in the rising wind and decided she must have headed to the mainland because of the storm. He wished he could see inside the garage to confirm her car wasn't there, but he imagined her staying in a mainland motel overnight, where a dog wouldn't be welcome. She must have locked her dog inside to be safe.

There was a dog flap set in the back door. The dog could come outside if it wanted to, but it obviously wasn't interested enough in Josh's knocking or calling to investigate. Fair enough, Josh decided, thinking of his own dog's fear of storms. He'd check again in the morning but he could do no more. He'd headed home, hunkered down in his office and immersed himself in his work.

Technology's role in medicine had always fascinated him, and the use of external robotic skeletons in the hope of restoring function to patients with spinal damage had become his passion. After his own accident it had been easy enough to leave hands-on testing to his staff. Retreating to the complexities of techno-science, he led his team from the seclusion of his office. He drove to the city when he was most needed. He attended overseas conferences, but otherwise he worked alone.

The project he was working on was vital and enthralling, but it wasn't enough to block out the storm. Dudley—the misbegotten mutt he'd been landed with when he'd bought this place—didn't help. He was cowering under Jock's office chair in what Josh imagined was the doggy equivalent of the foetal position, and his whimpers were getting louder.

'It's okay, boy,' he told him, but Dudley looked at him as if he was a sandwich short of a picnic and went back to whimpering.

By dusk the phone lines were out and his generator had cut in to augment battery storage from his solar power. This place was designed for self-sufficiency. Josh had power for refrigeration and lights, a slow combustion stove providing central heating and hot water, plus enough driftwood to keep both the stove and the open fire in the living room lit for months. He had a pantry and freezer full of supplies. His very expensive satellite dish was still giving him connectivity to the outside world if he needed it. Dudley might be worried, but he wasn't.

'Let's cook some dinner,' he told him.

Dudley was still looking at him as if he was nuts. He was under Josh's chair and he was staying there.

'Wuss,' Josh told him, but got down on his hands and knees and started scratching Dudley's ears. Dudley just whimpered.

Okay, he'd bring out the big guns—Dudley's favourite thing in the whole world. Josh lay on his back, patted his chest and waited.

His strategy worked. The scrawny kelpie gave a final worried whine, but this was a ruse Josh had used since he'd found the half-starved, flea-ridden mutt when he'd moved here. The anxiety-ridden dog could never resist. Now he inched forward from under the chair, then slithered cautiously up onto Josh's chest. Josh rubbed Dudley's spine in the way dogs the world over loved, and hugged him tight.

Which worked both ways. Josh might be self-reliant, he conceded, but the storm was a big one and he wasn't completely impervious to it. A hug from a dog was okay.

'We're both wusses,' he told Dudley, and Dudley signified his solidarity with a lick from throat to chin. *Bleah.*

'Dinner,' Josh said, grinning as he wiped away spit. Dudley heaved a resigned sigh that said he ought to worry more about the storm but maybe he'd put dinner first. Josh hugged him again, then headed to the kitchen, with Dudley slinking cautiously after him. He filled Dudley's bowl with kibble, then decided to check outside. He'd closed the shutters this afternoon, making it impossible to see through the windows, but now he cautiously opened the back door.

Josh's house, made of stone and hunkered among a couple of rocky outcrops, still seemed solidly safe, but outside seemed just plain scary. The wind was screaming. Debris was blasting against the walls. Josh's instinct was to close the door fast—but then he paused. There were car lights heading along the track from Moira's house, down toward the bridge.

Had Moira had second thoughts and come back for her dog? He hadn't seen her return, but then his windows had been shuttered. She must have come back, collected her dog and decided to retreat again.

Across the bridge? His vague worries about his elderly neighbour suddenly coalesced into fear.

He'd had qualms about the bridge when he'd bought this place, but a call to the local council had reassured him. An unmanned but essential lighthouse on the far side of the island meant the bridge always had to stay connected. Council had budgeted for a rebuild in the next financial year.

But this wasn't the next financial year, and no one had predicted a cyclone this far south. There'd be waves smashing against the pilings, and Josh had seen the ancient timbers creak and sway in the last storm. Which hadn't been as bad as this.

Now he was watching the car lights head toward it, and he found he'd forgotten to breathe.

He was overreacting, he told himself. The bridge had withstood weather for decades and it'd take the car less than a minute to cross.

For a moment a car's headlights illuminated the timbers as the car slowed. Moira had obviously paused to assess the situation.

The decision was made. The headlights inched forward, onto the bridge itself.

And then lurched violently and disappeared.

'Hell.'

And that was the least of the swear words he uttered as he hauled on his boots and headed through the internal door to the garage. He hit the remote on the doors, the wind blasted in—and seconds later he was out in the teeth of the storm.

At least his truck was sturdy. He'd bought it because it was tough, because he valued the ease of driving along the rough tracks to the island's isolated beaches. Now he valued its sheer weight.

He thought of Moira's tiny sedan. No one should be driving in these conditions, and the swerve of those lights... They'd pointed upwards and then disappeared.

He was gunning down the track like a madman. If the bridge had gone... If Moira's car had crashed into the sea...

There'd be nothing he could do. He knew it even before he reached the bridge. The channel across to the mainland was deep and fast flowing. This side of the island was in the lee of the storm but even so, the waves would be crashing through with force. A tiny car, submerged...

He needed help.

He didn't have it.

The phone lines and cell-phone connectivity had failed hours ago. With self-sufficiency in mind—and because he relied on video conferencing for his work—Josh had paid the horrendous price for satellite connection, but anyone in that water would be dead long before outside assistance could arrive.

He reached the bridge—or what was left of it. His headlights lit the scene and he saw a storm-washed wreck.

The bridge had crashed, its timbers now a jumbled mass, tilted sideways into the sea, already separating and being washed away.

A car was in that jumble.

It was still on this side, though, in the water but only just. The bridge must have crumbled almost as soon as it was fully on its timbers.

And it wasn't Moira's car. Moira's car was white. This was a tiny, indeterminate red thing. The car he'd seen occasionally visit.

And whoever was in it was in dire trouble. Its bonnet was almost submerged. Timbers were all around it and waves were thumping the wood. The car was slewing sideways...

He was out of his truck before he knew it, plunging down the bank, around the mass of loose planking, leaving his headlights playing the scene.

A massive plank was wedged against the driver's door. It was being shoved by more timbers. The car was being pushed further in.

He could see a face at the driver's window. A woman's face, framed by a mass of copper-red curls. A mask of terror.

He couldn't get to her.

He stopped for a millisecond, giving himself time to evaluate. Training kicked in. From the moment he'd enrolled in medical school, procedure had been drilled in, over and over. No matter what the emergency, assess the whole situation before acting.

This must be the world record for speed assessment, but it was worthwhile. The waves were hammering the plank against the car so strongly it'd be useless to try to reach the driver's door and attempt to pull it away. He couldn't do it. But the plank was angled, and the biggest force of the waves would be at the front of the car, where the water was deepest.

It felt counterintuitive but he backed away, further up the bank from the driver's door, to the far end of the plank holding the door.

Could he? He had no choice. He got behind the end of the plank, trying to brace himself against the water, against the blasting wind. He pushed with all his might.

The force of the water at the other end was now his friend. He could feel the timber tremble, then shift…

And suddenly move. The plank was suddenly caught by the current, tumbling out to midstream to be tossed away to the sea.

That left the little car without the plank's protection from the waves, but at least it wasn't wedging the door closed.

He surged in and grabbed the door handle. The woman inside was obviously pushing. He pulled—no, he hauled. The water was holding it shut, but with their combined strength the door finally opened. He shoved it back against the water's force, made his body a wedge to stop it slamming shut again and reached in.

The woman was struggling. She was youngish. Soaked. Small but bulky. Terrified.

He grabbed her, hauled her out to him, steadied her.

'Is there anyone else in the car?' He was yelling but the wind was tossing his words to oblivion. He put his mouth hard against her ear. 'Is Moira in there?'

'No. But her dog's in there.' Her yell was fear-filled, loud enough to be heard. 'On the back seat.'

'No one else. Sure?'

'Just the dog.' She was pushing against him, struggling to reach the back door handle.

His first instinct was to fight her, to simply drag her up the bank and get her safe, but she'd already grabbed the handle. If they were hit by another of the timbers...

But they had this moment. There was a chance...

He had his arm around her, and her bulky midriff helped, making their combined bodies a barrier against the water's force.

'Pull,' he yelled, and she tugged. The door swung wide and the surging water held it open.

But with both doors open, the car was starting to move.

'She's on the seat,' the woman screamed, but Josh's priorities had suddenly changed. As he'd held her he'd realised her midriff wasn't the squishy waist of plumpness. It was the firm mound of pregnancy.

She was caught between two doors.

Triage kicked in. He hauled her away from the car, to shore and then up the bank, ignoring fierce, fiery protests. 'Get yourself safe,' he yelled. 'Are you nuts? Your baby... Get into my truck!'

'The dog...'

'Now!' he yelled, and she relented, allowing herself to be shoved to safety. But on the bank, instead of heading to the truck, she turned back to him with anguish.

'The dog...' she screamed. 'Maisie... Please...'

He looked back, torn. The car's bonnet was starting to swerve downstream. He had milliseconds.

He lunged back into the water, reaching the car

again, groping into the back seat, knowing his chances were tiny.

His hands met a great lump of wet fur. Limp. Injured?

The car shuddered and moved.

Somehow he had her, by collar, by scruff. She came free with a rush, and he staggered and almost fell.

Another wave crashed into his legs. He went down to his waist in the water, but held position, held dog.

The car shifted more, slewing sideways. His arms were full of dog. He was struggling to find his feet.

And then the woman was back, staggering into the wash, grabbing his arm. 'Let me help.'

'Get back.'

'No. Move!'

She didn't release his arm. She was hauling him toward the bank and her extra force helped. Somehow he was on his feet. She was holding him, tugging.

And then they were staggering out of the water, surging upwards, not stopping until they were up the bank, not stopping until they collapsed in a sodden heap against his truck, safe from the wind.

As if on cue, there was a crash of timbers. In the beam of his headlights they watched another plank smash against the car.

The car rolled and tumbled and disappeared in the wash of white water.

And was gone.

For a moment neither of them spoke. Josh was having trouble breathing. Maybe he'd forgotten how. He sat slumped against the truck, his arms full of dog, feeling…gutted.

Unbidden, the thought came back of another accident, three years back. Of sitting just like this, waiting for the ambulance. Of hopelessness. Of despair.

'Thank you.'

The woman's voice cut across his thoughts, dragging him out of his nightmare. He thought of her trapped in the car as the water rose. Of her terror. He could feel the blackness...

Get over yourself, he told himself fiercely. This is a happy ending. Nothing like last time.

It was almost still in the lee provided by the truck, though maybe that was just comparative. It was quiet compared to the blast of wind in the open. Just standing was hard. How had they managed to do what they'd done?

'What the hell were you doing, trying to cross the bridge?' he snapped. Emotions were coalescing into a wave of anger. He saw her flinch, and hauled back himself.

'Sorry. We're safe. Explain later. Where's Moira?' She'd come from Moira's house. He'd expected Moira to be in the car. Why else would she be here but to take Moira to safety? But if Moira had already left... Had Moira sent her to fetch her dog?

'Moira's dead.' Her voice was flat, no inflection, leaving no doubts. Shocking.

'What the...?'

But if he was shocked, soaked, bruised, how much more so was this woman? The headlights weren't much use this far around the car but there was enough light for an impression. The woman was...youngish? She had coppery red hair, curls dripping to her shoulders. Not tall. Not plump either, as he'd first thought. She was wearing pants and a loose top, which was now clinging wetly. She looked very pregnant.

He needed to bundle her back to the house and get her warm. There was also the issue of a limp dog. Injured?

But triage... Moira. Dead?

'Explain,' he said, curtly. If Moira really was dead there was nothing he could do, but he'd heard enough anguished screaming from relatives during his medical career... 'He's dead, Doctor...' to know the diagnosis wasn't always right.

But she must have heard his doubt because it was addressed straight away.

'I'm a nurse,' the woman managed, and he heard the strong lilt of an Irish accent. 'I'm a midwife but I know death when I see it. Moira's my great-aunt. She's a loner, and she hates me coming, but she has a heart condition so I visit when I can, like it or not. When I heard the forecast I rang to ask her to evacuate. She told me where to go. Then this afternoon she rang me back, in a state. She sounded terrified, gaspy. She wasn't feeling well and asked if I could come. I suggested an ambulance but she snapped my head off. So I came. She... she was sitting by the kitchen fire, the dog at her feet. Almost peaceful. It took me two hours to get here but by the look of things I suspect she'd been dead for almost that long.'

'I'm so sorry.' It seemed appallingly inadequate.

'I hardly knew her.' Her voice was almost a whisper. 'But she was all the family I had.'

He thought suddenly of his dog, of fear and of the need for the contact of another living thing. There was so much bleakness in this woman's voice.

Triage. Sympathy would have to come later.

He rose and heaved the dog into the back seat. For the life of him he couldn't see what was wrong with her.

She was a golden Labrador, fat, heavy, limp. She raised her head a little as he moved her, her huge brown eyes meeting his. Had she been struck by timbers? It didn't make sense, but what did make sense was getting them all out of this weather.

With the dog in the back seat he half lifted the woman to her feet and helped her into the passenger seat. Then he headed for the driver's side, which was no mean feat when that was the weather side.

The wind was still rising. If it got any stronger... He blocked the thought as he headed home. Home, with its remote-control garage doors, with its heat, with its safety.

'Where are we going?' the woman managed.

'To my place. The house you can see from Moira's.'

'But it's empty!' She said it almost as an accusation. 'Moira has your phone number on the fridge. I told her to ring you, but she said she couldn't. When I got here I looked across and there wasn't a light on. You think I would have tried to cross the bridge if I'd known I could get help there?' Her teeth were chattering so hard she could hardly get the words out, but indignation came through, loud and strong.

'I'm very sorry,' he said and he meant it. 'I shuttered the place down at lunchtime. I also tried to check on Moira but no one answered my knock. That's Moira through and through, though. I should have left a light on.'

'It might have been helpful.'

'It might.' He hesitated. 'You didn't think to stay at Moira's until the morning?'

'She's dead.'

'I get that, but—'

'But I didn't want to stay with my dead great-aunt.'

Her indignation was still there. 'It felt like I had to let someone know, and I didn't know the bridge was going to crash. And the forecast says it'll get worse before it gets better. And then there's Maisie…'

'Maisie?'

'The dog. She's in trouble.' She glanced into the darkness of the back seat and indignation faded. 'I… Moira says…said…you're a doctor. Do you know anything about delivering puppies?'

'Delivering puppies…'

'Obstructed labour,' she said briefly, and her voice faltered, shock and stress flooding back. 'I'm sorry,' she said after a moment. 'I'm not…at my best. And I'm a midwife but I know nothing about labour in dogs. I could feel contractions half an hour ago, but they were getting weaker and so was she. The phone connection seems to be dead so I couldn't phone a vet. I couldn't get onto the internet to find out what I might be able to do and she's going to die and she's a lovely dog. And Moira's dead, which makes me feel sick to my stomach. And I'm freezing and I'm eight months pregnant and I'm scared. I *was* terrified. Thanks to you, I'm not any more but I'm still scared.' She took a deep breath, fighting against hysteria, and decided on indignation instead. 'And you should have put your outside light on.'

'I'm very sorry,' he said again.

'Thank you.' She took another breath and he could almost hear her gritting her teeth. 'If I were a heroine in a romance novel I'd have disintegrated into hysterics by now and left this whole mess to a knight on a white charger. But I needed him two hours ago. Now I'm over it. I don't know you from Adam but you've done all right so far, and I'm grateful. You're all I have in the knight on a white charger department, so please keep right on rescuing. Maisie's depending on you. I'm depending on you. You're all we have.'

And she put her face in her hands, gave one fierce sob and subsided.

CHAPTER TWO

SHE DIDN'T DISSOLVE into hysterics. She allowed herself
that one, single sob and then she hauled herself together.

Somehow.

At least she hadn't been swept out to sea. How many
times had she struggled for silver linings over the last
few months? She was fighting for one now. Not being
swept out to sea had to be close.

Oh, but she was cold.

But she was safe. This truck was built for toughness
rather than style, but its engine sounded reassuringly
powerful and it beavered its way along the track as if
the storm wasn't trying its best to shove it backwards.

And the man beside her…

He looked as tough as his truck, she thought.

He was tall and broad and the hands on the steer-
ing wheel looked weathered, large, capable. His mouth
was set in a grim line and his deep eyes were focused
fiercely on the track ahead.

There seemed to be a scar running across his forehead, around his left eye to the base of his ear. It added
to the aura of toughness. The impression she had was
of strength, competence and certainty.

His ancient sweater was soaked and streaming water.
His deep black hair was plastered across his fore-

head but the soaking just seemed to add to his aura of strength.

A knight on a white charger? Maybe not, but give her a hero with a serviceable truck any day. The thought made her hiccup on something between a laugh and a sob and he glanced at her sharply before returning his attention to the track.

'Don't you dare.'

'What?'

'Swoon or have hysterics.'

She almost managed a smile. 'Sorry. I didn't mean it.' Her teeth were chattering so hard it was almost impossible to speak but she forced herself to go on. 'If the books I've read are any indication of the remedies for either, isn't it a bucket of cold water? I've just copped an ocean.'

She saw his grim mouth relax a little. Half a smile?

She could see a light ahead—he must have finally put an outside light on. The sight was infinitely reassuring.

She needed this man's help. She needed to make herself sound sensible.

'I'm Hannah Byrne,' she told him. 'I'm a midwife, working at North Queensland Regional Hospital, and if the sticky note on Moira's fridge is to believed, you're Josh O'Connor. A doctor. Doctor of medicine?'

'Yes,' he said curtly. 'I insisted Moira keep my details. It would have been a sight more useful if she'd phoned me rather than a niece two hours' drive away. Two hours ago the lines were open. I could have been there in five minutes.'

'It would have nearly killed her to phone even me,' she said, and faltered. 'I guess...it did kill her.'

'Her stubbornness killed her,' he said bluntly. 'She

knew I was home. If she managed to ring you she could have rung me.'

'Maybe dying at home's what she wanted anyway,' Hannah said softly. 'She would have hated hospital. All those people… She can't…couldn't stand people. I think she only rang me because she was frightened about Maisie. She was old and she was ill. I can't… I can't grieve.'

'You *are* grieving,' he said matter-of-factly, and she closed her eyes.

'I guess…for what could have been.' She hauled herself together again. 'But today… She obviously didn't feel well enough to drive Maisie to the vet, but I suspect it would have killed her to contact you. A stranger. A man…'

Her voice trailed off as she thought of the old woman as she'd last seen her, slumped by the fireside in death, her hand trailing down to touch her dog by her side.

But then they were at the house. Josh flicked the remote and the garage door slipped up seamlessly. The inside light went on automatically and Hannah blinked in the shock of unexpected light.

'You have power.'

'Solar power augmented by batteries and a generator.'

'Oh, my.' She took a deep breath. 'And phone?

'Normal coverage seems to have been cut but I have a satellite.'

'A satellite phone? You can call for help?'

'I doubt help would be forthcoming,' he said, driving into the garage. 'Not in this storm. The latest forecast is for the cyclone's eye to pass within a hundred kilometres. This is going to get worse before it gets better.'

But as the garage door slid quietly down behind them the noise from the wind cut off. Just like that.

She was sitting in a silent, well-lit garage. With no storm.

Safe.

Maisie. She turned to look into the back seat. The big dog was still with them. She was looking at her with those huge eyes. Dependent.

Josh was right, though. There was no way they could call for evacuation for a dog.

Or for a great-aunt who'd died from natural causes.

She'd been shaking before but suddenly, weirdly, the shakes grew worse. Shock, fear, worry, and reaction from everything that had gone before was suddenly overwhelming. Her body seemed a trembling mess. She put her hands on either side of the seat and held on, trying to ground herself, trying to haul herself together.

But then Josh was around her side of the truck, and before she knew what he was about he'd lifted her out bodily.

'What...?' Her voice came out as an unidentifiable squeak. 'Put me down. I'm okay.'

'You're not okay,' he said, striding with her across the garage. Somehow he edged the door open, carrying into the house, lowering her a little to brush light switches on as he went.

She had a first impression of solidity, of stone floors, massive beams, of comfort. They entered the living room and she saw a fire in the hearth blazing with heat. She saw two great settees, club style, squishy, and a massive crimson rug.

A lanky, brown and black kelpie-like dog had been lying by the fire. He launched himself toward them, his skinny tail spinning like a gyrocopter. 'Back,' Josh ordered, and the spinning tail was instantly tucked between his legs. The dog cast Josh a look of deep reproach and retired back to the fire.

But Josh didn't pause. He was through the living room and out the other side, down the passage.

She felt warmth as they went. Central heating? Gorgeous.

Josh was pushing another door open. A bathroom. A wide, open shower. A bath.

A bath!

'A bath will be safer than a shower,' Josh suggested. Before she could respond he lowered her onto a stool and hit the taps. A gush of water streamed out, creating glorious steam. 'Otherwise I'll have to hold you up in the shower.' But then the impetus stopped. He knelt beside her and gripped her hands, his dark eyes meeting hers in concern. Professional concern? 'Hannah, tell me. Are you hurt in any way? Did you get hit when the car was swept down?'

Suddenly he'd turned into a doctor. Up until now he'd been a rescuer, a stranger with strength when she'd needed it. Now there was professional incisiveness.

'I… No.'

'Did you have your seat belt on?'

'Yes, but…'

'Can you feel your baby? Any movements?'

'I think so.' She faltered. Her hand went to her swollen abdomen. 'In the truck… I felt her kick. I'm sure…'

'Would you let me check? If it's okay with you I need to listen to make sure she's okay. I have a stethoscope.'

'You really are a doctor?'

'I am,' he told her. 'A neurosurgeon—not that that's any help now. But my med training included Babies for Beginners. Will you let me examine you?'

'I... Yes. Of course.'

'Can you pull that sweater off while I fetch my gear? Or can I help?'

'I can... I can do it.'

'Back in ten seconds,' he told her, and slipped out of the room.

She tugged off her soaked sweater. The relief as its soaked, heavy weight disappeared was indescribable. Then her bra... There was a qualm, but she made it short. *Sod it, he's a doctor,* she told herself. He'd have seen worse things come out of cheese. She looked at the bath, which was already a quarter full. Gently steaming.

Irresistible.

He was a doctor. She could play the patient.

She kicked off her sneakers and tugged away her saturated pants. She left on her knickers—he might be a doctor but a girl had some standards—and she couldn't wait a moment longer. She lowered herself into the heavenly, heavenly water.

He walked back in and she was in the bath.

Almost naked.

Steam was rising around her. Her damp, copper-red curls were dripping in tendrils to her shoulders. She was cupping the warm water to her face, and he could almost feel her relief as the heat made contact with her skin.

She was Irish. He'd heard it in her voice and he saw it now on her skin. Irish complexion, porcelain white, smooth, flawless. Her breasts were full, beautiful. Her figure—probably diminutive before—was gorgeously rounded with pregnancy. As her hands dropped from her face she looked up at him and he saw details for the first time. Green eyes, wide and clear. A generous

mouth and firm chin. A snub nose and a smattering
of freckles.

'Stuff modesty, this is irresistible,' she told him, and
managed to smile. He could still hear the shake behind
her voice but there was no doubting the courage behind the words.

This was a woman who'd driven for two hours in
filthy weather to check on a great-aunt who didn't like
her. A woman who'd risked her life to save a dog.

Who was looking up at him now, almost naked,
beautiful...

Trusting.

Because he was a doctor, he told himself harshly.
That was why she trusted him. It was amazing what a
medical degree conferred.

'Can you help Maisie?' she faltered, and he hauled
his thoughts away from her—or a little away from
her—and focused on priorities.

'She's still in the truck.'

'Josh...'

'If you're a nurse then you know the drill,' he said.
'People before animals.'

'I'm fine.'

'And your baby?' He hauled the stool up beside the
bath and fitted his stethoscope to his ears.

She subsided. He was right. She had been wearing
a seat belt and it would have tightened hard across her
belly as the car had lurched downwards. She felt another
flood of fear, this time almost overwhelming, but Josh
already had his 'scope on her belly. listening intently.

And then smiling.

'You want to listen?' he said, and moved the ear-
pieces to her.

She listened.

The warm water was still gushing into the bath. Any minute now her belly would be totally submerged. The warmth… The feel of Josh's hands as he fitted the 'scope into her ears… The *wush-wush* of her baby's strong, regular, wonderful, miraculous heartbeat…

She was suddenly stupidly, idiotically crying.

She didn't cry. She never cried. Not when Ryan had walked out on her. Not when her father had told her of the reception she'd get if she went home. Not once.

Now, though, the tears slipped down her face and she had no hope of stopping them. And then Josh was dipping a facecloth into the warm water and putting it into her hands, propelling it to her face. Asking gently, 'Where does is hurt?' and waiting with patience while she hauled herself together to say she was fine.

'You've been lucky, though I'm betting you'll ache in the morning. I can see bruises on your arms—that must have been from when you were trying to get out—and I'll bet you have others.' He had the stethoscope back and now he listened to *her* heart. 'Good,' he said. 'Mum and bub, hearts beating almost in sync. Lovely and strong.'

The relief was good. The relief was great.

'But Maisie,' she managed, because that's what her mad dash over the bridge had all been about.

'I'm going.' He motioned to the bars at the side of the bath. 'Use these if you need to get out.'

'Geriatric bars?' She almost had herself back together and was able to take in the bathroom. To say it was generous was the least of it. The shower was walk-in. The bath had innocuous silver rails running its length. The floor was lined with soft green rubber, unnoticeable unless you'd spent your career in hospitals and recognised hospital-grade non-slip surfaces.

'I live on my own and I'm not stupid,' Josh told her. 'They're not geriatric bars, they're sensible bars. If you knew how many injuries I've treated from people slipping in bathrooms… Use them, Hannah. Promise, or I need to stay here until you're out.'

'I'll use them.'

'Good girl.' He pulled fluffy white towels from a shelf running beneath the basin and hung them on what looked like a heated towel rail, and then motioned to a bathrobe hanging on the door.

'Use that if you need to get out before I return, but don't rush,' he told her. 'Don't let the water get any hotter than it is now.' He handed her a plastic jug from the same shelf. 'You might want to rinse your hair. Stay where you are until the shakes stop completely. I'll take care of Maisie.'

'Josh, this place…this equipment…you have everything.'

'I like to be prepared,' he told her, with the hint of a smile. 'Like your aunt, I value my independence and this place has been built to provide it.'

Then he stooped and touched her face, brushing the backs of his fingers gently across her cheek. It was a feather touch, no more. A touch of reassurance. 'You're safe now,' he said gently. 'You take care of you and your baby, and leave everything else to me.'

And he walked out.

She was alone. She was in Josh's care.

Involuntarily her fingers strayed to touch her cheek where his fingers had brushed.

There was no reason at all for her to put her hand where his fingers had brushed…as if it had been a gift beyond measure.

No reason at all.

* * *

Triage.

Dog.

Himself.

He was soaking and despite the warmth of the house he was starting to shake. If he'd been alone he'd be in the shower, enjoying the same hot water that was doing so much good to Hannah. But Hannah's dog was in trouble and she'd almost lost her life saving it. The dog had to come first.

Or almost first. He wasn't stupid and he could hardly function when he was sodden and freezing. He ditched his clothes, towelled himself dry and grabbed more pants, a sweater and thick socks. Then he headed back out through the living room. Dudley rose to greet him. With obvious reproach.

'Sorry, mate.' He bent to give him a swift hug. Dudley had been a bundle of nerves when he'd found him and this wind wasn't doing his nerves any good now. But Josh had a sick, wet dog in the car and the fireside was the obvious place to bring her.

'Needs must,' he said apologetically, and carried Dudley's basket into the laundry. He gave him a chew bone and an extra hug, then firmly closed the door. He knew Dudley would shake again but he couldn't help it.

Hannah's dog… Moira's dog…was still where he'd left her. When he pulled open the truck door she raised her head to looked at him, huge brown eyes almost pleading. Then her eyes filled with panic. Her sides heaved. He laid a hand on her sodden fur and felt it ripple with a contraction, then lose strength. The panic faded and her head fell back, all strength lost.

Trouble.

A layman would be able to sense that this dog was in

deep distress. Even the way she responded as he lifted her from the truck... He was a stranger, yet there was no hint of protest. Now the contraction was past, she was totally limp.

He carried her through to the living room and laid her in front of the fire. Then he grabbed an armload of towels from the laundry—which meant another apology to Dudley—and rubbed her. Her thick coat meant that getting her totally dry was impossible but he had to get her warm enough to prevent shock.

Or more shock.

As he towelled, her abdomen tightened again. Her tail was up, her rear distended.

The birth canal seemed to be slightly open but he could see no sign of a pup. In a human he could do a manual examination. In a dog?

Hannah had found her in trouble. She'd said she was a midwife and she'd have done her own assessment. If things had been progressing normally, she wouldn't have made the mad dash over the bridge. Maisie must have been like this for at least an hour, probably a lot longer. Since before Moira had called Hannah?

He knew nothing about dogs.

Internet. Thank heaven for satellite phones. He fetched his laptop, did a fast search and found enough to realise how dire Maisie's situation was.

'What's happening?'

He hadn't noticed Hannah's arrival. She was in the doorway, wrapped in his big, fleecy bathrobe. Her wet curls were tied up in a towel, with wisps of red escaping. She was staring worriedly down at Maisie.

'It has to be obstructed labour,' he said briefly.

'Yeah.' She crossed and sank beside her dog, who

whined a futile greeting and then went back to staring sightlessly at the pain within.

'I don't know what to do,' she told him. 'I tried to do an internal examination but there's no room. If there's a pup stuck it's still high in the birth canal. Too high to manoeuvre. Oh, Maisie...' Her voice broke.

'You love her?' It sounded harsh but he needed to know.

'No. Or maybe.' She shrugged. 'It's just... I've only been in Australia for a few months. Moira's my only relative here and she didn't want anything to do with me. But my Gran back home asked me to check on her, so I did, like it or not. Moira was never pleased to see me but even that first time Maisie was all joy to have a visitor. Every time I came Maisie's been greeting me like I was her new best friend. It sounds pathetic but she seems...more family than Moira was.'

He got it.

She did love this dog.

It made things more complicated.

'I need to phone a vet,' he told her.

'The phones don't work.'

'My satellite connection keeps mine working.'

That made her eyebrows hike. She sat back on her heels and stared at him, accusing. 'Really? Why didn't you give that number to Moira?'

'To ring someone on a satellite connection when normal coverage is out then you need a satellite phone yourself,' he said absently, still thinking of options. 'Moira only had a landline.' He frowned as she bent over the limp Maisie. Hannah herself was *very* pregnant. 'Hannah, your baby...you'd tell me if you were having contractions?'

'As if that'll happen,' she said, swiftly indignant. 'I

have at least four weeks to go and any baby of mine has more sense than to come now.'

He smiled and moved on. 'Good. Can you keep rubbing Maisie? I want her as dry as possible. I'll call the vet from the kitchen.'

'Won't any vet be hunkered down with the cyclone?'

'I have research friends all over the world,' he told her. 'Including veterinarians. I'll choose somewhere where it's daylight and sunny. Keep her as warm as you can while I find us some help.'

The easiest option with a dog this far gone, with its mistress dead, was one he could handle. There'd been a seal wounded on the rocks only weeks before, far too badly injured to recover. He'd figured what to do and he had the drugs to do it. But Hannah's face, and her words—'She seems more family'—had had an impact. There'd been real distress.

She'd almost lost her life trying to save Maisie. The least he could do was try.

Tom Edmonton, Melbourne based, was involved in the same research Josh was doing, though he'd been working with dogs with spinal damage. He listened to Josh's story and then gave his considered opinion.

'Josh, that's real trouble.'

'Tell me something I don't know.'

'Equipment? Drugs?'

'I have some. Tell me what I need.'

'I can't,' Tom admitted. 'I haven't coped with a pregnant bitch for years. But we have working vets in this building. Claire Chapter's one of our senior partners. I'll see if she's available.'

'Tom, I need help fast. We're running out of time.'

'And if she dies? Given what you've told me, you know that's the likely option.'

'Just put me through to Claire and let me try.'

CHAPTER THREE

HANNAH SAT BY Josh's wonderful fire, soaking in the warmth, listening to the wind howling outside, savouring the sensation of feeling safe—and agonising over the dog beside her.

Why was her heart so gutted because a dog was dying?

When she'd walked into Moira's house and found her aunt dead she'd felt grief for a life filled with bitterness, but she'd felt no deep wrench of her own heart. But Maisie…

She remembered the first time she'd met the dog. She'd just arrived in Australia. After three years of travelling, she and Ryan had found jobs at North Queensland Regional Hospital. She had a local great-aunt. To an increasingly homesick Hannah, the prospect of visiting Moira had seemed a little piece of home.

It hadn't worked out that way. Firstly Ryan had refused to come with her—*'Didn't we leave Ireland to escape family?'*—and then Moira had shown resentment at the intrusion and nothing else. Only Maisie had greeted her with joy.

Because Hannah had driven two hours to get to the island she'd been reluctant to leave straight away and said so. 'Can I take Maisie for a walk and check out the island?' she'd asked.

'Do what you like,' Moira had snapped. 'As long as you don't bother me. Stay away from the neighbours, too—I won't have you gossiping to anyone about me. Get her back before dark and then be off.'

So Hannah and Maisie had walked for a couple of hours, checking out the windswept wilderness of the island, with Maisie chasing sticks on the beach, racing like a crazy thing, running circles round and round Hannah, making her laugh. Then sitting beside her on the beach while Hannah felt comfort from her big, solid body. Over the ensuing visits, each one received just as coldly by Moira, Maisie had seemed to listen as Hannah had explained homesickness and Ryan's insistence that they weren't over wandering yet, and her increased doubts about a relationship she seemed to be holding onto by her fingernails...

It had been Maisie she'd spilled her heart to when Ryan had left. It was Maisie who'd listened after that last appalling phone call from her father.

Stupid, stupid, stupid.

And now, as she sat before Josh's fire, rubbing the dog's damp fur, she found her heart twisting with fear.

She needed this dog to live. Please...

And finally Josh was back, filling the doorway. He was a big guy, weathered, tanned. The scar on his face had been stitched well—maybe if he wasn't so tanned it wouldn't have been obvious. He was wearing faded jeans and an old Guernsey with frayed cuffs, rolled to the elbows to show muscled arms. His dark hair, still damp, seemed to have been cut short and then outgrown its cut. It looked tousled, as if he'd used fingers instead of a comb.

A doctor? He looked for all the world like a fisherman.

He tossed her a bundle of clothes. 'Jogging pants, socks and windcheater,' he told her. 'They'll be huge but they're the best I can do. If you're up to it…you said you're a nurse. I'll need your help.'

'What…'

'I can try for a Caesarean,' he told her. 'I've talked it through with someone who knows.' He knelt by Maisie and met her look head-on. 'Hannah, the vet I talked to… Claire…says after this time, and with the shock, chances are we'll lose her, but I'm willing to give it a try.'

She stared at him, stunned. 'Equipment? Drugs?'

'I told you, I'm a man who likes to be prepared. About two minutes after I moved onto this island a yacht came in too close and hit the rocks. One of the yachties broke his leg. Compound fracture. It was midnight and the two doctors over the bridge are elderly and don't do callouts. It took an ambulance two hours to get here. Meanwhile I didn't have the right gear to keep him out of pain, and I had to hurt him like hell to get the leg aligned to maintain blood supply to his foot. After that I applied for remote status and put together a kit that'll cope with most emergencies. Caesareans for dogs weren't on my list but Claire's done some fast research and I have gear she thinks I can use.'

'Can we?' It was hardly a whisper.

'Hannah, I don't know,' he said honestly. 'She's in a bad way already. The drugs I have all have the capacity to cross the placenta, which must compromise the pups. As well as that, prolonged labour prior to delivery causes maternal compromise. Claire tells me puppy mortality—even maternal mortality—has to be faced. But the only alternative is to put her down now.'

'No! Please.'

'Then I'll need help. Are you up for it?'

'Yes.'

He nodded, then lifted the big dog and turned toward the kitchen. 'Make-do operating theatre,' he told her briefly, and it was as if they were already a theatre team. 'Scrub at the kitchen sink. Two minutes, Nurse, stat.'

She was left to scramble into his clothes and turn into a professional.

He was a professional. Well, almost.

He'd hauled off his ancient sweater and put an apron over his T-shirt. It was white, with printed flames flickering up the sides. The caption read: *Caution: Extremely Hot.*

She blinked and he grinned.

'My older sister has a warped sense of humour.' The smile died. 'She lives in New York now and doesn't see me...as I am. Unsurprisingly it's never been used. I don't have scrubs so this'll have to do. I don't have another for you but the clothes I gave you are clean. There's antiseptic scrub at the sink, clean towels and disposable gloves.'

He motioned to Maisie, who was now lying limply on a sheet on the kitchen table. 'This is the best I can do as a theatre environment. Luckily the light's decent. I've injected morphine. She's far too passive already, but she's going to need analgesia as she comes out of anaesthesia.'

'Anaesthesia?' she queried. She, too, had moved into professional mode. In normal circumstances, on a guy like this, that apron would have her distracted to say the least, but the sight of Maisie lying helpless turned her from a soaked and a pregnant wuss into the nurse she was trained to be.

'I'm using propofol,' he told her.

'You have propofol?' General anaesthetic? In a doctor's bag?

'I told you, I'm ready for Armageddon here. Fixing my injured sailor wasn't pretty. I hoped that by getting my kit together I'd pretty much guarantee never to need it again, but here we are.'

She was thinking ahead, not liking what she was thinking. 'You'll need intubation.'

'I will, and that's where you come in. I have oxygen. I have intubation equipment. I don't have monitors, of course, so it'll be up to you to watch her like a hawk. Not that there's a lot I can do if her breathing fails but... well, let's just hope.'

He'd started working as he talked, rolling the almost limp dog onto her back, working with soapy water and a razor to shave her abdomen. He used slow, smooth strokes, as if he was trying to calm her rather than prepping for surgery. She wasn't reacting. The morphine must have kicked in fast, Hannah thought—or else Maisie was so far gone she couldn't react.

Either way, Josh was moving on, knowing his course.

'I'll also need help with the pups if there are any alive,' he told her. 'I've put towels in the oven, lowest setting with the door open. Claire says the foetal membrane should be removed and the umbilical cord clamped and severed. In a normal birth, the pup's chest is compressed, expelling fluid from the respiratory tract and stimulating the first breath. That doesn't work in a Caesarean so it's over to you. If it's not breathing then rub hard with clean towels to encourage respiration.

Claire says rubbing the hair backwards can help. I also have a suction bulb to clear mucus if you need it.'

Then he hesitated and his voice gentled. 'Hannah, you do need to be prepared for dead pups, though. Claire says after this time there's every chance we've lost them all. Also, we're looking at multiple births and there's only the two of us. I'm sorry, but we need to be harsh and fast in assessment, saving the fittest. You can't spend time on a pup that doesn't look viable if the next one I deliver looks like it has a better chance.'

She nodded, feeling ill. 'Got it.'

He'd tugged the table close to the kitchen bench and had already laid out equipment. She checked it fast. 'You *are* prepared.' Deep breath. 'If I'd known you were here and had this... If Moira had known...'

'Moira had every chance to ask for help,' he said, and she heard anger behind his words. 'She made bad decisions and you've been left with the consequences. That's what happens when people are—' He stopped, the anger she heard building cut off short. 'Enough. Are you ready?'

She did another fast visual of the equipment, then headed for the sink.

'Yes,' she told him, slipped seamlessly into the professional mode he'd assumed. The howling wind outside, the weird feeling of being in a domestic kitchen rather than a hospital theatre, the shock of the last few hours, even Josh's crazy apron...they all slipped away.

There was only a doctor, a nurse, and a patient and pups whose lives were in their hands.

She was good.

Professional assessment. Acceptance of limitations of equipment. Of limitations of themselves. Brief questions and then moving on. She helped him set up the IV for fluids without a question, and she moved fast.

She accepted how compromised he was and acted accordingly. The less time Maisie spent under anaesthetic the better her chances, and as for the puppies... they'd be struggling already. He wasn't going there.

He'd expected to help her with intubation but as he turned to help she motioned him away.

'Got it.'

Her voice was solid, grounded, practical, and he had a sudden sense that this woman would never promise what she couldn't deliver.

It was up to him.

Go.

Josh had performed Caesareans during surgical training—of course he had—but that was years ago, and a Caesar on a dog was a very different thing. He found himself thanking his stars that Maisie wasn't a mini-poodle or a chinchilla. At least a Labrador gave him space.

Claire's instructions were still echoing, listened to and held. 'I can stay on the line and talk you through it,' she'd said. 'But, honestly, Josh, you'll need to work too fast to listen.'

One final glance at Hannah, ready with her intubation gear. One final check of Maisie, lying semi-comatose from the combined effect of prolonged labour, shock and drugs.

'Let's get you safe, girl.'

And then there was no time to think, only time to follow Claire's echoing instructions. She'd sent him pictures and they were now burned into his consciousness, almost into his fast-moving fingers.

He made the incision from the bellybutton to the

pubis. So far, so good. Now for the foray into the world of Claire's diagrams and instructions.

A dog's uterus split into two forks—horns, Claire had called them. Canine reproductive anatomy differed dramatically from that of humans and he thanked his stars he'd taken the time to study those pictures. Maisie's need had been urgent but going in blind would have been a disaster. Still, he had to work fast.

Carefully he lifted the uterus and incised, just enough to lift the first pup out. This would have been the pup lodged in the birth canal, taking the pressure of the pups behind. One brief look told him it was dead.

He laid the pup in a bowl beside him, his curt nod without looking up a silent communication to Hannah of the outcome.

Next.

The next pup seemed lifeless but not distended. Was there hope? He had no time to assess—that was Hannah's job. He detached the placenta and handed it over.

The next pup moved in his hand as he lifted it clear and the sensation was like a jolt of adrenaline. He handed it over, but in his peripheral vision he saw the second pup had been laid aside.

Damn.

He wanted more fingers. He wanted more assistants.

He had time for nothing.

When he was sure there were no more pups in the first horn he moved to the next. Another pup. Another movement and he heard the faintest of whimpers. He had no time to react.

Another. Two more.

Done.

Seven.

He had the count solidly in his head, checking and

double checking that the placentas were all clear. Leaving one inside could spell disaster.

He had no idea how many pups were alive.

Hannah had kicked a chair to the head of the table and was now sitting down. She was still monitoring Maisie's breathing, but in the sitting position she'd been able to lay the pups on the towel on her lap. She'd lifted a hand and received each pup in turn, but he had no idea what was happening with them.

He still couldn't pause to find out. Claire's instructions were still in his head. He needed to close fast, using subcuticular stitching so as to not interfere with nursing of the pups.

'Josh…' Hannah's voice was urgent. 'She's coming round.'

'Let her wake up,' he said, inserting the last stitch. 'I'll take over. Attend to the pups.'

She scraped back her chair so he could access Maisie's head to supervise the removal of the intubation tube. The big dog gagged. Josh lifted the tubing clear, then watched as Maisie's eyes fluttered momentarily—and breathing resumed.

He almost sagged with relief.

But of course he didn't. When had he ever? He knew this feeling, the sudden drop of adrenaline after lifesaving surgery. He'd learned it was momentary—he needed to brace and then move onto the next thing.

Which was the pups.

'How many viable?' he asked.

Hannah had turned to the oven and was gently placing her armload into its warmed interior. He'd made a nest of towels and she was placing them in, one by one.

'Four,' she said softly. There were two wee bodies

laid aside on another towel, another in the bowl. She looked back at them in sadness.

'Let me see.' He had an almost overpowering longing for the city hospital he'd trained in, for skilled paediatricians and neonate nurses, for incubators, for at least one staff member for each baby during a multiple delivery.

He checked the three lifeless forms and knew nothing could be done. Gently he laid the first little body with its siblings and folded the towel around them all.

Four out of seven was a miracle all by itself. Aching for more was stupid.

Hannah stood to take over monitoring Maisie, and he knelt by the oven, checking the clamping of umbilical cords, getting rid of the remains of the birth sacs. Getting his head in order.

Four viable pups. One live bitch. It was far more than he'd hoped for.

Finally he stood and faced Hannah.

She looked totally wiped. Her face was as white as a sheet—or whiter.

She was staring down at the towel covering the dead pups, and her body seemed slumped in grief.

Shock must be taking its toll. What she'd gone through, and eight months pregnant herself...

He lifted Maisie down onto a sheet on the floor. The dog was dazed, stilled by the combination of shock and morphine.

'Stay with her while I organise a bed for her,' he told Hannah. 'I have two dog beds but they're both deemed to be Dudley's and I don't want property disputes. She needs a nest of her own, where the puppies can be introduced to her as soon as possible. Claire says sooner— her instinct to nurse has to be allowed to kick in fast.

She nodded, mute, and almost unconsciously he put

out a hand and cupped her cheek. 'Hey,' he said softly. 'You did great.'

'You did greater.' It was a hiccup of a whisper and he knew she was fighting back tears.

'Yeah, and I didn't find a dead great-aunt and nearly get drowned and I'm not eight months pregnant. I performed a Caesarean. All in a day's work.'

'You know, I'm very sure it's not.' His hand was still on her cheek and she lifted her own hand to cover it. 'Thank you,' she whispered.

And, hell, it was all he could do not to take her into his arms and hug her.

Maybe he should. She was shocked, shaking, distressed. Surely any normal human being would have hugged.

But the feel of her hand over his was creating sensations he'd fought for years to overcome. He didn't need this. Contact? Concern? Closeness?

He lifted her hand away and smiled down into her eyes. Which might have been a mistake as well.

He'd meant his smile to be one of reassurance, a gesture that she didn't need to touch him, to comfort him.

But she met his gaze and the smile faltered. Her eyes were direct, true.

'Thank you,' she whispered, and shifting his gaze seemed a bigger effort than shifting her hand.

'Moving on,' he said, suddenly harsh because there were things happening that he didn't understand—didn't want. 'I'll fetch that bedding. You're in charge, Nurse.'

She managed a smile back at that, accepting his weird foray into professional titles without a murmur.

'Certainly,' she said meekly, but with a trace of a twinkle that warned that in normal circumstances she was anything but meek. 'Anything you say, Doctor.'

CHAPTER FOUR

IN THE YEARS since the accident, Josh's half-sister had been amazing, supportive, loving, full of advice as he'd built this place, but grief was always between them. Finally Madison had cracked.

'I can't stay here, Josh. I have a job offer in New York. I need a clean break.'

She'd left, but not before leaving most of her gear with him. 'You have a huge garage. Why would I pay rental on a storage facility?' So now one side of his garage was packed with boxes, all labelled by his neat-freak sister.

And if his neat-freak sister could see her boxes now she'd have kittens.

He had puppies. Needs must.

Her boxes labelled linen were now empty. He cut the biggest to form a makeshift crate, put it in front of the living-room fire and filled it with Madison's pink towels.

In the kitchen Hannah was watching over an increasingly wakeful Maisie. He lifted the dog and carried her through to the fire. Hannah followed, and blinked as she saw the pink nest.

'Hey, how do we know the pups are girls? Sexist

stereotyping? Surely this is risking all sorts of neuroses in later life.'

He grinned, his first relaxed grin of the night. Hannah was smiling, too, teasing, and he thought, Wow, the courage of this woman...

'People who use my garage for storage do so at their peril,' he told her. 'My sister, Madison, has a twisted taste in aprons and a sexist choice of bath sheets. We're stuck with it. Let's get these babies settled and deal with their psychological trauma later.'

He laid Maisie into the prepared crate, then pushed an armchair up beside it. 'You're in charge of supervising,' he told her. 'Sit.'

'Josh—'

'No argument. Sit.'

She sat.

He returned to the kitchen and double checked the puppies. Four tiny pups, each a miracle in its own right.

The sad little bundle to the side was a tragedy, but compared to what might have been... Don't go there, he told himself. The last three years had been all about shoving unwanted thoughts aside—needs must to survive.

He carried the living pups into the living room and cautiously set them beside their mother. Maisie stirred and tried to look around at them. She made a huge effort and nosed them with interest, then flopped back down again.

The puppies squirmed against her, nuzzled, instinctively seeking what they needed. And found it.

And as they started to suckle, the tension seemed to ooze from Maisie—and from the two humans watching.

Josh found himself smiling. He glanced down at Hannah and she was smiling too. Mistily.

'Oh, Josh…'

'We did good,' he said, and dropped a hand on her shoulder. It felt okay.

More than okay, he thought suddenly. The feeling of peace… The presence of this woman…

Was suddenly disturbing. This didn't make sense.

Why was he thinking about peace? This was a crazy night. The storm was still building. The wind was howling around the house and the crashing of the sea was truly scary.

He thought suddenly of Skye and Mick and their three kids on the far side of the island. They'd been resolute in refusing help, but they hadn't expected the storm to be this bad. This side of the island was slightly sheltered. Theirs…not so much.

But there was nothing he could do now. His truck had rocked with the wind when he'd driven to the bridge, and the track to Skye and Mick's consisted of little more than sandy ruts. They were on their own.

'What's wrong?' Hannah asked, and he realised she'd been looking up at him in concern. He must have been frowning.

'Just…indeterminate worrying,' he told her. 'Something about a cyclone hovering around my house makes even a grown man uneasy.'

'Even a grown woman,' she agreed. 'Josh, the house on the far side of the island…'

'Moira told you about the Fordes?'

'Mick and Skye? I met them once when I was here, walking Maisie,' she told him. 'When your house was in darkness and I needed help I thought of them, but the track looked too dodgy.'

'I saw them earlier today. I asked them to ride the storm out here, but they said they love a good storm.'

'With kids that age?'

'Their decision.' He couldn't stop his voice sounding harsh. Putting kids' lives at risk...

Like he had?

'Hey, earth to Josh,' Hannah said, and he fought to get his face under control. He'd been too long answering. Too caught up in the past—again.

'I guess there's not a lot we can do about it now,' she said.

'Sadly not. Even if we knew they were in trouble, the truck will never make it there in this weather. And as for contacting authorities... Chopper? Boat? Not a hope. There's no way anyone can reach them until the weather eases. There's nothing to do but wait.'

'Right.' Then she hesitated and then looked...sort of hopeful? 'Josh, I know this is presumptuous when you've been so good already, but would you have what's needed for... I don't know...cocoa? Toast?'

Cocoa. Toast.

This was what he needed. Practicalities to drive other thoughts out of his head.

'When did you last eat?'

'Breakfast. I thought I'd have something at Moira's but there's something about a dead great-aunt that makes food drop down the list of priorities.'

His smile returned. Black humour was almost universal among medics—used as a release. He knew Hannah would be feeling gutted as well as shocked to the core by what had happened, but humour was a defence. He'd seen it time and time again in emergency departments and operating theatres throughout his career, and he knew how much it helped.

It helped now. It helped him.

'Then cocoa and toast are coming right up,' he told her. 'Maybe even something a bit more substantial.' He hesitated. 'Give me a few moments, though. I need to turn the kitchen back into a kitchen.'

'Let me help.'

But again his hand rested on her shoulder, pressing her down.

'No. Hannah, Maisie's still drug affected. She has her puppies and they need to be with her, but she might roll. Claire was firm on the need for supervision post-op, so you're the Maisie Monitor.'

'But—'

'No buts.'

'But Josh, this is your living room. We've just… taken over. Maybe you could put us all in the laundry.'

'Dudley's in the laundry.'

'Dudley?'

'My dog.'

'Oh, that's right. I saw him. Josh, it's his house.'

'So I should put Dudley here and put you and your dog and her babies in the laundry? I can see Dudley agreeing, but not me. Besides, tonight Maisie and her pups need monitoring, possibly all night, which means shifts, and if you think I'm going to spend the night in the laundry…'

'There's no way you're doing shifts. Josh, she's my responsibility.'

'She may well be,' he agreed. 'But I got very wet on your account. You then allowed yourself to be brought to my house, and you're about to partake of my toast and cocoa. Which means you're accepting that I've accepted responsibility for you. Hannah, you're eight months pregnant and you've had one hell of a day. Back off now and let me take over.'

'I think…' she said unsteadily. 'Maybe I already have.'

'Excellent,' he told her. 'Then keep on with more of the same.'

The kitchen was a mess. There was nothing for it but to go through it like a dose of salts. He missed the 'good ole days', he thought ruefully as he cleaned. As a neurosurgeon working in a major teaching hospital, he'd been able to walk from Theatre leaving a small army of hospital staff to clean up. Now he was it. Neurosurgeon and janitor all in one.

The sad little bundle of dead puppies was his nemesis. He looked down at it for a long moment, feeling strangely gutted. Claire had told him to expect them all to be dead, but still…

Since Alice's death he'd been thrown by all sorts of things, some totally unexpected. Now, looking down at the tiny bundle, he felt the grey void surge back.

Move on, he told himself harshly. He'd spent the last three years working out that the only way to rid himself of this void was to block out the world with activity. He'd dived into his research with a fierceness that left his colleagues stunned.

But research wasn't an option now. He carried the little bundle through to the garage. He'd bury it in the morning—or the morning after. By the sound of the wind he might be stuck inside for quite some time.

With Hannah. Who needed feeding.

Activity, he thought gratefully, and his freezer, his microwave and his frying pan co-operated. Half an hour later he was carrying dinner into the living room. Sausages, bacon, eggs, fried tomatoes and toast.

He gave Hannah a plate and hauled a chair up to the fire to join her. She was staring at her meal with astonishment.

'Wow!'

'Chef extraordinaire,' he told her modestly, then spoiled the effect by grinning. He tackled a sausage but she was still watching him, open-mouthed.

'What?' he said.

'Has anyone told you there's a cyclone outside?'

'Yeah, but not inside.'

'So you have everything you need.'

'I hate shopping,' he said simply. 'A once a month supermarket hit, big freezers and a cold store and I'm done. I have three more weeks before I need to worry about starving.' He paused, reflecting. 'Unless this cyclone hangs around. One stranded midwife, one lactating bitch and four puppies might cut our time frame down a bit. Ten days?'

'I'm not staying,' she said hurriedly. 'Or no longer than I must. As soon as the wind dies I'll take Maisie and the pups back to Moira's.' She hesitated. 'Though Moira's body…'

'That might be complicated,' he told her. 'We'll need to contact the authorities. Do you know if she was seeing a doctor?'

'I have no idea.'

'There's a small clinic at Stingray Bay over the bridge,' he said, thinking it through. 'That's where we all do our shopping, so I imagine it's where she'd go if she did see anyone. We need to see if a local doctor's prepared to sign off on her death on the basis of her medical history, or whether we need to call in the coroner. But, Hannah, it'll have to wait. I've just checked the forecast and it's not pretty. The cyclone's moving slowly. You need to accept that you're stuck here for a day or two.'

She closed her eyes. 'I'm so sorry.'

'I'm sorry too—that your dinner's getting cold. Eat.'

She managed a smile and ate, but in silence. He could see cogs working. He could almost see plan after plan being inspected and rejected.

There was no choice. She was truly stuck.

And so was he.

He didn't enjoy visitors. Since Alice's death he'd withdrawn more and more.

'I hate to see you so isolated,' Madison had said sadly as she'd left for New York.

'It's what I need.'

'Yeah, but I hate that it's what you need. Just remember there's a world out there waiting for when you come out the other side.'

'There isn't another side.'

'There is,' she'd said resolutely, and given him the naff apron. 'For when you're ready,' she'd said, and hugged him and left, and all he'd felt was relief at being alone where he could manage his demons in his own way.

But being alone wasn't in the equation now.

'Is there anyone who'll be worrying about you?' he asked Hannah. He eyed her pregnant abdomen with a certain amount of caution. There must be a dad somewhere, but early in his medical training he'd learned to ask questions with care. 'Do you have friends or family who'll be anxious when you don't get home tonight?' He motioned to his phone. 'My satellite phone can call normal numbers. If communications aren't down on the mainland then you can use it.'

But she shook her head. 'It's not a problem. I share hospital accommodation with other nurses, but they'll assume I've hunkered down to stay with Moira.'

'What about at work? If you don't turn up...'

'I won't be missed. I started leave on Friday.'

'Because of the baby?'

'They wouldn't let me work closer to my due date.' She sighed. 'The downside of working in the same hospital as my obstetrician meant I couldn't lie about my dates.'

'Would you have lied about your dates?'

'Of course,' she said simply. 'I want all the leave I can get after the baby's born.' She grimaced. 'I'm just a wee bit skint.'

'Because you're alone?' he asked gently.

She flushed. 'I'm okay.'

'But you're skint. And you don't have anyone worrying about you. So... You want to tell me why an Irish nurse with a hermit great-aunt is eight months pregnant with no one who'll worry if she doesn't come home at night?'

But she didn't react as he expected. Her green eyes flashed sudden defiance.

'That sounds like a counselling type query,' she said, softening her words with a tight smile. 'I've already copped it from our hospital almoner. "So, Hannah, how are you feeling, facing pregnancy alone?" As if it helps, talking about it. So how about you, Josh O'Connor? You want to tell me why an Australian surgeon is hunkered down on a practically deserted island in a house that resembles nothing as much as Fort Knox?'

'It doesn't,' he said, startled. 'Fort Knox?'

'I haven't seen Fort Knox,' she admitted. 'But this building... Is this what architects call minimalist?'

'Simple,' he retorted.

'Or austere, bleak, spartan. Every time I visit, this place seems to be blending with the rocks even more.'

'That's what I intended,' he said, faintly pleased.

'To be invisible?'

'I... No.'

'You're hiding?'

'No!'

'Neither am I, but I'm stuck. I can't go back to Ireland. It's here or nothing. So you...is it here or nothing for you, too?'

'You're channelling your hospital almoner?'

'Maybe I am,' she said, and grinned, then rose to gather the plates. 'Sorry. I know it's none of my business. Can I make you a cup of tea?'

'That's my job.' He rose but he rose too fast. She'd stepped forward to take his plate. They were suddenly too close, standing with only a plate between them.

She was still smiling, looking into his face. He saw freckles and wide green eyes and a tumble of fiery curls. He also saw defiance. And courage?

There was a story here. He knew it. Maybe it *was* because he had ghosts of his own, but he knew them when he saw them.

'Hannah...' Involuntarily he put a hand on her shoulder but the movement was a mistake. She stepped back fast and his hand fell.

'Sorry.' He frowned, his impression of the ghost deepening. Just shadows, he told himself. Ghosts didn't exist.

Which meant Alice didn't exist.

Her smile had completely disappeared. 'I just thought... I don't need hugging.'

'I wasn't about to hug you.'

'No. You touched my shoulder, that was all, but I'm touchy about touch. It comes from living with a bunch of carey-sharey midwives. *Tell us how you feel, Hannah. No, really, let's have a cup of cocoa and you can tell us all about it.* When what I really want is a glass or two of good Irish whiskey and to be taken out to a pub with a decent band.'

'It's a bit awkward getting to a pub right now,' he said apologetically. And the whiskey...'

I know. This baby means I can't drink alcohol.' She sighed. 'So cocoa it is, but not so much of the touchy-feely as we drink it, if you don't mind. I'm over it.'

'Aren't we both?' he said dryly, and her smile returned.

'Then sit,' she told him. 'You're on Maisie watch while I figure out your kitchen.'

'I can make tea much faster.'

'But I need to feel useful,' she retorted. 'You have no idea how much I want that.'

CHAPTER FIVE

WHEN SHE'D WALKED OUT, the kitchen had felt like an operating theatre but there was no sign of the drama that had played out here now. Josh would have had to clear things to make dinner but he'd gone the extra mile. World's fastest scrub! The room was meticulously clean.

And then she thought, The guy's a neurosurgeon. Neurosurgeons were famous for being meticulous.

A couple of times during basic training Hannah had been a gofer during neurosurgery, and she'd been blown away by the skill and intensity during microscopic surgery. She'd watched Josh deliver the pups and and she'd thought, The guy's good. Now she looked around the gleaming kitchen and she thought, No, the guy's a step above good.

But he was a neurosurgeon with ghosts. There had to be ghosts, she decided. Why else was he hunkered down in Fort Knox?

She'd wondered a couple of times about her great-aunt's neighbour but Moira had put her firmly in her place.

'I wouldn't be impertinent enough to ask. There was a woman here when he first came,' she'd admitted. 'But that didn't last. When did it ever? That scar…maybe she hit him. Good luck to her, I say. Men!'

That had been all Hannah had been able to find out, and in truth she hadn't been much interested. But now, thinking of Josh, she found herself very interested indeed.

But it wasn't about the way she'd felt when he'd put his hand on her shoulder, she told herself. Or the feeling when he'd carried her. Or when he'd checked her baby and reassured her, with all the gentleness in the world. Um…surely it wasn't? It couldn't be.

'It's just because we're stuck here together,' she said out loud. 'We might be here for a couple of days. We need to get to know each other.'

Then she grinned at herself. 'Really? Hannah Byrne, you're a terrible liar. He's fascinating. But after these couple of days you'll never see him again. His story's none of your business.'

But… a little voice said at the back of her mind. He asked about me so he wants to know. Fair's fair. And if you're staying, surely you need to establish he's not someone a woman needs to defend herself from with a kitchen knife.

Ooh, who's being dramatic? she answered herself.

She grinned, admitting ruefully to herself that she could be using thoughts of Josh to drive away thoughts of the terror she'd felt only hours before—of her great-aunt dead in the house a few hundred yards away, of the storm, and of the bleakness that seemed always just around the corner.

Her great-aunt had been cold and uninterested, but she'd been family and in some ways that had seemed important. It had been a tenuous link to home, but a link for all that. Now it, too, was gone.

She needed to focus on something else and Josh O'Connor seemed a good substitute. Even a great substitute.

'Okay,' she said, taking a deep breath. 'Let's make tea and encourage the man to talk. See if you can. Go for it, Hannah Byrne.'

Back in the living room, Josh was sitting on the floor, stroking Maisie's ears. Maisie had pretty much recovered from the anaesthetic but the morphine would still be working. Her pups were nuzzling her teats with greedy contentment, she was settled in a nest of fuzzy towels and her eyes were half-closed as Josh's hand worked its magic. She looked…

Pretty close to orgasm, Hannah thought, and why not with a guy like this stroking her head? She bit back a grin and laid her tray on the coffee table.

'Right,' she said. 'Decision.'

'Decision?'

'Yep.' She tossed cushions on the floor and settled beside him, because with cushions, rug, open fire, a contented dog and pups—and this man—where else would she want to be?

'I've decided,' she said as she settled. 'You've asked about me and I've decided to tell you. On condition.'

'On condition?' He looked startled, and suddenly wary.

'Tit for tat,' she said blithely. 'You want to know why an Irish midwife is stuck on Camel Island with no one to ring to say I won't be home tonight? Then I want to know why a neurosurgeon with the skills you have is hunkered down on Camel Island with—as far as I know—no one even worrying that there's a cyclone bearing down on you. Plus you have a very interesting scar on your face, which my Great-Aunt Moira supposed was put there by one angry wife. Or a lover. Either way, her dislike of men said you deserved it. In order to clear your name, I need your story. So here goes, Dr O'Connor. I'll tell you mine and you tell me yours.'

'For heaven's sake... I have no intention of talking of past history.'

'Fair enough,' she agreed equitably. 'Let's do tea and silence. Or we can talk about the weather. There seems to be quite a lot of weather about lately.'

'Hannah...'

'I really don't mind,' she told him. 'But it seems unfair to ask me if I can't ask you.'

His hand stopped its stroking and he turned to look at her.

She gazed calmly back. He had lovely grey eyes, she decided. Deep and calm, but a bit bemused right now. As if he wasn't used to being challenged.

'I guess as a hermit you don't get to talk about your past very much,' she said kindly. 'Maybe it's horrid. But I'm betting it's not so different from a thousand stories I've heard as a midwife. I imagine as a neurosurgeon you hear hardly any stories. Your patients will be nicely under anaesthetic while you operate. Me? I get to hang around women in extremis, sometimes for a long time, and, wow, the stories I hear would make your eyes pop. Not that I pass any on,' she said hastily. 'Button lips, that's me. I take stories to the grave.'

'I watched you try that tonight,' he said, still wary but his mouth twitching into the beginnings of a smile.

'So I did,' she said cordially. 'But I survived, and I wouldn't mind adding to my store of gory tales to carry to the next dunking. So what about it, Josh O'Connor? I'll go first if you like.'

He stared at her for a long moment. He really did have amazing eyes, she thought. The way they held... The way they searched hers, as if he was seeing inside...

She wanted to look away, but she didn't. She held his gaze and tilted her chin.

'Both or none,' she said.

'You should give me yours for the free board and lodging I'm providing.'

'That's not playing fair.'

'I can be mean when I want to be.'

'You know, I'm almost sure you can't,' she said thoughtfully. And then she sighed. 'But you have a point. That was a great meal and the bath was something else. If you really want to know...'

'Suit yourself.'

'That *is* mean,' she told him. 'To ask and then act like you don't want to know anyway.'

He shrugged and went back to stroking Maisie.

He really didn't want to know? Well, stuff it, Hannah thought, because suddenly the need to tell him the reason she found herself where she'd never thought to be, why she felt so stupid, so isolated, so helpless... It felt overwhelming.

He might not be the least bit interested, but something deep inside was insisting she needed to explain.

He *was* interested.

Okay, more than interested. He badly wanted to know.

This interest went against everything he'd tried to instil in himself since Alice's death.

Cut yourself off. Don't care.

But Hannah was right. He'd asked, and his question had backfired.

I'll tell you mine if you tell me yours.

She'd no longer demand but fair was fair. Already he was purging parts of his story in his head. He could give her a brief outline, no emotion, just facts.

And then she started talking and he somehow forgot about focusing on his hang-ups and was caught in hers.

So why was she alone?

'I'm not here through choice,' she told him. 'If I had my druthers I'd be back in Ireland.'

'Right,' he said cautiously. 'So why aren't you?'

'Because my family doesn't want me.' Her voice had turned bleak. 'I'm not welcome.'

'Why ever not?'

'In case you haven't noticed, I'm pregnant.'

'I had actually noticed,' he conceded. She managed a smile, but the bleakness was still in her voice.

'But did you notice there's no ring on my finger?' she asked. 'No? Maybe to you it's not important, but in my father's eyes, having a baby out of wedlock is right up there with giving the finger to the Pope. Worse. You know, if I'd had an abortion and told him, no one else knowing, I'm guessing he'd have been appalled but I'd still be welcome home. A few rounds of the rosary beads and we'd move on. But coming home as a single mother… I can still hear my father. "You've brought shame to the whole family, Hannah. Get rid of it, get it adopted, do what you like, but don't bring it near us. Keep your dirty business out of our sight and let's hear no more about it."'

'Ouch.'

'You said it. Ouch doesn't begin to describe the way that made me feel.'

He thought of it for a while, of the hurt, of the long-held prejudices that still had the power to cause rifts deep enough to drive family apart.

'Your mother?' he ventured.

'Mam thinks what Dad tells her to think and there's an end to it. So does my sister. Bridget and I were close as kids, she'd love to be an aunt but she has the spine of a jellyfish. I have a gran who I love to bits but she's in a nursing home in Dublin, not in a position to give me support.'

'But surely you have friends,' he said, puzzled. 'So few people think like your Dad any more.'

'Of course, but Ryan and I have been travelling for so long we've lost touch. Then there's the fact that I'm an Australian.'

There was a pause at that. He looked at her flaming curls, her freckled nose, her green eyes, her almost translucent, very Irish skin. Plus there was her lilting Irish accent.

'I can see that,' he said dryly, and she managed a smile.

'I'm not indigenous Australian, of course, but there's plenty of folk here with my colouring and accent. There's no want of Irish immigrants in Australia. Thirty years ago my family were immigrants, too. Failed immigrants, though. They came, they saw, and they scuttled back home as fast as money allowed.'

'As bad as that?'

'Dad declared it's a place full of heathens whose only God is the sun. He hates the beach, you see, so why he moved to Queensland… It was ridiculous. But they came at a low time in the Irish economy. Dad's a builder and he was out of work at home. Aunt Moira— Gran's sister—was already over here and she talked of how wonderful it was. But by the time Mam and Dad arrived, Moira's marriage had failed. Moira suffered from the family trait of "what will people think?" so just when Mam needed her most, she retired into her hermit existence and didn't want anything to do with my parents. Which left Mam alone. Mam hated the heat. She was dead lonely and after I arrived she seemed to sink into depression. Dad loathed the climate, loathed not having his local mates, his local pub. The experiment therefore failed. Home we went, with the only remaining legacy my Australian passport.'

'I assume that after all this time, you'd have an Irish one as well.'

'Yes, but it doesn't help the money side of it,' she told him, and sighed. 'Okay, let's get the second part—the Hannah-is-an-idiot story—over. You sure you want to hear?'

He could say it was none of his business. He should.

'From the top,' he said, and she flashed him something that was something akin to a glower.

'Okay, but I'll keep it short,' she told him. 'There once was a girl called Hannah who fell in love with a toe-rag called Ryan.'

'A toe-rag...'

'Gorgeous to look at, charming, carefree, all the things my serious, dour family isn't. Ryan wanted to see the world and so did I. I felt so confined at home. Even after I trained as a nurse, Dad seemed always to be looking over my shoulder. I love our village, our community, but I couldn't stand his control. Even when I moved to Dublin he was always finding an excuse to visit, to judge. Oh, the fights we had... And Mam and Bridge...their passive acceptance of his every decree makes me feel ill.'

'So maybe it was part rebellion, but I fell for Ryan

and off we went. Ryan's a trained paramedic, so with my nursing training we could find work wherever we went. We lived pretty much hand to mouth, moving from country to country, working just enough to let us travel to the next spot. But we did have fun.'

'After a couple of years, though, I was getting more and more homesick. To be honest, I was also starting to have doubts about our relationship. Ryan's the eternal Peter Pan. Where there's fun and adventure, Ryan's your man, but responsibility...not so much.'

'There's another ouch.'

'You said it.' She gave a wry smile. 'Anyway, instead of going home, Ryan convinced me to come to Australia. "One last adventure," he said, "before we settle down to boring domesticity." I was in two minds, but I made a quick visit home and nothing had changed. The way Bridget was turning into another version of Mam, I couldn't stand it.'

'So we came. "Let's stay for a while," Ryan said when he saw the beaches, the climate, plus the number of Irish in the pubs. "A year in the one place. Will that do for you, Hannah?" I was unsettled, uneasy, but Moira was here and I knew my gran worried about her. I thought I'll have a touch of family. And, as opposed to my parents, I love the sun and the beach. So we applied for jobs and settled—and then I found I was pregnant.'

He was watching her face. Seeing pain.

'So,' he said, cautiously now. 'I assume not planned?'

'Of course, not planned.' That came with a snap of anger. 'What do you think? That's exactly what Ryan threw at me, too. He said, "You planned this!" like I'd planned a murder.'

'Maybe not the best of reactions.'

'Not when he'd brought home a norovirus from his

stupid night at the stupid pub with his stupid mates, which I guess is why the Pill stopped working. And it was Ryan who said I was being paranoid when I said not tonight because we needed extra levels of contraception for the rest of the month...'

She stopped, took a deep breath, moved on.

'Sorry. Too much information. I just can't think of Ryan without knowing what an idiot I was, and for how long. One day I'll remember him for all the fun we've had, but not yet. Things are too raw. Because the moment I told him I was pregnant and I wanted to keep our baby, he said, "It's your baby, sweetheart, not mine." I woke the next morning to a note on the fridge and that was the only trace of him left.'

'Oh, Hannah.'

How to respond? A hug in sympathy? He didn't do hugs and, besides, there was enough defiance in her eyes to tell him a hug would be a bad move. For both of them?

She decided for him.

'So moving on,' she said, doing just that. 'I decided I'd go home but I was dumb enough to tell my family about my pregnancy before I booked the flight. Which was probably just as well. Dad told me exactly the reception I'd receive if I went home pregnant without a ring on my finger. Moralistic? You'd better believe it. It seems tar and feathering's too good for the likes of me. No, don't look like that. I've faced it now and I'm staying put.'

'Alone.'

'You know, I'm probably less alone than I'd be in Ireland,' she admitted. Also less needy. There's sense in my decision to stay. The hospital here's short of midwives and they've liked my work. They'll hold my job and I can stay on in hospital accommodation. There's a creche I can use after my baby's born. Plus, because I'm an Australian citizen, I can access your government's wonderful maternity payments. That's made the decision to stay a no-brainer. If I went back, well, I've been away for three years and I'm out of touch. I have hardly any savings. I'd be trying to find a job when I already look pregnant—how likely is that?—and I'd need to find accommodation. You think that'd be easy in my position? This decision is all about pragmatism.'

'But it still leaves you isolated.'

'I have friends here,' she said defensively.

'Friends who won't worry that you're not home tonight.'

'Will you cut it out?' she said, and huffed. 'I'm doing well, thank you very much. I have my life sorted.'

'Except you're lonely.'

'What's wrong with that? You're the one who thinks being a hermit is a great life choice. So there you are, Dr O'Connor. You have my whole life story, or just about the whole if we're not including the Ferris wheel incident of two thousand and six. So what about you? You want to tell Auntie Hannah or are you still being pig stubborn?'

'Pig stubborn?'

'Pig stubborn. Give.'

'I'd prefer to hear about the Ferris wheel incident.'

'That's not going to happen,' she said darkly. 'It was very undignified, and I didn't even have my best knickers on.' She sat back on her cushions and skewered him with a look that said, *Don't mess with me.* 'So now it's your turn. I know I agreed we could make this one-sided but I've changed my mind. Start with the scar,' she told him. 'Not a Ferris wheel? A lover with a kitchen knife? Something worse?'

'Car accident,' he said, grudgingly.

'When?'

'Three years ago.'

'Bad?' She shook her head. 'No, that's a crazy thing to ask. I can see by your face that it was bad, and it's not the scar I'm talking about. I'm guessing really bad. Life-changing bad.'

'My sister died.'

'Oh, Josh…'

What followed was silence.

It wasn't a bad silence, though, he conceded, as it stretched. The fire was crackling in the hearth, seeming somehow to mute the noise of the storm. In this room, with Maisie's soft ears still under his hands, with the slight smell of newborn puppies, with the faint mewing sounds of their nuzzling…with this woman sitting waiting with her patient, non-judgmental eyes… It was okay.

She was okay.

Where others would have jumped in with horror, with sympathy, she sat silent and waited for him to tell or not to tell. It was his choice and whatever he decided, he knew it would be fine by her.

'My fiancée killed her,' he said flatly, and waited for a reaction. He didn't get one. The wait stretched on until finally she cracked.

'Well, that sounds dramatic but I'm assuming stupidity or mistake rather than malice. You might as well tell me the whole story.'

Her response almost made him smile. Stupidity or mistake…a combination of the two.

'Aisling's a neurosurgeon as well,' he told her. 'A good one. Her father's a politician with clout, and she's always had family money. She's smart, beautiful, witty, and she has pretty much everything she wants in life. And for a while she wanted me.'

'That was…good for you?' she ventured, and he shrugged.

'Good, like Ryan was for you? Maybe stupid doesn't begin to cut it for both of us.'

'Ryan and I had a very good time,' she said, almost defensively, and he shrugged.

'I guess we did, too. We were surgeons at the top of our game. We had money, skill, respect and egos the size of large houses. Aisling also had the car of her dreams, an Aston Martin, arguably the world's most gorgeous four-seater sports car. Don't think the four-seater was because she was thinking of a family, though. She has two standard poodles, one white, one black, who sit in the back of that car like royalty.'

'Yikes,' she said, bemused. 'That's some picture.'

'Yeah, and I bought right into it,' he said grimly. 'To be honest, her image suited my ego as well. Anyway, the short story is we took my little sister out to dinner one night. I have…had…two sisters. Madison's older than me, actually my half-sister. Alice was an afterthought, conceived in a dumb attempt to save my parents' marriage. She didn't—how could she?—but she was loved, mostly by Madison and me. When she was eighteen she came to stay with me while she was on a break from uni. She thought Aisling was awesome, and Aisling played up to her. We went out to dinner one night and Aisling drove. By then our relationship was showing signs of strain. Aisling had Alice to sit in the front and I copped the poodle seat.'

'Ouch.'

'The back seat in an Aston Martin's hardly suffering,' he said with a smile that contained little humour. 'I was tired and I guess I pretty much zoned out. Then Aisling's phone pinged with an incoming message. I couldn't see what was happening, but it seemed Aisling was reading and texting while talking to Alice—and heading straight into oncoming traffic.'

Hannah's breath hissed in. She'd know, Josh thought. Every medic, every paramedic, every cop, every member of every devastated family knew by now that texting while driving was the new 'drink driving' stupidity. He closed his eyes for a moment as horror flooded back, as it had done over and over, for the last three long years.

He thrust it back with an effort. Who wanted to go there? Not him.

'So that's it,' he said flatly. 'Aisling veered at the last minute and the passenger side copped the brunt of the impact. Aisling escaped almost unscratched. I was left with a compound fracture of my left leg, bruises and the laceration you can still see on my face. And the knowledge that Alice was dead.'

'Oh, Josh...'

'So that was that,' he said, forging on grimly. 'Aisling's family spent a fortune on lawyers. She managed to get off with a suspended sentence, which she can ignore and get with her life. But Alice...' He stopped.

'Hell.'

'It is, isn't it,' he said roughly. For a moment he let the ever-present guilt wash over him, the self-loathing for the man he'd been, for the lifestyle he'd drifted into without thought for the consequences. Aisling had been driving but where had he been? Not looking out for his little sister. Not caring enough.

But then his thoughts were interrupted by a piercing howl, starting low but building to a yowl of despair, echoing ghost-like above the noise of the storm. 'Uh oh,' he said, seizing the distraction with gratitude. 'Dudley.'

'Dudley?' she said, startled out of the horror of the story. 'That sounds like the Hounds of the Baskervilles.'

'I've locked him in the laundry, but he hates this weather. Now he's started he may well howl all night.' He eyed Maisie and her pups and came to a decision. 'I thought it'd be better to keep the dogs separate, but looking at these puppies…'

They both looked. The pups were a squirming mass of patchwork, brown and black and cream. The littlest one had momentarily lost its teat and was squirming to reattach. They had a glimpse of a tiny face, black with tiny brown eyebrows, a creamy white chest and matching paws.

'You know, I'm guessing these might not be pure-bred Labrador,' Josh said mildly.

'You mean…?'

'Total number of dogs on this island equals two, and Dudley's brown and black. Do we need to be Einstein to figure the rest?'

CHAPTER SIX

IT WAS GOOD to have a distraction. Or was it?

Their combined stories had hurt, though Josh's was far more gut wrenching than hers. She'd watched his eyes and seen bone-deep pain. The scar was stretched tight over his lean, almost sculpted face, but she knew it wasn't the old injury that was hurting. To lose his sister...

She had a sister back home, still living with her parents, but there'd be no use asking for her support. Once upon a time she and Bridget had been inseparable, falling in and out of scrapes but best of friends all their childhood. As adults, though, Bridget had finally caved in to her father's bullying, while Hannah's rebellious streak had seen her move further and further away.

For the last few years she'd felt like she'd lost her, and she ached for her, but at least her sister, her family, were still intact. To have it any other way seemed unthinkable.

She had an almost irresistible urge to lean forward and take Josh's pain-etched face between her hands, to hold him, to hug him close. As a midwife she knew the power of touch. A woman in labour desperately needed someone to cling to, to grab, to swear at, to know they'd be there whatever. If there was no 'someone' then often a midwife had to step in and be that person.

She wanted to step in now, but Josh was looking intently at the puppies and his body language was telling her to keep her distance. His pain was his business.

Another howl echoed above the noise of the storm. Maybe the rising sound of the storm was sending Dudley to the edge of the dog's tolerance.

The storm should be uppermost in Hannah's mind, too, she thought. However, this situation, this man… Josh himself…was enough to drive the threat of the storm to the background.

Josh was focusing on the puppies because he wanted her to move on. Past the pain of his background. To present practicalities.

Or maybe to present mysteries. A golden Labrador with puppies that were golden—with patches of black and brown.

'I'll get him,' Josh said, and headed into the back of the house.

In two minutes he reappeared, and by his side was the dog she'd seen momentarily as she'd arrived. A skinny, black and brown mutt—almost a kelpie but not quite. Josh had him on a short lead. He was cowering against Josh's leg, as if he needed the comfort of human presence.

He took a couple of steps into the room and then stopped. Stiffened.

And Maisie's head lifted.

Another dog. A threat to her puppies?

Apparently not. Dudley whimpered and pulled forward. Maisie's tail thumped up and down against the rug.

Cautiously Josh let Dudley pull him across to the hearth. Maisie's tail still thumped.

Dudley sniffed, nose to nose. His tail, previously tucked coward-like under his chest, tried a tentative wag of its own.

He sniffed the pups.

Josh was ready to tug him away at the first sign of aggression on either dog's part, but there was none. Sniffing done, Dudley flopped down on the hearth beside Maisie.

Both dogs almost visibly relaxed.

'I guess...' Hannah ventured, awed and a little emotional '...we seem to have settled paternity.'

'Right,' Josh said grimly. 'Like I needed that.'

But Hannah grinned. 'Hey, at last, some good news. That means half the puppies are yours.'

'No!'

'Of course they are,' she said, cheering right up. The responsibility for a dog and four pups was already starting to weigh on her. 'Sharing's awesome. Doesn't the dad have to pay until they finish university, or whatever the doggy equivalent is? Do we need to bring in lawyers, or can we reach an out of court agreement?'

'I don't... They're nothing to do with me.'

'DNA testing it is, then,' she said, her smile widening. 'You stand not a snowball's chance in a wildfire of getting out of this one. Spay your dog, Dr O'Connor.'

'He's not my dog!'

'Really?' She raised her brows.

'And he's neutered!'

'Is that so?' she said, trying for bland, but the corners of her mouth twitched into an irresistible chuckle. 'You know, as a midwife I've learned to accept what people tell me about paternity, but in this case... I'll go bail we're looking at the biological parents.'

'Oh, of course they'll be Dudley's,' he said with

a groan. 'But half the fault will be Moira's. Why she didn't tell me she had an unneutered bitch…'

'Did you tell her you had an unneutered dog?'

'She knew. And he's neutered.'

'Really?' Her eyebrows gave a polite, disbelieving quirk and he sighed.

'Okay. Quick background. I bought this land two years ago. It belonged to a guy who was a bigger hermit than Moira, and even older. He had an almost derelict hut over the ridge from this place, and he needed cash to settle debts and reserve a spot in a decent nursing home when he needed it. He didn't want to sell but it seemed he had no choice and he'd reluctantly talked to a realtor. I came and chatted and we agreed I could buy, on the condition he could stay where he was for as long as he wanted.

'I headed overseas. My house was built by contractors, well out of sight of his hut. Then, just before I arrived back, his son contacted me to say the old man had had a stroke and was finally moving. The day I arrived he was gone and Dudley was on my veranda.'

She winced. 'A dumped dog.'

'I hadn't even known he'd had a dog,' Josh told her. 'When I went over to the abandoned hut I saw why. There was a stake in the back yard with a kennel, with a circular rut around the stake, trodden a foot deep. It seems Dudley had been pretty much chained full time. The son had obviously unchained him and left. When I saw Moira she shouted at me to do something. She'd been tossing him food since the old man left but she wasn't taking any more responsibility.' He shrugged. 'So I fed him, dewormed him and tried to settle the worst of his neuroses. A couple of months back I finally decided he'd be mine for life and had him neutered, but it seems…' He looked down at the squirming pile of pups. 'Not soon enough.'

'Well,' Hannah said, watching him, thinking…well, thinking good things. 'Well, well. I'm starting to think you're a very nice man, Dr O'Connor. You're a man prepared to haul drowning women and dogs out of cars. A man prepared to deliver pups by Caesarean at a moment's notice. A man prepared to put a stray midwife up for the night in the face of a truly appalling storm. And a man prepared to take on the responsibility of a litter of unwanted puppies.'

'Hey, I didn't say…' he started, startled, but her smile widened.

'You didn't have to. I'm starting to figure you out. Squishy in the middle is you, Dr O'Connor.'

But then she winced. She'd been nestled on the floor but her back, never friendly at this stage of pregnancy, reminded her that it didn't like being in this position— or indeed any position for very long. And it had been bumped. She'd been bumped.

She felt safer than she'd felt at any time since her toe-rag of a boyfriend had walked out on her, but right now a wash of weariness hit her like a wall. A twinge of back pain became an unbearable ache, and the need to sleep was almost overwhelming.

And Josh saw.

'You're exhausted,' he said, rising, holding his hands down to hers to help her up. 'I shouldn't have kept you talking. Let's talk about puppy custody tomorrow. Right now, it's bedtime.'

'Do you…? Is there a spare bed?'

'There is,' he said, grasping her hands. 'Madison helped design this house and she supervised its furnishings while I was overseas. Which means there's a

Madison bedroom that's furnished with every conceivable luxury—at my expense, of course.'

He tugged her up. She rose and was suddenly close. Very close.

Too close?

And, strangely, all at once the storm seemed louder. Despite its ferocity, it had somehow become an almost unnoticed background to the domesticity of the fire, of the meal, of the dogs and the shared confidences. Now suddenly she was aware of the gusts blasting around the building, and of spatters of whatever was being hurled against the roof, against the shutters.

She felt herself shudder. It must be the after-effects of the day, she thought, of the nightmare she'd been through.

And then she felt her knees sag. For heaven's sake, what was happening?

But Josh's hands were holding hers and his hold tightened. His hands dropped to her waist to stop her falling.

What on earth... He was too close—*she was too close*—but she wasn't pulling away.

This man had saved her and he seemed...her rock.

It was as much as she could do not to cling.

Um...whoops? She *was* clinging. Why didn't her knees want to hold her up?

'Hey,' he said softly, speaking into her hair, still holding her strongly. 'You're knackered. I shouldn't have let you sit up for so long. It's bed for you, sweetheart.'

'I'm not... I'm not your sweetheart.' Memories of that appalling note from Ryan...

And he got it. 'Of course you're not,' he said gently. 'Let's put it another way. You're exhausted, Hannah Byrne. Plus you're battered, bruised and eight months pregnant. So let's delineate our roles in the future. For the duration of the surgical procedure we've just performed I've needed you to be my colleague. We've debriefed afterwards, sharing personal confidences that might or might not assist us to move forward in a professional capacity. We've also decided on the welfare status of four newborns with previously indeterminate parentage. But the professional need for Hannah Byrne has ended. She's off duty. She's now an eight-month pregnant primigravida in my care. So, Ms Byrne, as your consulting physician, it's bedtime. Now.'

And before she knew what he was about he'd lifted her into his arms and was carrying her toward the bedroom.

He'd done it when they'd arrived. It had discombobulated her then when she'd been discombobulated already. Now...discombobulated was too small a word for it.

She felt weak, dumb, out of control...and cherished.

And it wasn't such a bad feeling, she decided as he strode down the passage with her in his arms. She had no intention of staying weak, dumb and out of control, but while she was, while her knees were like jelly and while she had the stupid shakes...why not lie back in this man's arms and savour the strength of him? Savour the feeling that she was safe, cared for, and there was nothing she needed to do but submit?

Oh, right. How politically incorrect was that? Helpless maiden being swept up by knight on white charger...

She couldn't help it. She giggled.

'What?' He kicked the bedroom door open and carried her over to the bed. Somehow, using one hand to hold her, he tugged back the covers and laid her on clean sheets. How did he do that?

'You need a horse and a suit of armour and a lance,' she managed, and he looked puzzled for a moment and then grinned.

'I doubt I'd have been able to pull you out of the water if I was wearing armour. And you...you should have been wearing a flowing gown and...what's that thing all good maidens in distress wear on their heads? A mantilla?'

'I left it at home,' she said mournfully, and then she took his hand and got serious. 'Josh, thank you so much.'

'Hey, that's fine,' he said gently. 'It's not every day I get to play knight errant.'

'You did it brilliantly,' she told him, and then she couldn't help herself. For some dumb reason her eyes welled with tears and she found herself tugging his hand against her cheek. 'I'd be dead without you.'

'Not you.' He stooped and laid a finger on her cheek. 'You'd have saved yourself and your dog because that's the kind of woman you are, Hannah Byrne. Don't you forget it. Now, is there anything else you need?'

'An alarm clock,' she managed, swiping away a dumb tear. 'Give me four hours' sleep and I'll take over the next Maisie watch.'

'I don't have an alarm but I'll wake you.'

'Promise?'

'Of course.'

She eyed him suspiciously. 'Why don't I believe you? Josh, please...'

'I'll call you when I need you,' he told her, and then, before she realised what he was about, he kissed her gently. On the lips.

It was a fleeting kiss. Maybe meant for forehead rather than mouth? It was the sort of kiss a parent might give a child as they said goodnight.

It burned.

Her hands flew to her lips and she stared up at him in confusion.

She saw matching confusion in his gaze. He backed away from the bed as if…he was afraid?

'Goodnight,' he told her, hurriedly now. 'Madison's set up the en suite with everything a guest could possibly want. Feel free to use anything—I know she won't mind. Call me if you need anything else.'

'There's nothing.' Her voice sounded funny. She felt funny. He was at the door, looking like he needed to bolt but he wasn't sure how to. 'I… Thank you. Goodnight Josh.'

'Goodnight, Hannah,' he said, and left and closed the door behind him.

He returned to the living room and sank into the fireside chair. Outside the wind was screaming, but here seemed a cocoon of warmth and safety. Even Dudley, who'd spent the day cowering and whimpering, seemed to have relaxed. He lay a little back from Maisie, enough to give her and her pups room. His eyes were mostly closed, as if in contentment, but every now and then they'd lazily open and glance across at the little family in their pink nest.

Checking on his woman?

That was sort of like *he* was feeling, Josh conceded, as the idea occurred that he'd kind of like Hannah to be settled on the settee, here in this room, so he could watch over her, too.

Which was crazy. Hannah wasn't recovering from an anaesthetic. There was no risk to her baby.

Why did he feel so protective?

It was natural, he told himself. He'd hauled her out of danger, she had been in trouble and he was only human.

The storm was doing its best to destroy his house. He was appallingly concerned for Mick and Skye and their children—his helplessness to do anything about their plight was doing his head in. He'd been landed with yet another needy dog, plus four puppies.

His mind stayed stubbornly on Hannah.

He wanted her where he could watch her. The fierceness of the storm made him feel like gathering close everything he cared about…

Cared?

Yeah, okay, he cared, he conceded, raking his fingers through his hair. But only for tonight, no longer. He'd made a vow not to care.

Even Madison… He loved his big sister but Alice's death lay between them like a wall of ice, and there was nothing that could be said or done to break it.

His parents had been disparate, a couple who should never have married. They were currently overseas, his mother climbing an Alp somewhere—he'd need to check Facebook to know where. His father was no doubt doing something important for the government—in Vienna? Or was Vienna last month?

He'd been buying into their life. He'd thought it through over the last pain-filled years, remembering the whole successful surgeon, ego-driven idiot he'd become. He couldn't think of it now without revulsion.

His parents had flown back for Alice's funeral. They'd made a token attempt to be there for him during the worst of his convalescence, but when he'd told them he was managing fine—he wasn't—they'd disappeared again with relief.

His sisters, though, had been his real family. They'd always been a part of him, his core, so of course Madison had stuck around. She'd always be there for him, and he for her, but the pain they saw reflected in each other's eyes was enough for both of them to acknowledge the ice wall.

He only had to glance in the mirror to know how much pain loving another could do. How easily he could get hurt. His wall was his survival mechanism.

Why, tonight, did it seem like he hated it?

It didn't matter. The wall was there.

He rose and poured himself a whisky. Whiskey. Irish. Both Dudley and Maisie watched him cross the room and then come back to them.

'It's okay, guys,' he told them. He stared down into his Irish whiskey and grimaced. 'I know my boundaries. My place is on this side of the wall.'

CHAPTER SEVEN

SHE WOKE TO the sound of crashing. Something was hitting something. Something tinny. Something loud.

It took her moments to struggle out of sleep, to figure where she was, to remember the events of the night before. To remember that this place was built like a fort. That Josh was somewhere in the house, keeping things safe.

Josh. Storm. Banging.

Her room had wide windows but they were strongly shuttered. Chinks of light were making their way through the slats, though. It must be morning.

Josh had been going to wake her.

Had he slept himself? He wouldn't have, she thought. She knew enough of the man to know that he'd have been too aware of the risks of Maisie rolling.

How did she know?

She just did.

But, drat, she'd had enough of his heroism. She could have taken a dog-watching shift. Did he want to make her totally beholden to him?

That wasn't a kind thing to think, she decided, but as she rose and stomped across to the en suite she was not enjoying the fact that Josh O'Connor was playing the martyr.

The sight of herself in the mirror stopped her short.

She'd taken Josh at his word when he'd said Madison wouldn't mind her using her things. She'd found a nightgown big enough to fit over her bump, and fluffy one-size-fits-all slippers. Josh's bathrobe—she guessed it had to be his because it was brown and anything belonging to Madison seemed to be pink or lavender—made her look almost respectable. She was a bit sore here and there, but mostly she felt fine.

She didn't look even close to fine.

Her car's airbag had gone off as the bridge had tumbled. It had slammed into her face, and she'd had to fight it off as she'd struggled to get out. There'd been timbers at head height.

Her face was a myriad of scratches and bruises.

If she'd been a nurse on duty and someone like her had arrived in Casualty, she'd have been calling for back-up.

It was all superficial, though, she thought, studying bruises and scratches with a professional eye. Bruises always looked worse the day after. There was nothing there to excuse Josh from his promise to wake her for puppy sentry duty.

Except she was eight months pregnant.

Again her professional self intervened to give her a lecture. If the roles were reversed she'd have broken her promise, too.

It didn't make her feel any less guilty, though. He'd put his life at risk by saving her. Her dog, her problems, had had him sit up all night.

She wouldn't yell at him. She'd just go out and tell him to get some sleep now.

She tucked his bathrobe more securely around her bump. It really was the most gorgeous bathrobe—and did it smell ever so slightly of him? Whatever, for some dumb reason it made her feel…hugged? Maybe that was too big a word but, whatever, she felt not only warmer in it but safer.

Chiding herself for ridiculous thoughts, she headed out to the living room.

The fire was burning low and the dogs were soundly asleep, Maisie in her nest, Dudley just out of it but his nose almost touching Maisie's.

Four tiny, blind worms of puppies were lying peacefully attached to their mother's teats. A family of dogs, seemingly utterly content.

No Josh.

She frowned.

The dogs woke as she opened the door, raised their heads to look a polite enquiry. Nothing to see here, their look said. Maisie knew her well, and Dudley had obviously accepted her as part of the furniture. Two tails gave perfunctory wags and they returned to the important task of sleeping.

Hannah smiled. Maisie's instant alertness, her tail wag and then her contented return to sleep told her the effects of the anaesthetic were well past. They looked like dogs who needed nothing.

So had Josh headed to bed?

She made her way cautiously back down the passage. His bedroom door stood open.

No Josh.

His bedroom was an almost complete opposite to Madison's. The bed was made with military precision. There were no paintings. No photographs. Nothing personal.

She took a fast mental tour back through his house, remembering only tasteful prints. The unknown Madison, she thought, imagining Josh's older sister leafing through online catalogues while Josh let her do as she willed. She could almost hear his brief—'nothing personal, nothing that hurt too much to remember.'

She thought back to her own cramped room, her nursing accommodation. Yes, her family had hurt her, but still every spare inch was covered with memories, of friends as well as family. She hadn't been able to stick things on the walls so she'd bought sheets of plaster board and propped them up so she had almost enough space to fit every face she wanted to remember.

This chopping off of his past…it seemed almost like an amputation. She thought of patients she'd nursed in the past after losing limbs. Of phantom pain that stayed with them for ever.

Oh, Josh…

But where was he?

She walked through to an empty kitchen thinking, had he gone to try and help the artists on the far side of the island? Surely not. She wasn't even game to open a door to see what was happening.

But she did head to the internal door leading to the garage—just to check—and drew in her breath as she saw the space where his truck should be.

Oh, hell. More heroics?

But even as she thought it, the remote-controlled door started swinging upwards and she had to retreat as a blast of wind almost knocked her back into the house.

She waited, knowing he had to have time to drive in and close the door to give him a weather seal so he could get into the house. What she wanted, though, was to rush out and…

And what? Yell, that's what.

He'd put himself in harm's way. Without her.

Josh.

She hardly knew the man. What was she about, leaning against the wall, her body shaking as if she'd been in danger herself, all over again.

The sounds of the wind blasting into the garage ceased. The truck door slammed and seconds later Josh opened the door into the house.

He looked appalling. He was wearing the same pants and sweater he'd been wearing the night before but they were soaked and coated with debris. His deep black hair, wavy when she'd last seen it, was standing almost upright. His scar was almost disguised by grime.

He'd opened the door with his left hand. His right was held tight against his sweater, and she could see bright crimson welling underneath.

'What the hell have you been doing?' Okay, that was not the way she'd been trained to react to injury. She should be calmly neutral, non-judgmental—whatever—but she was still shaking and her professional self had deserted her.

'Being dumb,' he told her, and then he grinned. 'But wow it's wild outside. There's a massage place in town that advertises salt scrubs. They should ship clients over here right now.'

His eyes were smiling, encouraging her to relax. Her voice had been shrill. Verging on hysterics? She took a deep breath and tried again.

'So you thought you'd pop out and see what hundred-mile-an-hour wind feels like? Josh, what have you done to your hand?'

'Cut it on tin,' he said, ruefully, glancing down at his blood-soaked sweater. 'I did it just then. A sheet of corrugated iron was trying to batter its way against the shutters on the windward side of this place. Left to its own devices, it might have pierced them.' His smile appeared again, reassuring despite the filth of his face. 'Nothing to worry about, Hannah.'

'You went out in the truck—to remove tin?'

'No.' His smile faded. 'I'm worried about Skye and Mick and the kids. The wind's died a little since last night. I thought… I'd check.'

She was watching his hand. The bleeding was sluggish. Instinctively she reached out and caught it.

'Are you sure it's only your hand?

'I'm sure.' He tried to pull back but she was having none of it. A gash was running from wrist down to his thumb. 'It's okay, Hannah,' he said, gently as if she was the one who was hurt. 'It's just blood.'

'Let's get it cleaned up,' she said, a bit unsteadily. 'So, Mick and Skye…did you reach them?'

'No,' he said, gentleness gone. 'The track's washed out and I can't see where to go. The first sandhill saw me bogged. It's taken me half an hour to get back here.'

Anger flooded in, fierce and strong. 'You tried that on your own? You could have been killed.'

'There's a note on the fridge,' he told her. 'I figured the worst that could happen was that I'd be stuck in the truck until the storm petered out. Which it should do by late this afternoon, by the way. I was safe.'

'Yeah, safe,' she muttered. The cut looked jagged. Dirty. 'This needs stitches.'

'I'll pull it together with Steri-Strips.'

'It needs more than Steri-Strips.' She was trying to lighten her voice, but the shake was still there. 'So isn't it lucky your first rescue was a nurse who has a nice line in needlework?'

'Hannah…' His good hand came up to grip her shoulder. 'It's okay. We're safe.'

'I know I'm safe,' she retorted. 'But for you to do such a stupid thing without me…'

'I'd hardly take an eight-months pregnant—'

'Nurse.' She practically yelled. 'Can you forget the eight-months-pregnant bit? I'm a nurse. Get into the kitchen and let me fix that hand.'

'The dogs—'

'Are fine. Safe, warm, happy. Thanks to you.'

'I wish—'

'Yeah, that Mick and Skye and the kids are the same. I get that. But you've done your best and there's nothing more you can do until the storm eases.' She hesitated. 'You said…this afternoon…'

'I still have satellite connection,' he told her. 'Amazingly the dish on the roof seems to be staying in place so I can see the forecast. The worst of the cyclone went through about three this morning but it's slow in moving away. By this evening, though, it'll still be windy but negotiable.' He hesitated, then added…

'Hannah, I've been onto the authorities. They know of your aunt's death. They also know of my concerns about Skye and Mick. There's nothing they can do, though. No helicopter or boat can get near the island in this weather. And… I checked on your aunt. I've laid her in her bed, covered her, done what I can.'

It took only that. All this and he'd taken the time to give her aunt the decency of dignity in death. Had he known how much the thought of her aunt still slumped in her chair had been doing her head in?

'I… Thank you.' It had almost killed her to leave her aunt. That he'd done this in this storm…

'I figured I had to check on her before I rang the authorities.

'In case I'd made a mistake?'

'I know you well enough now to accept mistakes aren't your style.'

'Really?' she said, and glanced down at her swollen midriff and winced. 'If you want to believe that...' She took a breath and managed a smile. 'Okay, hold that thought. I don't make mistakes and I'm a very good needlewoman. You have local anaesthetic in that amazing medical kit I saw last night? Everything I need? Then let's get you cleaned up and sutured before I remember just how many mistakes I've made in the past and find myself suturing your hand to your left ear.

He sat at the kitchen table, his hand on a towel. Hannah sat beside him.

She'd brought in a table lamp so she could see better. She had her instruments set out neatly beside her. The local anaesthetic had taken effect, her head was bent over her work and she was concentrating. Fiercely.

It'd be unusual for midwives to suture, Josh knew, but suturing would have been part of her training. Sometimes in the pressure of emergency rooms, with multiple casualties, there was no choice but to hand the job of stitching to a competent nurse.

And she was competent. There'd been no hesitation in the way she'd faced the task, neither had there been hesitation in her use of the anaesthetic. She'd double checked with him, but he had the feeling it was only a formality. Her care with cleaning, debriding and now stitching was as skilful as any surgeon's.

He was no longer watching his hand, though. He was watching her. The copper curls wisping around her face. The smattering of freckles on her nose. The tip of her tongue emerging at the side of her mouth, a sure sign of concentration. Her fierce green eyes...

A woman to be reckoned with.

The unknown Ryan should have had his head read to abandon such a woman, he thought suddenly. What an idiot.

He watched her face, her intentness, her total focus, and he thought…

She was so alone. She needed…

What he needed?

What was he thinking? He dragged his thoughts back into line with a jerk. He was a loner. He'd made that decision and he had every intention of sticking to it. Just because one needy female had crashed into his life in a storm…

Was she needy?

Of course she was. She might come across as fierce and competent, but she could surely use his help.

Maybe he could help her without getting involved himself?

And that was a dumb thought, too. Why was she needy? She'd organised herself a job, accommodation, childcare. She had friends.

Who didn't care for her as they should. She was a woman who deserved to be cared for.

She was tying off the last of the sutures now, and the compulsion to put his hand on those bright curls, to feel them slip through his fingers, was almost overwhelming.

No!

He was tired, he decided. His normal defences were down and, besides, he didn't even know this woman.

Why did it feel like he did?

Why did it feel like he wanted…?

He couldn't want.

'Right.' She popped a dressing over the stitches and

beamed her satisfaction. 'It's a beautiful job if I say so myself. But now, Josh O'Connor, it's time for bed.'

It was so much what he was thinking that he blinked, but her smile wasn't the least bit sexy. It wasn't the least bit…inappropriate. She was smiling kindly, like she'd just patched up a kid with a scraped knee and was telling said kid what to do next. Bed meant just that. Bed.

'Shower first,' she told him. 'But keep that hand dry. Use a surgical glove and hold it out of the water. Then hit your bed and stay there until you've hit the other side of exhaustion.'

'I'm not—'

'Exhausted? Pull the other leg, Josh O'Connor. I'll wake you if I need you. I promise that, and I keep my promises, unlike some martyr doctors I could mention.'

'I didn't promise.'

'I believe you did,' she said serenely, and stood and started clearing the table. 'So what are you waiting for? Go.'

What was he waiting for? He stood, and for a moment the world rocked a little. He was exhausted, he conceded. But still…

Did he want to go to bed and leave this woman?

'Go,' she said, putting her hands on her hips and fixing him with a glare fierce enough to skewer. 'You're wasting time.'

'Yes, ma'am,' he said weakly.

He looked at those fierce eyes, those dimples, those gorgeous freckles and he didn't want to go at all.

But as the lady said, he was wasting time. It hurt but she was right. He took a deep breath, snagged a surgical glove from the box on the table—and went.

CHAPTER EIGHT

HE WOKE TO the smell of cooking.

Someone…something?…was licking his face.

Ugh.

He fought his way to consciousness and shoved. Dudley fell to the floor, rolled, found his feet, put his forefeet back on the bed and started licking again.

'Dudley!' The stern female voice had Dudley glance around briefly, but the dog's tail wagged, with every sign of continuing his display of slavish devotion.

Then Dudley saw the plate on the bedside table and launched himself at that.

But Hannah was fast. She grabbed the dog's collar and was hauling him back before he'd even had time to investigate.

Not that there was anything to investigate. Pre-sleep, when Josh had emerged from the shower, there'd been tea and toast beside his bed. He'd eaten them with gratitude but had slipped into sleep almost before he'd known it. Now all that was left on the plate was crumbs, and Dudley practically drooped with disappointment.

'I'm so sorry,' Hannah said regretfully. 'The catch couldn't have engaged when I—'

'Sneaked in with my tea and toast?' he finished for her. 'You're forgiven. What's the time now?'

'Two p.m.'

He glanced at the bedside table and almost yelped. He'd slept for hours.

'It's lunchtime if you want it,' she told him. 'Cornish pasties. They might not be Irish but I love 'em. That's some food stockpile you have. Every ingredient I needed. Yay.'

'You've been cooking,' he said, fighting the feeling he'd woken in some parallel universe.

'It's what I do when I'm stressed,' she told him. 'And it works for Dudley as well. Maisie's been deserted but I've promised her one—or even two—so that's okay.'

Parallel universe didn't begin to describe the way he was feeling, he decided. He swung back the covers and then thought…hell, he was only wearing boxers. For some stupid reason he was blushing like a girl.

But Hannah wasn't reacting like a blushing girl.

'Hey, nice pecs,' she said, matter-of-factly. 'How's the hand?'

'Fine,' he told her.

'Liar. Use some paracetamol. The pasties will be done in five minutes.' She hesitated and her smile faded. 'Josh, the wind seems to be dying. I don't know how to work your internet to find out if it'll rise again but I thought—'

'I might be able to get across to Skye and Mick's.'

'I thought *we* might be able to get across to Skye and Mick's,' she said severely. 'There's no I in Rescue.'

'Team talking?' he said, and found himself grinning. She was so sure. So brave. Here she was, eight months pregnant, hauled from a sinking car and yet ready to head out into danger again. 'There's no I in Sense either. The I has to stay home and guard the dogs.'

'The dogs are doing fine without me, and they'll be

even better after Cornish pasties. That's a great little courtyard you have, by the way. Though it's a bit small. As the only place they can safely relieve themselves, by the time this wind eases you might find your grass with a hundred burn patches.'

'You're changing the subject,' he growled. 'Hannah, you're not coming with me.'

'It's windy but not dangerously so,' she said serenely. 'The island's not so big that if we get bogged I can't walk home. There's no bridge between here and Mick's. Plus...' Her voice faltered a little. 'Josh, this storm has been terrifying and their side of the island would have borne the brunt of it. If their house didn't hold up I can't think of anywhere safe they could have sheltered. I hope I'm wrong but...well, two medical professionals might be more use than one.'

'Hannah—

'Enough arguing,' she said, as if the argument was indeed concluded. 'Stop distracting me with those pecs, get yourself dressed and into my pasties and then we'll go play Medics to the Rescue.'

The pasties were amazing. He hadn't tasted pasties like this since... When? Since he'd been a kid and his grandma had cooked for him. She'd let him help, he re-membered, and weirdly that memory was all wrapped up in the way he was feeling now.

His parents' marriage had been stormy, to say the least. His grandmother's house had been a sanctuary.

This kitchen, with the warmth from the Aga oozing gentle heat, with the dogs nosing around...even Maisie had struggled in to investigate these glorious smells... with this woman wearing his ridiculous apron...

Mostly with this woman, he thought, and had to give

himself a fierce mental shake. She's nothing to do with you, he told himself. She's a woman you're helping. Nothing more.

A woman he was helping?

She was giving leftovers to the dogs, washing oven trays, lifting another batch of pasties from the oven...

He wasn't helping her. *She* was bringing his kitchen to life.

He blinked and tried to focus on his pastie, but the sight of Hannah...

His apron was sitting over her baby bump, its slogan protruding like a neon sign. *Caution: Extremely Hot.*

She was eight months pregnant, battered and bruised. A woman he'd rescued and who needed care. How could she be...hot?

Ridiculous.

'I've made a heap of pasties,' she told him happily. 'Mick and family may well need feeding.'

'If they're okay.' He was struggling to focus on anything other than that crazy apron. And her smile.

'As you say,' she said, her smile slipping.

'Plus they're just as likely to be vegans.'

'Vegans who've been blown to bits by a storm and haven't eaten for a couple of days might well swallow their scruples,' she retorted, but looked doubtfully at her pastie pile. 'I can hardly scrape the meat out now.'

He grinned at her look of dismay. She really was gorgeous.

But she'd moved on. 'Josh, the weather...'

'I checked online while I was dressing,' he told her. Man, these pasties were delicious. 'The wind's easing back a bit. The cyclone's moved out to sea but the edges threaten to blast in again tonight. Not as bad as before, but up to fifty or sixty knots. You're right in thinking we have a window. Maybe three or four hours. The truck's solid. Over and back, collect the Fordes and bring them back again.

'We?' she said, cautiously.

'We,' he agreed. 'As long as you're careful. And follow instructions. And don't do anything that'll put either you or your baby at risk.'

'Yes, Doctor,' she said meekly, but she was smiling and he thought there was nothing meek about this woman.

Nothing meek at all.

The island itself was a mess. Low-growing salt bush had been wrenched and hurled across the island in great tangled heaps. The sand had shifted, so there were vast ridges that hadn't been there before.

He drove cautiously down to the stone wharf and then along the shoreline. The wharf had been used to supply the lighthouse in days when lighthouse keepers had lived here, and it'd been used to land building supplies for his house. It'd be needed again now, he thought—it'd be the only access until the bridge was rebuilt.

Would he need to buy a boat?

But he was getting ahead of himself. Or using the ideas to distract him from what lay ahead.

And from the woman who sat beside him.

Like him, she was concentrating on the track, and he thought she was almost driving for him. He'd seen this look before in fellow medics as they strode toward an emergency room after a call, knowing something grim was waiting, as though concentrating could let them see what lay ahead.

She'd argued with him to let her drive—'Josh, your

hand'—but had subsided when he'd told her it didn't make sense, that he knew the island and she didn't. Now, looking at the mess around them, her look was bleak.

'They're sensible,' he told her. 'They'll have found shelter…somewhere. Or maybe the house has held.'

They jolted over the last ridge, and he stopped the truck, staring aghast at the devastation below.

The house hadn't held.

It had been built in a tiny bay, a picturesque piece of magic, with turquoise water and a wide curve of gorgeous sandy beach. When he'd been here in the past he'd been almost blown away by the beauty of the location, and by the simplicity and charm of the wooden cottage Mick and Skye had built themselves.

There was no charm about the cottage now. There was no cottage. The base of the fireplace still stood. A couple of walls did, too, although they leaned drunkenly inwards.

Smashed furniture, clothing, the detritus of living was scattered around the whole bay.

'Oh, no,' Hannah whispered, and he glanced across at her blanched face and wondered if his matched hers.

He could see no one. Where were they?

The wind was still whistling, sand sweeping across the devastation. The sea was a maelstrom of white and grey. Nature reclaiming its own?

No.

Part of him didn't want to go any further. Like that was going to happen. Reluctantly he steered the truck down to the house site, parking in the lee of the tiny amount of protection the chimney gave.

The truck was surrounded by shattered glass, ripped corrugated iron, mess.

'Just lucky Madison left her gum boots,' Hannah managed, striving for a lightness she must be far from feeling. Here was the almost universal black humour medics were famed for, a sole defence when your guts felt like they were being ripped out. She held up a foot to inspect a pink boot with yellow ducklings emblazoned on the side. 'Emergency services, eat your hearts out. Bulletproof vests have nothing on ducklings.'

'My sister got them for rock-pool paddling. She has a warped sense of style.' Josh's gaze was sweeping the bay, as was Hannah's. Searching. 'Block your ears.'

He put a hand on the horn and blasted, then blasted again. The truck's horn was so loud the sounds of wind and sea faded in comparison.

He stared out again. Nothing.

Where could they have gone?

The Fordes' car, a rickety sedan, was parked away from the house, pointing inland. The windows of the car were smashed and the doors on this side blasted open. Had they tried to leave, then abandoned the car in mid storm? What were their options then?

Had they huddled together to keep safe and then been buried in the mass of shifting sand? He felt sick.

Why hadn't he insisted they stay with him? Why hadn't he picked up the kids and carried them away bodily?

'You can't save people from themselves,' Hannah whispered. 'Josh, you did what you could.' And then she paused. 'Josh, look!'

And at the edge of the curve of the bay, where the sandhills rose steeply, they saw a figure. The blowing sand still formed a gritty fog, but whoever it was was waving.

It was an adult, either Skye or Mick.

'Stay here until I see what's happening,' Josh said, pushing open the truck door and heading for the sand-hill.

'Pigs might fly,' Hannah muttered, and headed after him.

It was Skye on the ridge. Josh reached her first and as Hannah came up behind she saw her fold into Josh's arms. Josh held her tight and hard for a long moment. He'd know, Hannah thought, that the most important thing after terror was contact. Unless someone was bleeding out or not breathing then the reassurance that they weren't alone was crucial.

For long moments he stood and held her. She was dressed in ragged shorts, T-shirt and bare feet. Her long blonde hair was a matted mess, her neck, her legs, her arms a bloody tapestry of scratches.

Finally Josh put her back, holding her tightly by both shoulders, his strength seemingly holding her up.

'You're safe now, Skye. You know I'm a doctor, and Hannah here is a nurse. Where are the others?'

She looked wildly up at him. Her face was as scratched and bloody as the rest of her, but the damage looked superficial, Hannah thought. Her eyes were wild but clear, and her breathing was fast but not shallow.

She saw Josh do a fast visual assessment as well. Moving on...

'Where are they?' Josh asked again, and Skye gave a gulping sob and grabbed his hand and started tug-ging. Back across the sandhill that'd been hiding her.

He reached back and grabbed Hannah's hand they struggled forward. This storm was no longer danger-ous but struggling in soft sand when being sand-blasted was hard. The duck gumboots weren't great footwear.

It'd be easier if she took them off but she wasn't stupid—with this amount of debris she'd be another victim in moments.

But she was damned if she was being towed. She gritted her teeth and got her feet moving.

She let her hand stay in Josh's, though. Linking was sensible.

And it made her feel…

Oh, for heaven's sake, she was in emergency mode. Focus on what lies ahead, she told herself, not on the way this man's hand was making her feel.

Then they crossed another sandy ridge and even the feel of Josh's hand faded to nothing.

One man and three kids.

They were crouched in the lee of a rocky crag. It wasn't much of an overhang, though, just enough to deflect the worst of the wind.

The two older kids were holding what looked to be a horse-hair blanket over their heads, forming a canopy to increase the range of the windbreak. A younger child was crouched between them, fists in her eyes, sobbing.

A man lay prone on the ground. A body? Hannah's heart gave a sickening lurch, but then he stirred, groaned and reached out a hand, as if to comfort the littlest child.

'It's okay!' The group hadn't seen them but Skye's faltering cry made them look up. 'Dr O'Connor's here,' she gasped. 'He's even brought a nurse.'

And then she sank to her knees, sagging in a culmination of relief and exhaustion.

The wind was still blasting. The kids looked scratched, battered but mostly uninjured. The littlest one looked a ball of misery but her sobs alone said that there shouldn't be a life-threatening injury.

The man, though... He'd slumped back onto the sand, his face grey. Josh was already slithering down to him.

Triage.

What was Hannah's first priority?

They had one blanket, and for such a group it provided little protection. The kids' faces looked stretched, their eyes too big for their faces, red-rimmed from the sand. Dehydration?

Josh was bent over Mick, focused on his need. Skye and the kids needed her attention, but Josh needed equipment and they all needed water.

She'd seen Josh load a water container into the back of the truck, plus medical equipment. Also, if the truck was here they could use its bulk as a partial wind break. She had no idea what was going on with Mick, but triage said the truck was essential.

'Do you need me now or will I get the truck?' she asked Josh. He didn't look up.

'Truck. We need gear. Drive it around the sandhill and come at us from behind. Don't try to come straight up and over. Drive slowly, taking the lowest slope rather than the quickest route. If there's any doubt stop and walk back. And, Hannah, treat yourself with care. Take every step with thought.'

He glanced back at her then, as if he was torn about letting her go. It seemed that with all the demands around him, with a myriad of conflicting needs, she and her unborn baby were still in his mix of priorities.

She blinked as their gazes met.

Go with care, his look said, and as she turned and stumbled back to the truck, for some stupid reason she felt her eyes welling with tears.

It was such a small thing, to have someone care as

Josh was caring. And it wasn't as if it was personal. It was medical triage.

But it felt personal. For Hannah who'd felt appallingly alone from the moment Ryan had walked out the door, from the time her father had slammed the phone down on her, cutting her off from her entire family—this felt huge.

'So you're overreacting. Go get the truck and stop being ridiculous,' she muttered, but she muttered under her breath because talking to herself with sand blowing into her face was not a good idea. Also thinking of Josh…like she was thinking…was even less of a good idea.

Focus on now. On putting one foot after another into the shifting sand. Her boots were filled. Her feet were ridiculously heavy but it'd be useless to stop and try and empty them. The truck was too far away and Josh needed the truck and its contents quickly.

'So stop thinking and move,' she told herself, but she had a feeling that every part of her, right down to her feet in their ridiculous duckling boots, wanted her thoughts to stay exactly where they kept on drifting.

CHAPTER NINE

MEDICAL PRIORITIES TOOK OVER. Her thoughts might stray as she struggled back to the truck, but driving the vehicle across the sandhills took every ounce of concentration she possessed. They never had roads like this in Ireland, she thought grimly. Josh must be really worried to have sent her to get the truck rather than do it himself.

But she made it. She parked the truck beside the huddled group, trying to position it to block the worst of the wind, then hauled open the back and tugged out the container of water.

She filled a tin mug and handed it to Skye. 'Wash your mouth out and drink,' she told her. 'Lots. Then get the kids to do the same.'

'Mick...' Skye sounded despairing.

'I need to help Dr O'Connor,' she told her. 'We'll take care of Mick. Your job is to get water into the kids.'

She filled another mug and carried it to Josh. Whose face was grim.

'I need you to drink a bit of this, mate,' he told Mick, but Mick groaned and turned his head away.

Josh lifted his head, ignoring his clenched lips, the greyness of his face.

'Open your mouth,' he told him. 'I know how much pain you're in but I need to get the sand out of your mouth. Priority, mate. We'll get morphine on board but your airways need to be clear first. Open.'

This was a new Josh. Decisive, authoritative, someone not to be reckoned with. It was no surprise that Mick obeyed.

She headed back to the truck and grabbed the medical bag. By the time she returned, Mick's mouth at least was clear of sand. 'Spit,' Josh was ordering. 'One more mouthful and then we'll let you swallow.'

She set down the bag and then tried herself to assess. The rug was lying over Mick's legs. She lifted it with care and had trouble keeping her face impassive.

Mick had been wearing jeans but they were almost shredded. His legs looked as if something had sliced into him. Both legs looked a bloody mess.

She touched his feet. He was wearing sandals. One foot seemed fine.

The other was distinctly cooler.

She glanced at Josh, his eyes met hers and she knew he was already way ahead of her.

'He and Skye laid over the kids in the worst of the storm,' Josh said curtly, as he held the mug to Mick's mouth again. Mick drank now, but the ashen look on his face didn't change. 'Skye told me. When the house collapsed they headed here and stayed. Mick lay on the windward side all night, bearing the brunt of the wind to protect his family. A sheet of iron slammed into his legs. Deep lacerations and I suspect a compound fracture.'

She nodded, careful to keep her face impassive. Major rule of training—don't scare the punters. She replaced the rug and headed for Josh's bag, using her body to protect its contents from the blowing sand as she searched for what she needed.

'Hey, being eight months pregnant does have its uses,' she quipped to those around her. 'I make a great windbreak.'

There were strained smiles, which was reassuring.

What did Josh need? She forced herself into medical mode, into nurse mode. Swabs. Morphine. Syringe.

The wind was still fierce. The truck wasn't enough to provide protection, and her body wasn't all that great at withstanding its blast either.

Her mind was heading in all directions. Mick's legs had stopped bleeding, but a pool of darkened blood lay in the sand under him. It represented a lot of blood and his colour reflected that. He'd need an IV, plasma, a saline infusion at the very least. And...compound fracture?

She handed over the swabs and syringe and started gathering IV equipment. But Josh stopped her.

'Not here,' he told her. 'There's no way I can get a stable line in with this amount of sand and wind.' He hesitated and she could see his mind working—in a direction he didn't like? But when he spoke his voice was bland. 'Hannah, can you stay with Mick while I take Skye and the kids back to the house?'

'Of course.'

She already knew why. While she'd been battling to get the truck over the sandhill, she'd been thinking transport and she already knew what Josh had obviously figured.

They needed to get these guys to safety—all of them. But the truck was a four-seater for midgets—the back seat was tiny, with a tray at the back. Her first thought had been that Josh should take Mick to safety but then he'd have to return for them, leaving Mick alone. Not safe, not after this amount of blood loss.

Next option. If she took Skye and the kids back to the house first, it'd take her an age to get back, even if she didn't get caught in a sand drift.

Third option. She stayed with Mick and kept him alive while Josh did the first run. It was hardly a safe choice. If Mick was to go into cardiac arrest…

There was no choice.

'There's everything you need in my kit,' he told her, his gaze meeting hers and holding it with a solid message. He meant defibrillator, adrenaline, equipment for resuscitation.

Please, God, don't let me have to use them.

It was a silent prayer but she could see by Josh's face that he knew what she was thinking.

'Just don't go into labour,' he said, smiling with a confidence he must be far from feeling. 'Mick, I'll put a rough splint on your leg to hold it steady, but then I'm taking Skye and the kids back to my house. To safety. We need to make two runs because my truck's too small to fit you all and I want your legs to be stretched out. Hannah's a trained nurse and she'll keep you safe until I get back. My house is solid, warm, with everything we need. You've done a great job, mate. The morphine will kick in any minute. Skye and the kids are already safe. See if you can drink a bit more water, then lie back and let the drugs do their work.'

'Safe…' Mick muttered.

'Yeah, you've done it,' Josh told him. 'Care's now over to me and Hannah.'

'Hannah…'

'She's a nurse in a million,' Josh told him. 'There's no one I'd rather leave you with.'

The wait for Josh to return seemed to take for ever, but the drugs took hold and Mick seemed to drift in and out of awareness.

He mustn't have slept all night, Hannah thought. He'd been holding his body over his little family, taking the brunt of the storm himself.

'You're a hero,' she told him as she encouraged him to drink more.

'It's Doc O'Connor who's the hero,' he muttered thickly. 'Who'd'a thought a doc would come to this island? Gossip says he's too damaged after that damned accident to work. Doesn't look damaged to me.'

'Nor to me,' Hannah said stoutly, reflecting, not for the first time, how emotional trauma often left a far worse damage than physical. 'We're lucky. He'll stabilise your leg properly and keep you out of pain until we can get you to hospital.'

'You his partner?'

'No.' The idea gave her a sharp jolt. 'I'm Miss Byrne's niece. Josh rescued me as well.'

Luckily Mick was too fuzzy to ask more questions. He lay back and let the morphine send him into a dozy half slumber.

Hannah sat beside him and tried not to feel how uncomfortable she was. Her baby was kicking—hard.

'You don't like being sand blasted either,' she said under her breath. But then she thought, *Her baby*.

It was an emotional punch. She'd pushed through this pregnancy by putting one foot in front of the other, concentrating on practicalities, but in a few weeks a little person would enter the world. A little person solely dependent on her.

The idea was terrifying.

Would she be able to ring her mother? Her dad would slam the phone down if she tried. Even her sister… She and Bridget had been so close all their lives, but Bridget had caved in, in the face of her father's rage-filled bullying. When Hannah had tried to call, Bridget had whispered his reaction. 'Your sister's shamed us,' he'd told her. 'You'll have nothing to do with her or you'll leave this family as well.' There'd been a few furtive calls but their closeness was gone.

Desolation hit like a wall, but then Mick stirred. She needed to refill his mug—for every mouthful he seemed to spill three—and she went back into putting one foot after another mode.

Finally Josh returned, and with that went any time for reflection. He brought a decent piece of wood, and carefully replaced the rough stick he'd used as a first urgent splint. He administered more pain relief, then they laid the truck's front passenger seat down and manoeuvred Mick aboard.

It sounded simple.

It wasn't.

'Right,' Hannah said at last as she squeezed into what was left of the back seat. 'Home.'

Home.

It was a strange word. A strange concept. Josh was battling to keep the truck on the rutted track. The last thing they needed now was to overturn, but Hannah's hand was holding Mick's wrist and she was watching him, keeping tight obs on his pulse. He could stop being in doctor mode for a moment and let the strangeness of the word drift.

He was going home.

With hangers-on.

When he'd left, Skye had been feeding the kids—there was nothing vegan in the way they reacted to Hannah's pasties. She was staggering a bit, and still dead scared for Mick, but she had her filthy, sand-coated kids around the kitchen table and was doing her best.

'As soon as you've eaten I want you all in the bath or shower,' he'd told them. 'I need to do a full check of all of you but not until the dirt's gone.'

He'd then done a swift dog check. Thankfully his laundry was big. The dogs had been less than impressed when he'd shifted them—Maisie had even given a low growl—but a couple of leftover sausages had done the trick. The last thing he needed was any of the kids venturing into the living room and facing a bitch with pups.

Then he'd headed back to Mick—and Hannah. Now, waiting for him was Skye and three battered children, plus two dogs and four pups.

At home? A sanctuary?

He'd never thought of it as a sanctuary. He'd thought of it only as an escape. Now that escape would be crammed with people he didn't know, kids, dogs, medical needs, dog needs.

And Hannah.

What was there in this woman that made his world seem to settle. That made him feel that, yes, this would be chaos but she'd be there.

He glanced in the rear-view mirror and she saw, she smiled and she gave him a quick thumbs up before turning back to say something to Mick.

She should be frightened herself. Instead she was calm and practical.

When he'd asked her to stay with Mick—at eight months pregnant, the day after she'd almost drowned, after her aunt's death, after terror, while crouching behind a sandhill being blasted by gritty wind, she'd simply said, 'Yes.'

Not even a falter in her calm demeanour.

If he was in the market for a relationship... For a woman...

Which he wasn't, he told himself fiercely, astounded that such a thought could surface at such a time. He put a hand up and traced the scar on his face, as if to remind himself of consequences.

'Are you okay?' Hannah asked from the back seat. 'Is your hand hurting? Would you like me to drive?'

It took only that. After all this, she was concerned about him.

''We're nearly there,' he said, too curtly, but she smiled.

'That's great, Josh. You hear that, Mick? We're nearly home. Well done, us.'

CHAPTER TEN

THE NEXT COUPLE of hours were focused on medical need and little else.

A clean Skye, draped in Josh's bathrobe, met them as the truck turned into the garage and helped them lift Mick into the kitchen.

'I've put the kids into the big bedroom,' she said, apologetically. 'I hope that's okay. They're asleep already. What can I do to help?'

Her face was bleached white as she looked at her husband. With cause, Hannah thought. With the amount of blood loss he'd suffered, Mick looked dreadful.

'Go to bed with the kids,' Josh said roughly as they got the semi-conscious Mick into the kitchen, onto their rough operating table. 'Skye, you know I'm a doctor and Hannah's a nurse. We have everything we need and there's nothing more you can do. Mick might need you when he wakes up, though, so the best thing you can do now is sleep.'

She left, reluctantly, but she looked almost dead on her feet.

Josh was already inserting a drip. Mick had been drinking but not enough. He needed fluid resuscitation—saline. Josh was swabbing everything three or four times over. The sand was insidious.

The morphine combined with blood loss combined with dehydration was making Mick drift in and out of awareness. As Josh started removing what was left of his pants, though, he groaned and grabbed. Hannah caught his hand.

'You're okay, Mick,' she told him, as she'd told him over and over in the past hour. 'You're safe. Dr O'Connor's good.'

'Mick, we're going to put you to sleep for a wee while,' Josh said. He was inspecting Mick's legs, his face carefully impassive.

Hannah had seen this look any number of times with medical personnel.

Don't scare the patient.

His look scared her.

'Fancy yourself as an anaesthetist?' he asked, and sent her a look she read from years of experience.

'I don't need to fancy myself,' she retorted. 'I'm superb.' She managed a grin and held Mick's hand tighter. 'You have two of the best medical personnel in Australia treating you, Mick. Skilled, professional—'

'And modest,' Josh said, rising to her smile. 'Don't forget modest. Mick, we might have to knock something off your Medicare funding for fixing your leg on the kitchen table instead of in a nice, shiny theatre, but never doubt our ability. Give us a minute to get the worst of the sand off us—we don't want to be shaking sand into our neat handiwork—and we'll have you to sleep and sorted in no time.'

'It still hurts,' Mick faltered. 'And I can't feel the toes on my left foot.'

'That's why we're here, Mick. Leave it to us.

* * *

A compound fracture. Multiple lacerations. Compromised blood supply to the foot.

He should be in a major hospital with orthopaedic and vascular surgeons, plus a team of highly skilled nurses, Hannah thought.

There was no such option.

Almost as soon as they had everyone safe in the house the wind started rising again. The forecast was for another few hours' blow. Josh made a fast call, placing them in the queue for evacuation, but there was no chance of that until morning.

Which left Hannah working as anaesthetist while Josh fought to stabilise the fractured leg and, more importantly, to repair the compromised blood supply to the foot.

How he did it with the equipment he had available to him, Hannah had no idea, and she couldn't watch to find out. All her attention was on Mick's breathing, on his thready pulse, on what she had to do to keep both things stable. Anaesthetics were not part of midwifery training. Luckily she'd been in a lot of theatres in her time. She'd paid attention, but still she was well out of her comfort zone. Josh was incorporating her in his scope of responsibility, though, giving curt orders, aware of her tenuous hold on the situation.

Hannah concentrated fiercely on what she had to do—but on the tiny part of her brain that was still capable of other thought, she could only wonder at this man's skill.

He was working fast, obviously acutely aware of the need for minimal anaesthetic when not only was his anaesthetist a midwife, but he lacked any of the superb technology used in modern theatres to monitor the patient's condition. And he was talking to Hannah as he worked, possibly aware that it settled her—at least made her as settled as anyone doing what she was doing could be.

'There are splinters of bone pushing against blood vessels,' he told her. 'The fracture itself seems relatively easy to align but the splinters are doing the damage.' There was a long silence with intense concentration on both their parts, and then a sigh of satisfaction. 'Got it. You b… That one's been kinking the main artery. There's a surge to the foot already.' Another silence and then… 'It's regaining colour. You beauty. I think we're home and hosed, Hannah. Pulse?'

'Still steady,' she told him. Every sense was directed at Mick's pallid face, his breathing, his heart rate.

'Right, let's get the leg splinted before it can shift again. There's more I could do but I don't want to keep him under for a moment longer than I can help. Though I reckon that drip's already doing its job. Amazing what hydration can do.'

That was aimed to make her feel better about the risks. It was true, though. She wasn't imagining it. Mick's colour was already improving.

Josh was splinting, then turning to deal with lacerations. So many…

He swabbed and cleaned and pulled them together with Steri-Strips. 'They'll need decent stitching when he gets out of here, but it's too risky to keep him under for longer.'

His leg was going to look like patchwork for ever.

But there was a for ever, Hannah thought, and she felt almost light-headed. How lucky were they all that Josh had been on the island?

He finished and helped her to reverse the anaesthetic.

'Amazing job, Dr Byrne,' he told her as Mick coughed and choked and then started breathing for himself.

'It's you who's amazing,' she told him. 'To have the forethought to have this equipment here... To have the skills...' She found herself blinking back tears. She thought of this little family and how they'd be if Josh hadn't found them. She thought of where she'd be...

She couldn't help it, she put her arms around Josh and hugged. Hard.

It was the most unprofessional action...

She didn't care. He held himself stiff in her arms but she didn't care about that either. She knew enough of this man to know his ghosts, his pain, his need for isolation wouldn't want her close, but, dammit, she needed to hug him. She buried her face in his chest, she wrapped her arms around as much of him as she could hold—which wasn't as much as she'd have liked because her bump got in the way—and she hugged and she hugged and she hugged.

He hadn't been held since Madison had left, and he hadn't enjoyed being held then. The guilt as his sister had held him had been almost overwhelming.

There was no guilt here. There was only...fear? Fear to hug back? Fear to accept warmth and friendship—for surely that was all it was?

It was also reaction, he told himself. Hannah had had an appalling couple of days. She'd risen to the challenge brilliantly. Her reactions to everything thrown at her had been little less than mind-blowing, and now she was hugging him.

Like Madison, he thought. Madison hugged him to give him comfort and he didn't deserve comfort.

But as Hannah continued to hold he felt more. She was holding and holding, her face was buried in his chest and he realised she was taking comfort, as well as giving it. Almost involuntarily his arms wrapped around her and he found himself hugging back.

He was still watching Mick, but the big man's breathing was settling. His eyes hadn't fluttered open yet but they would.

Mick was safe. They were all safe.

This woman had made it possible.

His head seemed to bend of its own accord, and he found himself letting his chin rest in her hair. He wanted more. He wanted to bury his whole face in her tangle of curls. He wanted to lift her, hold her, protect her…

Claim her.

There was a dumb thought. Primaeval and sexist and wrong on so many levels. Stupid. She was nothing to do with him and she'd be gone tomorrow. He needed to get back to his solitude, to the way of life he needed to keep himself sane.

But for one sweet moment he allowed himself to forget the fears, the promises. He allowed himself to savour the feel of her, the warmth and strength of her hold, the sensation of giving and receiving. Of almost merging.

He could feel her heartbeat. She must be feeling his as well. It felt good. Right. Perfect.

As if it was meant.

But it wasn't meant. It was shock and trauma that had created the moment, and sanity surfaced. He sensed rather than saw Mick open his eyes and he wasn't sure if it was Hannah who tugged away or him, but either way suddenly they were separate beings. Emotion was put away.

They were back to being professionals with a patient emerging from anaesthetic.

'Skye...' Mick croaked. 'The kids...'

And that's what loving's all about, Josh thought as he adjusted the drip and Hannah did the reassuring. It's blind terror, exposure, where someone's death can cut you in two and destroy more than your life.

All he had to do was remind himself of that appalling moment when he'd realised Alice was dead. At the grief etched onto Madison's face.

Solitude.

He needed to get back to it, fast.

He needed to get all these people out of his house. Including Hannah.

Hannah lay in bed and felt guilty. Josh O'Connor was starting to look hunted.

Not only that, his house was filled to bursting. And he must be exhausted.

Skye and the kids were in Josh's big bed. She was in Madison's. Mick was on the settee in the living room. The dogs had the laundry.

Josh was keeping watch over Mick on one of the small fireside chairs. Hardly a base for sleeping. But when she'd demurred, offering to take the first shift, Josh had told where to go. 'Get into bed and sleep,' he'd told her. 'The last thing we need is for exhaustion and stress to bring on early labour.'

He was right, but now... She glanced at the bedside clock. Three a.m. She'd had almost seven hours' sleep. Surely he'd let her now.

But even as she thought it she heard footsteps padding along the corridor. Light footsteps. Skye?

She might be in trouble. Josh had given them all painkillers but they'd be wearing off now.

She could do this for Josh, at least, she thought, and tossed back her covers to intercept her.

She didn't make it. Skye already had the living-room door open and was looking worriedly across to the settee.

The room was lit only by firelight and one small lamp. Hannah could see a shape on the settee—and Josh sitting upright by the fire. He rose as he saw Skye.

'There's nothing to worry about,' he told her gently. 'I've just put more morphine into his drip but he's sleeping naturally. Everything's okay.'

'I know,' Skye said, faltering. She was wearing one of Josh's T-shirts, Madison's knickers, and nothing else. Her hair was still tangled and wild and she had sticking plaster across one side of her face, but she looked across at her husband and her expression firmed. 'That's why I'm here. I've slept solidly. The kids are okay. They're such a bundle of arms and legs in that bed that they'll comfort each other if they wake. Now I'd like to take a turn watching over Mick.' And then, as Josh hesitated, she held out her hands as if in supplication. 'Josh, I need to.'

And Josh got it. Hannah saw his face soften and she understood. Skye must have thought they could all could die. Mick had covered her and her children with his body. He was her husband and she loved him.

She needed to take a hand in his care.

Josh rose, smiling. 'That's great, Skye. Do you need painkillers yourself? No awards for bravery, now. Yes or no?'

'I could use something,' Skye admitted. 'But nothing that'll make me sleep. I want—'

'To watch over Mick. I understand.' He bent over his truly impressive box of medical supplies and produced a couple of pills. 'take these with water. There's a pitcher here and a glass. If Mick wakes up, see if you can encourage him to drink. The drip will be keeping him hydrated but his mouth was dry so long it'll be like sandpaper. Yours too, I'm guessing. And if there's anything you need, if there's anything worrying you at all, come and fetch me. I'll be in the kitchen.'

'I promise.' She took the pills like an automaton and sank down beside Mick. She took his hand and held it and Hannah and Josh might as well not have been there.

With one last, long look, Josh slipped out of the room. Hannah had backed into the passage.

'In the kitchen, huh?' she said as he closed the door, and she saw him start.

'Hannah…'

'I was coming to offer what Skye's providing,' she told him. 'I've been usurped. But no kitchen for you. You must be dead on your feet.'

'I'm okay.'

'You're not okay. Is your hand hurting?

He'd almost forgotten his hand. 'No.'

'That's great. Bed, then.'

'There's not—'

'A bed? There is. Madison's bed's a double. In you go and sleep. I'll tell Skye where you'll be if she needs you, but she can find me first.'

'Hannah, you need sleep more than me.

'I've had it. I'm fine.'

'You're not fine. Hannah, I will not sleep while you sit up.'

'Ditto for me,' she said serenely. 'Which leaves one

option. We share. I'm going to make myself some tea and toast first, though. Would you like some?'

'I...' He hesitated and then shrugged. 'Yes.'

'Good boy,' she said, and he blinked.

'What, am I a kid?'

'For the purpose of the exercise, yes.'

'Hannah, we can't—'

'Have wild hot sex while sharing a double bed?' She grinned. 'How did I know you were thinking that?'

'I wasn't!'

'What? Not horny as hell over an eight-month-pregnant woman in your sister's stretched-to-bursting too-frilly nightie when you're almost dead on your feet with fatigue? I don't believe it.' Her grin widened. 'But I'll risk it. Go on, get yourself into bed. I'll check the kids and the dogs, make tea and toast, and bring you some. But what's the betting you're asleep before I return?'

She was right. He slept.

She'd taken her time in the kitchen, wanting Josh to settle. Then she'd made him his tea and toast and carried it through to the bedroom.

One look at the unconscious Josh had her returning to the kitchen with the unwanted snack. 'Hey, I'm eating for two,' she told herself with satisfaction, and enjoyed her second snack almost as much as her first.

Finally it was time to return to bed, but a part of her was niggly with unease. Her suggestion to share was surely sensible but there was a little voice saying it was unwise.

'Oh, for heaven's sake, even if we managed to have hot sex there'd hardly be consequences,' she muttered at last, and tiptoed to the bed and slid under the covers.

He had his back to her. Madison's bed was a double but only just.

As she slid in beside him their bodies touched and she felt him shudder.

He was wearing only boxers. His chest, his arms were bare, and she couldn't mistake the tremor.

'Josh?'

No answer. He seemed deeply asleep.

So why the tremor?

She lay in the dark, listening to the storm outside but thinking of this man's history. Of a trauma that had never been forgotten. In the last two days he'd come appallingly close to more tragedy.

There was no weakness in this man. She knew it but she also knew he'd built his armour so his strength could be rebuilt from within.

Not from without. Not by needing people. Not by accepting...care.

She felt the tremor again. There was probably no need for her to intervene, but if this was a nightmare...

Of course it was a nightmare.

She was a nurse. It was her job to care. To stop nightmares.

That was a good, practical way of looking at it, she thought, and before she could think further—because why would she?—she edged closer and wrapped her arms around his broad back. It was a bit tricky with her bump, but it felt okay.

It felt right.

He was still shuddering. She tightened her hold and whispered against his skin, 'Josh, it's okay.' She could feeling her breath waft back at her. 'Everyone's safe. All's well, Josh, love. Sleep, sleep and sleep.'

And for a moment she felt him stiffen. Had she woken him?

'It's only me,' she whispered. 'Your inconvenient friend, Hannah. I'll let you go if you want but, Josh, the kids are safe. Mick and Skye are safe. Even the puppies are safe. You've saved us all. You did good, Josh. Now sleep.'

And blessedly she felt his body relax. His breathing eased, deep and steady.

'Sleep,' she whispered again, and the feel of his back, cocooned against her breast, seemed to have the same soporific effect on her.

She slept.

CHAPTER ELEVEN

JOSH WOKE TO SILENCE. The constant howling of the last two days was gone, and in its place…peace.

And warmth.

He had a woman in his arms.

Hannah.

He had no memory of her coming to bed. Or maybe he did. He recalled a whisper of a sensation, and then her touch, the sound of her soft voice and his dreams abandoning him. Then only sleep.

But somehow in the night he must have stirred, moved, held her in turn.

She was lying facing him, her curls splayed on the pillow, her face lovely in sleep.

Lovely. She truly was.

His arm was lying under the soft swell of her breasts, cradling her. How had that happened?

He was so close he could feel her breathing. He could feel her warmth under her flimsy nightgown.

He felt more at peace than he'd felt for three long years, or maybe even longer. For ever?

Which was crazy. This was the result of exhaustion, he thought, plus the release of the tension and the danger of the past few days.

Sunlight was edging through the chinks in the shutters. Morning. He needed to check Mick.

As if on cue, there was a wail from somewhere in the house, not of distress but of indignation.

'He's finished the Vegemite. I wanted Vegemite on my toast.'

'Uh-oh.' Hannah stirred and woke smiling. Or maybe, like him, she'd been awake and savouring this extraordinary moment. Smiling inwardly even before she opened her eyes. 'Do you not have back-up Vegemite, Dr O'Connor? I call that a major fail. You realise you could well risk a report to the medical board.'

'Not guilty,' he said. He should remove his arm, but it seemed to have no intention of moving. Nothing felt like moving. Here was peace.

Here was…home?

With difficulty he forced his mind back to practical. 'Vegemite's my staple,' he managed. 'There should be two more jars in the storeroom.'

'So who gets up to tell them?'

'Let 'em eat honey,' he murmured, and she chuckled. She had the most glorious chuckle.

But then… 'Mick,' she said, and they both knew the moment had ended. If there'd been any problem, Skye would have come to tell them, but it was over four hours since Mick had had a proper check. And with the wind gone, it was time for the outside world to intrude.

Mick needed medical evacuation—that leg needed to be set by an expert—and they could all leave with him. Skye had told them last night that her mother lived in the city and would welcome them. They could stay with her while Mick recovered and they tried to figure what to do about their ruined home.

Moira's body would be removed by the authorities,

to await a coroner's report and burial. With that link to the island gone, Hannah would return to her hospital apartment to await the birth of her baby.

Maisie and the pups were probably officially Hannah's. Could she keep them in her hospital apartment?

Regardless, he'd be left with his solitude. Which was what he wanted.

Wasn't it?

Hannah lifted his arm—with reluctance?—and edged back, rolling to her side so she could read his face.

'Help will come now?'

'We're on a priority list. The sea will still be huge but there'll be choppers. Mick needs skilled orthopaedic surgery to stop permanent damage to that leg. With a death and a serious injury I imagine we'll be top priority. I've said six people need urgent evacuation. Plus there's Moira.'

There was a moment's silence and then…

'Josh, can I stay?'

He stilled. His gut said yes. It was so much what he was thinking.

But then sense took over—of course it did.

'Why would you want to stay?'

She sat up then, tugging the covers up to her breast, as if she was putting distance between them.

'A few reasons,' she said diffidently. 'And before you say no, I'm not asking if I can stay here. Not in your house. But someone has to clear Moira's house and that someone needs to be me. There'll be all sorts of things that need to be organised. And Maisie and her pups… I don't know if I can look after them where I'm living now.'

'It's not safe for you to stay,' he said, automatically in

medical mode. 'You're eight months pregnant. There's no bridge.'

'But once the sea settles—and it should settle within the next twenty-four hours—the jetty will be useable. I know there are water taxis at Stingray Bay. I could call one the moment I go into labour. There's a medical clinic at the Bay, so I'd have immediate help, and if a taxi's not fast enough I could get an ambulance to Townsville. And, of course, if the weather even looks like turning again I'd leave immediately.'

'It's a bad idea.'

'It's not ideal but when else am I going to deal with this?' she reasoned. 'After my baby's born? Moira's house will be a mess, and who knows how demanding my baby will be? And there's no one else—Moira cut herself off from everybody. I need to spend a few days here, sorting and cleaning. I'll organise a funeral for Moira over at Stingray Bay, then pack up anything of value, get rid of the perishables, lock it and leave. I've already organised a bigger apartment in Townsville. I just need to get permission to have Maisie there. You know, in the long run Mick and Skye might be interested in Moira's house, but that's for the future. I don't even know what her will says. She might have left the house to a dogs' home for all I know, but for now the responsibility must be mine.'

'You really have been planning.'

'Just a little,' she said, and her face lit with a trace of mischief. 'I wasn't all that tired, and for half an hour or so earlier on you were snoring.'

'Snoring! I couldn't have been.'

'Definitely snoring,' she told him, her smile widening. 'But I wouldn't worry. Extreme exhaustion can make that happen. I hope you're feeling better now. Your hand?'

'It's fine. I'm fine,' he told her, and he had to acknowledge that he was definitely feeling better. Something about the way she was smiling at him...

He had a woman in his bed. In her bed.

Hannah.

Smiling.

For a moment he was totally, absolutely distracted. What he was feeling...

What he was feeling had to be shoved away. He turned away, almost abruptly, and snagged his jeans from the floor, focusing on pulling them on. A man needed to be dressed. A man needed separation.

But her words replayed in his head and he knew separation had to be postponed.

'You can stay here,' he said gruffly, hauling on his T-shirt. 'Here, Hannah, in this house. I have no idea what damage the storm's done to Moira's house...'

'It's a solid house,' she told him. 'Even if there is a bit of damage I can cope, though I might need to borrow some of your supplies. That's why I'm asking your permission.'

'And you might need my help if you go into labour?' He kept his back to her. For some reason it seemed important to keep this impersonal.

'I might,' she admitted. 'I guess...okay, I wouldn't suggest this if I didn't know you'd be here. But I weighed it up and decided that with your support the plan would work. It is asking a bit of you, Josh, so if you say no...'

'I do say no, at least to part of it,' he said heavily, and then he turned back to her. Damn, she was so lovely. Tousled from sleep, in that silly frilly nightgown, her bedclothes pulled up like she still needed defence...

She made his heart twist as it had no right to twist. As he had no intention that it could ever twist.

'If you must stay then you stay here, in this house,' he told her. 'In this stage of pregnancy I'd be needing to traipse across every half-hour to check you haven't collapsed with an antepartum haemorrhage.'

'As if that's likely. You wouldn't have to.'

'I'm responsible, even if you're not,' he snapped, and then regrouped. He was standing now, looking down at her, thinking how young she looked. How vulnerable. How alone.

Do not get sucked in. Do not care.

Too late. He already did.

'You'll stay in this house,' he growled. 'Or you'll leave the island. That's an order.'

'Surgeon ordering nurse.'

'No,' he said, and relented. 'Friend caring for friend. But the choice is still the same. You know I have the room. I can help you with the heavy things, emotional and otherwise. We'll do this together, Hannah, or not at all.'

She gazed up at him and he saw her blink. And then blink again, fast. A single tear trickled down her cheek and she swiped it away with what seemed anger.

'Stupid,' she muttered.

'Me?'

'My emotions. Forget it, I'm over it. Josh, do you mean it?'

'I mean it.'

'Then thank you,' she said gratefully. 'I accept with pleasure.'

After that, events of the day took over. There was little time for introspection, no time to doubt the wisdom of what he'd just promised.

Josh found the Vegemite—seemingly the most urgent of priorities. He checked on Mick, who was still dazed, shocked and hurting.

Skye was in pain, too, with bruising pretty much all over her. She and Mick had protected the kids superbly but at huge cost to their own bodies.

'And I'm about two minutes pregnant,' Skye admitted, and Josh winced. If they'd known that he never would have let her sit up the night before.

'So is everything feeling normal?'

'Actually…cramps…'

'How pregnant are you?'

'I haven't had a check yet, but I think…about eight weeks?'

Damn, why hadn't she said so last night? Josh had checked bruises and lacerations, asked if there was anything else.

Why hadn't he asked about pregnancy?

'Because you're a surgeon?' Hannah said when he told her. 'Don't beat yourself up. I imagine there'll be forms with boxes to tick if any fertile lady comes within your treating orbit. Where are forms when you need them?' She checked and reassured both Josh and Skye herself. 'There's no sign of an ectopic and you didn't get hit in the stomach. The cramps are easing but we'll take no chances.'

Skye was tucked back in bed, with Hannah reassuring her that with shock and lack of water, tummy cramps would probably have nothing to do with the pregnancy. Regardless, Josh put in a call to increase their need for priority assistance. Without Skye acting as Mum, Hannah and Josh were caught between medical need and the needs of three traumatised kids.

Hannah came into her own here, too. These were good kids, but they were stressed, and Josh watched

with admiration as Hannah managed to settle them. She
got them baking—'Because I'm Irish and I can't stand
toast and Vegemite.' She made a huge batch of cookie
dough, and by the time the medevac chopper landed
they were loaded with a tub of Very Weird Cookies.

'For your grandma,' Hannah told them before they
trooped across to the chopper. Toby, the eldest at ten,
seemed the most traumatised, and with his parents both
on stretchers, he gripped Hannah's hand and clung.

'You know your Grandma's going to be at the hospital when the helicopter lands,' Hannah told him, crouching awkwardly to give him a goodbye hug. 'Your mum's
on a stretcher because she got more bumps than you,
and she's sore. Your dad has a broken leg and a few cuts,
but both your mum and dad are going to be fine. The
doctors and nurses will look after them, and Grandma
will look after you.

'You should come with us,' Toby whispered, unwill-
ing to let go the only security he seemed to have.

One of the medics came across to collect Toby and
heard. She smiled down at Hannah, her professional
eyes perusing Hannah's obvious baby bump. 'You can
come too if you want. You certainly meet our criteria.'

'Thanks, but no,' she told her. 'Josh will look after
me, just as Grandma will look after you, Toby, and so
will your mum and dad, just as soon as the doctors
have patched them up. You've had a huge adventure.
When you get to Grandma's, will you draw me a picture of you all at her kitchen table and send it to us?
I'll stick it on Dr Josh's fridge. It's a very bare fridge.
It needs a picture.'

'Okay,' Toby said, squaring his shoulders a little now
he was faced with a task he could handle. 'I'll get the
others to draw, too. And maybe Mum when she's bet-

ter. She paints awesome pictures.' His chin wobbled. 'All her pictures... They'll have blown away.'

'That's one of the reasons Dr Josh and I need to stay,' Hannah told him. 'As soon as you're gone we'll drive over to your house and see how many of Mum's pictures we can collect. There'll be lots of other stuff to find, too.'

'I'd like to help.'

But your job is to look after your mum and dad and the littlies,' she told him. 'They need you.'

Toby's shoulders squared still more. He sniffed—just once—and then pulled himself together and allowed himself to be lifted up into the chopper.

'Brave kid,' Josh said as they watched it lift in a blast of down-draughted sand. 'And well done, you.' His arm came around her again in an almost unconscious gesture of protection.

She stilled and then consciously removed his arm.

'Well done, us,' she told him. 'Next...'

Next Josh insisted that she rest while he headed back over to the ruined cottage to see what he could salvage. She sort of rested, but not much. Her brain seemed to be wired, as if expecting something else bad to happen.

She wanted to go...home? But where was home?

It felt like nowhere.

The initial chopper was for emergency evacuation but the chopper for Moira's retrieval was different. In the expanse of outback Australia, hearses were useless, and this island was now so remote the same need applied. The unmarked chopper arrived later that afternoon, an official with it.

The official was officious, and apart from a brief question or two to Josh, he wanted to talk to Hannah alone. Josh left them be and returned to desultory clearing up. Sand was everywhere.

When Moira's shrouded body was stretchered to the chopper, he headed back over.

Hannah was standing on the veranda, watching them go.

He did better this time. He didn't put his arm around her. He just stood beside her as the chopper became a speck in the sky and was gone.

'It's all organised,' she told him bleakly. 'Autopsy because she hasn't been to a doctor for years, then, when the death's cleared as being from natural causes, her body will be released to the funeral home in Stingray Bay. He says probably within a few days. I'll let my family know, but they won't come. If it's okay with you, I'll stay on until then and clear Moira's belongings. As long as the sea's settled I can get a water taxi and go back to Townsville from there. It'll hardly be a big funeral. There'll only be me.'

'There'll be us' he told her, and the urge to put his arm around her again was almost overpowering. 'I was her neighbour, and as long as I'm welcome I'll be there.' I'll be with you, he thought but he didn't say it. It wasn't Moira who seemed alone now. It was Hannah.

'It's a shame Maisie'll be too busy to attend,' he told her, seeing her bleakness and aching to drive it away. 'Maisie's the one who loved her, and she loved Maisie. Moira wasn't totally alone. And she knew you cared. Sometimes even a breath of family is enough.'

'Is that what you have now? A breath of family?' She caught herself and dashed her hand across her eyes. 'Sorry. I didn't mean… You don't have to answer.'

He managed a smile. 'It's okay. And my sister Madison is more than a breath. She's a blast.'

'Bossy?'

'You'd better believe it.' But as he said it he thought of Madison's brusqueness and her dictatorial pronouncements and he thought she hadn't been like that before Alice's death. Or not so much.

He hoped she wasn't driving people away with her façade. Had he caused that, too?

'Hey, Josh, don't look like that.' Hannah sounded startled and he realised her bleakness had been replaced by concern. 'You've done good. We've both done good.'

'We have.' But he couldn't get rid of the bleakness fast enough—or maybe he didn't want to, because pain helped him keep the shutters up between him and the outside world. Shutters were important.

And Hannah seemed to sense what he was thinking. That alone was good.

'I might clear up here a bit now,' she said, striving for matter-of-fact. 'I'll start with the light stuff, clearing the fridge and things. I'll come back for dinner. Is that okay?'

'Of course.'

'But something simple. A can of something on toast. Don't you dare go to any bother. Then I'll help with the mess over there.'

'You won't.'

'Then I'll come back here and work until dark.'

'You're eight months pregnant, Hannah. You'll be sensible.'

'Then I'll go to bed,' she said. 'But I won't disturb you any more than I have to.'

'You won't disturb me.' What a lie!

'I already have,' she told him, with a rueful smile. 'I know it and I'm very sorry. It's just a few more days, though, Josh, and you can resume life as you know it.

I'm not going to land me or my dog or my pups on you one day longer than I must.'

'Hey, I have responsibility, too,' he said, striving for lightness. 'I concede Dudley's the father.'

'So he is,' she said, suddenly cheerful. 'So we should split the litter down the middle. Dudley gets two, Maisie gets two. As soon as they're weaned I'll bring them back, but I'll do it in the dead of night. I won't disturb you any further. It'll be a true secret baby thing. You'll wake up one morning and there'll be two puppies in a basket at your front door.'

'You'll have your baby by then.'

'So I will,' she said, still cheerful. 'So it might not be me who does the dumping. I hear you can rent a man-with-a-van. Do they deliver puppies? Then there's the issue of no bridge. It'll take some figuring but I'll work it out.

'I'm sure you will,' he said, still in the bleak voice he couldn't seem to get rid of.

'Right,' she said, and visibly braced. 'Next. House cleaning. Off you go and do yours, Josh O'Connor, and I'll start with mine. See you at dinner.'

And she gave him that same cheerful grin, headed back into Moira's house and closed the door.

She didn't hear him leave. Maybe he was still standing on the veranda.

And she... The smile had slipped from her face the moment she'd closed the door. She leaned against it and it was all she could do not to slump to the floor.

She was shaking all over.

Somehow she managed to get herself into the gloomy living room, sink onto Moira's overstuffed settee and bury her head in her hands.

It was stupid to shake. There was no reason.

Why did it feel as if she'd just closed the door on her only link to sanity?

'It's reaction,' she told herself. 'It's the storm. Plus half drowning, and rescuing kids and Mick and Skye, and saving the puppies. And Moira's death.'

Moira. She'd been a fiery, hard loner but she hadn't kicked Hannah out when she'd come. Neither had she looked at Hannah's obvious pregnancy with disgust.

Moira had been family. Not much but a little.

Now...

Who else did she have?

Almost unconsciously her fingers lifted her phone from her pocket. It had been useless since she'd arrived on the island, it had got wet with the dunking, but suddenly the bars on the front told her connection had been re-established. And she still had charge.

It'd be early morning back in Dublin, she thought. Her family would be awake. Her sister would be about to leave to work.

Dear God, she missed them, and it wasn't just them. It was the village, her town, the whole feeling of belonging. 'I'm too old to miss my mother,' she whispered, but it didn't help.

She phoned.

Her parents still only had a landline. It rang and she waited, imagining her father leaving the breakfast table and heading down the hall. Grumbling. He hated being disturbed before he'd read his paper, but the job of answering the phone was his alone.

'Yes?' When finally he answered the word was a snap.

'Dadda?'

'Is it you?' She heard his breath hiss in. 'Have you got rid of it yet? Your mother wants you home.'

'Could I speak to her?'

'I told you, you're not part of this family until I know it's gone. What do you want?'

'Aunt Moira's died.'

There was a silence on the end of the phone. Then... 'God rest her soul, then, but she's made it clear she's nothing to do with us.'

'Could you tell Gran?'

'We'll not be telling your grandmother. We saw her last weekend and she's slipping.'

Gran. No!

'Da, just how sick is she?'

'Your grandmother's health is nothing to do with you,' he snapped. 'Nothing in this family is until you get rid of whatever shameful thing it is that you're carrying and come home.'

The phone went dead and she was left with bleakness.

During their childhood her father had been a harsh and autocratic parent, a manipulative bully who'd long since turned his wife into a defeated husk. Hannah and Bridget, though, had found ways to have fun despite him. Sometimes it had seemed as if he'd hardly noticed the two little girls who'd learned to be mouse-like in his presence, but as they'd reached adulthood, his need for control had closed like a vice.

Hannah had escaped, to Dublin, to study nursing. Then, as his interference had escalated, she'd left to see the world—with a man she'd fallen for for all the wrong reasons.

Bridget, though, had caved in. 'I'm sorry, Hannah, but I need to stay. I love our village and I love Mam.

You're making your own life but I don't have your courage. I couldn't bear the yelling. You and Gran both stand up to him, but I can't. I need my home.'

Home. Where was it for Hannah? Among a pile of cheap furniture in hospital accommodation in Townsville?

What sort of home was that?

She tugged open Moira's curtains and Josh was sweeping sand from his veranda. He must have seen the movement because he raised his hand and waved.

She didn't wave back. The way she was starting to feel about Josh, it was all she could do not to leave this gloomy house and head back over there now. To ask him to hold her. Ask him to give her the comfort she craved.

He'd already saved her life. What else was she asking?

She was asking nothing.

She headed into the kitchen. Josh had already done a cursory clean—when he'd come over the day before to check? There were few signs of the drama that had taken place.

She moved to more practical things. A garbage bag and the fridge. She moved slowly because she ached.

Josh was now shovelling banked-up sand from under the eaves. Surely that wasn't his most urgent task. Was he doing it so he could keep an eye over here? Or to let her know she wasn't alone?

That was fanciful. And she wasn't alone.

Bridget, her sister, would be at work now. She worked for a local solicitor, a friend of their father, and she wasn't supposed to take calls at work. But needs must. She rang and Bridget answered. Cautiously.

'Oh, Hannah, love, are you well?'

'I'm well. Bridget...'

'You haven't had the baby?'

'No.'

'But you'll come home after you've had it? Will you be getting it adopted?'

She sighed. 'No. Bridge, did Dad tell you Aunt Moira's died?'

'Has she?' Bridget sounded distracted.

'He didn't tell you? Bridge, what's wrong with Gran?'

All through their childhood Gran had been their haven, their one true thing. Hannah had been ringing her all through her time away, and she'd been a source of love and comfort through the whole nightmare of her pregnancy.

'She's been losing weight and now they say she has cancer. Terminal. They've just moved her into this hospice place.'

'Oh, Bridge...' She hadn't even known of the weight loss.

'I need to go,' Bridget whispered. 'Love you, Hannah.'

'Bridge...' She cut across her sister's dismissal, her need urgent. 'Will you send me details of where Gran is and keep me in touch? Please. I need to know these things.'

'Dad says I mustn't.'

'Will you disobey him? For me?'

A deep breath. A sound that could have been a sob but then...

'I will, Hannah. As long as you let me know...when the baby's born.'

'When *my* baby's born.'

'Yes,' Bridget whispered. 'My niece or nephew. Good luck, Hannah. Bye.'

She disconnected.

She could still see Josh on the veranda. Dudley had come out to join him. They were both standing...as if on sentry duty?

It helped.

'I can do this,' she muttered, and rose to fill a bowl to start wiping the shelves. 'I can do this alone.

Especially if Josh was at her back.

'I don't need him,' she muttered, but he was there, and she thought if he wasn't...

He wouldn't be for more than a few days.

'But I'll take what I can get,' she told the empty fridge and started cleaning.

CHAPTER TWELVE

HE TOOK HER back to Townsville. Hannah objected but how could he not? Her wreck of a car was still mixed with the wreckage of the bridge.

Josh's truck was stuck on the island, but he organised a water taxi to collect them on the day of Moira's funeral. All of them. When they reached the mainland he settled bedding in the back, parked it in the shade and left the dogs to sleep while Hannah said goodbye to her aunt.

The service was short to the point of brutal. Hannah and Josh were joined by a director of ceremonies, a couple of funeral parlour employees and an almost empty church.

Hannah clung to Josh's hand during the service—she needed to—but as they left the cemetery she made one last bid for independence. 'Josh, let me take the van. You go back to the island.'

How could he?

'I've hired the van to be returned here,' he growled. 'How do you think you'll return it if I don't come?'

She bit her lip. 'But I'm so beholden already.'

Which was the last thing he wanted her to feel. This woman had so much on her shoulders.

And when they reached the city he discovered she had more.

Apparently, she'd been sharing an apartment with three other nurses, but she'd made arrangements to move into a bigger apartment, by herself, before the baby arrived. The move was supposed to have happened two days ago and her room in the shared flat was already spoken for.

'We moved your stuff for you. Just collect the key from the janitor,' a bright young nurse told them, eyeing Josh curiously before heading off on her own business. So they found the janitor, collected the key and unlocked the ground floor apartment door.

She was met with her belongings, carried into the living room and no further.

He could tell she was mortified but after one glance she pinned on a bright smile and faced him.

'Josh, thank you. I'll be fine now. If you could…if you could carry Maisie and the pups into the laundry. I think there's a laundry… Regardless, you need to get back. Thank you for everything.'

He looked around the apartment with distaste. They'd walked through a scrappy courtyard to get in so at least Maisie could be let out, but the place itself… Ugh.

It'd be all she could afford, he thought.

Could he offer to help financially? He took one look at her set face and knew how such an offer would be received.

But he could help in other ways.

'I'm staying until you're sorted,' he said, eyeing her pile of 'stuff'. Even her bed was a mess. It had been disassembled for the shift and was now a base, four legs, a plastic bag of bolts and screws that looked ominously small, and a mound of tangled bedding.

'I'll be fine,' she repeated, but she couldn't make herself sound like she meant it.

'Pigs might fly.'

'Josh, no. I can manage.'

'I know you can manage but you don't need to.'

'My friends will help me.'

'I'm thinking your friends are the ones who tossed your belongings in here,' he said grimly, and then he shrugged and smiled. 'Don't make this into a big deal, Hannah. Dudley needs a bit more dad-bonding time anyway. We'll stay overnight, help you get this place in order and then disappear from your life for ever.'

'For ever?' The words came out as an almost instinctive reaction of dismay. He saw the flash of what might have been fear, quickly quashed. 'I'm sorry. Of course for ever. Don't mind me, I'm pregnant.'

'Yeah,' he told her. 'You're pregnant and you need help.' She was three weeks from her due date, he thought, and she was alone.

She was in a hospital apartment. That was reassuring. There'd be midwives and doctors close by, but still...

Apart from a brief stint in basic training he'd had little to do with obstetrics but one thing he did remember was the memory of labouring mothers clinging like a drowning person to their support person.

Who was Hannah's support person? One of the people who'd dumped her stuff in here?

'I'll stay tonight and then leave but it doesn't need to be for ever,' he growled. 'If you need me again...'

'I won't.'

'That's up to you,' he told her. 'You decide.'

* * *

It could have been a nightmare. Instead it was almost fun.

She'd been through a nightmare, but Moira's funeral had seemed a marker to end it. She was off the island. Josh had made phone calls to the insurance company and a replacement car was on its way. Maisie was safely delivered. The pups showed every sign of being gorgeous and it should be easy to find them great homes. She had Maisie with her permanently, and she kind of liked having Maisie.

It was almost dark. Josh was staying the night.

Josh was rebuilding her bed.

'Stop it,' she scolded herself, and she darned near said it out loud. This man was a good Samaritan. There was no way that part of her should think... Was thinking...

'No!'

'We have one bolt left over,' he told her and held it up, looking concerned.

'We bought it cheap,' she told him, struggling to haul her disordered thoughts into order. 'Maybe they gave us extra.'

'They're flimsy bolts but they all seem to have a match.' He heaved the mattress onto the base, sat, then cautiously bounced. 'I'm no engineer but it seems sound enough,' he told her. 'I think it should hold.'

'You think?'

'Mattress on the floor, then?'

'No,' she told him. 'Do you know how hard it is for me and my eight-month bump to get up from the floor? What's the worst that can happen? I descend in the night? And, Josh, speaking of nights... We bought our couch second hand and it has springs where there aren't supposed to be springs.'

'Cushions on the floor for me, then,' he said cheerfully. 'Dudley can be my pillow.'

'Josh, you can't.' Oh, her thoughts... Back, girl. 'Maybe you could get a motel?'

'I'm far too clutch fisted.'

'I'll pay.'

'Then you should be more clutch fisted,' he said severely. 'Hannah, I was a Scout. I did camping and everything. I can sleep on two twigs and a reef knot.'

'Really?' She relented and chuckled. 'Okay, cushions on floor, but only if you use some of my pillows. They're my indulgence. I have six.'

'Deal.'

She was still dubious, worrying about it while they made up the bed, unpacked enough boxes to find the kettle and ordered in pizza.'And beer for me because I deserve it', Josh decreed.

Then he decreed that she go to bed. She was, in fact, exhausted.

'I'm heading out to the late-night supermarket to get provisions for breakfast,' he told her.

'I could come.'

'Or you could sleep. What would you rather do, Hannah? Honest?'

She looked into his face and what she saw there demanded honestly. This wasn't a man she could lie to.

'Sleep.'

'Wise,' he told her, grinning. 'Though a bit more risky. If sometime in the night that bed decides it needs its full complement of nuts and bolts...'

'Then I'll descend a whole eighteen inches onto mattress,' she told him. 'Josh, thank you.'

'Think nothing of it,' he told her, and he leaned forward and kissed her on the tip of her nose. 'Sleep. You need it and your baby needs it. Maisie and her babies are already asleep. Dudley and I are in charge of the maternity ward.'

And he chuckled and left her, and she went to bed.

It felt so good, to lie here knowing Josh was coming back, even if it was just to sleep on her living-room floor.

He was leaving tomorrow. For ever?

'Then I'll take tonight,' she told herself, and wished she could take more. Which was an entirely inappropriate thought. She shoved it away with reluctance, and finally she slept.

With her finger just touching her nose.

He came home and the place was in darkness. Dudley watched with interest as he unpacked groceries, but the two mums were asleep.

Dudley got his reward, a bowl of chopped steak. Josh took the same in to Maisie, who woke enough to receive it with canine gratitude. Dudley settled beside her.

Josh came back into the box-filled living room and surveyed the lumpy settee with misgivings.

Cushions on floor, then. He could do this.

Why was he doing this?

Three years ago he'd made a vow not to get entangled with anyone. No one, period. The pain of waking up in a hospital bed to find Alice was dead, seeing the naked grief on Madison's face, being helped into a wheelchair so he could go with her to identify Alice's body in the morgue...

Hearing his big sister's sobs of utter, desolate loss...

Then there were the bleak faces of his parents as they'd flown in for the funeral. The fixed cheerfulness of Madison as she'd determined to get on with her life...

He'd caused it. It wasn't just Josh who was hurting. Pain had washed outward like ripples in a pond. To get involved like that again... To care...

He still cared for Madison—of course he did—but he'd never allow his actions to hurt her again, neither would he enmesh himself in anyone else's life.

The fact that Hannah needed him...

She didn't need *him*. She needed practical help, that was all there was to it. He'd be gone tomorrow, and she could get on with her independent life.

She was like him, he told himself. She'd been hurt and she needed to build her own armour.

In a foreign country, with a newborn baby, with a dog and four puppies...

Only two puppies would be her responsibility, he told himself, and puppies could be rehomed. Hannah could exist with a newborn and a dog. Maternity payments were generous enough for an Australian citizen. She'd get by. She didn't need him.

He rolled over and buried his head into one of her pillows.

Did it smell of her?

He thought it did.

Sleep was nowhere.

She mustn't need him.

He lay in the dark and told himself over and over why what he was thinking was stupid, dangerous, impossible. He knew it was.

And then the bed collapsed.

One minute she was sleeping the sleep of the dead. The next there was a crack of timber and she was unceremoniously tipped sideways. The floor was carpeted. Her fall was little more a slide as the mattress slipped from the collapsing bed. The pillows fell after. Disoriented, she lay where she'd rolled, with a couple of pillows rolling on top of her.

'Hannah!'

Light from the living room flooded in. Her bedroom light was flicked on and she winced. It wasn't so bad, here on the floor. What she resented more than being tossed unceremoniously out of bed was that light. She wasn't hurt. She had her pillows. Left to her own devices, she'd simply close her eyes again.

'Hannah!'

She heard fear in his voice and it woke her right up. Josh…

'I think I know where that bolt went,' she managed, a trifle woozily. 'You shouldn't have left me in charge of the leg on this side.'

'You're okay?' He was bending over her, his face etched with concern. 'Hell. Hannah…'

'I fell from eighteen inches,' she managed. 'Onto carpet and pillows. Call the fire brigade. Paramedics. Lawyers. I'm sure I can sue someone. This bed's definitely faulty.'

There was a sharp intake of breath and then silence. She heard him audibly regroup.

Her head was still buried in pillows. She should wiggle round and face him but for some reason…well, for some reason she didn't.

'You're sure you're okay?'

'I'm sure.'

'Oh, Hannah…' His voice broke and as it did so a part of her seemed to break as well.

How was it possible that she knew this man so little and yet so well? She heard his fear. She heard the history of anguish.

'Hey, I really am okay. She turned and smiled up at him. He was bent over her, so near. So near... 'Only I think the rest of the night's going to be mattress on the floor.'

'Right,' he said, and he was suddenly in charge again. Surgeon with a plan. 'Lie still.'

'There's no need.'

'Lie still,' he growled, and she subsided because, to be honest, lying in a tangle of bedclothes and pillows on the carpet didn't seem such a bad fate. Especially when Josh was doing his 'man in charge' thing. She almost smiled.

But he was already busy, hauling the broken bed out from under the mattress and propping the base against the wall, where it stood like a crazy art installation— *Modern Man's Technological Advances in Bed-Making.* Then he stooped and started remaking the 'bed mattress' with her in it.

He tucked in the corners of the bedding. He rearranged the pillows. Finally he tugged the sheet and blanket up to her chin and smiled.

Catastrophe averted,' he told her. 'We'll buy you a new bed tomorrow.' And his smile deepened and he leaned forward and kissed her on the nose.

Again.

On the nose.

And her nose was still tingling from the last time.

His eyes were warm and caring, twinkling with the ridiculousness of the situation but also...well, the caring went deep.

It had no business going deep. She knew he didn't want to care and she didn't want him to care.

Liar.

But the caring wasn't all one way. She looked up into

his eyes and she saw concern behind the laughter, and also a trace of fear.

He'd heard the bang as the bed had collapsed and he'd been with her in seconds. This man had seen fear close up and seen the after-effects of it.

Josh…

She was cocooned back in her neatly ordered bed-clothes. Josh had ordered her world so she could drift safely back to sleep. While her man watched over her?

Her man.

He was no such thing but, oh, the way he smiled at her…

Enough. A woman had only so much self-control and she'd reached the limit. If it was daylight, if she was properly awake, if this didn't seem like some hazy, amazing dream then maybe she'd have more control, but this was a dream. Josh was so close.

She needed him closer.

Josh.

She put her palms on either side of gorgeous face and drew him down. Was he resisting?

'Josh,' she whispered, and there was no question.

'Hannah,' he whispered back, and then his mouth met hers and there was no space for words.

There was no space for anything but each other.

CHAPTER THIRTEEN

SHE STIRRED AS the first rays of morning sunshine glimmered through the sagging venetian blinds. She needed to do something about those, she thought sleepily, but not yet.

Nothing yet.

She was cocooned in the arms of Josh O'Connor and in this space, in this time, who had cares for saggy blinds?

She'd gone to sleep with her arms entwined around his neck—she was sure of it. At least, she thought she was sure. She'd lost herself, totally and surely, the moment his mouth had met hers. Their clothes had somehow disappeared. Skin against skin, they'd seemed to merge, fitting together like two halves torn apart by trauma and now magically come together.

Twin souls.

There was an overstatement, she thought sleepily, but she felt her face lift into a smile of warm, sated contentment. Her spine was curved against his chest. At some time during the night she must have turned away from him, which must surely have been sensible as her swollen belly surely couldn't fit breast to chest. But she hadn't been aware of it. She hadn't been aware of anything but her need to be closer and closer and closer...

Sense, though, had prevailed. Sort of. They were both sensible adults—sort of. Their mutual need for warmth, for comfort—for each other?—had only gone so far. Somehow they'd held onto a last vestige of sense.

'I'll not,' Josh had murmured at some time during that sweet night. 'No precautions. Eight months pregnant...'

'You can hardly get me pregnant again.'

He'd chuckled and held her closer, his mouth claiming her, his body doing the same, but the final joining hadn't happened. They were medical professionals. They knew the rules.

Rules, Hannah thought. Where were they now?

They had to be reinstated.

She was eight months pregnant with another man's child. Josh had all but told her he wanted no commitment, ever. This was nothing but a night of comfort, a mutual taking and giving before reality inserted its ugly head.

And it was still happening. It was still now. His arms still held her. For a few last glorious moments she could block out the world and let herself imagine this was how life was. For always.

'Awake?' His voice was scarcely more than a breath and she responded by a tiny stirring against him. Oh, if this was for ever... If this man loved her...

He cared for her. That had to be enough, she told herself. He'd saved her, he'd helped her and this last night he'd held her in what was surely mutual need. He held her still and her body was responding with an almost animal instinct. Here was her place, here was her home.

Here was her man.

He wasn't her man. They were lying on a tumbled mattress on the floor of a sparse hospital apartment.

This was *her* home. This was *her* reality. But his hands were holding her spooned to his body, and his mouth was doing something delicious to the nape of her neck.

Oh, the feel of him... The desire to turn and claim what they'd both somehow decided it wouldn't be sensible to claim, to surrender her body totally to his magic...

Except it wasn't her body. It was already claimed, by the child of another man, and they both had the sense to know it. At least she did, but if his mouth kept doing... what it was doing...

'Josh...' she managed, and he released her just enough so she could roll in the cocoon of tumbled bedclothes and look at him.

Mistake. He was so near. He was so... Josh.

'I need to get up.' It was so hard to make herself say the words, but indeed the words were true. She had to somehow tear herself from the fairy story. Someone was kicking her bladder.

'Of course you do,' he said, and smiled, and that smile was almost her undoing. 'Let me help.' He pushed the bedclothes back and rose—and the sight of him...

Dear heaven, the sight of him... What would she give to be taken back in time, to be free, untrammelled, in a position to fight for what she wanted.

She would fight for this man.

Maybe she'd lose—probably she'd lose because he'd made vows for a good reason. Maybe his scars couldn't be mended but, oh, she could try.

But not now. He tugged her up, and as she rose she was achingly aware of the bulk of her body. As he pulled her up, breast to chest, she was still apart from him, pushed away by the bulk of her pregnancy.

History that couldn't be undone.

You need to focus on your baby, she told herself, and

as if on cue she felt her belly tighten, and a stab of pain ran across her back.

It'd be a Braxton-Hicks contractions, common in late pregnancy. A reminder that this was no time to add complications to her life.

Complications like Josh?

She snagged the sheet and tugged it around her, then pulled back, aware of an overwhelming desire to weep. She wouldn't. What sort of message would that give him?

'That was some night,' she managed, and somehow she even managed to lean forward and bestow a kiss on his gorgeous mouth. It was a feather touch, no more, a signal to both of them that she understood boundaries and now was the time now to restore them.

'Hannah…'

'Bathroom,' she said, because those stupid tears were welling, like it or not, and she would not cry. 'Then coffee? Have we unpacked coffee yet? There's an imperative. And the dogs… They've been stuck in the laundry all night. Bathroom, coffee, dogs. We need to get this day started, right now.'

And before he could respond she tucked her sheet tighter around her and fled. Into the bathroom where she could close the door, lean heavily against it and figure how to breathe again.

He tugged on jeans and windcheater, wondering how the hell he'd ended up holding a gorgeous, naked Hannah in his arms all night. Wondering how he'd had the strength not to take her as his body had screamed to take her. All the way. Total commitment.

Love?

There was the nightmare. It was both an impossibility and the answer to all his questions.

Quite simply, the way he felt about Hannah was the way he'd vowed he'd feel about no one. That he could love enough to hurt…

He'd seen hurt in Hannah's eyes then. Had she expected to be slapped?

He could never slap her—but hurt her? 'You already have,' he said harshly, out loud. 'You're raising expectations you can't meet.'

So step away now?

He hauled back the memory of opening his eyes after surgery, confused, dazed, seeing Madison's face.

'Alice,' he'd said, and what he'd seen on his sister's face was all the answer he'd ever need.

'And Aisling?' Somehow he'd asked that next.

'She's fine,' Madison had whispered, and the look on her face was a mix he never wanted to see again. Despair. Heartbreak. Blame.

He'd thought he and Aisling were a perfect pair but the risks… What price had his family paid for his stupidity? What price had *he* paid? Pain and pain and pain. Yet here he was, standing in the bedroom of a woman he hardly knew, feeling a tug he'd vowed never to feel.

Be practical! He could help her—of course he could. He could finance a better apartment. He could make her life easier.

She wouldn't let him. It was all or nothing with Hannah—he knew that—and he'd let too much slip for her to forget his backstory. She had her pride. He'd had to work to convince her to take this much.

But he was a friend. Surely she'd let him help.

A friend? The way she'd slipped into his arms last

night? The way he'd felt as he'd held her? He could still feel...

No. Memory slammed back, almost like a guillotine. Memory of searing loss. How could he expose himself to that risk again?

A voice in the back of his head whispered, You already have.

'Then back away.' He said it out loud and the sound of his voice jarred him into the present, into practicalities. 'Move on. Get this place organised and then get back to your island. You've played the good Samaritan and nothing else is needed. You can see by her face that she gets the boundaries. Tell her. Talk to her. But whatever you do, get out of here, Josh O'Connor, before every one of your resolutions turns to dust.'

Hannah was still in the bathroom. He could hear the sound of running water.

Hannah in the shower. Her naked body...

'Cut it out!' He said that out loud as well and headed for the laundry to let the dogs out. Hannah's courtyard was minuscule. How could a bitch and four puppies use only this as their outside space? There'd be no lawn left for Hannah to sit in the sun and play with her baby.

That was Hannah's business, not his.

He headed back to the kitchen and rooted through boxes until he found kettle and mugs and coffee. Muesli? Ugh. What he'd really like was a decent fry-up. He'd seen a convenience store last night, only a block from here.

He headed to the bathroom door. The shower had stopped.

'You feel like eggs and bacon?' he called through the door. 'Or would you like to go out for breakfast?'

No answer.

'Hannah?'

'Josh…' And the way she said the word had him pushing the door wide, regardless.

She was bent over the hand basin, gripping it fiercely with both hands. Her sheet had fallen to the floor but she was in no mind to care. Her entire body was rigid.

'Hannah…'

'It's coming,' she managed. 'Josh, my baby's coming. So hard… So fast… Josh, please… Help me, Josh. Help…'

And everything else was nothing.

The contractions were deep and strong right from the start. This was to be no labour where Mum could stay home, rest between contractions, wait until they were five minutes apart and then think it was time they made for the labour ward. Hannah's next contraction came three minutes later, the next two. And in between her body was rigid, fierce with expectation of pain.

And fear. He could see it and he could feel it as he carried her back to the bedroom.

This woman was a midwife. She knew birth almost better than anyone, but right now she wasn't a midwife. She was a first-time mum and she was terrified. Professionalism had gone out of the window.

And Josh?

He didn't feel like a doctor either.

In the time after the accident, when his role had been patient rather than doctor, his fears had been those of anyone facing the unknown. Being on the outside, looking in, was a very different experience from the opposite—surrendering control.

He felt way out of control now. The sight of Hannah in pain was doing his head in. He set her back on their collapsed bed and she grabbed his hands like she was drowning.

'Stay with me,' she managed. It was a fierce order, but it was a helpless plea.

'Try and get rid of me,' he told her. 'I hauled you and your baby out of that car and I'm all for happy endings. You can't throw me out of this movie at three quarter time.'

She managed to chuckle but it was a wavery laugh, turning into a pain-filled gasp. 'Josh...'

'Yeah, whatever's happening's happening fast.' Stupidly he was having trouble keeping his voice steady. He placed a palm on her rock-hard belly as the next contraction started to roll through. 'Hannah, let's get you across to the hospital. By the feel of these contractions, he or she isn't mucking around.'

'I... Yes... I'm booked in...' And then the full force of the contraction hit and his hands were caught again.

Afterwards he'd find scratches where her fingernails had dug into his palms, but he didn't feel pain. He held her, willing strength, willing confidence, willing courage, and she closed her eyes and moaned, and he felt that he'd never been in such a position of trust...

He'd seen births before—of course he had, throughout his training. He'd seen birth partners gripped like this, held, sworn at, shoved away and then grabbed again...

He'd never understood until now that being in this position was an honour above all others.

'You need to let me go, Hannah, love,' he said, gently now as the contraction eased. 'A mattress on the floor with no equipment is scarcely the optimal place to give birth. I need to find you a bathrobe and get you to where you need to be.'

'Us,' Hannah gasped. 'Oh, Josh, please... Get us.'

'Of course us,' he said, and he heard the break in his voice as he said it. 'Hannah, we're in this together. It's you who has to do the work but I promise you, I won't leave you.'

He was there. Somehow he got her across to the hospital but he was still there.

As educated, as prepared as any woman giving birth for the first time could be, nothing had prepared her for this. Her body had been taken over by a force she had no control over. Her contractions had started strong and kept right on, wave after wave of power and pain.

In the birth room with her were two of the hospital midwives, women she'd worked with, women she counted as her friends. She could feel their empathy, their support, their skill.

A doctor flitted in from time to time, muttering things like 'Progressing nicely, keep it up...' The white coat at the end of the bed barely made an impression. It was just the midwives and Josh.

Josh.

She had no right to ask him to stay, but she had no intention of letting him go. *Now* was entirely selfish. She'd take what she needed to birth this baby, to have this little one safe in her arms, and what she needed was strength.

And Josh gave it to her. He sat beside her for what seemed hour after interminable hour. He let her grip his hands in a death grip during contractions. How did that help? She only knew that it did.

He murmured to her. He held her when she needed to be held. He listened to her swear—she didn't even know she knew these words. He was just there.

Josh. Her hold on sanity. Her hold on life.

He was no such thing but that's what he felt like and she wasn't letting go for a moment. And when finally, finally that last moment came...

'One more push.' Josh was right there, firm, sure, her rock in a sea of pain. 'You can do this, Hannah. We can see your baby. Just one more push and you'll have him safe in your arms.'

And she looked up into his face, stern and sure, compassionate, caring, but ruthless in his certainty for what she had to do—and she pushed.

And one appalling minute later she heard a yowl of indignant protest and a tiny, slippery miracle of a baby was lying on her breast. Warm and wanting, mewing a tiny baby sound, already nudging towards her nipple.

'You have a daughter...' Josh's voice was faint, seemingly far away.

'A daughter.' Her focus should be all on this tiny slip of a brand-new person, but it seemed there was room still for that ever-present awareness of Josh. He'd slumped back in his chair as if he, too, was exhausted.

He'd been with her every step of the way. He'd saved her life and her daughter's life and he'd been...here.

'Josh, thank you,' she whispered. 'Oh, love, thank you.'

The *love* slipped out before she could stop it but she was blinking back tears and she had no room to care. Her daughter. *Her daughter!*

'She's perfect,' one of the midwives breathed. 'And red hair, just like her mum. A proper little Irish lass for you to love and cherish. Oh, well done, both of you.' And she'd included Josh because for now he was her partner and no midwife would begrudge him that title.

'All Hannah,' Josh managed, gruffly. 'All awesome

Hannah.' And he put his head down in his hands and held it perfectly still.

'Don't you dare faint on us now,' the midwife said, but she was smiling. At some time during the hard, fast labour they'd learned he was a doctor and there'd been teasing. 'It's always the strong ones who go down.'

'I won't faint,' he said, and he lifted his head and met Hannah's eyes and smiled. 'You're brilliant, Hannah. Your daughter's brilliant. Two tough, gorgeous women ready to face the world.'

She smiled back at him, mistily, her hands cradling her baby, her world expanding by the moment. She'd done it.

They'd done it.

'Does she have a name yet?' the midwife asked. 'Or will you need time to get to know her before deciding?'

'I've decided,' Hannah said, smiling and smiling. Life was good. Life was great. Josh was right, she and her daughter could face anything.

'Her name's Erin, after my grandmother,' she said. 'Erin is strong and brave and I love her very much. Both my Erins. And if it's okay with Josh...' She smiled at him, almost shyly. 'I'd like her second name to be Alice, because if it wasn't for Alice you wouldn't have been on that island and Erin and I would be...be dead. Because of Alice, Erin is here and safe. And I love the name. Is that okay with you, Josh?'

Was it okay?

Surgeon bursts into tears in patient's bedroom? Not quite. He managed to nod, to stoop and kiss her—and then he staggered out into the corridor and let it all out.

It was just as well this wasn't his research hospital. Here no one knew him. He was just another visitor.

Why did he feel so much more?

CHAPTER FOURTEEN

SHE'D ASKED ENOUGH of him. Josh needed to be back on the island—there was still mess for him to sort there—but when he demanded who else would look after Maisie and her pups she simply caved in.

How could she not? She had no one else.

She needed to be back in Ireland—she ached for the support the community would have given her. But her father was still abusive, domineering.

She rang and left a message telling her parents they had a granddaughter. No one picked up. She knew they had caller recognition on their phone. It was useless trying to ring further.

She rang her grandmother, who sounded weak and frail, but here at least was a loving reception for her news. Gran wept and told her she was lovely and brave and she loved her, and please could she send a picture of her namesake and she'd hide it under her pillow if her father visited.

'If?' Hannah queried, and there'd been a long silence.

'He and your mother don't come so much,' her grandmother admitted at last. 'Not since I told your father he was a bigoted bully for the way he's treating you. Well, I've told him often enough in the past but I might have got really angry this time.'

'Oh, Gran…'

'It's what he is,' the old lady said resolutely, and then broke off as a fit of coughing consumed her. She couldn't speak again, and finally Hannah disconnected and rang the nursing staff.

'Please… I'm her granddaughter in Australia. Could you check with her for permission and then let me know if there are any changes in her health?'

'She's definitely slipping,' the nurse warned her. 'If you want to see her then you need to come soon.'

These were words that made Hannah feel bereft, for how could she come? The impossibility of travel slammed home.

Bridget rang, but it was a faltering, guilt-ridden call. 'I heard your news from Gran. She's so pleased, so touched that you called her Erin. Hannah, I'd love to fly over and see you but…'

But. There were so many *buts*. She thought of the welcome most babies received in the small town she'd been raised in, and she ached for that community for her daughter.

But she held her baby daughter close, and Josh was in and out of her room, always seeming to be there just when she needed him, and she decided there was nothing to be done but accept Josh's offer of help and worry about tomorrow tomorrow.

Two days after Erin's birth he was there to take her… home? It didn't feel like home—a barren apartment that she'd left in a pile of boxes and chaos—but it'd be her home and her life from now on.

They walked the block and a half from the hospital—the advantage of living in a hospital apartment. Josh carried Hannah's holdall and Erin's carry cot. Hannah walked beside him, cradling Erin. She felt sun on her face, a gentle wind, the strangeness of being outside hospital with a new little life. She felt...weird.

Josh opened her front door for her and she felt a whole lot more weird.

She'd left a barren, utilitarian, chaos-filled space. Now...

The little kitchen was brightly welcoming, with benches clear of clutter, her mass of boxes gone. A shiny yellow kettle sat on the hob, a bunch of white daisies on the counter. Grimy windows had been cleaned to let sunlight stream in. Curtains now replaced her appalling venetians, fresh, new, yellow and white stripes. Gorgeous.

Giving Josh a look of wonder, holding her precious bundle close, she ventured further.

Into the living room.

What little furniture she'd had had been cheap and nasty, bought or scrounged by herself and Ryan when they'd thought they'd be here for not much more than a year. There was nothing cheap or nasty in what was here now.

Her horrid sofa was gone. The lounge was dominated by a club settee and two matching armchairs, old-fashioned floral, the kind that hid all sins, the kind that said, Sink into me, this is where you belong. Piles of cushions beckoned even more.

'I can even sleep on it,' Josh said proudly. 'It's long enough and there's not a single piercing spring.'

'Oh, Josh...'

'Look at the rest,' he told her.

The rest...

A woollen mat, deep pinks and soft lavender, covered the previously barren floor. A big television was wall-mounted—what had happened to her tiny squint-to-see-it model?

There were wall lamps, a coffee table with a few enticing books scattered on it, and on the wall was a print of a watercolour, the *Cliffs of Moher*, wild and beautiful, a painting that spoke of home but yet was so beautiful in its own right that it didn't cause pain.

'This wasn't all my work,' Josh admitted as she gazed about her in wonder. 'I rang Madison. She sent me a plan.'

'You rang your sister—about me?'

'I said I had a patient who needed cheering up.'

A patient... Right. Madison would know he hadn't treated a patient personally for years. What would Josh's sister be thinking?

But Josh was opening the bedroom door. What else?

What else took her breath away. Her bed had been miraculously rebuilt—or was it a new bed? Beautiful new bedding.

The serviceable bassinet she'd bought from a charity shop and scrubbed until most of its paint was gone had been replaced. In its place was a vision in pink, a pile of cuddly toys on the stand beside it, a change table, a mobile of teddy bears, a wombat nightlight...

'Madison didn't help me here,' Josh said proudly. 'This is all my own work. Plus a little assistance from the lady in the shop down the road. You'll be thrilled to know I'm now a gold-class client of Cocoon My Baby. You want to see the pram?'

She could hardly speak but she didn't need to. Josh was opening the laundry door. On the far side of the laundry she saw a gleaming new pram-cum-stroller, one she recognised as being far beyond the realms of anything she might have afforded. But she hardly had time to see, for out of the laundry tumbled the dogs. Dudley and Maisie surged out to wag and lick and wiggle. Inside she saw a big, soft dog bed, with four tiny occupants. There was another bed for Dudley. And the door...

'I talked your landlord into letting me put in a dog door,' Josh said modestly, and Hannah thought of the crusty hospital property manager and thought how much money would have had to change hands before he'd have allowed this. 'Oh, and I've been talking to your neighbour. Ruth loves dogs but has never summoned the courage to own one. We've thus removed two boards from your dividing fence. Her courtyard is bigger than yours so now they have what almost counts as a respectable run. Payment may possibly be first choice of pup but Ruth's great. I wouldn't be the least bit surprised if she's over first thing with a casserole.'

She was speechless.

She had her tiny daughter. She had her dogs. She had a perfect home and it seemed she had a neighbour.

She had Josh.

No. She didn't have Josh. He was gorgeous, kind, caring, but she didn't have him. Oh, but what he'd done for her...

'I'll stay for a couple of days,' Josh said. 'Just to see you settle in.'

'I... There's no need.'

'Do you want me to?' Was it her imagination or did she hear a note of anxiety?

Did he want to stay?

'Of course I want you to,' she managed, and it was too much. She sniffed back a sob and hugged him, or hugged him as much as she could. He hugged back. She and her daughter were enfolded in this man's arms. The dogs wuffled and wagged around her legs and her face was buried in Josh's sweater.

Josh might not be here for ever but he was here now, and here seemed definitely home.

The next few days were chaotic, filled with the fuss of babies and puppies, filled with crazy domesticity. If they'd been true partners it would have been the start of the rest of their lives, but somehow the boundaries they'd both recognised the morning Hannah had gone into labour stayed in place.

The boundaries were unvoiced but they didn't need to be voiced. He lay on the sofa and listened to Hannah coo to Erin during the night feeds and he felt apart. As he'd vowed to be apart. Three days later, with Hannah and her baby as settled as mother and newborn could be, they both knew it was time for him to go.

'You've done so much for me already,' she told him. 'It's time you got back to your own life.'

Sense told him it was the truth.

It had made him feel great that he could help her. That he could make her little apartment into a home. That he could cook for her, that he could care for the dogs, that he could watch dumb television while she nursed her tiny Erin. That while she slept he could take her baby and nurse her himself, giving Hannah much-needed rest.

He'd done it for her, he told himself, and if his heart had twisted as he'd managed to get the tiny newborn bundle to sleep against his chest…well, maybe that was satisfaction in being needed as well.

But if he didn't leave now, would he ever? To make her dependent on him… No.

But he could fill her needs one last time. On that last

morning he rose early, made her eggs, toast soldiers and coffee—he'd already discovered her favourite breakfast—and took it in to her.

Erin was asleep. Hannah was looking amazing, in pink PJs with purple sumo cats. Her curls were tangled by sleep, she was surrounded by a sea of pillows and she looked cross.

She was staring down at a contraption that looked like some sort of plastic breast. He saw tubes, plastic bags, a wad of tissues—and a glower from Hannah that would have seen off lesser men than him.

'It's the work of the devil,' she muttered. 'But I will conquer it.'

'Conquer what?' But he'd already figured it out. He set her breakfast on the bedside table and perched on the end of the bed as she abandoned the contraption and tackled her egg with relief.

'Bloody breast pump,' she told him darkly. 'I stick it on and nothing happens. Nothing. Then I take it off and milk flows everywhere. But it's early days yet. Roslyn's coming over later this morning—you remember the midwife who was there for me at the end? She's a lactation specialist and has promised to help.'

He frowned. 'So why do you need a breast pump?'

'For Ron.'

'Ron?'

'Later Ron,' she said, and grimaced. 'Forward planning.'

'You're scared your milk might dry up?'

'Not in a million years,' she said, as she dipped a toast soldier and cast another dark look at the equipment. 'I seem to have more milk than a dairy full of Friesians, and I'm planning to take advantage of it. I'm training my body to think it's feeding twins. Whenever Erin finishes, my plan is to pump what's left over and freeze it. That way, when I go back to work in six weeks the women in the hospital creche will be able to feed her my milk.'

What was there in that to make him seem to freeze himself?

'In six weeks,' he said slowly. 'Hannah, you can't go back that soon.'

'Of course I can. Lots of women do. I have a good job to go back to, I had a lovely normal birth and I have creche arranged onsite.'

'But surely you don't want to.'

'You think I have a choice?' Her eyes flashed anger but then she caught herself. 'Sorry. That was uncalled for. But it's a reality, Josh. I'm a single mum on a limited income, but I'll be fine. You've set me up brilliantly and as soon as I can get this contraption working all will fall into place.'

'I can help you financially. That'd give you space to spend more time with her. Hannah, let me—'

'No.' She said it almost harshly. 'Josh, enough. I've needed you and needed you and needed you, but you need to allow me to regain my dignity, to get on with my own life. We're fine, Erin and me. I won't hang on your sleeve a moment longer.'

'I don't mind.'

'No, but I do.' She took a deep breath. 'I can't allow myself to depend on you any more, Josh. You don't want that and neither do I.'

He didn't want to be needed?

He didn't. He'd made that vow three years ago. Almost unconsciously his fingers moved to the scar running down the side of his face. He thought of the first time he'd felt it—as a dressing. His hand had gone to the dressing almost before he'd opened his eyes. Then he'd woken and Madison was there, and the pain he'd seen in her eyes had been bone deep.

He looked down at Hannah, who was consciously focusing on her toast fingers. He looked at the tiny bundle in the bassinet beside her.

How could he let her continue to need him? He'd hurt her. Eventually he must.

'It's okay,' Hannah said gently into the stillness. 'I get it, Josh. You need to be alone. For what you've done… Josh, I'll love you for ever, but now it's time for you to go.'

It was.

Somehow he made it out of the room. Somehow he was packed and he and Dudley were in his truck, and Hannah's apartment was a dreary block of bricks disappearing in the rear-view mirror.

'I'll be back to visit,' he'd told her.

'Of course you will,' she'd said in a voice that had been none too steady. 'There's a little matter of two puppies that are legally yours the moment they're able to leave their mum. Eight weeks?'

'I'll be back before that,' he told her.

She took his hands and she kissed him. Lightly, though, a fleeting kiss, and he hadn't had the courage to take it further.

'A quick visit only,' she said gently. 'Josh, thank you but I no longer need you.'

His truck disappeared into the distance. She walked back inside and closed the door behind her.

And sank onto the floor and buried her face in her hands.

Why did she want to sob?

'I love him.' She said it out loud and Maisie heard

and snuffled out to investigate the pain in her new mistress's voice.

'I'll get over it.' She hugged Maisie hard and Maisie licked her face in canine incomprehension.

She would get over it. He'd been her hero when she'd needed him and that was all. She was now a competent midwife, a caring mother and a responsible dog owner, with no need for Josh at all.

'And even if I do need him…because…

'There's no because,' she said sharply, causing Maisie to back off in confusion. 'Men. Who needs them?'

But Maisie was looking at the door. Dudley was gone, too.

'Oh, for heaven's sake, we need to move on,' she told Maisie. 'We need a snack. Or more than a snack. It's ten in the morning and neither of us have eaten for a whole two hours. We nursing mothers need to maintain our strength. Food's a much more important focus than men we don't need.'

But as she and her dog headed for the kitchen to check the fridge—which was loaded, thanks to Josh's generosity and forethought—Maisie kept glancing back at the door.

As did Hannah.

'They're gone,' she told Maisie, trying to sound sensible, determined, a woman in charge of her world. 'We need to move on. One ham sandwich coming up. Or two? Anything we want, Maisie, girl.'

Anything we want?

She moved into ham-sandwich production but still her eyes kept drifting to the door.

Anything she wanted?

She knew what she wanted, and it wasn't going to happen.

CHAPTER FIFTEEN

THE CALL CAME at seven at night.

None of his research team would ring him at this hour. It'd be Madison, Josh thought, as he abandoned the research paper he'd been wading through and reached for his phone. Four weeks ago he'd resented any interruption, including calls from his bossy big sister. Now he was grateful. It was so hard to keep his focus on his work.

It was so hard to keep his focus on anything but a woman and a baby in Townsville.

'Hi, Madison,' he said into the phone.

'Josh, it's Hannah.'

His breathing seemed to stop.

Why did this woman have this effect on him? Why did his world seem to stop when he heard her?

He'd been to Townsville twice since he'd left her. Well, he'd had to. His team was based at the university, and while he was dropping in it would have been surly not to detour to see how Hannah, baby and dogs were going.

He'd played with the pups, getting bigger and cheekier every day. He'd held Erin, feeling the newborn smell of her, cradling her, being amazed at the changes in her. He'd given Hannah time to wash her hair or duck out to the shops, or do whatever was hard with a newborn baby. He'd stayed when he'd been useful, but when there was no need for him he'd had no place there.

But now this. The phone call. What was wrong? Something was. He could hear it in her voice. He could almost see her, at this time of evening maybe already in her PJs, because that was the most comfortable outfit she owned. Her crazy sumo cat pyjamas? He needed to block that vision.

Why was there panic in her voice?

'What's wrong, Hannah?' And then, because this was Hannah… 'What can I do?'

'Oh, Josh…' She hiccupped on a sob and his world seemed to still.

He thought of Erin as he'd last seen her, a bundle of milky contentment. He'd cradled her while Hannah had taken herself off to get a haircut, and he'd looked into her little face and felt a tug so strong he'd almost panicked.

'I'll come,' he said, and he heard Hannah gasp and then struggle to pull herself together.

'No. I… It's not that urgent. At least… Josh, I don't know how to ask.'

'Then take a deep breath and tell me what's not that urgent,' he told her, his heart rate settling a little. Nothing appalling, then?

'It's Gran,' she told him, stuttering a little as she got the words out. 'In Dublin. You know I've told you about her. Josh, she's dying. They rang from the hospice this afternoon. She's still conscious but she's fading. The nurses say…well, they can't make guarantees but she's not eating and she's refused a drip. But, Josh, she's asking for me.'

And in her voice… Desolation. Loss.

Love.

'Then you have to go,' he said calmly. 'You'll need money for the fare. No,' he said as she tried to break in. 'It would be my privilege.'

'Josh, it's not the money,' she told him. 'I wouldn't ask…after all you've done and I'm not completely destitute. I do have some savings. But, Josh, I can't take Erin.'

He thought that through. Four weeks old… Yeah, there'd be complications.

'We'll have to fast-track a passport,' he told her. 'I know a lawyer in Canberra…'

'I already went down that path,' she told him. 'It's been three hours since the hospice rang and I've been trying every which way since. Josh—Ryan's name's on Erin's birth certificate. In retrospect I shouldn't have put it there, but I thought… I hoped…'

'That he'd want some contact?'

'He's her father.' It was a despairing gasp but once again she gathered herself. 'Apparently, I need to get his permission to take Erin out of the country. No exceptions. But I've rung everyone I can think of, his parents, his friends, and no one knows where he is. He's still in Australia, they think, but no one knows for sure and the nursing staff says Gran only has days. Oh, Josh, I need to go.'

'So you need me to care for Erin?'

She gasped again and then fell silent.

'That's what you need, isn't it, Hannah?' He thought of the impossibility of cutting through red tape for Hannah to take her baby back to Dublin. He thought of alternatives. This was the only one, and Hannah had figured it before him.

'There's no one else,' Hannah whispered, sounding

almost terrified. 'But, Josh, I can't believe I'm even asking. Of course you'll say no, but this is for Gran, not for me, so I thought… I had to try. I just…'

For Gran, not for me.

Of course not for her. This was Hannah, a woman with a heart as big as the ocean she had to cross to get home. A woman who'd use her scant savings—and by now he'd figured just how scant—to say goodbye to a dying grandmother.

What sort of reception would she get when she reached Dublin?

Cold, he thought. She'd visit her grandmother—if she was still alive when she got there—but then she'd be faced with a family who'd rejected her out of hand. Would she even be permitted to attend the funeral? Maybe not, he thought, but visiting her gran now, a woman who, despite being close to death, was still of sound mind, was surely an option. Hannah wouldn't be turned away.

He thought suddenly of Alice, of waking and finding she was gone. If he'd had those last few minutes to say goodbye…

'Of course I'll care for Erin,' he said, almost before he knew he was about to say it. 'When can you leave?'

'Josh—'

'Is there a plane tonight? That might even be possible. Our bridge is still down but the weather's calm. I can get a water taxi and hire a car on the other side.' He'd have to pay through the nose to hire a car at this time of night, but some things were imperative. 'I can be with you in two hours.'

'Josh—'

'You'll need to leave me instructions.' He was thinking ahead. 'How much milk have you expressed?'

'I... Maybe enough for a week? Maybe not quite. But I've already tried her on a bottle of formula because I'm supposed to be going back to work in two weeks. She doesn't like it much, but she takes it.' She sounded almost robotic, dazed beyond belief.

'That's great. It means I can augment with formula if I need to. I can ask for help from your midwife friends if I get into trouble.'

'They'll help,' she said, but she said it doubtfully. 'I did think that maybe I could even have her admitted but...'

'But hospitals are full of bugs.'

'And they wouldn't do it. Not for this. If I were ill...'

'You'll be ill if you don't go,' he told her. 'Hannah, let me check flights. Hang on.' He swung back to his computer and did a fast search. 'Yes! There's a flight to Dublin via Brisbane and Dubai, leaving at eleven tonight. I'll see if I can get you on. Flick me your passport details. I can do the rest.'

'Josh...' She was half laughing, half crying. 'You can't just drop everything. Tonight!'

'Hannah.' His voice turned stern. 'You want to say goodbye to your gran?'

Another deep breath. 'I do,' she admitted. 'Almost more than anything.'

'Then we're wasting time. You pack and write instructions. I'll book you on this flight, then call a water taxi and rip Jed away from the telly to organise me a hire car. We're running tight on time, so I suggest you take Erin to the airport with you and we'll do a handover there. Jed can organise me a baby seat so I can take her back to your place and we'll go from there.'

'Oh, Josh...' She was definitely crying now.

'Enough,' he said gruffly. 'Dudley and I will stay in

your apartment until you return.' Thank heaven it was a hospital apartment, he thought. How much did he know of newborns? He had enough sense to think he wanted the backup of a midwifery ward if things went pear-shaped. 'I'll need to pack as well. We both have things to do. Go for it, Hannah, let's move.'

'I can't—'

'Of course you can. Right, Hannah. Ready, set, go.'

She reached the airport before he did. The cab driver dropped her off and helped her with her baggage. She carried Erin into the departure hall, tucked herself into a quiet corner, sat on her suitcase and waited.

Fifteen minutes after she arrived, so did Josh.

He strode through the big glass doors and stood for a moment, looking around. He was a big man, dressed in jeans and a black T-shirt, a bit too tight. His leather boots had seen better days. He looked relaxed, his gaze calm and thoughtful. A man facing the prospect of coping with a newborn alone? Not so much.

He looked at ease. Confident. Sure.

In this sea of travellers dressed for travel, coping with the fussiness of checking in, of saying goodbye to loved ones, Josh stood apart.

He'd stand apart anyway, Hannah thought, and then his search located her. Their eyes met and he smiled, and she thought maybe she might cry.

Oh, this man…

'Hey.' He reached her and squatted down to look into her eyes. 'Hey, Hannah.' And he touched her face.

It was a fleeting touch, nothing more, and why it had the capacity to make tears spill…

'I'm sorry,' she managed. 'I can't…'

'You can't think, and why should you?' he told her. 'Sweetheart, you look done in.'

That brought a reaction. 'I do not!' She blinked back treacherous tears. 'I'm fine.'

'Good girl,' he told her, and lifted Erin from her arms. The little girl was wide awake, staring upward at the bright lights with wonder. But as she met Josh's eyes, her tiny face creased.

She smiled.

Her baby's first smile. At such a time...

Josh even had the temerity to produce a man-sized handkerchief and hand it to her. Was there no end to him coming to her rescue?

'Let's get you checked in,' he told her. 'You can have your cry out on the plane, but I'd advise sleep first.'

As if she could sleep on planes... But as he led her toward the check-in counter, instead of heading for the mile-long economy queue, he headed for crimson Priority.

'Josh!' she gasped. 'You can't. I can't!'

'What?'

'Go Business.'

'You're not,' he told her. 'First class or nothing.'

'But I can't pay you back.' This was ridiculous.

'I travel a lot,' he told her. 'By a lot I mean so much that I have points to spare. This is costing me nothing, Hannah.'

'Are you out of your mind?'

'I'm not.' They'd reached the counter and Josh tugged a sheaf of papers from his wallet and handed them over to a bemused clerk. 'We need your passport too, love.'

'Don't call me love!' What was there in that overused word that had her panicked?

'Sorry.' But as she fumbled for her passport he stood

watching her with a strange expression on his face. Dammit, she was blushing. Her passport came out of her bag with a rush and fell.

They stooped simultaneously but as her fingers reached the passport, she found she was gripped. Held.

Josh was cradling Erin in the crook of one arm. With his spare hand he held her wrist, compelling them both to stay stooped.

Her eyes met his, calm, grey, thoughtful.

'Hannah, I'm so sorry about your gran,' he said softly, while above their heads the lass on the check-in counter waited with the patience surely reserved for first-class passengers.

'I… It's all right.'

'It's not all right now, but it will be,' he said softly. 'You need to say goodbye to an old lady you love, and then let her go in peace.'

'Oh, Josh…'

'And now you need to gather your strength, go through those big doors and head to the other side of the world,' he said gently. 'And then come back to us. Home is here, and Erin and I will be thinking about you all the time you're away.'

There weren't people behind them—that was a blessing, for Josh's free hand had moved to cradle her cheek, firm, sure. He was propelling her face to his.

One of her hands held her dropped passport. The other was free. She should use it to push him away.

Why would she? How could she?

Came another slight tug, and somehow she was close. So close.

Close enough to be kissed? There seemed no choice.

His mouth met hers, warm, strong, wonderful. His free hand was in her hair and hers in his, so the kiss deepened. Somewhere below there was a baby, cradled between them, cocooned by their kiss.

It felt amazing.

It felt right.

It felt like…home was right here.

'I'm sorry to interrupt, but we're running close to time. We need to get you boarded.' The voice above them was apologetic but firm, and when they broke away and looked up, the girl was beaming a smile a mile wide.

'I do love a romantic goodbye,' she told them, and then she looked back at the papers Josh had handed over. 'I see your return ticket is open ended.' She beamed down at Hannah. 'I'm guessing you'll be back soon.'

'I… That's right.' Josh's hand tugged her to her feet and she felt herself blushing from the toes up. 'Very soon.'

'Well, with this to come home to why wouldn't you?' the girl said, not even trying to conceal a touch of wistfulness. 'Wow,' she said. 'All the way to Dublin and back, and your man and your baby to come home to.' She took Hannah's passport and did a cursory check. 'All's well here,' she told her. 'Gate five, boarding in fifteen minutes. I'm sorry sir,' she told Josh. 'You can't go through to the gates unless you're travelling. But you can kiss her again before she goes through Security.'

'I might have to,' Josh told her—and did.

She sat in her unbelievably luxurious seat, she looked out as the lights of Townsville faded behind her and thought, What have I done?

I've left my baby with Josh.

With a man she hardly knew.

With a man who'd done so much for her already.

She was already feeling sick about leaving Erin. Her arms felt empty. Soon her breasts would begin to ache, but in first-class luxury she should even be able to use her breast pump. She'd have to keep expressing if she wanted to breastfeed once she got home.

Home.

Where was home?

She was going home, wasn't she? To her country, to her family, to the people who'd been with her all her life.

Home was where the heart was.

Home was back with those fading lights. Erin. Maisie. Dudley and a litter of tumbling puppies.

Josh.

'Don't think like that. Don't!' She said it out loud, but in her cocooned luxury there was no one to think she was queer in the head.

He'd kissed her as if he loved her.

Well, that was nonsense. She had herself under control now, or almost. He'd kissed her because she was an emotional mess, because he'd wanted to reassure her, because he felt sorry for her.

Because he was quite simply the kindest, most wonderful guy she'd ever met.

So how could someone like Josh ever want her?

He didn't want her, she told herself, and she knew it was true. He wanted isolation. He wanted no more ties, and didn't she come with ties? She'd just landed him with a four-week old baby to care for. Plus two dogs and four puppies.

She thought of his gorgeous house and mentally compared it with her cramped one-bedroom apartment. He'd go spare. That he was doing this for her...

'How could I have asked it of him?' she demanded, out loud again.

'I had no choice and I gave him no choice.' She gave up on sanity and talked aloud anyway. 'So don't get any dumb ideas, just because he comforted me and kissed me goodbye. I might need him, and he might be everything a great hero needs to be, but I come with baggage up to my ears and he doesn't need baggage.'

'Baggage?' The flight attendant was suddenly right there, with a tray holding water, orange juice and champagne. 'Is there a problem with your baggage, ma'am? Can we help?'

'I... No.' She hauled herself together and thought stuff it and took a champagne—the first alcoholic drink she'd had since she'd learned she was pregnant. 'Yes, I do have a problem with baggage,' she admitted to the woman who was looking as if she really cared. That was also professional, she told herself. This woman was doing what she needed to do, as was Josh.

'I have all sorts of baggage problems,' she told the attendant, and managed a smile. 'But I can sort them. They're nobody's problems but mine.'

Josh opened the apartment door and carried the tiny, sleeping bundle of Erin inside.

Dudley came in on his heels and headed straight for the laundry door. There was a frantic whine from the other side, Josh opened the door and Maisie launched herself out joyously to greet them.

Followed by four wobbly, wide eyed puppies.

Josh stood in their midst and gazed around him. Hannah had done her best to leave the place presentable, but she'd been rushed and baby paraphernalia was everywhere. The fridge door, bare when shifted in, was now a mass of baby appointment schedules, to-do lists and fuzzy photos taken with her phone and printed on a low-quality printer.

There was a picture of Josh on his last visit, holding Erin, with Maisie looking adoringly up at him.

He was smiling.

He couldn't remember smiling. Didn't Madison say he never smiled?

Two of the pups launched themselves at a clothes horse standing by the window, trying to drag down the edges of a bunny rug. 'No!' Too late. The clothes horse collapsed and baby clothes went everywhere. Plus Hannah's clothes. Knickers, socks, feeding bra...

This felt weird. Far too intimate. Hannah's world was closing in on him.

He thought of Alice and the pain of losing her. He forced himself to keep thinking, biting on the pain like biting on a bad tooth, testing to see how deep the pain went. So deep.

He didn't need this. He didn't want this.

'So why did I kiss her?' He stared down at Dudley like his dog might give him some clue. 'I'm setting up expectations I can't meet. I can't let her keep needing me. I don't want anyone depending on me.'

Why not? Dudley seemed almost to be looking the question.

'Because I have baggage, and baggage hurts.'

And Dudley wagged his tail as if he totally understood, totally sympathised, and then a puppy grabbed his tail and he turned and growled. And then another puppy grabbed his ear. Maisie headed over to nose the pup on the ear away. Then Maisie's nose touched Dudley's and, as if he'd been commanded, Dudley caved in.

He sank to the floor and rolled over. In seconds he had pups all over him. Maisie sank down beside him,

Mum having time out, and Josh found himself smiling again.

Erin stirred and woke up, her eyes looking up at him with wide-eyed interest. Maybe a little anxious?

'Sorry, sweetheart, I'm all you have now,' he told her. We're just going to make the most of it.'

And here it came again, the smile. A smile just like her mother's.

He had baggage?

One baby didn't care.

Dudley had baggage?

His dog had obviously caved in on that as well.

'So I guess my baggage is there to be picked up when your mum stops needing me,' he told Erin, and then he picked up Hannah's wad of 'How to Care for a Baby' notes and stared at its bulk in astonishment.

'Does she think I'm an idiot? I'm a surgeon. If I can operate on a human brain, surely I can change a nappy.'

But…she was wet. And a man could just check.

'Okay, let's get this thing rolling,' he told Erin, and headed for the change table, collecting wipes, disposing bags and fresh nappy on the way. And the instructions. 'Let's just forget all about baggage for however long it takes to get your mum home. Then life can take over.'

CHAPTER SIXTEEN

'*ACUSHLA*... LOVE...'

Gran's voice was so soft Hannah could hardly hear her. She was fading fast. Hannah had been here for two days and she'd spent almost all her time at the hospice. Gran was clutching her hand, and Hannah was blessing everything that had let her be here. Mostly Josh.

All Josh.

'Show me the pictures again,' Gran whispered, and Hannah complied. She'd managed to connect her phone to the overhead television so Gran could lie in bed and see every image she put up.

She showed the pictures Gran most wanted to see. A baby named for her. Her great-granddaughter.

She had the images on a loop now, so she could talk Gran through them. Erin on the day she was born. Erin's first bath. A selfie where she'd held her baby while a sea of curious puppies took their first look.

Erin being cradled by Josh.

'Stop it there,' Gran whispered, as she always did when it came to this shot. 'Let me see.'

There was a long pause. Gran's breath was raspy, ragged, uneven, but her eyes were alive and wondering. 'Tell me again,' she asked for surely the umpteenth time. 'He's not your babe's father?'

'He's not. You know Ryan left me, Gran, when he knew I was pregnant.'

'Gobshite!' she said, and weak though her voice was, the word echoed with disdain. But then her tone changed. 'But this is Josh. A doctor. He's a lovely man—you can see it just by looking at him. And you'd be the one holding the camera, the one he's smiling at.'

'He is lovely,' she conceded, letting herself drift into that smile.

'And he's waiting for you to come home.'

Home. There was that word again.

Where was it?

'He'll make you safe,' Gran said, gripping her hand with fingers that held far too little strength. 'I know it. I can see it in the way he's looking at you. You'll be loved, my Hannah.'

'Gran—'

'Don't you tell me any different,' she said, hurriedly, with a hint of waspishness. 'I know a happy ending when I see one, and that's what we all need. A happy ending.'

'And a happy beginning?'

'Definitely,' her gran said and gripped her hand harder. 'I wish it, my Hannah. I wish it for you with all my heart.'

'Josh?' The call came at eight in the morning. It was Hannah, and her voice was laced with tears.

'She's gone?'

'A couple of hours ago. I was with her.'

'Your parents?'

'No. They've visited a couple of times but when they knew I was here… Gran insisted I stay so they kept apart.'

'You haven't seen them?'

'Once.' Her voice was stilted. 'Bridget a couple more times, but she's scared Dad'll find out. I'll not be staying for the funeral, Josh. I'm coming home.'

Dammit, what was her family thinking? He wanted to punch someone.

He wanted to give someone a hug.

Instead he moved to practicalities.

'Your ticket is open-ended. I'll book you on the next flight.'

'Thank you. Is Erin okay?'

'She's beautiful,' he told her. 'Turn your video on.'

'Not my end,' she said hurriedly. 'I'm a soggy mess.'

Dammit, he wanted to see her. What was a bit of sogginess?

'So's your daughter,' he told her, managing to keep his voice calm, and he flicked on video mode and positioned his phone so she could see her baby. Erin had been lying in his bed, having her bottle, when Hannah had called. He'd been thinking he should stir and change her—get dressed himself—but he'd been tickling her toes and somehow tickling took precedence.

Yeah, well, he wasn't about to tell Hannah that. She'd think he was totally besotted. Which he wasn't. He was here to do a job. Keeping Erin safe and Hannah reassured.

Only that.

He focused the phone lens on Erin and tickled again. Erin's tiny face creased into her gorgeous smile again and he heard Hannah gasp.

'Oh, Josh. Oh, baby. Oh, she makes me feel...'

'Like you're nearly home,' he said, surely and strongly. 'Two more days, love.'

'Please don't call me that,' she begged. 'It makes me feel more needful than I really am. Josh, after I get home I won't need you any more, I promise. What you've given me is a gift without price. You've been the hero to end all heroes but I won't be needful for the rest of my life. Will you bring Erin to the airport? We can swap over there, and you can go back to your island.'

'Is that what you want?'

'Of course it is,' she said, making her voice firm. 'I won't hang on you any more. I'm strong, Josh, really I am, despite the wimpy-ness you've seen. I can get back to delivering babies and looking after mine, and you can go back to your fantastic research. You know I've read all about it online? It sounds fantastic, what you're trying to do. I found your presentation in Boston on your team's website. The hope you're giving to paralysis patients...'

It needed only this. She was still consumed with loss—he could hear it in her voice—but within her grief she was remembering the hope on the faces of the patients who'd joined the early trials. He and his team were working to attach neural signals to external, robotic skeletons. They were so close...

His work was critical. He needed quiet. He needed isolation.

Did he?

'I need to go,' Hannah said, and he heard aching weariness in her voice. 'I'll catch some sleep now but, yes, please, to booking my flight home. But I promise, Josh, this is the last time I'll ask for help. My need for need is over.'

She disconnected and he lay and stared at the ceiling for a long, long time.

Erin was still soggy, but he was idly tickling her

tummy and she was making dumb little cooing noises that signified all was right with her world.

All wasn't right in Josh's world. His head felt like it might explode.

My need for need is over.

She didn't need him any more. That was great, wasn't it?

Of course it was. The vow he'd made, not to let emotional entanglements lead him anywhere that could cause pain, to him or to others, was surely as strong today as it had been when he'd woken up to find his sister had died.

His non-tickling hand ran over the scar on the side of his face. There was his reminder of the chaos emotional entanglement could bring.

But Hannah… He'd kissed her. He'd called her love.

He'd only done that because she'd needed comfort. She'd needed strength and warmth and practical help, and he'd provided it.

He could keep giving it to her. She still needed…

He stopped. His brain seemed to have hit the brakes and was refusing to go any further.

She still needed?

'Be honest,' he told himself, aloud. 'I still need.

'I can't need,' he said, bluntly across Erin's tiny murmurs. 'I won't put my emotional needs on her. Has history taught me nothing?'

His hand stopped tickling. There was a whimper of protest from beside him and he caught himself. Do what comes next, he told himself. Put emotion aside. Hadn't that been his mantra for years?

So he did what came next. He changed Erin and wrapped her in a fresh bunny rug. He dressed himself and then carried the almost-asleep baby out to the back porch to check on the dogs. It would have been more sensible to put Erin back in her bassinet for a sleep, but he wasn't feeling sensible right now. For some reason he needed to hold her.

The dogs were awake. The puppies had tumbled out of their basket, and the moment he opened the laundry door they were all over him.

He sat on the doorstep and fended them off from investigating Erin, investigating him. They headed down to tumble on the now-worn grass.

Maisie and Dudley flopped down beside him. Obviously after a night spent with pups, adult company was welcome.

This courtyard looked like a bomb had hit it, Josh thought. When the pups left he'd have to spend some time fixing it up, replanting.

Would Hannah let him?

She wouldn't. She didn't need him. She'd said it and he knew she'd meant it.

As he'd meant his oath never to entangle himself again in this thing called love.

> *When a man takes an oath...he's holding his own self in his own hands. Like water. And if he opens his fingers then he needn't hope to find himself again.*

At some time during his interminable convalescence he'd read Robert Bolt's *A Man for All Seasons,* and these words had resonated. For if he let himself love again then surely he'd lose himself entirely. How could he possibly risk it?

Then Dudley jumped up and licked his face, looking hopefully toward the food bowls. Reminding him of the prosaic. The ordinary.

'So I'm being a dramatist,' he told his dog, and took Erin back to her bassinet and fed the dogs and sat down at his computer to check flights from Dublin.

Hannah was coming home.

He needn't hope to find himself again…

He could drift…anywhere.

Or he could find himself with Hannah. And six dogs. And a baby. And complications and domesticity and a laughing, green-eyed girl who'd won his heart.

He needn't hope to find himself again…

He texted her confirmation of her flights, leaving the next day so she'd have time to have her sleep out before she left.

She texted back.

Thanks, Josh. For everything. But let this be an end to it.

An end?

Dudley was now lying at his feet, for some reason looking doleful. As if he knew this time of family was almost over?

Family. There was a word Josh had run a mile from.

He raked his fingers through his hair and headed back outside to look at the pups again. They were a suckling mass of sleepy contentment. Maisie looked up at him and wagged her tail and he thought, She's contented, too.

Dammit, he wanted to share.

Why couldn't he?

Close your eyes and jump.

All it took was courage.

If it was Hannah she'd jump, he thought. Hannah had courage for both of them.

Enough to share?

And all of a sudden he felt…small. Cowardly.

Stupid.

And with that feeling, suddenly things cleared. The ice wall was a thing he'd made to defend himself, to defend others, but if all it caused now was hurt… Dammit, surely he could kick it down? Or melt it? Or even climb it and see what was on the other side. Sure, he might fall, but why not try, because the only risk was to be left where he was now. The option made him shudder.

So…kick the thing down? Expose the other side?

'You've got to be kidding,' he said out loud, because that wall had been important for so long. Dudley and Maisie both looked at him in concern.

'I'm not kidding,' he told them, and went to knock on the next-door neighbour's door, because Ruth had offered babysitting and he needed a couple of hours. Now, before he lost his nerve.

Along with everything else, he thought.

But then he thought, What am I talking about? I'll only lose if I don't try.

Or if she doesn't want—

'Don't go there,' he said out loud, because Hannah not needing him was unthinkable.

But then he caught himself and stood for a moment while his thoughts caught up with him. While he acknowledged the truth.

He didn't need Hannah to need him.

He needed Hannah.

The plane landed at dawn.

It was an appalling hour to arrive anywhere, Hannah thought as she collected her baggage and made her way through Customs. She'd told Josh he wasn't to meet her. He'd protested, but she'd been adamant. The airport bus stopped right outside the hospital. She'd meet him at the apartment.

Everything's in order, he'd texted back. You'll find us shipshape and ready to move on.'

Which meant she needed to be ready to move back to the life she'd planned from the moment Ryan had left her. Single mum. Midwife. There was a complication with dogs, but she'd find homes for the pups. And she'd love keeping Maisie.

The thought should cheer her, as should the thought of being reunited with her baby.

It did, sort of, but as she made her way through the gates her legs felt leaden.

Fatigue? Probably. She should have slept on the plane but too much had happened. She was emotionally wired.

She sort of hoped Josh might have disregarded her instructions and come to meet her anyway.

He hadn't. The arrivals hall was a sea of anxious faces but as she tugged her suitcase through the throng there was no one she recognised.

Of course there wasn't. He'd reacted with anger to the thought of swapping Erin over at the airport and of course he was right. To take a sleeping baby out of her cot at this hour... No, he'd be at the apartment, packed, ready to leave.

As was sensible. He knew she didn't need him any more.

So think of practical things. Taxi instead of bus?

It'd cost her a mint, but maybe she could splurge. She was so weary.

But sense prevailed. The bus left every half-hour and

it stopped right by the hospital. She tugged her case toward the bus stop…and then stopped.

Stunned.

There seemed to be balloons where the bus should be.

Or maybe they were in front of where the bus should be. She couldn't tell. All she could see were balloons. Rainbow balloons, every colour she could imagine. And in the front of the balloons… Josh.

Holding a baby.

Her baby.

She dropped the handle of her wheelie case and it fell unheeded to the pavement.

Josh was here.

And it wasn't just Josh. What on earth had he set up on the pavement?

He'd brought her a playpen he'd bought when he'd furnished her apartment. 'I won't need that until Erin's at least a year old,' she'd told him, struggling to make him take some of the stuff back, to limit his generosity.

He hadn't listened, though, and it was being used now. He'd set it up on the pavement and tied balloons all around it, helium balloons so they waved and fluttered six to eight feet off the ground.

And the playpen was full of dogs—Maisie and Dudley and four balls of wide-eyed, waggy-tailed fluff: puppies who seemed to have doubled their size since she'd last seen them.

There was a bus behind the balloons. Her bus? People were gathered as if waiting to board but no one was boarding.

They were watching Josh.

Who was watching Hannah.

'I hoped you'd have the sense to catch a taxi,' he told

her as she stared. 'But I knew you'd catch the bus. My thrifty Hannah. Welcome home, love.'

And stupidly she said the first thing that came into her mind. 'I'm not your love.'

'That's something we need to discuss.' He walked forward to meet her. Erin was awake in his arms, interested, curious. She gave her mother a huge, toothless beam and Hannah thought any minute now her heart might melt.

Josh eased Erin into her arms, and she stood, gazing down at her baby, taking in every tiny detail, while Josh stood back and looked at them both like a genie might look at Aladdin. Beaming with genial pride. Ready to grant any wish she might make?

Which was nonsense. This was nonsense.

'Why?' she asked, her voice faltering with emotion and fatigue. 'Why have you brought the dogs? And Erin. And all this...stuff. Josh, this is crazy.'

'This is to stop me going crazy,' he told her.

The pups were going nuts. Maisie and Dudley had jumped out of the playpen and were leaping ecstatically around her. The puppies were trying to reach their parents. The bus passengers were looking agog.

'I had to bring them,' Josh said apologetically. 'They're family. I'm sorry about not being in the arrivals hall to meet you but there's some dumb rule about not letting animals past the entry door. So I set this up here. I did give your photo and my phone number to the guy organising the taxi rank in case you decided to be extravagant. If you'd turned up there, we would have done a sprint.'

'With all this stuff?' She was trying hard to make her voice work.

'These people were planning on helping me,' he told

her, and grinned at the sea of faces around them—the crowd was swelling by the minute with people were attracted by balloons and puppies. 'This gentleman...' he motioned to a thick-set airport security officer '...thinks he'd like to buy one of your pups. I told him he'd need be thoroughly vetted but so far Maisie and Dudley seem to approve.'

Hannah turned to stare. The guy in the uniform gave her a sheepish wave. 'I like the one with the white eye patch,' he told her. 'She's a ripper. I reckon I could train her to come to work with me.'

'Josh...'

'I know, it's too much to take in,' Josh said apologetically. 'But the thing is, I need to say something and I need to say it now.'

'Need...what?'

'Will you let this guy hold Erin for a minute?' Josh suggested, motioning back to the security officer. 'His name's Michael. He has four kids of his own and he's very reliable.'

But as if on cue Michael's radio alarm sounded. Michael lifted it and listened.

'Yes, we do have a situation down here but it's a minor domestic and it's sorted,' he said into the radio. 'No, I don't need back-up, sir. Yes, we'll clear it as soon as possible but I believe the lady is feeling faint, what with all the excitement. There's a doctor in the crowd. If I give them just a few minutes, sir, I believe we'll have the situation under control with minimum impact.'

He hooked his radio back on his belt and grinned at Josh. 'You heard. Ten minutes. Get on with it, Doctor.'

'Get on with what?' Hannah demanded, wholly bewildered.

'Making the lady not faint,' Josh told her. 'Hannah,

try not to faint while I say this because my medical reputation's at stake. Love, I have something to ask.'

'Josh…' She was struggling between laughter and tears. 'This is ridiculous.'

'It is, isn't it?' Josh said. 'And this bus leaves in ten minutes and Michael's superiors might send in the riot squad if we haven't dispersed. No pressure, love, but…'

Pressure? Her lovely steady Josh… Her hero… He'd lost it, she thought. There wasn't an ounce of sense in any of this.

Oh, but he was here, and he was smiling at her.

She was struggling for sense amid chaos. Okay.

Deep breath. She was, after all, a midwife, she told herself. Calming hysterical situations was in her remit. 'We do need to disperse,' she managed. 'Josh, where's your car? We don't need to keep these people here any longer.' Move away, her tone said. Nothing to see here, people.

But it seemed there was.

'We'd kind of like to know the answer,' Michael said. 'He's going to—'

'Don't you dare say it before I do,' Josh interjected. 'Sorry, love, I had to tell them or Michael here would have moved me on.'

'Too right,' Michael said, grinning, and he reached out and took Erin, and Hannah was so gobsmacked she let her go.

'What…?'

'Okay, this was maybe a dumb idea,' Josh conceded hastily. 'When I thought it through I hadn't factored in Security. But now we're here…'

'Now we're here, what?'

'Will you marry me?'

He said it in a rush, almost panicked, and it brought

them both up short. For a moment they stared at each other. Even Josh seemed too stunned to take it any further.

'Help, I didn't get that right,' Josh said, and there were mutters of agreement—and disapproval—from the onlookers. 'Can we try again?'

'Josh—'

'Shush, love,' he told her. 'I will get it right. Give me space.'

'Seven minutes max,' Michael warned, and Josh waved acknowledgement, but his gaze didn't leave Hannah's.

He delved into his pocket and hauled out a tiny crimson box.

He dropped to one knee.

'I can't believe I'm seeing this,' an elderly lady from the bus queue said. 'Ooh, it's giving me palpitations.'

'You can be my fainting lady if I have to explain this away,' Michael said kindly. 'You want to lie down?'

'I want to watch,' she said with asperity.

'Yes, but the bus is due to leave, and she hasn't even answered,' someone else said.

'Bus ain't leaving till she does,' a woman in a bus driver's uniform declared, and Hannah gasped and choked and looked down at Josh.

Who was looking up at her.

Who was holding a ring.

Who was holding her heart.

'Josh, don't…' she said falteringly. 'I can't. You know you don't want me. You're just kind and lovely and caring. You're a hero and you rescued me, but I don't need rescuing any more.' She bit her lip but she made herself say it. 'I don't need you.'

'Don't you, love?' Josh said tenderly, and suddenly

their extraordinary backdrop faded into insignificance. Everything faded to insignificance. There was only this moment. This man. Josh.

'You don't want marriage,' she managed, forcing the words out. 'And, honestly, Josh, I don't need it. I don't need you.'

'That's just it,' he told her. 'I've been thinking of all the ways you could need rescuing, racking my brains to think of any way I can be useful. And, honestly, Hannah, I can't think of one. But I'll try. I need to try because... Hannah these last few days... I've figured... my vow to stay isolated was just plain unworkable. Unthinkable. Or maybe it was thinkable until I fell in love.'

'Ooh,' said the lady with palpitations, but Hannah didn't say anything at all.

'You see, there's need and there's need,' Josh said, almost apologetically. 'There's physical need, like hauling you out of sinking cars and delivering babies and—'

'And sex,' some yahoo called out.

'Thanks,' Josh said dryly, but he caught her hands and smiled. 'Yeah, there's sex, and I'll admit that I've pretty much thought of that from the moment I met you. But there's the other need. The need that makes me ask—makes me plead—that you'll become my wife. For I need you, Hannah. When you found me—or when I found you—I was as near to a hermit as made no difference. I might have hauled you out of a car but you hauled me out of so much more. Out of an existence I look back on now with disbelief. When Alice died I pretty much closed down. It took you, my beautiful, funny, strong, wonderful Hannah, to show me how to open up again. To be open to my need as well as yours. To be open to love.'

Whew.

There should be a word bigger than gobsmacked, she thought dazedly. There should be a word to describe— the fact that her heart was about to burst?

'So what about it, Hannah, love?' Josh asked, and she looked down into his eyes and saw anxiety riding above all else.

He truly thought she wouldn't? It was enough to make her dizzy all over again.

'Two minutes,' Michael warned. 'They'll bring a squad.'

'Shut up,' the palpitating lady snapped, and Michael gave her an apologetic look.

'Sorry, but it won't do a mite of good saying we've got longer. There's other buses wanting to use this bay. So what about it, love?' he demanded of Hannah. 'Marriage or not? Put the man out of his misery?'

And Hannah stared around her at the sea of concerned faces, of these people she'd never met in her life. At her dogs. Her puppies. At her baby in the security guard's arms.

Home, she thought mistily. How could she have thought it was anywhere but right here?

And she dropped to her knees to face Josh.

'What about it, love?' she said, smiling mistily at her beloved. 'Shall we put them out of their misery?

'Hannah… Will you say…?'

'Of course I'll say,' she said, and then she tugged him into her and kissed him gently on the mouth. And then she tugged away.

'And of course I'll marry you,' she told him loudly, as the crowd roared their approval and he gathered himself together and tugged her into what he termed a proper embrace. An embrace that would have lasted… a lifetime?

'Time's up, people,' Michael said warningly.

'No,' Josh said, cupping Hannah's face in his hands and tugging her mouth to join his. 'Time's starting now.'

Baby steps.

That was what Josh had warned her to expect. 'This isn't a miracle, Hannah. There's so far to go. Every step forward seems to produce more complications but this... well, come and see.'

So she sat up the back in a conference hall at one of the most eminent universities in the world, while Josh and his team presented their progress.

Madison sat beside her, clutching her hand. For Josh's sister this was almost as huge as it was for Hannah. 'Of course I'm coming,' she'd said breathlessly when Josh had rung to tell her. 'Josh, I'm family.'

And there was yet more family, for unbelievably Bridget was outside, playing with two-year-old Erin. Erin couldn't be trusted to stay quiet during such an important presentation, but when Hannah had told Bridget she and Josh would be in London her sister gone very quiet. Two days later she'd rung back.

'I'll be there. I'm even telling our father. And I'm coming to Australia to visit,' Bridget had breathed. 'And, Hannah... Our mam... She says she has money Gran left her, and she might just use it to come, too. Can you believe it?'

She couldn't. She'd believe it when it happened.

Baby steps.

Which was what was happening in front of her. The team had left the stage, leaving only Josh and Oscar.

Twenty-year-old Oscar had been a surf fanatic, supremely fit, vibrant, active. A wave had dumped him into a sand bank four years ago and he'd been a quadriplegic ever since.

Three years ago, when he'd had been chosen for this first major trial, Oscar had simply been 'the patient' when Josh talked of him. Josh had carefully made his work impersonal. All the fittings and trials had been done by Josh's team, with Josh working on technicalities in the background. Two years ago, though—post-Hannah—the friendship between the two men had become deep and abiding, and Josh's research had flown because of it.

Alone on the stage, Josh was adjusting the last of the electrodes that wired Oscar to an exoskeleton.

The exoskeleton was a simple brace—or maybe not so simple—supporting Oscar's lanky frame. The first frame they'd built had been so bulky it had been impossible. They now had it down to twelve kilograms— they'd get it lighter—and it took only five minutes to fit.

A simple cap contained electrodes that sent neural signals from Oscar's brain to the exoskeleton. Because of day-to-day electrical interference—such as someone using a cellphone nearby—sensor patches were attached beside Oscar's eyes so he could adjust errant signals with vision.

The five minutes were almost up. Oscar, a big, eager kid, sat in his wheelchair, looking excited.

Josh looked tense. As he should. On this prototype lay hopes of massive international funding, hopes of helping so many.

Done. Oscar grinned up at Josh. Josh managed a tense smile back and stepped away.

Oscar was alone.

He wasn't completely alone, though. In the audience was Josh's team, men and women who'd put their hearts and souls into this research. The entire team seemed to be friends, as Oscar was a friend. They were all now Hannah's friends.

And Josh's friends.

Josh and Hannah's little family now lived right in Townsville. Camel Island would always be their happy place, their place of peace, but it was no place to be part of a community. Their new home, on the hills overlooking the sea, was full of dogs, friends, love and laughter.

And child.

Soon to be children.

Hannah put her hand on her belly and told herself and her unborn baby that they needed to cross their fingers.

Get it right, she pleaded. This was so important.

Josh was standing well back. It was clear to everyone that Oscar was completely unaided. The big kid grinned and let the silence hang. He had a sense of the dramatic did Oscar.

Finally, very slowly, his hand reached out for a glass of water on the tray beside his chair. His fingers grasped the glass. There was a moment's pause as he tested his grip before lifting, then he raised the glass and drank. And put the glass back on the tray.

He grinned again. Then, seemingly almost involuntarily, his hand moved upward.

He scratched the side of his neck.

There were gasps, and then a roar of laughing approval from the audience. This conference was for medical scientists from around the world, doctors and technicians who'd know that to scratch an itch was such a basic human need...

Oscar was laughing with them. Then, with supreme concentration because this was still incredibly hard— there was a way to go with this technology yet—Oscar slowly, slowly rose to his feet. He stood for a moment, steadied, and then took a step forward.

Another. A third.

And then Josh was moving across the stage to meet him. They stood silent, as if assessing each other, then both raised their right hands.

It was a handshake between friends.

It was a small thing.

It was huge.

The audience erupted but Hannah didn't clap. She'd subsided into her handkerchief.

Her Josh. Her wonderful, magical Josh.

No longer a loner.

A friend for so many.

What was happening on the stage seemed a medical miracle, but it wasn't merely a medical miracle. She emerged from a sob as Josh sought out her face in the crowd, as Josh smiled out at her.

He was her friend. He was her love.

This was their happy-ever-after.

* * * * *

RISKING IT ALL FOR THE CHILDREN'S DOC

TINA BECKETT

MILLS & BOON

To my supportive husband and family!
Thanks for sticking with me!

PROLOGUE

FIVE-YEAR-OLD ELEAZAR ROHAL'S mom kneeled in front of him and took hold of his shoulders. He couldn't remember the words she said, but he could remember the exact moment his universe changed forever. His gaze took in the serious men who stood on either side of her—men whose expressions made him fearful—and the way his mom's mouth trembled when she said she had to go away for a while.

He glanced to the side where his "Aunt Maddie" stood in the doorway and surveyed the scene, tears streaming down her face. When his mom finally stood, she nodded at Maddie, who came over and took his hand. Ellis shook it off, trying to move toward his mom instead. But she took a step back, staying just out of reach.

He stopped. "Mommy?"

"Be good, Ellis. Remember Mommy loves you. Now and forever."

Except she didn't, or she would have stayed with him.

Five years went by. Then Ten. And although Maddie was kind and loving, Ellis had never quite been able to erase the pain generated by his mother's abrupt departure or the fear that Maddie, too, might be taken away by people he didn't know. His questions about whether his mom was in jail or had been kidnapped had been evaded, and Maddie had simply repeated the words she'd said countless times before: Mommy had had to go away, but she would never stop loving him.

He never really believed it. And Ellis could never quite muster up feelings of love for anyone else. *Attachment disorder*. He'd heard the words whispered from behind closed doors. And although the label had eventually fallen away as he threw himself into school—excelling at subjects that involved science and objective reasoning—he never quite forgot what it meant: he was incapable of attaching to others in an emotional way.

But it was okay. He'd found other ways to cope. He'd done his best to banish the possibility of softer emotions—and had been quite successful, if his failed juvenile romances were any indication.

And now on the cusp of graduating from high school and moving into adulthood, he had some decisions to make.

All he knew was that he *would* figure out where he belonged in this world and take his place in it.

No matter how many years it took, or how many sacrifices he had to make to do it.

CHAPTER ONE

LYRIC WESTPHAL WAS LATE. Her phone's alarm hadn't gone off this morning and the shift from Pacific time to Eastern had totally screwed up her body's natural rhythm. And Atlanta had a completely different feel from Las Vegas. But this opportunity had seemed like a gift from heaven for both her and Alia, giving them the chance for a new start. Far from the memory of her sister's death and the circumstances behind it.

If only she could get to her appointment.

God, if she ruined her chances here because of her own lack of foresight, she would be crushed. She glanced at the seat next to her, where her notebook of ideas sat. Maybe it was too soon, but the hospital deserved to know what they were in for.

She swung into the parking lot of the sprawling hospital, found a spot and jumped from her car, clutching her notebook and heading for the entrance at a sprint. Thank God she'd worn low boots.

As soon as she got confirmation that she had the job and found a place to stay, her parents would fly with Alia, reuniting her with her niece. She never dreamed that at thirty-three years of age she would start a family under these circumstances, but she was already fiercely protective of her young charge. And as her dad's health was not the greatest at the moment, they'd made the joint decision that Alia would live with her. Far from Vegas, where she'd grown up. Far from where Lyric's sister had died.

She shoved through the front door, annoyed when a man stepped almost directly into her path, forcing her to swerve so quickly she dropped her notebook. She started to give him a sideways glance, before shelving it when she noted his tight jaw and raised brow.

Not his fault, Ly.

He bent down to pick up the book, glancing at the open pages as he handed it back to her.

"Thanks," she muttered, turning away to face the information desk in front of her and addressing the attendant. "I'm looking for Dr. Lawson's office—I have an appointment."

The man who'd started to walk away retraced his steps, head swiveling toward her. "Dr. Westphal?"

She blinked. How did he know her name? She didn't know him. She didn't know anyone here. And with those boyish good looks and reddish hair, she would have remembered him. "Yes. I'm Dr. Westphal."

The man glanced at the woman behind the desk. "I'll take her up."

She swallowed. He must work here. Or maybe he was even the hospital administrator. "Are you Dr. Lawson?"

"No. Lucky for you. I was just in his office, though. Waiting on you."

She closed her eyes. "I'm sorry. I know I'm late. It's just… It's been one of those mornings. I would have called, but I was driving and…" She sucked down a deep breath. "I'm Lyric Westphal. And you are…?"

"Ellis Rohal. If you decide to take the position, we'll be working together. I'm head of Pediatrics." He nodded at the notebook she clutched. "I take it that isn't an addition to your résumé, unless drug rehabilitation is an interest of yours?"

Oh, perfect. Not quite the way she would have liked this introduction to take place. He must have read some of what she'd written in her notebook. "It is, actually. I'd hoped to talk to Dr. Lawson about it."

His brows came together. "He's a busy man."

"I'm sure he is. I can assure you that I'm never— well, almost never—late."

"Good to know."

Although one corner of his mouth lifted, there was something brusque about his attitude, almost as if he'd already made a judgment about her without even getting to know her. Hopefully he didn't think *she* had a drug problem.

Maybe she needed to restart this meeting. When he stopped at the elevator and pushed the up button, Lyric held out her hand. "Let's try this again, shall we? Dr. Rohal, I look forward to working with you. *If* I'm offered the position."

There was a tiny hesitation before he took her hand. And when he did, she was sorry she'd gone that route. His grip was warm and firm, the slightest hint of callusing scraping against the sensitive skin of her palm, making her shiver. No way he'd gotten those from handling surgical instruments. He held her gaze, eyes seeming to search her features, before he released her hand in a hurry, for which she was glad. Because her heart was suddenly thumping out some funky rhythms.

Then they were in the elevator heading to the fourth floor with several other people. He didn't speak to her, which made her nerves ratchet even higher than they'd been when she entered those front doors.

She hoped Dr. Lawson wasn't as annoyed as Ellis Rohal seemed to be. Or maybe the good doctor was simply against her being here, although she had no idea why that would be the case. Pediatric endocrinologists weren't a dime a dozen, especially the ones who worked more on the behavioral side of the spectrum, although she dealt with plenty of other issues, as well, including abnormal growth issues and pancreatic insufficiency.

Once off the elevator, they turned a corner, and Ellis's long, easy strides made her feel like she was having to run to keep up. By now her knuckles were clenched around the notebook, and she suddenly regretted bringing it along. Maybe it really was too presumptuous of her to share her ideas before she'd even started working at the hospital. Ellis's attitude made her feel she was being accompanied to the principal's office after doing something naughty. And Lyric had always been kind of a Goody Two-shoes, to the amusement of her childhood friends.

Not so her sister, who'd always been wild and free. Only now did she realize that Tessa had been fighting her own demons.

Dr. Rohal reached a door, gave a quick knock and then entered.

The man inside leaned back in his chair, eyes crinkling in a smile that made her heave a sigh of relief. "Ah, so you found her."

This man sounded glad. The opposite of Dr. Rohal.

"I think maybe she found me." The man said it completely deadpan, as if she hadn't nearly careened into him.

"I'm very sorry for being late."

"Nonsense. I suspected you'd gotten lost. After ten

years of being here, I've still been known to take a wrong turn or two. It's a big place."

She smiled, very grateful he'd given her an out. "Yes, it is."

With graying hair and wire-rimmed glasses, Dr. Lawson might have been what most people pictured when they thought of hospital administrators. But there was a softness to his eyes that surprised her. As did his dismissal of her tardiness.

Unlike Dr. Rohal.

She'd thought the head of Pediatrics had left Dr. Lawson's office because he was sure she was a no-show, but he'd actually been sent to find her. That had probably annoyed him even more. He was evidently a man who didn't like his time wasted.

Well, while she'd gotten off on the wrong foot with him, she hoped he'd keep an open mind, especially since they'd be working together if she got the job. A prospect that made her a little queasy at the moment. Had this move been a mistake?

No. She'd promised herself that Alia would not go down the same path as Tessa had.

"Have a seat, and you can tell us a little about what brought you to Atlanta."

She dropped into one of the comfy leather chairs across from the desk, noting that Dr. Rohal remained standing, choosing to lean a shoulder against the wall next to him instead. From her seated position he seemed much taller than he had a few moments earlier, his lanky frame stretching toward the ceiling and calling her attention to those narrowed hips and long legs. Stuff she had no business noticing!

She shifted in her chair, suddenly aware of her own curves, which she'd always tried to play down. As a teenager, she'd wanted to be stick-thin, but her build would never allow for that, even though she tried to jog three miles a day whenever she had the chance.

Here's where things got tricky. She didn't exactly want to admit that she was only here because of an unspoken promise she'd made to raise Alia in a place that was far from where her sister had made so many missteps, one of which had resulted in her death, despite the last trip to rehab. The one Lyric had insisted on. Like other stints in different facilities, it had fallen short. As had Lyric's attempts to help her sister. That's where her notebook came in.

"Well, I actually graduated in Las Vegas, as you can see from my résumé, but I really wanted to come to a larger teaching hospital, where there were more opportunities to serve the community at large. I read about the position here at New Mercy and decided to apply."

"Our vigorous curriculum attracts some of the most promising students in the country. Are you interested in teaching, Dr. Westphal?"

She hesitated. "Please call me Lyric. And, yes, I'm open to teaching at some point, if the opportunity arises. Along with some other ideas." The notebook in her hand felt heavy all of a sudden.

"See, Ellis? Some doctors are willing to take on a few medical students."

"I've taken on my share." The other doctor's expression did not change. At all. No flash of humor. No show of irritation. Unlike when she'd bumped into him downstairs.

Dr. Lawson made a sound that made her smile, although she quickly erased it when the pediatrician aimed a look at her. And right on cue, she saw something sprint across his face. Although whatever it was disappeared as quickly as it had appeared.

"I did use the word *willing*," the administrator said.

Lyric would take on two hundred students if it meant she got this position and could reach her goals. The separation would be hard on her parents, but they understood her reasons and fully supported her. It would also give her dad some time to rest.

Her eyes strayed to the handsome doctor she would be working with if she was hired. She hoped he wouldn't be a problem.

As her glance lingered for a second longer than necessary on his broad shoulders and the craggy lines of his face, she swallowed. Maybe it wasn't him that would have the problem.

No. She'd just gotten out of a dead-end relationship and had no intention of starting something else. With anyone. Her five-year romance—if you could call it that—with Jim Riley had been one of the biggest mistakes of her life. And Alia had to be first and foremost in her life right now. The four-year-old had already been through enough. She needed stability. And love.

If Dr. Lawson was hoping Ellis would respond, he was disappointed. He stood right where he was, not looking in the least concerned.

These two men were good friends. She sensed it, despite Ellis's seeming nonchalance. That also made her uneasy. Dr. Rohal could make things difficult for her, in more ways than one.

"So, Dr.... I mean Lyric. I'd like to think I'm a pretty good judge of character. And your résumé and references are impeccable. I'd like to offer you the position. How much notice do you need to give your current hospital?"

Despite a quick thrill of elation, she tensed. "I've already resigned my position there." She'd had reasons she needed to make that cut swift and final. One of which was Jim. Besides, leaving had spurred her to work hard to find another position. It had also removed the possibility of being known as the doctor whose sister had OD'd on opioids.

"So you can start immediately?"

"Yes. I'll need a day off in about a week when my parents fly down, and I need to find a place to stay and a..." She shook her head, almost blurting out that she'd need to find a day care for Alia. It wasn't that she was hiding the fact that she was raising her niece, but she also didn't want to jinx her chances. Not when she was so close to fulfilling her goal.

"Great. Any questions? Anything else you'd like me to know?"

She swallowed, throwing a quick glance at Ellis before turning her attention back to the administrator. "I've toyed with some ideas for a community drug-abuse-prevention initiative, if you'd care to look at it."

"In that notebook you're carrying?" At her nod, he added, "Indeed I would. Why don't you leave it with me, and I'll glance at it after my scheduled meetings."

"Jack, don't you think we should be careful about just—"

Dr. Lawson cut off Ellis. "We will. But we've got that big grant earmarked for the children's unit. I'd say drug-use prevention could merit at least some of those funds."

Uh-oh. An inner voice told her the pediatrician already had his own plans for the grant money they'd received. She did not want to go head-to-head with him. At least not right away. "Please look it over and make sure it fits in with the hospital's plans for the community. The last thing I want is to seem like I'm coming in here with an agenda."

Ellis's head swiveled toward her.

Okay, so maybe she did have an agenda. But it was important to her.

"I like to know where my hospital staff's interests lie." Dr. Lawson reached a hand toward her, and she put the notebook in it, sending up a quick prayer that her arguments were persuasive and well laid out. Sometimes she let her emotions get ahead of her...at least, according to Jim.

Dr. Lawson's voice broke through her thoughts. "Do you have everything you need? The hospital has some overnight apartments, if you need to stay in one for a while."

"Thank you. I'm having my furniture shipped to me as soon as I officially have the position. And I do have a place to stay temporarily." She didn't mention that it was a hotel room.

"Like I said, consider the position yours. Let us know if you need help moving in."

Us? Her eyes tracked back to the pediatrician. She seriously doubted he would be willing to help. Besides, she didn't have much more than a set of bedroom furniture, a sofa and a dining-room table, along with a twin bed she'd purchased for Alia. Her mom was going to stay with her for a week or two to help her get settled and to stand in the gap while she looked for a preschool.

"Thanks again. I'm very happy to be here."

"Great. Ellis, can you show Lyric around and take her by Human Resources to finish the process? She'll need a lanyard as well as a sticker for her vehicle."

Lyric glanced again at the head of Pediatrics and found him with a frown. He hadn't known he was going to be playing babysitter and wasn't happy about it. "If you have other things to do, I'm sure someone in HR can give me a map."

"No, it's fine. We need to sit down, anyway, and have a talk about…expectations."

The slight emphasis on that word made a shiver go through her.

"Ellis, you go easy on her. She hasn't even started yet."

He gave the administrator a tight smile. "Don't worry. I plan to treat Dr. Westphal with the same kid gloves as the rest of the staff."

Lawson gave a quick snort of laughter. "That's what I'm afraid of." He turned his attention to Lyric. "Don't worry. His bark is much worse than his bite."

She doubted that. She bet his bite was every bit as bad. Maybe even worse. So what she needed to do was stay out of reach of those pearly whites and concentrate on doing her job until she could prove herself to him. She tossed her head and gave the pediatrician a look. "I'm sure we'll get along just fine."

And she intended to do that. No matter how maddeningly attractive the man was. Or the fact that being "bitten" by him had just taken on a whole new—and entirely dangerous—meaning.

Ellis sucked down a deep breath and tried to hold onto his temper. Temper mostly directed at himself. Ever since he'd run in to the new doctor in the lobby and she'd fastened those darkly lashed eyes on him, he'd been on edge, his attention drawn to her again and again. Even now there was a steely cord that pulled at something in his gut, making him notice little things about her, like the way her nose turned up at the tip and the dot of a beauty mark that sat just beside her left eye.

Not good. He was rarely drawn to anyone, especially not the people he worked with. That character trait—some would say character *flaw*—was so deeply ingrained that it had become comfortable. A safety zone that people didn't venture beyond. Or if they did happen to wander past that boundary, it didn't take long for them to retreat as quickly as they'd come.

The fact that Lawson might look at the ideas in her notebook and decide those were a better use of the funds than the equipment he'd requisitioned...well, that didn't help. The grant money wasn't endless. He'd always been a fan of requesting tangible items that could be used time and time again, rather than programs whose efficacy couldn't be measured or that were a one-time push that would be over in a flash.

Was there a drug problem in Atlanta? Yes, just like every major city across the United States. Did initiatives help? Possibly, but Ellis had always had difficulty with things that were subjective in nature. Another "perk" of his childhood.

"I need to run by my office to get something, and we can have that quick chat while we're there."

She seemed to stiffen beside him. "Listen, I brought those ideas as just that. Ideas. I'm not trying to take over. I had no way of knowing that the pediatric department had just received a grant."

He believed her. He'd wondered if Jack had mentioned the money during their phone interview. But her gaze was steady. "I was just surprised you brought a proposal with you. Did you spearhead an effort in Las Vegas, as well?"

"No." She paused, her hair sliding forward to hide

that freckle beside her eye. "But I wish I'd done more to address the drug problems when I lived there."

Her voice was so soft he almost missed the words.

"May I ask why?"

She shrugged. "Because we can't just rely on rehab programs. People sometimes go through that process multiple times and then fall right back into the same old habits—slide into the same damaged friendships. Rehab programs are a great tool, but they can't be the only one we use. I believe we need to break the cycle of addicts returning to old patterns. We need to help them form new connections. New friendships. Strong ones. Far from the drug culture. Help them find new jobs. Form new patterns of behavior through training, behavioral modification, medication. Whatever it takes."

He'd done the behavioral-modification route as a child. They'd even tried to teach him how to attach to people. But although Maddie had tried, he could see now that she'd been grieving, too, and had been focused on suddenly being thrust into the role of a single mom.

His instinct was to brush past Lyric's words, but she spoke with a conviction that made him stop and take a closer look at her.

"Once Jack is done with your notebook, I'd like to take a look at it, as well. I can't promise to change my mind, and I'll be honest and say that I already have plans for that money."

"I thought maybe you did. It doesn't have to be right away. I just wanted to let people know that this is something I'm passionate about."

His various counselors had been, too. But in the end, old patterns seemed to be too ingrained, the fabric of his life already woven. And now he didn't even try to change that—didn't want to.

He started walking again. "I can tell you are." Ellis thought there might be more to it than what she'd said, but he wasn't going to pry. Not yet. And since she leaned toward behavioral endocrinology, it made sense that she might look at addictive behavior in a way that others might not. His own childhood experiences with behavioral modification were tied to unhappy memories.

Five minutes later, they were in his office, which was a bit more plush than he would have chosen if he'd had any say in the decor. But Jack had reiterated what the higher-ups had already said. They wanted the hospital as a whole to have a welcoming feel. That included any space where one might encounter patients or their families, and since he did meet with people in his office, hc really hadn't been able to argue, even if he would have preferred a metal desk and simple folding chairs.

Instead there was a warm brown leather love seat with red throw pillows. He saw her glance trail around the room and wondered how those brown eyes were processing it. Did she see the decor as a waste of funds, like he did?

Finally she blinked and looked back at him. "Very nice."

"Have a seat. How different is New Mercy from your hospital in Las Vegas?"

"Pretty different. Las Vegas is a show world, so I think the city as a whole has a glitzy image to uphold. Including the hospital I worked at."

So her old hospital had been even more ostentatious than New Mercy? "And here I was wondering if you'd be uncomfortable with the money spent on decorating."

She shrugged. "It's part of today's medicine, I think. I'd be just as happy in a supply closet, though."

That surprised him. "So would I."

She smiled. "Wow. It looks like we agree on something. Finally."

Yes, it did, and he wasn't sure how he felt about that. Having an adversarial relationship with her seemed the less complicated path right now. Maybe he should try to hold on to that for as long as possible.

He rounded his desk and dropped into the high-backed office chair. "So it would seem."

They spent the next twenty minutes discussing the normal workings of the hospital and some of the research she'd done on addictive personality disorder. He was surprised that the dopamine used to treat some of the symptoms of Parkinson's were now suspected of causing gambling addictions in some of those same patients.

"I think I knew on some level that there could be a hormonal link in addiction, but I've not studied it enough to form an opinion one way or the other," he said.

He'd often wondered if attachment disorders were a result of more than just childhood trauma. Maybe some people were just wired that way. Like him.

"Behavioral endocrinology is pretty interesting. But it's impossible to say which came first. Drug use can also cause physical changes in the brain, which perpetuate addiction. So after the issue has been dealt with through rehab, a new form of addiction might pop up, like gambling or even eating disorders."

That made sense.

"Someday we'll have to have an in-depth discussion on that." And that had nothing to do with the way her eyes sparkled when she talked, or the way she leaned toward him when trying to make a point. It was almost worth trying to play devil's advocate just to keep the conversation going, except he didn't want to like anything about her. He hadn't been in favor of hiring her in the first place, felt like the department ran pretty smoothly without adding another cog in the machine. And he wasn't really interested in changing his opinion just yet.

Time to shift to a different subject. "You mentioned needing to find a place to stay. Have you met with a Realtor yet? Depending on what part of the city you want to live in, one-bedroom apartments are a little harder to find. I could give you the name of the person I used."

"That would be great. But I need a two-bedroom place. Not one."

She sounded like that was nonnegotiable. Was she planning on getting a roommate? Or maybe she had a child. He hadn't even thought of that. Or maybe she just needed an extra room. Whatever her reasons, it was none of his business.

He scrolled through his list of contacts until he reached the right entry. "Do you want to put the number in your phone?"

"Oh, yes, of course." She grabbed her purse and retrieved the phone from a front pocket. "Okay, I'm ready."

He read off the number. "His name is Dave Butler and he's with Great Properties Real Estate. He's a friend of mine."

"Thank you. I really appreciate it. Any tips about which areas I should look in?"

"It depends on how long you want your commute to be. As you saw this morning, traffic can be heavy."

Her fingers went to a simple stud earring, twisting

it one way and then another. "I'm not so much worried about the commute as I am about the…"

"The…?"

"I would like it to be in a good—as in fewer drugs— school system. It won't be as important now as it will be in the next year or so."

The next year?

He knew she was single. That much had come out during his discussion with Jack. But if she was pregnant, shouldn't he know that she might need to take a leave of absence at some point? She hadn't volunteered the information, and he wasn't sure he was even legally allowed to ask about it. If she wanted him—or anyone else to know—she would tell him.

And, in reality, he didn't want to know. The less he knew about Lyric's personal life, the better. He wasn't quite sure why that was the case, but some primal instinct was telling him to keep his distance from this one. Kind of hard to do when he would be working so closely with her. Possibly even warring with her about how that grant money was going to be spent.

But still…

"Is there something I should know?" he asked.

The fingers fiddling with her ear paused for a few seconds—seconds that told him volumes, although she probably didn't realize it. She didn't want to tell him, but was trying to think through her decision.

"Maybe. I didn't mention it, because I don't anticipate it affecting my work in any major way."

She took a deep breath and then the words came out so fast his brain had time processing them.

"I have a four-year-old who'll need to be enrolled in a good preschool."

CHAPTER TWO

A QUICK SUCCESSION of emotions scrolled across his face, the last of which was shock. "You have a…child?"

She forced her hand away from her ear and back into her lap, then clasping her hands tightly "Yes. And no. She's my niece. She'll be living with me—permanently. My mom will be bringing her as soon as I find a place to live. Which is why I want to locate a preschool that's not too far from my apartment."

This was something she'd be having to explain time and time again. But it was probably important for him to know where she was coming from. She twined her fingers together until they hurt, willing herself not to let him see the chaotic frenzy of emotions that were tumbling through her system. "My sister died of a drug overdose six months ago. I've been helping to care for her child on and off ever since she was born."

He leaned forward, planting his elbows on his desk. "I'm sorry. I had no idea."

The earnest words, coming from a man who'd seemed hard as nails for most of their hour together, caused a dangerous prickling sensation to gather behind her eyes. Damn. She did not want to cry in front of him. She wanted to be just as distant and unreachable as he seemed to be, except she just wasn't good at playing those kinds of games.

And she missed her sister. So very badly. Had missed her even before she died.

"Tessa went through various rehab facilities and nothing seemed to stick. Her experiences were why I changed my focus from simple pediatric endocrinology to behavioral endocrinology. If some of my sister's addiction patterns could have been redirected while she was still in her teens or even younger, maybe her life wouldn't have played out like it had. And I want to make sure Tessa's daughter doesn't feel abandoned. Either by me or by the system."

"Abandoned. I can see how she might feel that way."

Did he? Or was he just giving a conventional response because he didn't know what else to say? But when she looked into his green eyes, there was a dark flash of something she didn't understand. She chalked it up to an unattached man who had no clue about the struggles people like Tessa, or now, Alia, went through.

Except she didn't know if he was unattached. Nor did she care.

"So that's why I'm so interested in looking beyond the hospital and into the community, to see how I can make a difference."

"And if you can't make a difference?"

His words stopped her in her tracks. Was that what he thought? That it was a hopeless cause? She hoped not, because they definitely would not get along if that was the case. What it *would* do, however, was make her second-guess her decision to move to Atlanta and apply at this hospital.

"What do you think the answer is, then?"

"I have no idea, honestly. I treat the patients who cross my path. Period."

She blinked. Did he even realize how cold that sounded?

"So you have no interest in trying to change things? In trying to prevent some of those patients from ever needing to cross your path?"

"It's not that I'm not interested. I would just need to look at studies before diving into something I have no knowledge of."

Some of the tension drained from her. So it wasn't that he refused to get involved. He just didn't know anything about what she was trying to do. "I do have some statistics in my proposal, but you'll find it a bit of a nature-nurture paradox. Sometimes we can only effect change if we experiment with different methods. It's how some of our greatest advances in medicine came about."

"I'll be interested in looking at the numbers." He didn't sound entirely convinced, but then she didn't expect him to be. She would be the first to admit that she had a very personal reason for her interest in drug prevention. Ellis didn't come across as someone who was driven by emotion. Had he never experienced a heartache strong enough to motivate him to change something?

"That's all I'm asking for. I don't know the hospital or the community yet, so it may not even fit in what would work in this area. I plan on researching what's currently being done. Maybe my ideas would be redundant. If so, I'll accept that and be happy that there's work being done."

Lyric had done some research even before her trip to Atlanta. She thought there was room for a new approach, but Atlanta was turning out to be very different from Las Vegas. She had actually shared her ideas with her own hospital before she left, but obviously she would no longer be there to fight for them. And that didn't sit well. But Alia had to be her number-one priority for now.

Maybe in the future, she could go back to her home city and try to advocate for change. Only time would tell. But for now she was here. In Atlanta. And she would help where she could.

She thought of something. "Can I ask what you earmarked the grant money for?"

"New equipment. Updated record-keeping procedures."

Her head tilted. "Nothing for the patients themselves?"

"I'm sorry? Those would benefit the patients."

Maybe. But she would have expected at least one thing that addressed patient comfort, especially in the pediatric ward.

"Can I make a suggestion?"

"Another one?" But the smile he gave her took the sting out of the words.

She smiled back. "I could always make up another proposal."

"Not necessary." He leaned back in his chair, his gaze catching hers. "Let's hear it."

"Maybe something fun for the kids. Hospitals are already a stressful place. Is there anything we could do to ease their stay?"

"Other than trying to provide accommodations for the families?"

"Yes. Things like therapy animals. A visiting magician. Recognition of birthdays. Updated—as in brighter—decor in the hallways." She'd noticed there weren't very many things that set this wing apart from the other ones. "Maybe even have themes for the different sections of Pediatrics."

"Themes." He picked up a pencil and scribbled something on a pad. "I tend to think more in terms of actual physical benefits."

"I think some of those things would provide actual physical benefits. While also benefiting their emotional well-being."

"So says some of the other staff."

So people had already brought this up to him. If so, as a newbie, she probably wouldn't be the one to change his mind. "I'm not sure what your grant amount was, but surely a few hundred dollars could be used toward enrichment."

"Three million." He said it without a flicker of emotion. Not even the twitch of an eyebrow.

"Your grant is three million dollars?"

"It is."

Her brain swirled with possibilities, but she knew that in the end the decision wasn't up to her. It was up to him and, ultimately, the board of directors as to who would decide where the money should be spent.

As if realizing where her thoughts were going, he laid down his pen. "I can see that I may come to rue the day the hospital hired you."

Shock overtook her before she realized he was joking. It was there in the slightest twitch of those firm lips.

She laughed. "Then I will make it my mission in life to make sure you don't. And I do vow not to suggest a karaoke korner—corner spelled with a *k*—featuring show tunes."

"Surely that isn't actually a thing."

He tilted his head in a way that suggested he was flabbergasted by that notion, and he now looked almost too gorgeous for words. She swallowed, remembering the callused palm that had slid across hers earlier.

"Surely it is. And I'll be the first to admit that the kids love it. Especially the ones in the oncology ward."

"Karaoke korner...okay."

And without knowing why, she laughed again, realizing she might have waded into waters that were a little deeper than she'd expected. Time to trudge her way back toward shore, where the sand was firm and where her feet were far less likely to be pulled out from under her by some rogue wave. Like the one seated across from her, whose sudden smile threatened to do just that: pull her under. Way, way under.

Karaoke korner.

Exactly what kind of hospital had Lyric come from? One very different from New Mercy, that was for sure. Was he that much of a stick-in-the-mud? It looked like she thought he was. So did a lot of other people on his staff, but he really hadn't cared. His bottom line was saving lives.

But she claimed that those other things could help do that, as well. He'd shown her around and left her in the HR department to finish up some routine paperwork. But as he had, he'd been very aware of the plain walls in the corridors. Walls that, every once in a while, were punctuated with some kind of framed art. But even those pictures that were fun had a common theme: education. Frogs displaying healthy eating habits. Lions that suggested patients get out there and lead active lives. Not a karaoke korner in sight.

But maybe there should be. Not with show tunes. But kids songs? And fun games?

Something he'd not experienced a whole lot of during his childhood. Maddie had worked hard to provide for them, but it hadn't left much time for other things. Like vacations. Or birthday parties. Or Valentine's Day cards for his classmates.

Was that why he'd been so opposed to some of his colleagues' suggestions over the past several years? Because it reminded him of things he'd missed out on? And along comes Lyric and does just that.

Hell, what had he just let into his department?

He could almost swear that those second thoughts came from learning that Lyric was taking in her niece. A girl that, if he had to guess, had been abandoned, emotionally and physically, thanks to her mom's drug habit.

Ellis couldn't remember a lot about his own mother, but he could swear she was not a drug user. And his dad? There was nothing. He couldn't remember a time when a man had been around, and Maddie once told him even she didn't know who his father was.

He'd often wondered if his mom had become a spy or something for the government. But surely she would have eventually come back to find him or try to reestablish contact if that was the case. She never had. And Maddie had died when Ellis was in his early twenties, leaving him with questions that would never be answered. What she had left him, however, was a trust fund that had been established by his mom. It hadn't been an astronomical figure, but having sat in the bank for a decade and a half, it had accrued a healthy amount of interest.

Which again ruled out drug use and prison, because

he'd looked through the national database of prisons, looking for her name, but nothing had matched.

He sighed, irritated that these old thoughts had come back to haunt him. Could it be that he sensed a hurt in Lyric that rivaled the hurt he'd once felt over his mom's disappearance from his life? But his emotions over the past had gone cold long ago, while hers were still raw and painful. Her niece would be a constant reminder of what had happened to her sister. Probably the way Maddie had been a reminder that his real mother had left him without a single explanation.

A twinge in his chest jarred him, and he rubbed a palm across it. He didn't want to go back and relive any of that. So, time to think about keeping a bit of distance between him and the hospital's newest staff member. Any changes he implemented in his department would be because he felt they were needed, and not to make one Lyric Westphal happy.

Even as he thought it, he took out his phone and called his Realtor friend. The two of them had known each other since high school and had kept in touch over the years. Ellis didn't have a ton of friends, but he counted Dave among the closest. He'd asked Lyric if she minded if he gave Dave her contact information and she'd thanked him, saying she'd appreciate that.

"Hey, Ellis. I hoped I'd hear from you. You never gave me an answer about the game next week."

Damn, he'd forgotten about that. "Sorry, you're right. I've just been swamped. When is it again?"

He got through the preliminaries and agreed to go with his friend to the Braves game next week. He then gave a quick rundown on what Lyric said she was looking for, leaving out anything personal, like her sister's death.

"Ah, new love interest, buddy?"

And just like that, he regretted making the call. "No. You know me. I'm not interested in going that route." It wasn't that he hadn't gone out on dates or slept with his share of women. He had. But he'd never had a serious relationship and had no desire for one at this point in his life. Love and kids just weren't in the cards for him.

"Smart guy." Dave was divorced and had sworn over a few too many beers that he was never going down the aisle again. Although Ellis didn't believe him for a minute.

"So if you could give Lyric a call and steer her in the right direction—"

"Pretty name."

Yes, it was, but he wasn't about to admit that or the fact that he'd noticed a little more about her than he should have. He didn't need his friend getting the wrong idea and saying something to her. "I guess. She seems to be a competent physician. That's all I care about."

He didn't actually know how good of a doctor she was yet, but her résumé was impeccable and Jack would have checked her references. The hospital administrator was genuinely nice, but he was no pushover and didn't put up with poor performances from his staff.

"Stacy and I just broke up, you know. It was for the best, but about this new doc, any chance she's—"

"Dave…" He let a warning note creep into his voice. The last thing he wanted was for his friend to be unprofessional, especially after Ellis was the one who'd recommended the Realtor in the first place.

"Ah. Got it. Don't worry, I won't hit on your girl."

"She is not my girl." His voice tightened further.

Dave laughed. "Calm down, or I'm really going to start wondering."

"Don't make me regret giving her your name." He forced his voice to lighten. He knew it was just Dave's personality to joke, and had no idea why he was overreacting to it now. Maybe because something about Lyric made him bristle.

"I won't. Scout's honor."

With that they said goodbye and Ellis dropped his cell phone back onto the desk, wondering over the crazy day he'd already had. And with the full slate of appointments he had scheduled, it wasn't going to let up anytime soon. Putting Lyric and Dave firmly out of his mind, he concentrated on what he could control.

Medicine. He sighed and pulled the nearest case file toward him. It wasn't like he always had control of those outcomes, either. But sometimes all he could do was try his hardest and hope for the best.

CHAPTER THREE

TWO DAYS AFTER her furniture had been delivered, Lyric studied the radiographed images she'd received. They were of a child's left hand and wrist, with hormone test results slated to arrive sometime this afternoon.

She was pretty sure she knew what the results would show. That Jacob Sellers would need a little help catching up to his classmates. In the bottom one percentile of the norms for children his age, it was a good thing his parents hadn't waited to have him tested. Left untreated, he would fall further and further behind, and once his growth plates closed, there would be no chance of catching up. Unfortunately, treatment would include a daily shot—no fun for anyone—and she'd already called and left a voice mail for Ellis to update Jacob's family, since he was the one who'd called for a consult on the case.

Her meeting with Ellis's friend, Dave Butler, had resulted in her finding a cute little town house in only a day. She would rent it until she could find a place to actually buy. And the best part was, there was a preschool within walking distance. That would be hard to top. She'd told Dave to keep his ears open, but that she was in no big hurry to put in an offer on something else.

He'd been nice, and when their conversation turned to Ellis, who was a high-school friend of his, it had been hard not to be curious. She'd done her best not to ask any kind of personal questions, but she would love to know if he was always so... She wasn't even sure of the word she'd use to describe him—reserved with a touch of surly, maybe? Or if he was only that way with her. If Lyric had to guess, she would say that she wasn't his first choice as an addition to his department. Dave did say, however, that he doubted Ellis would ever marry.

She wasn't even sure how that subject had come up, but she'd squashed it the best she could. Especially since she didn't want Dave going back to Ellis with tales of how interested she'd been in his personal life. Plus, there was the fact that she'd probably be talking to Dave quite a bit more as he researched properties for her. Better to set the tone now, rather than be sorry later.

Her mom had gotten a great price on flights, and she and Alia were due to arrive this morning. She was going to come to the hospital and pick up keys to Lyric's place and then work on getting Alia settled in her new bedroom. Lyric's mom had bought some jungle-themed posters and bedding, and brought them along with them. It would give them something to do while Lyric was at work, anyway. And it would help her niece feel she'd had some input into what her room looked like.

Lyric's heart cramped. It should be Tessa who was sharing these special moments with Alia. It was so hard to believe she'd never see her sister again. She closed her eyes to blot out that thought, then stretched her back and shut down the screen of her laptop. Someone knocked at her door, and she stiffened for a second, before calling to whoever it was to come in.

Ellis entered her tiny office. "I got your message. So I was right to refer the patient to you?"

Was that supposed to be a rhetorical question? "The

radiographs of his hand do seem to support the insufficiency of growth hormones. I'm just waiting on the results of the blood tests."

The problem with measuring growth hormones in the human body was that they were released in pulses, so if blood was drawn at the wrong time, there might be a false negative. So Lyric had administered medication geared to stimulate the release of those hormones. To see if there were still lower than expected levels that, along with the hand and wrist X-rays, would indicate intervention was warranted.

"Good. When I talked to his parents, they seemed in favor of hormone therapy."

"Yes, they mentioned that to me, as well, when I spoke with them on the phone. I think they were glad to know the problem wasn't just in their imagination. And that there might be some treatment options."

Ellis rounded the nearest chair and lowered himself into it, his knees nearly touching the front of her desk. "Good. Let me know what his blood test shows."

"I will." Wow, the man made her already small space seem minuscule. He could just reach across her desk and…

And nothing.

Remember that wave, Lyric. You need to stick close to shore.

"Dave said you found a place?"

She hesitated, hoping that Dave wasn't as free in sharing his observations of her as he had been about Ellis. Not that she'd encouraged him. She hadn't. The Realtor had only gotten in a few brief summaries before she'd done her best to halt the subject. "I did—thanks for recommending him. He seems very…efficient."

Efficient? Really, Ly?

Ellis studied her face for a moment or two, and right on cue, she felt a surge of heat zip through her cheeks.

"Hmmm…maybe I shouldn't say anything, but Dave divorced a few months ago. And he just broke up with a girlfriend."

More heat scorched through her. Was he hinting that she should go out with his friend? Not happening. He wasn't really her type. She was more into… Her eyes tracked to Ellis. Oh, Lord.

"I don't think that's any of my—"

"Sorry. You're right. It's just that Dave sometimes acts before he thinks."

Unlike Ellis? She could very well believe that the pediatrician did nothing without mulling it over in his brain for a few thousand years.

Like Jim? No. Lyric's ex hadn't been merely cautious about deepening their relationship. He just hadn't been interested.

At all.

He'd been perfectly happy hooking up periodically and letting the rest just coast along. The day her sister died, he'd sent her a "condolence" text. The pain of that had been the last straw. She'd called him and broken it off, asking him not to come to the funeral. She couldn't carry a relationship on her own, and she'd been done trying.

As for Ellis, she had no idea how he handled relationships, nor did she care.

"I think we can all be guilty of impulsivity from time to time." Acting before she thought was probably how her sister had gotten hooked on drugs. It had made Lyric more careful about following her impulses. Not that she would ever be tempted to do drugs. Far from it. Even the time she'd hurt her back and her doctor had wanted to prescribe pain medication had been met with an upheld hand. No bones had been broken, so she'd relied on ibuprofen to help her get through the next couple of weeks.

"Maybe." Ellis's dubious tone made her more certain that he didn't want to be numbered among the people who bought candy in the checkout lane of his local grocery store. Or asked a woman out after meeting her for the first time. "I wanted to talk to you about something else, though."

Something besides Jacob Sellers? Maybe Dave really had said something that wasn't meant for public consumption. Her finger went to her earlobe, but since she'd forgotten to wear earrings today, she found nothing to twirl. She dropped her hand back to the desk. It was a bad habit, anyway. Good thing she didn't play poker, or she'd be broke in a matter of days.

"O-o-k-a-a-ay." She drew the word out. "What is it?"

"Jack wants a more in-depth proposal on your anti-drug initiative. One geared specifically for the greater Atlanta area. And he wants me in on it. We're supposed to take a couple of days and research what's already being done, taking one or two of those days to do a physical search of a couple of corridors known for their drug use."

"He does?" Shock went through her. She remembered the hospital administrator wanting to look through her idea notebook, but had expected nothing would come of it. Especially since Ellis had said he already had plans for the grant money. Did that mean he'd changed his mind? Or was he being forced to do something he didn't agree with? Maybe she should address that. "And you're onboard with this?"

Ellis propped an ankle on his left knee. "Let's just say I'm willing to keep an open mind."

She glanced at him, noting the slight furrow between his eyebrows. She wasn't sure if the frown indicated thoughtfulness or irritation. It did nothing to reduce his "wow" factor, though. If anything, it just made him more mysterious and harder to read. She'd bet this man had women throwing themselves at him from every corner.

And yet Dave had said it was doubtful he would ever marry.

Oh, no. You are not heading back to that subject, Ly. Because you are definitely not in the market for anyone, either.

Especially not with her young niece coming to live with her. She couldn't afford having someone who would pop in and out of her life at their leisure.

Still, her eyes slid down his straight nose and landed on his lips before she jerked her gaze to a philodendron she'd inherited from the office's last occupant. Man, she needed to water that thing. Its leaves were starting to wilt.

She forced herself to recall what he'd just said. Open mind. Okay. That she could deal with. "That's all I ask."

"I'm sure it's not easy to go into these kinds of things with hard fact and not let your emotions get wrapped up, especially since—"

"You're right. My sister was the reason I started thinking about this. She's even the reason that I decided to make the switch to behavioral endocrinology, but everything I've read or studied just reinforces the idea that we need to gear our efforts to a younger segment of the population."

She doubted Ellis let his emotions "get wrapped up" in anything.

"How young?"

"Well, certainly before they reach eighteen." She made a motion in the air. "It's kind of like Jacob Sellers's bones. We need to intervene before those growth plates close, to have the best chance at changing course. Once closed, those bones become set in stone. Literally. The longer a person uses drugs, the harder it is to change those habits. They become hardwired into our grey matter."

His propped foot jiggled a time or two, bringing her thoughts back to him as a person. From his perpetually mussed hair, to his strong thighs and narrow hips, he was put together in a way that defied logic and made it hard not to notice him. Lord, why couldn't he be some weaselly man with a nasal twang and twenty kids?

"Good comparison. And it makes sense. But we have a definitive treatment protocol for patients like Jacob. But drugs…"

"I know." Any warmth his first remark had generated was wiped away by the dubious tone that came after it. He was right. There was no easy answer. "But we have all kinds of conditions that don't have a cut-and-dried treatment. That doesn't mean we don't keep trying. Think about childhood cancers or even muscular dystrophy. We keep looking, keep researching, in hopes that someday we'll stumble on something that *will* work."

One corner of his mouth tilted. "I think you should have gone into apologetics instead of medicine."

Just like it had at other times, the very hint of a smile made her catch her breath and sent her thoughts spinning out of control.

I doubt Ellis will ever marry.

She banished the thought that somehow kept creeping in. It didn't matter to her one way or the other. "I don't like to argue with people, so that wouldn't be a good match for me." Nor would Ellis be a good match for her... if she were even looking for a man, which she wasn't.

"I haven't found that to be true."

Her teeth came down on her lip. He thought she was argumentative?

As if sensing her thoughts, he added, "You're very good at persuasion."

Okay, *persuasive* put a more positive spin on it. "Only if I truly believe in what I'm fighting for."

He leaned forward. "And what are you fighting for, exactly, Lyric?"

Maybe he'd said her name before, but she couldn't ever remember hearing it roll off someone's tongue in those low gritty tones before. It caught her off guard, making all rational thought crash through her brain's guardrail, making it hard to find anything to say that wouldn't sound crazy. Or overly personal.

Like asking him to say her name again.

"I'm fighting for..." The pause was long enough to become awkward, so she said the first thing that came to mind. "I'm fighting for people like my niece, who've lost a family member to drug use and who are in danger of becoming statistics themselves if there's no one there to catch them. Luckily she has other relatives who love and care for her. Who want her to grow up far from that kind of life."

He gave her a look. "She's one of the lucky ones, then. And the reason you moved from Los Vegas to Atlanta?"

"Yes." It was that simple and that complicated. Alia

deserved a chance at normalcy, and each day Lyric prayed she was making the right decision. Every city and town had drug issues, so hopefully she wasn't just trading one problem location for another. "I would do anything for her."

Ellis's eyes met hers, and for several long seconds she couldn't force herself to look away.

"I know you would," he said. "Let me know how I can—"

A soft knock sounded at the door, interrupting whatever he'd been about to say. He stood. "Let me know what Jacob's test results say, and we'll talk about when to take that research trip."

"Okay." She stood as he headed for the door and opened it. Something flew past him so fast that Ellis took a step backward, his head turning to follow its trajectory around the desk until the small form attached itself to Lyric's knees.

"Aunt Lyrie, Aunt Lyrie!" Her niece's mispronunciation of her name had always made her smile and today was no exception.

"Alia, you almost knocked Dr. Rohal down." She sent a quick apologetic glance his way just as her mom appeared in the doorway.

"I'm sorry, honey, I didn't realize you had someone here with you." Her mother's gaze went to Ellis.

"It's okay," he said. "We were just finishing up. You must be Lyric's mom."

"I am. Paula Westphal. And that little tornado is Alia. Sorry for her barging in like that."

"No need to apologize. I'm Ellis Rohal, one of Lyric's colleagues."

Colleagues? More like her boss. He definitely had

seniority over her and probably had the power to put the kibosh on her project. Hopefully he wouldn't, though.

Lyric knelt down to hug her niece, wrapping her arms around the little girl and dropping a kiss on top of her head. "I'm so glad to see you, sweetheart."

Her glance came up and found Ellis staring at her with some undecipherable expression. He didn't look mad. If anything, he looked taken aback. Probably from being forced to witness their family reunion.

She mouthed, *sorry.*

Ellis shook his head, mouth cocking up in that half smile that seemed to say "it's okay."

The silent exchange between them seemed intimate, somehow. Like trading secrets that they wanted no one else to hear.

Except these weren't secrets, and there'd been no reason for either of them not to say the words aloud. She suddenly wished they had, because ever since he'd come into her office, there'd been this weird awareness that had shimmered in the air. At least on her side. Ellis probably had had none of those thoughts.

"I'll let you go. If you could give me a buzz when those results come in, I'd appreciate it."

"Of course."

With that he was gone, leaving her alone with her mom and niece.

After going over to close the door, she motioned her mom to the chair Ellis had just vacated, while she scooped up Alia and moved back behind her desk. The child bounced on her lap. "How was your flight, Mom?"

"Good." She laughed. "Wow, do all of the doctors in Atlanta look like that?"

"Look like what?" She feigned ignorance and hoped her mom didn't go getting any strange ideas. She'd been the one who'd dried her tears after her disastrous relationship ended, even as she'd been grieving the loss of Tessa. Lyric would have thought she wouldn't be so quick to push her remaining daughter toward another man.

"Well, like the neon lights of a casino that draws folks for miles."

"Mom!" Her words were meant as an admonishment, except her mother was right. Lyric herself had noticed how gorgeous Ellis was. And as hilarious as it was to hear that fact talked about in Vegas terms, it fit. Because just like those casinos that lured would-be gamblers to come and take a shot at the jackpot, he was unpredictable and as hard to read as the dealer at any blackjack table.

"Am I wrong?"

No, she wasn't. "I don't think Dad would be thrilled to hear you talking about another man that way."

They were just words, though. Because her mom and dad were deeply in love and completely committed to each other. And with his current health problems, they'd grown even closer. Which made it that much harder to understand how Tessa had wound up where she had. She'd grown up in a home that was full of warmth and love, not what you'd expect of an addict. But it just went to show how important it was to provide a safety net outside of the family unit.

"Your father never has to worry and he knows it. Besides, your doctor friend is far too young…for me." She gave her daughter a sideways glance that said it all.

"No. Do not even get that look in your eye." Lyric was still in recovery. Not from Jim, but from the whole idea of love and how much of a crapshoot it all was. She wrapped her arms tighter around Alia, who was busy drawing on the calendar blotter that was on top of Lyric's desk. Good thing she used her phone to keep track of her appointments.

"What look, honey?"

"Ha! You know what look. I have this little munchkin to look after right now, and that's all I care about." Besides, Ellis wasn't the marrying type, according to his friend, and Lyric was no longer the friends-with-benefits type, no matter what she'd settled for in the past.

"Munchkins grow up."

She ignored her mom's remark, and said, "Do you two have time for lunch? Or are you too exhausted from the flight? I can give you the key to the town house, if you just want to go get settled in."

"How long do you have for lunch?"

"About an hour. Time enough to grab a bite and head back to the house, if you want to go that route, although I won't be able to stay long."

"Yes, we'd love it, and I'm sure Alia will want you to personally show her where her room will be. I left our luggage with the nice woman at the information booth in the lobby."

Good thing the child was too young to really understand why Mommy wasn't coming home. There'd been some tears the first several days, but since Alia had spent most of her time with her grandparents and Lyric by that time, it had just been a passing shower. Unlike the grief that Lyric and her parents had experienced. All those regrets...

She forced her brain back to her mom's comment. "Was the woman young and friendly with dark brown hair?"

"She was. And she had the cutest accent."

Probably the same woman who'd been there the day Lyric had arrived at New Mercy and almost crashed into Ellis. Only three days had gone by since that encounter, and she was already starting to feel strangely at home in her new environment.

Except for with Ellis, who disrupted her nerve impulses in ways she didn't understand. Like when he said her name. Or when he smiled and told her she was persuasive.

All she could do was hope it was due to the newness of everything. Since she'd been born and raised in Vegas, this was her first big move away from home. Combine that with the end of a dead-end relationship, and she was happier than she should have been. The last thing she needed to do was let her mom start filling her head with ideas that didn't belong there. She wanted her daughter happy, and Lyric understood that. But now was not the time.

And Ellis had probably not thought of her that way.

And she didn't think of him that way, either. Nor would she. She just needed to keep her eyes on her two life goals: raising Alia and joining the fight to end an epidemic that was destroying thousands of lives a year and leaving devastation in its wake. It wasn't smallpox or polio and there was no vaccine to prevent its spread. So as hunky as the head of her department was, she would fight him tooth and nail, if need be, if he tried to come between her and reaching those goals.

Two days later, Ellis went with Lyric to talk to Jacob Sellers's parents, although he was beginning to regret that suggestion. Watching Lyric's niece run over and hug her tight had made something in his gut shift. The little girl was about the same age as he had been when his mom left forever. Only this child's mother was dead and his was…

He had no idea what she was. But the impact on him had been the same as if she had died. Maybe worse, since she'd left without explanation or any attempt to contact him in the intervening years.

It had to have been awful for Lyric and her mom to have to somehow explain that Mommy wasn't coming home ever again. Except if she'd been a drug addict for as long as Lyric had said, maybe she'd never been a major presence in her daughter's life, anyway. Not like his mom had been in his.

Just outside of the exam room, he paused. "What was your niece's name again?"

Brown eyes met his, a slight flare of shock entering those dark irises. Or was that his imagination? He wasn't even sure why he'd asked the question. He wasn't likely to ever see the child again, so what did it matter? But it was too late to withdraw the words.

"Her name is Alia."

Alia. He mulled that over for a second or two. The syllables had a melodic lilt to them that fit the smiling little whirlwind that had swooped into her aunt's office and hugged her tight. Kind of like Lyric's name fit her. It was unusual and caught at his senses, making him want to say it. Again and again.

He turned his thoughts to something else before he did just that. "Did you find a preschool?"

"Yes. My mom took her this morning and will pick her up at two. I may need to find a sitter to help with that once my mom goes home."

He nodded. "The hospital has a database of services that provide transportation and after-care programs.

Or you could care for the bulk of your appointments in the mornings and reserve afternoons for office work."

"Are you saying I could bring her to work?"

What the hell was he doing? These were all things she could figure out on her own. Without his damn interference. "I'm saying you wouldn't be the only one who did that. And there are always other people around who could watch her for a few minutes here or there."

Her head tilted. "I don't know. I kind of want to keep my private life and work life separate, although it's all pretty new right now. Let me see what I can arrange. Although I will look into the database. Thank you."

Time to cut off this topic of conversation before he did something foolish, like offer to help watch the girl. Not that he would. He dealt with enough children on a daily basis without taking on the child of a colleague.

He wanted to help kids. Probably because of his own childhood issues—although he tried not to explore that train of thought more than necessary. But he made sure he kept that help on the medical side of the spectrum. Periodically watching Alia would not fall on that side, and he would be well served to do what Lyric said she was doing: keep his business life and personal life separate. Although Lyric's antidrug initiative had a little of her private life tossed into the mix, didn't it, since she'd lost her sister to drugs? He wasn't about to point that out, however.

"Shall we?" He motioned to the door of the exam room.

Once inside, they greeted Jacob and his parents. Ellis let Lyric take the lead, since she was the specialist.

"Well, as you know, the tests did show that Jacob may need a little help with his growth hormones. I wanted to explain what that will entail." She motioned them to seats, while she took the exam stool that was in the room. Ellis opted to stand.

He glanced down at where Lyric was leaning forward, her hands moving as she described the treatment protocol, dark hair shining under the harsh glare of the fluorescent lights. Propping a shoulder against the door, he wondered how things were going with Alia. Hopefully the child was settling in, although it had only been two days since she'd arrived in Atlanta.

Raising a child who wasn't your own was a huge undertaking. He probably hadn't appreciated Maddie's sacrifice enough. And with very little in return, honestly. He hadn't been an easy child. He'd been withdrawn and rebuffed her attempts to hug him. And yet she hadn't turned him over to the foster-care system, which now surprised him. Maddie had also never married. He had no idea whether that was because of him or because she'd never met the right person.

Lyric was Alia's blood relative, though, whereas Maddie had only been a friend of the family. But was it any different? The sacrifices were the same either way.

"We'll use Jacob's weight as a guide for the dosage, but it will have to be given daily with no interruptions to be effective."

"Is it a…um, shot?" Jacob's mom looked a little nervous.

"It is, but it's quick and easy. The hormone comes loaded in a kind of pen that, with a click of a button, injects the medication just under the skin. Some caregivers even wait until the child goes to sleep before swabbing the spot with alcohol and administering the injection. It's a tiny needle."

"What if he cries every time he gets it?"

"I can't promise he won't the first time or two. But

it's really a lot easier than it sounds. What we'll probably do is set a date for his first shot and have you bring
him in, and we'll help you administer it. We can have
a few practice runs with a pincushion so you can get
the hang of dialing in the dosage on the side of the pen
and then pushing the plunger." She smiled at each of
the parents and then patted Jacob on the shoulder. "I'm
sure he'll do fine."

If she was as good with her niece as she was in reassuring this young family, she was going to raise a kind
and responsible young lady. And if Alia's over-the-top
reaction at seeing her aunt was any indication, then the
child didn't have the same problems as he used to have
with attachments.

Used to have? He still did, although he did finally
come to love his Aunt Maddie, and was able to show her
affection just before she died of a heart attack.

But that didn't mean it came easy now. It didn't. If
Alia came running to him, would he stiffen up and
freeze? Teach her that love was something that was
rebuffed?

Hell. That was part of the reason he wasn't going to
have a family. He just couldn't run the risk.

Lyric set her laptop on the desk in the room. "There's
a video I want you to watch about the process that might
make things a little easier to understand." She pressed
Play and a canned presentation began to display charts
and statistics and ended with a demonstration of the
pen itself.

When it was over, there were a few seconds of silence, and Ellis said, "So what do you think? Dr.
Westphal has done an admirable job of describing the
treatment, but like the video said, it's a long-term com-

mitment. It's better not to do it at all than to start and decide you can't follow through."

Lyric agreed. "I want you to be completely comfortable with your decision whichever way you go."

Jacob's dad spoke up. "If we don't go through with treatment, how far behind will Jacob fall?"

"That's hard to predict, but it's doubtful he would ever catch up. He's not producing enough of the hormone on his own, so as the years go by, he'll fall further behind his peers. If he's comfortable with that and you are, as well, then I don't want to talk you into something you'd prefer not to do."

"Jacob has already mentioned wanting to be tall like his daddy. I don't want to let my fear keep me from giving him the best shot at a successful and happy life."

He understood that. Lyric wasn't letting her fear stop her from raising Alia. And Maddie had tried to do the same with him.

Mrs. Sellers looked at her husband. "I want to do this."

"Yes. So do I. We'll both learn how to give the injections and take turns if need be."

Lyric took one of Jacob's hands. "Will you help Mommy and Daddy with this?"

The boy gave a solemn nod.

"Well, it looks like it's unanimous. I'll look at my calendar and give you a call early this next week for a couple of practice sessions. You can either bring Jacob with you, or practice without him the first few times."

Mrs. Sellers glanced at her husband. "Can you get off work to come while Jacob is in school?"

"I'll make it happen. If you can give me about a week's lead time."

"That won't be a problem," Lyric said. "I'll get in

touch with the drug company and check with your insurance to see what they say."

"We'll do this with or without insurance."

Ellis spoke up. "If there's a problem, the hospital has a few funding programs we can explore."

"Thank you so much." Mrs. Sellers clasped her husband's hand.

A few minutes later, they said their goodbyes, and Ellis saw them out the door.

Lyric glanced at her watch. "I think they made the right decision."

"I think *they* think they made the right decision."

"You disagree?" Her head tilted to look up at him.

"No, but if it had gone the other way, would you have been just as supportive?"

She hesitated. "I'll admit, I truly feel it's in that child's best interest to undergo treatment. But they have to buy in, as well, or it won't work."

Maybe it was just the way he was built, but Ellis had always maintained a certain distance from his patients. He rarely got emotionally charged about diagnoses or treatments, always thinking of it as being professional and objective, something they were actually taught in medical school. Lyric was obviously strongly in favor of treatment in this case, but he was pretty sure she wouldn't have overridden the parents' wishes.

And in the end, he agreed with her. He thought it was in Jacob's best interest, too.

She was still looking up at him, and today there was no earring to twirl. He found he missed that. In fact, once or twice he'd had an urge to say or do something that would make her do just that: make those elegant fingers reach for her earlobe.

Hell, he needed to get out of this room before he

was tempted to do something besides meet her gaze for gaze. "I do think they'll stick to the treatment protocol. They're dedicated and want to do what they think is right."

"I do as well." She stared at him for another minute before glancing away.

He sucked down a breath. "Okay, I have another patient in a few minutes, so let me know when you schedule their first trial run. I'd like to be here."

Why? There was really no reason to. Was it because of Jacob? Or because of Lyric? Something told him he might not want to go searching for an answer to that question.

"I will."

With a raised hand, he turned and walked out of the room. As he did, he could almost swear he felt her bemused gaze follow him. If so, she wasn't the only one who was bemused. And he needed to shake off whatever was going on with him. And soon. Before he said or did something he couldn't take back.

CHAPTER FOUR

"I WISH YOU didn't have to leave so soon."

Her mom gave her a quick hug. "Me, too, but your dad has been holding down the fort for the last week and he has a doctor's appointment coming up. We both plan to visit during the summer. He's already put in for some vacation time. If that's okay."

"Of course it's okay." Her mom had insisted on sleeping on the sofa bed, despite Lyric's repeated offers to take her bed. Maybe she should tell Dave to look for a three-bedroom place instead so she could have an actual guest room. Or she could set up a cot for herself in Alia's room so her parents could have her room.

She'd already offered to take her mom to the airport, but she wouldn't hear of it, saying a taxi would keep Lyric from getting to her meeting late and that if Alia's preschool called she wouldn't be so far away.

Lyric was due to meet Ellis at a local coffee shop to plan their research trip. When she'd suggested meeting in one of their offices, he'd said it might be better to meet where things at the hospital wouldn't interfere and there'd be no interruptions. And he was right. Whenever she stayed home on her days off, things at home tended to pull at her and she ended up working all day instead of taking some much needed time off.

But she had to admit, she was a little nervous. This would be the first time she'd spent much time with him since that day in her office when Alia had arrived. And she'd had a weird reaction to him that day, which she'd chalked up to her imagination. At least she hoped that's all it was, because Jacob Sellers's parents were due to come in a couple of days from now for their trial run of administering the growth hormone. And for some reason, Ellis wanted to be there.

Didn't he trust her?

A horn honked out in front of the town house. "I think that's the taxi." Her mom gave her a tight squeeze. "Tell Alia we'll be back to see her soon."

Her mom had already told the child that. Several times, but there'd still been some tears from her niece on the way to preschool. If it weren't for Lyric's dad's job, she had a feeling her mom would already have her bags packed to move to Atlanta. And maybe that would even help with her dad's heart problems.

As it was, if things went well with things at the hospital, her dad might just put in for a transfer. Or take early retirement. Vegas had some bittersweet memories at this point for all of them.

"I will. And we'll plan video chats every few days."

With one last goodbye, which had Lyric tearing up this time, her mom disappeared into the taxi. After closing her front door, she wandered around the empty town house. She already missed having her niece's chatter and her mom's calm, steady presence. She was now on her own with her niece for the first time in her life. And, suddenly, she wasn't sure she could do it. She knew exactly how Jacob Sellers's parents felt. That whole vibe of knowing it was the right thing but not feeling sure you were capable.

Yes, you are, Ly. You have to be. That little girl has no one else and you can't expect your mom and dad to take on raising her. Not when you have the means...and no romantic commitments to interfere.

Breaking up with Jim actually couldn't have come at a better time, as painful as it had been at the time.

Going into the little girl's room, she admired the decorating efforts of her mom and niece. Her green comforter was scattered with various throw pillows and a couple of jungle animals—a sloth and an elephant, to be exact—were there to keep Alia company. Her gaze moved to the framed picture on the dresser. She went over and picked it up. It was a picture of Tessa and Alia, when the child was barely a year old. Her sister—although rail-thin—smiled down at her daughter as if she didn't have a care in the world, when in reality she was probably thinking about her next fix.

Fortunately, Tessa had had no problem leaving Alia in her parents' care, so there'd been no court battles, just a steady attempt to help their daughter beat her habit. A fight Lyric had joined in. But nothing had seemed to work. And now she was gone.

She hugged the photo to her and closed her eyes. "I'm sorry, Tess," she whispered. "So, so sorry. But I promise I'm going to spend the rest of my life loving your daughter and doing what I can to help others like you."

The picture went back on the dresser, her fingers trailing over it one last time. She was sure that at some point Alia would ask about her mom, and they would need to have a talk about what had happened. But today was not that day. And now she needed to go get ready for her meeting with Ellis and pray that he would help her keep the promise she'd just made to her sister and Alia.

* * *

He saw her the second she arrived. Dressed in dark jeans and a cream scoop-necked shirt, she looked tall and elegant, her dark hair almost grazing her shoulders. The cut was modern and almost choppy, the different-length strands curving this way and that, giving her an air of assured independence. And it was right on target with what he knew about her. She was stubborn and determined and didn't let much stand in her way.

If she had her way, she'd probably take this project on by herself, but that wasn't smart for more than one reason. First, she was emotionally invested in the outcome, because of her sister. And second, they needed to be able to sell this to the board, and for that to happen, it needed more than one supporter.

And Ellis wasn't positive he could give her that support. If they got into the neighborhoods and he didn't think the hospital was the right entity for the fight, he was going to speak up and say so. But he'd told her he'd keep an open mind, and he would. He'd already crossed three expensive pieces of equipment off his wish list to help leave some funding open. He just didn't want to be throwing money into a black hole that benefitted no one except those in administration.

He lifted a hand to catch her attention and she nodded, going up to order her coffee. This particular coffee shop was attached to a public library and also sold chocolates from a local chocolatier. He watched her peruse the glass-fronted case, pointing to something she'd spotted. The person behind the counter quickly packaged it up and handed it to her, along with a beverage. She then made her way over to his table.

Sliding into the seat across from this, she smiled.

"I love this place. I'll have to bring Alia here. She can check books out and get a hot chocolate."

He nodded at the small box. "Looks like you got a little more than hot chocolate."

"Yes, unfortunately. Turtles are a weakness of mine. And I got a cappuccino with a shot of vanilla—not hot chocolate—to go along with it."

"Turtles?"

Up went her eyebrows. "You've never had a Turtle? Ever?"

"I take it we're not talking about a reptile."

She opened the box. "Here. Try one. It's milk chocolate with caramel and pecans. They also make them in dark chocolate with several different kinds of nuts."

He took one and waited as she also selected a chocolate. She bit into hers, a long string of caramel coming off the candy. Part of it landed on her lower lip. She chewed, her tongue darting out to sweep away the stray stickiness.

Ellis's mouth watered, the reaction having nothing to do with the candy and everything to do with what he'd just witnessed. He'd thought meeting on neutral ground had been a good idea, but now he wasn't so sure. He popped his own candy into his mouth and bit down.

She was right. It was good. The slight bitterness of the pecans blended nicely with the sweetness of the caramel and chocolate.

She paused with the rest of the candy near her pink lips. Lips that looked far softer than they should. A fleeting thought circled his skull. Would he be able to taste the caramel that had rested there moments earlier?

"Good?" she asked.

"Very." There was a little too much emphasis on that

word, and he wasn't sure if it had to do with the candy itself or his ridiculous imaginings.

"I can see this is going to be a dangerous place to hang out."

Yes, it was. At least after this. She didn't mean the two of them, though. Of that, he was certain.

"Several parents of my patients have mentioned this place, and I thought it would be a good chance to check it out." Right now, he was pretty sure he should have picked a different day to do that.

"Alia will love it."

"How is she doing, by the way?" He hadn't seen the child again since that day in Lyric's office.

"Great. She loves her preschool so far. My mom went home this morning, so things will be a little more challenging than they were, but we'll manage."

"Let me know if I can help." *What? Where had that come from?* "And don't worry about being late or needing to leave early."

"Thanks. Hopefully that will be very rare, and I'll make sure it doesn't interfere with my work. I'm still looking for a sitter for the weekends or for days that the school is closed." She cleared her throat, taking a sip of her coffee and then lifting a tote bag she'd brought with her onto the table. "I brought a notebook to keep track of what we've done and the sections of town we've visited. Anything I should know?"

The next twenty minutes were spent with Ellis pulling up a map on his phone and sharing the research he'd done on the different areas. She added the work she'd done on social resources in the greater Atlanta area along with a list of rehab centers she'd found online.

It seemed they'd both come prepared. He liked that.

"So what do you think needs to happen, exactly? Where do you see holes in the system?"

"Well, in Vegas I would have loved to have schools take a trip to rehab centers, or maybe have addicts who have successfully kicked their habit mentor at-risk students. I think that might work here, as well, since I didn't see anything like that being done."

"And who would select these students? I can see a danger in it appearing to be profiling."

"I'm hoping parents will step up and recognize problems in their own households. People who want to get help for their kids before it's too late."

He could see the value in that. She really had done a lot of thinking and researching without him asking and despite having her niece to take care of. A sliver of admiration worked its way under his skin, making itself known each time she said something new.

"So can we set a date to go through these six areas?" He made a note to himself to get a dose or two of naloxone to take with them, just in case, although he hoped they didn't run into any cases of opioid overdose while they were out.

"My schedule is probably lighter than yours is right now, so if you can give me a date, I'll put it in my phone."

Glancing through his calendar, he realized she was right. He had few completely open days, except for the weekends. "Any chance you could go on a Saturday or Sunday?"

"I have Alia at home on weekends. If you map out some areas, maybe we could go at separate times and report our findings to each other."

He thought for a minute. "I'd rather try to be on the same page, if we can. It's hard to bounce around ideas by text, when we're not both experiencing the same things at the same time."

Experiencing the same things? Something about that sounded off to him, although he couldn't really put a finger on why.

She laughed. "Any chance your friend Dave has kids and could schedule a play date with Alia?"

He really didn't want her relying on Dave, and again, he wasn't sure exactly why. "He doesn't have kids. Sorry."

"Well, we're at an impasse then, it would seem. You're busy during the week, and I'm busy on weekends."

"Most of my surgeries are in the morning. I can juggle my schedule and get three or four hours over the course of a couple of afternoons. That would give us a good start. What time do you have to pick up your niece in the afternoons?"

"Preschool ends at two, but they have an after-care program that in extenuating circumstances can hold them until six. They need at least a day's notice, and I would rather not go that route every day, but periodically it would be okay."

"All right." He looked at his calendar again. "We have Jacob's parents two days from now, but how about tomorrow and then again on Friday?"

"That should work. I'll let the school know."

"Can I give you a ride back to the hospital?" The offer came out before he could stop it, but really, it was the polite thing to do.

"I drove, but thanks. I'll see you at the Sellers appointment, then, if not before." She nodded at her little box. "Would you like another for the road?"

"I'm good." He really didn't want to risk seeing her

bite into another one. Especially after watching her lick the sweet center off her lips. Because as much as he might deny it to himself, he hadn't been able to stop himself from imagining kissing that bit of caramel off her. Something he was never ever going to do. Which is why it was better to not even leave the door open for thoughts like that.

He stood. "I'll see you later, then."

"Okay, sounds good." And as she opened the lid of the box and took out another chocolate, he turned on his heel and headed for the exit, and an escape that right now looked sweeter than that whole damn box of candy.

CHAPTER FIVE

LYRIC HAD NOTIFIED the preschool that she wouldn't be in to pick up Alia until sometime after four. She hoped her young niece wouldn't get worried, although she'd talked to her about it the previous evening, so she was prepared.

Waiting at the front of the hospital for Ellis, she found herself a ball of nerves all over again. What was it about this man that made her react like that?

Maybe it was the way his gaze had dipped to her mouth when she'd been eating her candy and gotten some of it on her lip. She'd gone very still, not realizing she was holding her breath until his eyes came back up to look past her.

God. Her whole body had vibrated in a way she didn't recognize. And that was scary.

As if knowing she was thinking about him, Ellis came striding down the hallway, dressed in jeans and a black polo shirt. He looked amazing, making her wish she'd brought that box of candy with her. Except she'd gone home and eaten the whole thing in almost a sitting. Just so she wouldn't have to think about what had happened anymore.

"Hi, sorry I'm late. Surgery ran a little longer than I expected."

She couldn't stop a smile. "Not a problem. I haven't been here long." Was it her imagination or was the lady in the reception booth checking out Ellis? It was the same young lady who'd been there the day she'd arrived. She hadn't noticed it then, but she'd been a nervous wreck after arriving late. "And it's good to know that I'm not the only one who can be delayed."

"Touché." He evidently didn't need to ask what she was talking about. "I thought we'd take my car, since I'm more familiar with the area."

His eyes never even strayed to the information booth, which made some of Lyric's tension slide away, although that was ridiculous.

"Good, because I'd probably get lost, even using the GPS on my phone."

Making their way to the parking lot, Ellis stopped in front of a shiny, black BMW. Her eyes went big. "This won't stand out at all. Maybe we should take the bus."

"It'll be fine. We won't be going into the worst of the worst areas, since they're the farthest away from the hospital."

She nodded and waited for him to click open the locks from a keypad on the side of the car. Sliding into the leather seat, she found herself inhaling before she realized what was happening, and tried to catch his scent in the vehicle. And she did, along with the smell of warm leather and…coffee. She spied a cup in a holder, a small curl of steam coming from the vent on the lid, obviously from a different coffee shop than the one she'd met him at yesterday. Her mouth watered, wishing she'd brought one of her own.

"I'm jealous. I didn't even think of bringing coffee."

"I brought that for you, actually. Cappuccino with a shot of vanilla, right?"

She blinked. He remembered what she drank? "Thank you. You didn't get one for yourself?"

"I had an espresso. It was quick to drink."

She picked up the cup and took a sip. "Mmm, perfect. I guess I should have brought some Turtles in trade."

"Look in the back."

She twisted around and spotted a small familiar box. She gulped as something in her tummy started tingling at the way he'd looked at her the last time they'd had Turtles.

Not the marrying kind, remember? And neither are you. Now.

But why did it have to be marriage at all?

Because she'd already done the casual-relationship thing and it hadn't been satisfying. At all. But maybe that was because she'd been expecting something deeper, when Jim had had no intention of making their pillow talk into anything permanent.

"You didn't have to get me those."

He started the car, turning to look at her with a raised eyebrow. "Oh, Lyric. Who said they were for you?"

She laughed. "They are addicting, aren't they?" As soon as the words were out of her mouth, her laughter dried up. It was crazy how she used to be able to shoot those words out like they meant nothing. "Sorry. That wasn't very funny, given the circumstances."

"Hey…" His hand touched hers, those funny callouses making themselves known again. "You have to keep some separation or it'll drive you crazy."

"And you? How are you able to keep separate from things that hurt?"

He took his hand off hers, a muscle in his jaw pulsing. "I think some people find it easier to stay emotionally detached."

Was he saying she couldn't? That stung, but she wasn't going to let him know it. She decided to change the subject.

"Can I see your hand?"

"Excuse me?"

Oh, Lord. Why had she asked that? She was supposed to be going for something less personal, not more. "Sorry. I noticed you have calluses and wondered what they were from."

And why had she noticed that in the first place? She'd shaken hands with hundreds of men and never thought twice about what their palms felt like.

Maybe he did yard work, or sailed or something.

He turned one of his hands over and glanced briefly at it as they pulled onto the interstate. "I do a little woodworking in my spare time."

"Woodworking?" It took a second for the words to compute.

"I make furniture, actually."

"Wow. I didn't know people did that much anymore."

She pictured him leaning over some piece of wood and slowly working it, his hands gliding over each inch of it, feeling the warmth and life he was breathing into the piece. A shudder rolled through her before she could stop it. Maybe it would have been better if he *had* simply raked leaves to get those calluses.

He shrugged. "Let's just say I find satisfaction in something being finished. Something that has nothing to do with sickness or death or trying to diagnose something you've never come across before."

"I can understand that."

She hadn't been searching for pieces to the puzzle that made up Ellis, but felt like she was holding a couple in her hand right now. "At least you don't have to worry about getting emotionally involved with a piece of wood."

Except she'd imagined him doing just that, hadn't she? Or was the wood merely a substitute for something very different?

Darn it, Ly! Don't go placing yourself on this man's sawhorses.

"You're right. You don't get emotionally involved."

She needed to stop this train of thought. Right now. "So where are we going first?"

"Merit. It's the neighborhood on our list that is closest to the hospital, but it's also the area with more resources. We're about five minutes away."

A mile or two later, he took an exit and turned onto a quiet street. Right away, Lyric saw graffiti on the overpass they'd just exited. But the houses didn't look as run-down as she'd expected. "Are we there?"

"Yes. We're headed to a high school that has a reputation for drug use."

Another turn, and she spotted a large brick building with sign out front saying it was the Merit high school. They drove by at a fairly slow rate, noticing a police presence on two of the neighboring streets, along with a lot of other parked cars.

"Looks like maybe they're working to combat the problem, too."

"I would say that's the case, as well," he said. "I don't want to cruise by more than once or we'll look suspicious. Let's move a little farther out on the grid."

Just then, students started pouring from the entrance like a hose that had suddenly been turned on full blast, and the school-zone light started blinking.

Two of the kids that passed them lit up cigarettes as

soon as they were across the street, despite the police presence. Several others followed suit.

"Hell, why do they do that to themselves at that age?"

She understood exactly what he meant. Lyric had found Tessa smoking on more than one occasion when she was in middle school. Besides being illegal, Lyric had found that it became easy to swap one addiction for another, since they all caused dopamine levels to rise, rewarding the user with that feeling of being normal and happy. But the younger they started, the more they wanted to recapture that feeling and hold onto it. Lyric was convinced that smoking had started the ball rolling with Tessa. Maybe it didn't with everyone, but there was a connection with addiction and genetics. Maybe Tessa had inherited something and smoking flipped a switch in her brain that opened the door and transformed something from taboo to "normal."

The police weren't doing anything, but then again, they were probably looking for something much worse, like dealers. They left the school zone and did a slow circle, eventually going farther and farther away.

"Hey, there's a rehab facility. And it's not very far from the school, either."

"There are several in the area from what I saw online."

"I guess we could contact them and see if they have any kind of programs to help mentor school-aged kids. I almost feel like we need to start at the middle-school level, or maybe even younger."

She jotted down the name of the rehab center, making a note to give them a call later on today. They passed a group of about ten kids who were standing in a tight circle. "That's weird. Wonder what they're doing?"

There were no police on this block and a shiver went

through her. Someone had his phone out, held way up high like he was filming something. A fight? No, she didn't see any commotion going on. She turned her head as they went by, still trying to figure out what was bothering her. She suddenly saw a ripple of activity. Then she realized someone had emerged from the group and was yelling for help. Screaming, actually.

"Stop, Ellis! Something's wrong."

He pulled over immediately, maneuvering between two parked cars. Someone sprinted from the scene. This person was older. Slick-looking. She didn't like it.

She was out of the car in a flash, rushing toward the group, even as Ellis popped his trunk and took out what looked like a medical bag.

"What's going on?" she asked the nearest person.

"Who are you?" A belligerent teen blocked her path.

"I'm a doctor. Is someone hurt?"

A girl ran over to her and grabbed her arm. "A man was trying to show her how, and she suddenly fell over."

"Trying to show her how to what?"

Scared eyes stared into hers. "How to find a vein."

Oh, God. A million thoughts went through her head. Had the person actually injected her with anything? Pushed in an air bubble? "What was in the hypo?"

"I don't want to get her in trouble." By now the crowd of kids realized an adult was on the scene and scattered faster than she would have believed possible, leaving the girl she was talking to and another girl on the ground. Two other girls stood back, gripping each other. They looked no older than fourteen. Her sister's face swam before her eyes.

"I need you to tell me. Her life depends on it." Holding on to the girl, she dragged her to the victim just as Ellis reached them.

He motioned to one of the two girls who were watching. "Call 911." When neither of them moved, he raised his voice and pointed at one of them. "Do it! Now!"

The girl nearest to him pulled out her phone and dialed.

"She's not breathing," Ellis said. "Start CPR."

The girl she was holding moaned. "No, Alisha! Oh, my God." She looked Lyric in the eye. "It was heroin. Please help her."

Getting on the ground beside the stricken girl, Lyric found the spot in her chest and began compressions. "We need naloxone."

Ellis was already in his bag just as she heard sirens, but she kept counting down the number of compressions. He came over with a needle of his own. "I've got it. Stop compressions for a second."

Swabbing her arm with alcohol, he injected the life-saving medicine while Lyric started compressions again. Ellis fitted a manual breathing device over the girl's mouth. Lyric stopped so he could pump a couple of breaths and then started back up. "One, two, three, four, five, six…"

They should know in just a few minutes if it was effective.

A uniformed officer hurried over to them, and Ellis quickly explained who they were, telling the man they'd administered naloxone.

Just then the sound of a ragged breath came from the girl on the ground. She turned her head and vomited.

"EMS is on their way," the officer said.

The girl who had called 911 was long gone, but the friend of the downed girl was still there sobbing. He turned to her. "I need her name and an emergency contact number."

"She's my sister…" She sobbed wildly. "She's not going to die, is she?"

Shock roared through Lyric and a sense of déjà vu almost overcame her. She'd assumed the other girl was just a friend. She swallowed, trying to keep her mind on her patient.

Ellis was next to her, checking pupillary reactions and taking her pulse. She glanced at the girl standing over them. "Are you using, too?"

"She's my baby sister."

Lyric bit her tongue as a million ugly words came to mind. She'd done everything in her power to help Tessa kick her habit and to find an older sister actually helping the younger one to follow in her footsteps… She couldn't begin to understand that mind-set.

"Are. You. Using?" She made her voice hard.

"Not for very long." She looked at Lyric through brown tearstained eyes.

"Listen to me. Your sister could have died. If we hadn't gotten here when we did, she would have. Is that what you want?"

She shook her head, but didn't say anything.

The officer put his hand on the girl's arm. "She's right. Your sister is very lucky. We're going to call your parents, and then we're all going to sit down and have a long talk, okay?"

"Y-yes."

EMS got there and took over care, writing down the information from Ellis's syringe. "Lucky you were on the scene."

Ellis looked at Lyric and nodded. "It looks that way. I don't normally carry naloxone with me, but since we were doing research in this area for the hospital, I decided to bring a couple of doses, just in case we ran into something."

She hadn't even thought of bringing any. Then again, she hadn't expected to find someone OD'ing on the street.

But Ellis had come prepared. His speech about staying emotionally detached came back to her. Maybe she really did have a problem.

"An older male ran from the scene, while another person filmed the situation on his phone," he said to the officer. "You might want to see if you can find the person, if you need a visual when you investigate."

"We'll do that. Thanks."

She remembered seeing someone with the phone pointed toward the scene, too. What kind of sick individual recorded someone who might be dying?

Had someone filmed Tessa's last fix?

As soon as the girl and her sister were loaded into the ambulance and the sirens faded away, Lyric stood on the sidewalk shaking, arms wrapped around her waist, while Ellis finished giving the police officer a statement. God. She hoped he didn't need her to do the same, because she was going to come apart, if so.

She sucked down one deep breath and then another, and prayed she could make it home before she made a total fool of herself in front of Ellis and whoever else happened by.

Ellis glanced over at Lyric after the officer had him sign his statement. Something didn't look right. She looked totally alone standing on the sidewalk, and her eyes...

Stricken. He'd seen that same expression on the face of parents who'd been told there was no hope for survival for their child. But the girl from today had survived. And maybe she and her sister had both gotten the wake-up call they needed. Lyric should be relieved they'd happened across the scene. And yet there was no evidence of that on her face.

"Do you need anything else?"

"No, sir, we'll contact you if we do. Thanks again for stepping in to help."

"It's part of my job."

Yes, it was. So why did this feel like something else? At least on Lyric's side.

He walked over to where she was standing. "You okay?"

"Yeah, fine." She even nodded as if she needed to emphasize that fact.

"I'm beginning to think you're right about the need for some mentors or something. Today never should have happened."

"No. It shouldn't have."

He frowned. He was right. There was something going on with her. "Let's get back to the car."

"Can we just walk for a few minutes? I need some air."

The air was pretty warm and humid this time of year, but he nodded. "Sure. Let me just put my bag away and lock the car."

"Oh, I'm sorry. I'm sure you need to get back to the hospital."

"I'm good." He glanced at her for a minute. "Tell you what. There's a park not too far from here—it's a quick drive. Why don't we go there? We can save the rest of the locations for another time or Friday, like we talked about."

"Thank you. That sounds wonderful."

He stowed his medical gear and they climbed in the

vehicle. Less than fifteen minutes later, they were at one of the smaller parks that dotted Atlanta's scenery. The entire way, Lyric had been silent. Maybe it was the crash after the rush of adrenaline from administering CPR.

"This is beautiful." She climbed out and looked around at the greenery.

"It is. Some of the five-Ks I've participated in have been in this park."

"I can see why."

He tried looking at the area as if seeing it for the first time. A paved path meandered through patches of trees and grassy areas, a solid white line dividing it in two. Park benches were planted along the way at regular intervals.

He knew from coming here that there was also a dirt running path with hills and planned uneven areas for those who wanted a more strenuous workout. The park was popular because of the various activities it offered, as well as distance markers that helped keep track of how far you'd gone. Even now a few runners passed by, despite the heat of the afternoon sun.

They entered through the gates, and a sign informed them that the area was patrolled on a regular basis. Lyric nodded at it. "I'm glad to see that."

"I should have warned you that some of the areas we'll be visiting are rough. Sorry you had to see it on your first trip."

She stopped and looked at him, blinking. "You think I was scared?"

He thought through his words carefully. "No, I think it was an emotionally charged situation and adrena-line—"

"Adrenaline had nothing to do with it." Her flat tone held a warning.

"What then?" He was trying to understand, but somehow failed to grasp what she meant.

"My sister OD'd. I've often wondered if she could have survived had someone in the vicinity had a dose of naloxone." Her lips twisted. "And yet, I never even thought to bring some with us."

"Hey, I almost didn't, either. It was sheer luck that I packed it."

She took a step closer, her expression softening. "Ellis, you saved that girl's life."

He swallowed, looking into eyes that were moist with emotion. Some answering sentiment appeared out of nowhere, the sensation odd and unfamiliar. And yet it felt right. Sliding a finger under her chin, he tilted her head. "So did you. You kept her alive until the naloxone could take effect."

"I felt totally paralyzed, as if I were experiencing my sister's situation firsthand. I was scared we weren't in time. And when she took that first breath, God..." Her chest rose, as if mimicking what the girl had done. "I thought I was going to fall to pieces."

"But you didn't."

"You have no idea how close I was."

"She's alive. That's all that matters." He cupped her face, noting how exquisite her bone structure was as he brushed a bead of moisture from beneath her eye. "I'm sorry it couldn't be the same for your sister."

"What happened to staying emotionally detached?" Her smile was shaky. "Looks like you're not always as gruff as you appear."

"Gruff, huh?" He smiled. "I've been called a lot of things, some not very nice, but I think that's the first time I've been called that. At least to my face."

His gaze trailed to her lips, watching as her teeth

caught at the lower one in a way that made things tighten. He remembered the caramel from the coffee shop. How he'd thought about kissing it. Kissing her.

"Maybe it's because of how you were the day we met."

He had been kind of a bear that day. But his mood was more from hearing that the grant money his department had been promised might have to be shared for something that wasn't on his list. But he was beginning to think maybe it should have been. That girl from today had probably been transported to New Mercy, and someone from Pediatrics was almost assuredly going to be called on to help with her care.

"I'm surprised you didn't call me a stronger word than that."

"How do you know I didn't?"

His smile widened. "In that case, I won't ask." The tips of her hair brushed across his fingers, feeling silky soft, her skin warm despite having just left an air-conditioned car.

"Maybe Dr. Lawson was right. Your bark was worse than your bite."

"Don't be too sure about that."

Suddenly he knew his crazy fantasies were going to come to fruition. He was going to kiss her. The combination of their back-and-forth banter and having her so close were doing a number on him, and he was finding it harder and harder to resist.

If he was going to back away, he needed to do so now.

He stayed rooted in place instead.

"Lyric?"

"Mmm?"

She looked relaxed and comfortable, whereas moments earlier she'd said she'd been at a breaking point. He wasn't sure if he'd made the difference or if it was just the passing of time. But it was also the first time he could remember her not looking like she was on edge, waiting for something to happen.

He liked it. Wanted to keep this version of Lyric around for a while.

And so he did what he'd been wanting to do for the last half hour. He leaned down and kissed her.

CHAPTER SIX

THE SECOND HIS mouth touched hers, Lyric felt the earth shift under her feet.

His lips were warm and firm, just like she'd imagined they'd be. And, yes, she had imagined them. Time and time again, despite the numerous cease-and-desist warnings she'd sent to her brain.

Her efforts had failed and now she knew. And the kiss was every bit as heady as the stray images she'd intercepted inside her head.

Not good. Because she didn't want to like the kiss. She should shove him away and ask him what he thought he was doing. But she didn't. Because she was a very willing participant in what was happening. In fact, she didn't want it to stop…wanted it to keep on going for ages.

Her arms crept up and rounded his neck, as if she was afraid he might suddenly pull away. But, so far, he was showing no signs of moving.

Something whizzed by them, a bicycle, probably, but she didn't care, didn't stop to make sure they were out of the way of passersby.

He shifted his angle and the thought ran through her head that even his kiss was gruff. As if it had taken him by surprise, and he hadn't been able to stop himself. His teeth nipped at her bottom lip, making her edge even closer, the languid warmth in her tummy changing to something that churned with heat. And need.

She was pretty sure he'd started off with the intention of comforting her. And she'd wanted the comfort. Until the word *more* whispered through her head. She'd needed more, and it was almost as if he'd heard her thoughts and was giving her what she wanted.

Her fingers slid into his hair and found it warm and crisp, a muffled groan coming from him when she explored deeper.

A giggle sounded nearby, and she realized it hadn't come from her. Or from him.

That made her pull free with a gulp. Ellis was just as quick to let her go. Her eyes searched the area and saw a couple walking side by side, hands clasped. The girl glanced back at them with a knowing smile.

Oh, Lord. Did the woman think Ellis was her boyfriend? Her lover?

He was neither.

A flash of panic came over her. She had Alia to think about. And all his talk of emotional detachment came back in a rush.

What had she been thinking? She stepped back in a hurry. "I'm so sorry. You were right. After the adrenaline and everything..." She waved her hand around as if she could grab the rest of the explanation out of thin air. She found nothing. Except worry. Worry that she would ruin everything, and he would send her packing. Worry that her first week with Alia would be overshadowed with thinking about what had happened.

"I'm the one who should be sorry. You were upset. And I knew better."

She blinked. "You didn't do it on purpose."

"No. Of course not. But I sensed you weren't yourself. I never should have kissed you."

"I'd like to think we both got caught up in the moment." It was the truth. Because once his hands cradled her face, she was a goner. If he hadn't initiated that kiss, she almost certainly would have. So she was really as much, if not more, to blame for what happened as he was.

She continued, "Well, at least we both realize it was a mistake." It had been, hadn't it? Or was she making too big of a deal about it?

"I don't make a habit of kissing coworkers. And it won't happen again."

Was he worried she would go to HR and report him? Not very likely. She didn't want anyone to know what had happened. And he really hadn't done anything wrong. Neither had she.

So why did she feel guilty?

Because she had a young niece who needed her right now. And one thing Alia didn't need was the confusion of seeing her aunt kiss someone and wonder if that "someone" was going to be a fixture in their lives. Thank God she'd broken things off with Jim. Although she almost certainly would have once Alia became her responsibility.

And she was not going to repeat her mistakes with someone else.

"I'm sure you don't. Neither do I. So I vote that we forget about it."

"Forget about it. Sure."

There was an odd note to his voice, but if she had to guess what he was feeling, she would say relief. Because that's what she was feeling. Right?

Of course.

"Do you still want to be there when I meet with Jacob Sellers's parents?"

"Yes, unless you think that would be a distraction."

It would, but she didn't want him to know that. And by the time that appointment rolled around, her feet would be back on terra firma and today would be just a faint memory.

"Of course not. Besides, we agreed to forget about what happened."

"Sounds good. Let's get back to the hospital. I'd like to check on the girl who OD'd and see how she's doing."

"Could you call me and let me know once you find out?" Right now she needed to get away from him. Because the longer she stood in this park and looked at him, the less likely she'd be to keep her resolution of putting this behind her. Because even now, there was a voice at the back of her head that whispered, *That resolution begins tomorrow, right? Not today. So why not just have that one last little binge before the fasting begins?*

Fasting? Ugh. This was more than just going on a diet. This was a knife slice that separated what had happened today from what would happen in the future.

"I will."

So they made the trek back to the car in silence, for the most part. However, Lyric was painfully aware of everything about him as they walked and as they drove back to the hospital. And that did not bode well for putting this behind her. But somehow she had to. For her sake. And for Alia's. The little girl did not need any more turmoil in her young life. Lyric had to put her own wants and needs on the back burner for a while. No matter how hard that might prove.

* * *

Ellis stood outside of the door to Lyric's office two days later. The overdose victim had survived, much to everyone's relief, and both the girl and her sister were now getting the counseling they needed to hopefully prevent this from happening again. He'd debated a couple of times since then about pulling back from the Jacob Sellers case, but knew if it wasn't that situation, there would be others that would require him to work with Lyric.

He'd beat himself up several times over the past couple of days. He wasn't quite sure what had happened. He'd seen grief before. Many times, in fact, but he'd never allowed any emotion to come between him and his objectivity.

Maybe it was the fact that those emotions had even arisen that had caused this. Ellis normally had to work on summoning some semblance of compassion, so it was the fact that this had seemingly erupted out of nowhere that had shocked him and made him act impulsively.

And he didn't like it. He preferred his old style of dealing with things, even if it did earn him adjectives like *hard-nosed* or *emotionless* from some of the staff.

There was nothing to do but knock on the door and face her. It had to happen sometime. Maybe he shouldn't have worked so hard on making sure their paths didn't cross. Because this was not the best setting for making that first contact.

He almost groaned aloud as the thought made the memory of another "first contact" arise.

Forcing his knuckles to strike the surface of her door, he rapped twice, hearing her call out for him to enter.

When he did, he found the Sellerses already in the room and Lyric holding an orange.

On the computer screen that faced the couple was a diagram with various subcutaneous injection sites circled.

He greeted the couple and asked how Jacob was doing.

"He's been asking when he can start getting his 'growing medicine.'"

Lyric smiled. "That's a good sign. I really think he's going to do just fine."

Ellis wondered why she hadn't brought in one of the practice mannequins, although he knew the old standard was an orange. He glanced at his phone, thinking maybe he was late, but he wasn't. It was still five minutes before their meeting time. He tried not to be irritated that she'd started without him, but recognized that it didn't make sense for her to just sit there with the couple without actively doing what they'd come there for.

She obviously didn't always run late, like she had that first day.

"So as I was saying," she said, pointing to the areas on the screen. "Any of these sites are fine, and we already talked about rotating where you give the injections."

She handed an injection pen to Mrs. Sellers, while she held the orange. "Since you said you'll probably be doing the majority of the injections because of work schedules, we'll start with you. Do it just like I showed you."

Mrs. Sellers did great setting up the needle and dialing in the amount of growth hormone. But when she got to the part where she had to push the plunger, she hesitated. "You're sure it won't hurt?"

"It's best to just push it with purpose. He'll barely feel it. A good option would be to wait for him to go to sleep, as I mentioned last time we met."

He was impressed with how matter-of-fact and confident Lyric was. And that confidence seemed to transfer to the husband and wife as they both succeeded with their practice injections.

Soon they were done and out of the room.

"That went well." He watched her clear away the items they'd used, putting the trash in one receptacle and the needle in the portable sharps box she'd brought into her office. "We do have a practice mannequin, if you want to use it."

"We might next time, but I wanted them to become familiar with the pen itself without having to worry about where exactly to give the injection. 'One skill at a time' was one of my instructor's mottos. I've tended to find that to be true."

It made sense. He glanced at her to see if there was any hint of being uncomfortable around him. "I saw you started early."

"I did. Sorry. They were in the waiting room, and I was done with the patient I'd been speaking with. I thought we'd just get started. I hope that was okay."

"Of course. How's your niece doing with her new preschool?"

Lyric made a quick face. "Not as well as I'd hoped. She's started crying every day when I leave, although she's fine when I go to pick her up."

"Are you bringing her here after preschool is over?"

"I have been, only because I'd rather not bombard her with having to switch from one day-care setting to another on top of the move and everything else. I hope that's not a problem."

"Not at all. I was the one who suggested it." He softened the words with a smile, hoping they hadn't come across as condescending.

Only now did he notice that she had slight smudges under her eyes…and she only had on one earring. A testament to how hard a time she was having adjusting? An unfamiliar pang went through him at the thought that she might throw in the towel and go back to Vegas. "Did you lose a…?" He motioned to his own ear.

She reached up and touched one lobe and then the other, the action sending a jolt through his chest.

Then she rolled her eyes. "Oh, God. It's just been one of those days." She smiled back. "You know, when nothing goes according to plan?"

He did indeed. He'd had one of those two days ago, when his trip to one of the project sites had gone spinning out of his control. He certainly hadn't planned on kissing her. Or reviving a child who'd overdosed. "Yes, I do. Those days are never fun."

Well, that wasn't strictly true. The kiss had been pretty awesome, although that made it dangerous, not fun.

Lyric undid the tiny diamond in her other ear and dropped it into her desk drawer. "Thanks for noticing. Hopefully no one else has."

Why *had* he noticed it? Maybe because he was used to seeing her twirl those little dots when she was uncomfortable. Or maybe it was just boredom. But today she hadn't even tried. Did that mean she was becoming more comfortable with the hospital? With him?

Doubtful. Because he was still just as on edge around her. Maybe even more than he'd been before.

All because of that damn kiss.

Today she wore a black scoop-necked blouse and

cream trousers that hugged her hips just enough to bring his attention to them.

Or maybe that was just his mind roaming through areas that he'd marked as restricted territory.

She set the orange on her desk. He glanced at it with a frown. "Are you going to eat that?"

"I was. The pen was a dummy, so no actual serum was injected and the needle was sterile. I don't like to waste food."

He grinned. That was such a Lyric thing to say. And how had he even known that? Or that she'd managed to make him smile when he wasn't feeling particularly cheerful? "I hope that's not your actual lunch."

"No. I'll grab something on my way to pick up Alia." She bit the corner of her lip. "Can I ask you something?"

He tensed but held onto his smile. "Sure."

"If I'm ever busy with a patient during the time I need to pick her up, do you know of anyone at the hospital who is trustworthy and who would be willing to be added to the approved pick-up list at the school? I don't have any relatives here, and don't really know anyone all that well yet. They could just bring her here to the hospital."

Before he even had a chance to entertain other possibilities, he heard words emerge from his mouth that had no chance of being retracted. "I can, if you think it will help. Most of my surgeries are in the morning and surely we won't both be tied up with patients at the same time."

She frowned. "Are you sure? It won't be forever. I'm hoping she'll settle into a routine and will eventually be able to be enrolled in an after-care program. Just right now I can't see my way to—"

"It's fine. I don't mind." It really wasn't fine, but he'd

already said the words and couldn't really take them back. "What do I need to do?"

"I'll need you go to with me to the preschool so they can get a picture of you to put in their files along with your signature—and mine, of course. So if we could set a day and time to do that—"

"I'm free now, and—" he nodded at the orange "—I haven't had lunch, either, so why don't we grab that bite on the way. Or do you have another patient to see right now?"

"No, the Sellerses were my last scheduled patients. But I do have paperwork to catch up on this afternoon, so I thought I'd bring Alia back here and let her play on the floor while I work."

"Good. Do you need to wrap up anything before we go? You said she gets off at two, right?" It was almost twelve thirty now.

"She does get off at two." She hesitated. "Are you sure? I wasn't hinting for you to volunteer, I honestly was just looking for suggestions. I just haven't had time to make many friends yet…" Her voice trailed away, as if she was embarrassed by that fact. "It takes me a while. Lucky you—you're the only person I really know here."

A sliver of awareness went through him. She only knew him?

It meant nothing. He'd been at this hospital for years and could still count the number of friendships on one hand. Dave Butler was one of the few people in his life that he would consider a close friend. It wasn't that he spurned friendships so much as valued his work above those kinds of relationships. It was where he felt the most comfortable.

And the fact that he'd impulsively kissed Lyric? It

was not like him at all, and the warning was clear: he needed to be careful.

"I'm sure you'll make friends once you get a routine down. And it's not like I'll be picking her up every day. It might happen, what...once?"

"I hope not even that. But the preschool really wants an alternate in case of emergencies, such as if school is released early because of bad weather or other unforeseen circumstances."

"I can understand that. Not that we get much snow here. But when we do, it pretty much qualifies as a natural disaster within some government offices."

She laughed. "Good to know. Vegas is like that, too. It does snow every couple of years, but it rarely sticks."

"Anything special I should know about Alia? Will she be afraid of a stranger picking her up? Should I be around her a time or two—with you there, of course—so she gets used to me?"

"I hadn't thought about that. She has been a little weepy, recently. I don't want you to end up with a wailer on your hands."

"Wailer?" He felt even less sure about his suggestion now.

"Sorry, I'm kidding. And I really don't want to impose on you. But if you'll go with me today, so she can see you again and maybe interact with you a bit, that would be helpful. You're a pediatrician, so it's not like it'll be a stretch for you to talk to a kid."

He was a pediatrician, but that didn't mean it wouldn't be a stretch. At the hospital, he had a goal to work toward. But with Alia...?

Wait. Maybe he could approach it like he did the kids at work. Treat this as a problem that needed a solution. Lyric's niece needed someone reliable who would be there in the event that her aunt couldn't. The goal would be to help her feel safe.

The snatches of memories he had from when his mother left were of abject terror and a sick certainty that the same men who'd taken his mom were eventually going to come and take him or Maddie away. And he would be left completely alone. No child should have to experience that, so if he could help Alia feel safe and secure—even in this small way—he was going to try.

Otherwise she might contact Dave and ask him to do it.

Where had that come from? Maybe because Dave had actually called a few days ago and asked if it would be inappropriate for him to ask her out. Ellis had had no choice but to say he had no opinion one way or the other—which wasn't entirely the case. And he had no idea why.

The image of her unhooking that earring swung around to haunt him again. And if Dave plucked those tiny studs out of her ears?

A queasy feeling roiled around inside of him.

Lyric hadn't mentioned having plans with anyone. And during that kiss he'd shared with her, she had definitely been kissing him back. Which had been part of the reason he hadn't come to his senses and pulled back sooner. Because the way she'd kissed...

Hell! No thinking about that.

Surely if she'd had a date with someone else, she would have said so afterward.

He realized she was looking at him. Waiting for him to respond to whatever she'd said. "I'm not sure about it not being a stretch, but I'll certainly do my best not to traumatize her."

"Traumatize her?" She cocked her head. "How would you do that?"

He'd meant it as a joke, but maybe subconsciously his thoughts about his own childhood had translated themselves into the conversation. He made something up. "By telling her 'Dad jokes.'"

"Don't you have to be a dad to do that?" Her features had relaxed. Surely she didn't think he would actually say something to scare her. Then again, despite her words, she didn't really know him. And if she did, maybe she wouldn't be so quick to agree to his name being on that list of alternates.

"Hmm...you've never heard any of my jokes."

"I can't picture you actually delivering a punchline. To anything." She laughed again, the light sound again pulling at something inside of him. Her brown eyes sparkled, and she tossed her head, sending strands of glossy hair flying in all directions.

It was probably the most carefree he'd seen her since she'd started working at New Mercy. He liked it. A little belatedly, he realized he was still in her office, and the door closed. And she was standing not five feet away from him, while snatches of internal conversation were starting to make themselves heard in his head. And what they included would definitely not be on their lunch menu.

"We'd better go or that bite to eat will be smaller than my appetite."

Especially since his appetite was starting to expand into other areas. And that bothered him. A lot. His relationships with women—like the rest of his life—were things that were arranged with almost clinical precision. They didn't just "happen."

She hesitated. "If you're sure."

"I wouldn't have offered if I wasn't."

The words were a little shorter than he meant them to be. But this was real. There was no going back now—not without an awkward explanation that he'd rather not give. He repeated the argument that his signature on a piece of paper would not likely come to anything, and this would all be just an empty exercise. At least he hoped so. Because having his picture on a file that gave him responsibility over a young child...

He sucked down a quick breath. He'd assumed he'd never have anything but a medical responsibility for anyone. Especially a kid who had undergone a trauma similar to his own. Well, he was not going to screw this up.

"Okay, thanks again." She came forward and touched his hand, her fingers light, before she moved past him to the door. "It's a relief not to have to worry about that."

She might not be. But he was, now. But he would go, and in doing so put Lyric's mind at ease about her young niece. And maybe he could prevent the child from experiencing the fear of abandonment that he'd once felt. That alone made his offer worth it. And since he and the endocrinologist would be working closely together, it would prevent there being any hard feelings at this short juncture in their working relationship.

Because he was pretty sure, there would be plenty of other chances for that to happen. Especially if he couldn't get his heart back in line with what he knew to be true: that Lyric and Alia were not permanent fixtures in his life. And they never would be.

CHAPTER SEVEN

LYRIC SAT ACROSS from him at an Italian eatery that was within a ten-minute drive from Alia's preschool. She'd been so worried about that kiss turning things between them into an untenable situation, but it didn't seem to have. Unlike her, Ellis had evidently brushed it off as insignificant, at least from his attitude. She wasn't sure whether to be insulted or relieved.

Relieved. This is not a situation, like with Jim, where you wanted it to mean more than it did.

In this case, she definitely did not want it to mean anything.

"I met with Dr. Radner, and she wants us to work some cases together. I guess I should have run that past you first," she said.

Dr. Theresa Radner was one of the psychiatrists at the hospital, so it would be natural for them to collaborate on some of the cases involving children.

"No need to run it by me. Maybe talk to Jack about it, just to see if that meshes with the rest of the needs of the hospital."

He said it as if it didn't matter, but there was the slightest hardening to his tone that made her wary.

"You don't sound thrilled by the idea."

"I don't really have any thoughts about it at all. I see where you're coming from, though."

No change in his voice.

Now she was sorry she'd brought it up. Would he change his mind about being Alia's alternate for pickup? Well, if it took something as little as that to change his mind, maybe it would be better if he wasn't on the list at all. "If you're worried about it interfering with my work in Pediatrics, it won't. But since the behavioral aspect of my degree is important to me, I think the other behavioral departments should be able to call and ask for a consult, don't you?"

"I do. And like I said, it's not my decision. Ultimately, it's Jack's."

So was he saying that Jack might be the one with the problem? Because that's not what it sounded like to her. "Do you think he'll object?"

Ellis stared at her for a second as if he was going to refuse to answer. Then finally, he said, "I doubt it. The two departments have just had different focuses, that's all."

"Aren't both focused on helping children?"

"Of course." He took a bite of his ravioli and glanced over her shoulder, avoiding meeting her gaze.

Despite his words, she was feeling more and more like he was the one with the problem. And she couldn't for the life of her guess why that might be.

So she followed his example and ate for a minute or two before trying again. "I also thought she—specifically—might have some thoughts on my project. I'm still at the brainstorming stage of how things might work."

"I get that. And you don't have to justify your reasons. I'm sure it will be fine."

"Okay, that's great." It wasn't really, but what else was she going to say? She really needed to tread carefully and not forget that she was the new kid on the block.

The waitress came over and asked how the check was going to be divided. Before she could say anything, Ellis said it would be all together. When the woman left, he added, "I'm putting it on the expense account, since we've spent almost the whole meal talking business."

"I'm sorry. That was my fault. I'm sure the last thing you want to talk about is work while on your lunch break."

"I like my job." He shrugged. "It's the most important thing in my life, and I don't see that changing anytime soon."

Almost exactly what Dave had said about him. But surely he wanted to get married eventually. Although Dave said that wasn't the case.

None of her business. As long as he didn't stand in the way of her goal, she would stay out of his personal life.

And that kiss?

That wasn't delving into his personal life. In fact, she hadn't learned very much personal about the man at all, other than that he was a great kisser. But he already knew a lot about her. Much more than she shared with most people. And that made their professional relationship pretty lopsided. But she didn't have a choice.

Or did she?

"I can tell you like your job. Did you always want to be a doctor?" So much for not asking anything personal. Except people asked that question all the time. It didn't mean she was trying to pick the padlocks on his personal life.

"Not always. I was just good at the sciences in school and seemed a natural fit."

An odd answer. Most people went into that line of work because they wanted to help people, not because they were good at science. But it wasn't like there was a right or wrong answer to that kind of a question. "And pediatrics?"

This time he hesitated. "I think I wanted kids to have a good start in life and this was one way I could help with that."

There was a conviction in his voice that hadn't been there when she'd asked her first question. It seemed like instead of getting to know him better, each revelation made him even more enigmatic than he already was.

The waitress brought back their check and Ellis signed for the meal. She was surprised to see that over an hour had gone by since they'd arrived. Alia would need to be picked up in just fifteen minutes.

"I've been keeping track, don't worry."

Had he read her mind? Because she doubted he was talking about the tab. "Thanks."

What else could she say?

A few minutes later they were at the school and asking how to add someone to the pickup list. Once the forms were filled out, the director pulled out a small digital camera and took Ellis's picture. Lyric cringed at the uneasy look on his face.

This all felt a lot more official than she thought it would. As if she was signing over Alia's care to someone else. She wasn't. At least not permanently. And her mom was on the list, too, and had gone through the exact same steps. But it hadn't seemed weird then. Not like now.

She glanced at Ellis, suddenly feeling like she was

making a terrible mistake, like she'd just opened her life to someone again. Which was ridiculous. She hadn't. She would have asked any number of people in Vegas to do the same.

But those people were her friends, and Ellis was…

An acquaintance. One she'd kissed. One she might have done more with had they not been in a park or interrupted. But it would have been a one-time thing. Something that didn't really mean anything to her emotionally.

And that kind of terrified her. Is that how Jim had seen her?

Evidently, since when she asked where he saw their relationship in five years, the surprised widening of his eyes had said everything. He hadn't seen them anywhere, and certainly not married.

The school administrator thanked them for coming. As if she now saw them as a couple. Lyric wanted to set her straight, but not in front of Ellis. Maybe she could explain that they were just friends later on.

Even though they weren't friends. Not really.

He followed her as she walked toward the door of Alia's classroom. The bottom half of the Dutch door was closed, but the upper part was open, allowing a clear view of what was going on inside the room. The children were bent over some kind of project on their desks. They were drawing. No chaos, no crying. It looked like everything was being done in an orderly manner.

She breathed a sigh of relief, feeling for the first time like she'd made the right decision after loads of self-doubt.

And the decision about Ellis? Well, that wasn't so cut-and-dried.

Alia's teacher came over, looking impossibly young

with her blond hair pulled back in a ponytail and a smock over her clothes. Her aide continued to help the children.

"Hi. She's doing great today. Very little crying."

Lyric clasped her hands in front of her. "I am so glad to hear that." Alia had not even looked up at the door. Instead the tiniest tip of her tongue stuck out in concentration. A huge wave of love washed over her. This child was hers to raise. To protect. To cherish. And she was going to do it for all she was worth.

I'm trying, Tessa. Believe me, I'm trying.

And part of that trying was making sure she kept her priorities straight.

"Let me see if I can tear her away from her artwork."

"What are they drawing?"

Her teacher smiled. "Something they wish for."

Lyric kept her own smile plastered on her face, although a quiver went through her. Was Alia aware enough to have drawn a picture of her mother and wish she was with her and not an aunt? Or was she wishing for a father of her own?

She squelched the urge to look at the man next to her.

Ridiculous. She'd probably drawn a picture of a tree or beach or something. She glanced back to see that Ellis was still behind her. She'd half expected him to turn around and stride in the other direction. Probably the last thing he'd wanted was to get involved with someone who'd taken on her sister's child and promised to raise her.

Well, that was okay, because he *wasn't* involved with her. He was simply a name to put on a required piece of paper. An emergency fill-in.

Kind of like Lyric was? Her heart cramped. She had

to stop thinking like that. She loved her niece and would do anything for her.

A minute later, Alia had her backpack on and came running toward the door, a sheet of paper flapping in her tiny hand.

"Auntie Lyrie! I drew a picture for you."

The teacher opened the door, and at the last second, Lyric remembered she needed to introduce Ellis to her, just in case. "Ms. Taylor, this is Ellis Rohal, he is on my emergency contact list. If I'm ever stuck at work, he has my permission to pick Alia up from school."

Ms. Taylor stuck out her hand. "Nice to meet you. Alia is a special child."

"Nice to meet you, as well."

She was sure he didn't know how to respond to the other part of the teacher's greeting. She realized the enormity of what he'd agreed to do.

Lyric knelt down and hugged her niece, glancing at the paper she was holding out to her. "What's this?"

"It's my new kitten. I wished for her."

Relief and dismay both shot through her system. Relief that the picture was not of Tessa and dismay in that Alia was used to having a dog for company at her mom's house. She hadn't even thought about her wanting a pet here. "Your kitten?"

"Do you like her?"

Lyric forced her gaze to the drawn image on the paper. An all-black shape that might have been a kitten was in front of a girl's stick-figure legs. Alia, probably. And holding Alia's hand was a much taller figure with short dark hair and a skirt. Her heart underwent several more layers of pain. Her sister was a blond, like Alia's teacher. And her mom was gray. So that meant the person in the picture was…her.

Oh, God. Her eyes moistened to a dangerous level, threatening to spill over before she caught hold of herself and forced back the tide.

"I do like her." She stood and turned to Ellis. "Alia, this is a friend of mine—his name is Ellis. You met him once before at my office. He's going to pick you up if I ever can't."

Ellis held out his hand. "Very nice to meet you officially, Alia."

Putting her tiny hand in Ellis's much bigger one, she gave it a careful shake. "Do you have a kitty?"

He shook his head. "I don't, I'm sorry."

"It's okay. I'm getting one. You can come visit her."

Ellis shot her a quizzical look. "I'll have to ask Auntie Lyrie if it's okay."

Hearing him say her name like Alia did made Lyric's chest tighten.

"It's okay, right, Auntie Lyrie?"

"O-of course." Too late, she realized the question had been in reference to him coming to meet her kitten. "But we'll have to see about the kitten. I would hate for her to get lonely when we're not there."

Alia shot Ellis a glance. "Maybe he can stay with her."

"No. He can't. Because he works at the same place I do."

"Oh." The child's face fell.

"But we'll talk about maybe getting a pet." Something that didn't take as much work as a dog did sound pretty appealing. And Lyric missed her parents' dog, too; they'd gotten her not long after she started medical school.

She said goodbye to the teacher, who threw her an apologetic glance, probably because of what Alia had drawn, but it wasn't the woman's fault. She was pretty sure they hadn't coached the kids on what to draw. On impulse, she asked, "Do you know if there's an animal shelter around here?"

"Yes, there's one about a mile from here on Route Fifty-five."

Maybe she would go after Ellis dropped them back off at the hospital.

"I know where it is." The words came from the man beside her. Oh, God, had he thought she'd been hinting that he drive them there?

"Oh, I wasn't implying that you should—"

"I know you weren't. But it's close. If you're really thinking about getting a pet, that is."

She was. At least now. It would be something for Alia to love. A tiny companion who could help the child as much as the child could help a lost or abandoned animal.

She was pretty sure her sister would have approved.

Tessa, this should be you. Why? Why?

But, of course, there was no answer.

Suddenly she was sure of her decision. Maybe Lyric needed something to help her with her grief as well. Some little helper who'd replace sadness with at least a little joy.

"I wasn't thinking about it, but it might be the perfect thing for her. But what about your car?"

"It'll be fine."

Alia put her hand back in Ellis's. "Are you getting a kitten, too?"

"No, but I'll come with you to see what they're like, if that's okay." He looked a little uncomfortable, but he wasn't shaking off her niece's grip. The warmth that had gone through her belly at the park seeped into her again, making her nervous. As did seeing Alia holding his hand. What if she got attached to the man?

Wasn't that another one of her reasons for leaving Vegas? Even though she'd broken it off with Jim before deciding to raise Alia, she'd been half worried that he wouldn't give up and might try to win her back if she stayed. She was pretty sure she would have said no, but why chance it? Part of the reason she'd stayed with him for as long as she had was out of a sense of loneliness. But she'd come to realize he hadn't filled it in any real sense, and she'd finally accepted that he never would.

Neither would Ellis.

So she'd make damn sure he wasn't around Alia enough to break her heart. She was sure he wasn't any more anxious to be a fixture in their lives than she was to have him there. There was nothing to worry about. As soon as they got done at the animal shelter he would be back out of their lives. Or out of Alia's, anyway. And that's all that mattered.

The visitation room at the shelter was busy, surprisingly enough. And the child had not let go of his hand, except for on the drive over there. This wasn't quite what he'd signed up for, but it wasn't like he could just shake her off.

And he was the one who'd offered to drive them over here in the first place. But Lyric had looked stricken when she'd looked at that picture her niece had drawn. He glanced at her now as she peered through the cattery window, where felines of all shapes and sizes were tucked away in different corners or perched on a huge cat tree.

"Are you sure this is what you want to do?" he murmured in a low voice so that Alia couldn't hear. "An animal is a long-term commitment."

"I know. And I actually think it is. But if we find one, I can come back in my own car and pick him or her up."

"Why?"

Her mouth twisted. "Well, you've gone from coming with me to the preschool to volunteering to take us to the animal shelter. I know you said you would, but I don't like asking you to transport him or her, if we find one we agree on."

We agree on.

He knew she was talking about Alia, but the words sent a dart through his midsection. Hell, he'd done this to himself, but at the time it had seemed the right thing to do. And it wasn't like he could back out of it now.

Nor did he want to. Not really. He liked Alia's hand in his more than he wanted to admit, which was part of what made him so uncomfortable. Maybe because he'd once been this child. Or at least had a similar story.

Alia placed her hand on the glass window, and a big scruffy tabby—a slight hitch in his step—moved closer. He seemed to size up the child through the barrier, and then in a surprising move pressed his cheek against the clear surface and rubbed against it.

"Auntie Lyrie! He likes me. Can we have this one?"

Lyric's eyes widened before meeting his. "I don't know, honey. I thought you wanted a kitten."

"He *is* a kitten. And he loves me. He really, really does." The grizzled cat chose that moment to repeat the gesture, and Ellis could almost swear he could hear the animal's purr through the glass.

Lyric knelt and stared at the animal through the glass. "I'm not sure…"

The cat head-butted the glass again, sliding the side

of his face over the area where Alia's hand was again. "Please, Auntie Lyrie. He'll cry if we leave him here."

Subtle blackmail? Surely the child wasn't old enough to use tools like that. But Lyric had mentioned that Alia cried when she left her at day care.

Could an animal feel abandonment, like a human?

"Well, let me ask and see what he's like."

She went over to the desk, leaving Ellis alone with the girl. "*You* like him, don't you?" she asked.

He evaded the question as much as he could. "He seems to like you, that's for sure."

"No, he doesn't. He *loves* me."

Damn if the cat didn't sit in front of them as if waiting for Lyric to come back with her verdict. There was an obvious problem with one of his back legs, and as he looked closer, it seemed that his tail had a slight crook to it. Had he been injured?

Looks like that's two strikes against you, bud.

The cat looked up—as if he understood exactly the odds he was up against—with a suddenness that startled Ellis. And yet, he'd still tried to make a connection. A lump formed in his throat—a rare surge of emotion that he hadn't felt since...

Hell. If Lyric didn't take the cat home, he might just have to do it himself. He'd never really thought of having a pet, preferring his independent life, but this wasn't really about him needing companionship so much as it was about the cat needing someone to take care of him. When you had fifty cats in one space it was hard to give them all an opportunity to be adopted, especially one that looked a little rough around the edges.

He'd noticed the more desirable cats had index cards on the window identifying who they were. As his eyes wandered across the groupings, he didn't see anything on this particular cat.

Lyric came over with the attendant, and he found himself almost hoping she would say she didn't want the cat. She sighed and glanced at him. "He's older. And he probably won't want to play with you very much, Alia. Why don't we look at some of the kittens?"

The child glanced up and fixed her aunt with a look that was far beyond her years as the cat limped a few steps away from them as if knowing he was about to be rejected and was distancing himself first. Ellis shouldn't know how the cat felt, but he wondered if he hadn't done some of the same things, because of his mother's disappearance. It's what reactive-attachment disorder meant, right? That if he didn't attach to others, he couldn't be hurt.

"He's hurt. He needs us."

Ellis knelt down. "What if I said I would take this cat home and help him, and you could help another kitty. One that needs someone like you to play with."

"Ellis…" His name came from the woman standing above him. "You don't have to."

"I actually want to. Unless Alia has her heart set on him. Does he have a story?"

The attendant said, "Well…this is Max's second time at the shelter. He was adopted once—a few months ago—and…" She glanced at Lyric as if asking for something.

"Alia, why don't you come with me to look at the kittens while Ellis talks to this nice lady about Max."

"You promise you'll help him? And that I can see him?"

"I do."

The child let go of his hand and went with her aunt to another cattery, where younger cats were.

The attendant handed Ellis an index card that looked like the others that were stuck to the glass. He soon saw why it was not on display. By the time he finished reading it, the knuckles of one hand had curled in on itself in anger and disgust. The decision was made. "I'll take him."

"You can go into a visitation room with him if you want. Even though Max has been through the wringer, he has stayed just as sweet as ever. We all love him here and…" She sized him up. "We want to make sure this never happens to him again."

"It won't. You have my word. Or better yet, you can send someone to check on him from time to time and make sure he's being well treated."

The woman's lip trembled. "Thank you for giving him a chance. He truly deserves it."

In the end, two cat carriers went into his BMW. One with the grizzled old man who'd earned a second shot at happiness and one with a kitten named Shiloh. They were as different as night and day. Shiloh was a multicolored calico who was as spunky and lively as Max was laid-back.

Lyric made sure that Alia was buckled into the car seat and when Ellis went to open the door for her, she stopped him with a hand on his arm. "Thank you. That cat didn't deserve what happened to him, and I was afraid that as much as Alia might have wanted to adopt him, she might hurt him without meaning to. I'll teach her to be careful, but a kitten is a better choice for us." Her hand squeezed for a second and let go. "I guess under that gruff exterior lays a soft heart." She grinned. "I'm talking about Max, of course."

No, she wasn't. But he liked it. And hell if he didn't want to extend that moment of contact between them. He'd better figure out a way to take a few steps back before he wound up with more than a cat. That wouldn't be fair to Alia or her aunt. He did not do emotional attachments, despite Lyric's statement. And if he tried, he had no doubt that he would end up hurting them both. He wasn't sure he could attach to a cat, much less a human being. And from what Lyric had told him about Alia, she, like Max, deserved someone who could love her the way a parent loved a child. This was not some science experiment that you could play with and then toss out and start again. This was Alia's life.

He decided that unless the child asked to come over and visit Max, he wasn't going to offer. It was one thing to be a contact person on a list at a day care and another thing entirely to spend a lot of time with them. So he'd done his good deed for the year and would try not to step up and do anything else.

With his hand on the latch, he gave a pull and opened the door for her without a word, effectively breaking whatever moment there'd been between them. "We need to get the cats home. Do you need me to stop and get anything for yours?"

She glanced at him and then shook her head. "Nope. Alia and I can do it when we pick up my car. There's a big pet store that'll let us bring Shiloh in so she won't have to sit in the car. I'm pretty sure we're going to be in there for a while. Thankfully, my landlord accepts pets."

He hadn't even thought about that, since he owned his place. "I'm glad it worked out for you."

She tilted her head with a frown. "Is something wrong?"

He was acting like a jerk. Well, maybe not a jerk exactly, but he knew he'd gone from friendly to stand-offish. But he wasn't sure how to step back any other way. "No. Just didn't expect to wind up adopting a cat."

"Oh, God, I am so—"

"No, I didn't mean it like that. It was my decision and no one else's. And Alia was right, the cat needed someone. And you were right that he needed an adult. At least at this stage, until he's fully healed."

The cat's background had included the fact that a teenager had swung him around by one of his back legs, effectively snapping one of the bones. No vet care had been offered and the bone had healed badly. Fortunately a neighbor had reported a later incident, and the cat had been seized and returned to the shelter. But his tail had been broken so badly that it would be permanently crooked and he was very touchy about having it messed with. He could see why. Ellis would be touchy, too.

In fact, he was, too, just about things other than his physical well-being.

He forced a smile. "It looks like it was fate that we were both there when we were. Max will get a home where he no longer has to worry about being hurt, and Shiloh gets a home where she can run and play to her little heart's content."

"Thanks for offering to let Alia visit him. I promise she won't abuse the privilege."

He was hoping she'd forgotten about that. "It's fine."

It wasn't, but at least she was cognizant of the fact that he wasn't interested in a swinging-door policy.

After closing the car door, he went around to his own side and got in, started the engine and backed out of the shelter's parking lot. And then he headed back the way he'd come just a few hours earlier. When life had been simpler and when he'd had only himself to worry about.

He'd wondered if hiring the behavioral therapist was going to mess up his grant plans. It had, but not in quite the way he'd thought it would.

If he wasn't careful, this could cost him a lot more than a few pieces of expensive equipment. In fact, if he'd had a heart, he was pretty sure it would be in mortal danger.

So he would just have to make sure that that particular organ had no chance of being resuscitated. By Lyric, her niece or anyone else.

CHAPTER EIGHT

SHILOH BOUNCED OFF the couch and into Alia's arms, much to the child's delight. Despite Lyric's reservations, this had been the right decision after she'd seen the picture her niece had drawn. Hopefully things would continue to go well. A week had passed and Alia was no longer crying when she went to preschool, maybe because she knew that her kitten was at home waiting for her. And her interactions were suddenly a lot more vibrant, according to her teacher. She'd insisted on bringing a picture of Shiloh to class, and Ms. Taylor had taped it to her cubby space, where Alia could see it every time she took something out or put it back.

"We have to go, honey. We'll be late to school."

"Okay." She put Shiloh back down on the couch. "'Bye, Shy. I'll see you after school."

With that she ran toward the door with none of the usual complaints. When Lyric told her mom they'd adopted a cat, she was thrilled and said Lyric's dad was as well. Alia had always loved animals.

What she didn't tell her mom was that she had gone to the shelter with Ellis, since her mom would immediately start formulating various scenarios that would wind up with Lyric married in them. She'd done the same thing when she was dating Jim and, unfortunately,

Lyric had gotten caught up in some of those fictional worlds and started to actually believe in fairy tales. Well, no more. She was a little older and a whole lot wiser. At least she hoped she was.

Once she dropped off Alia at school, she headed to work. She hadn't seen Ellis in a couple of days, but that wasn't surprising, since his mornings tended to be a whole lot busier than hers were. At least at first. Lyric was rapidly catching up to him in that area as more and more people heard of the new behavioral endocrinologist's presence at the hospital. He'd warned her that she would have to manage her time in order to not be overrun with patients and doctors needing opinions.

And she had met with the hospital's psychiatrist—with Dr. Lawson's approval—and found her to be very friendly and knowledgeable. Whatever reservations she'd sensed from Ellis hadn't been mirrored in the administrator's position. Maybe it was a territorial issue. Except, contrary to what she might have thought when she'd first met him, he really didn't seem to be.

Oh, well. It didn't matter. What did matter was that Theresa Radner and the behavioral department were behind Lyric's efforts to start a mentoring program that was coordinated by some of the local rehab centers. So far she'd called the one in Merit, the district she and Ellis had visited. And if he didn't have time to go with her to the rest of the areas, Dr. Radner had offered to help her check them out. A bonus was the psychiatrist knew several of the directors of the rehab centers and could act as a liaison between New Mercy and the centers.

She breezed into the hospital, her mood light for once, anxious to get her day started. She exited the elevator onto the fourth floor and headed to her office, only to find Ellis outside of it waiting for her.

"Am I late for something?" She glanced at her phone. She'd been extraordinarily careful to be on time ever since their first bristly meeting.

"No, just wanted to catch you before your day started."

"It looks like yours already has."

He shook his head. "I'm just an early bird, although my new roommate has been keeping me up late at nights."

Shock made her go very still. His new roommate?

As if sensing her surprise, his eyebrows went up. "Max? The cat? Surely you haven't forgotten our trip to the shelter."

Before she could stop it, every muscle in her body seemed to relax at once, threatening to send her slithering to the ground. She quickly stiffened her back. "Of course. I thought maybe you'd rented out a room or something."

The or-something part was really where her head had been parked. Although to find a special someone a week after they'd kissed? That would have changed her view of him, although she wasn't sure why. The kiss had meant nothing. To either of them.

Right?

Right. She'd learned her lesson when it came to that. She wasn't going to let herself get caught up in those kinds of mind games ever again. Nor was she going to let her mom blow things out of proportion, which is why she'd kept things such a secret.

"No, I think two curmudgeons are enough for one bachelor pad."

"I think you're probably right. Especially two perpetual bachelors. Although *curmudgeon* is a pretty apt term as well."

"You've been talking to Dave."

Oh, great. She really didn't want him to think she and the Realtor had been gossiping about him. She had only talked to Dave one other time since signing the lease on her place. He'd called to see how things were going and to let her know if she ever needed someone to talk to, to feel free to contact him. She didn't need someone, so she'd never called him back. She'd halfway wondered if he'd been hinting at wanting to go out on a date with her, but if so, she wasn't interested. He was a nice guy, but he certainly wasn't…

That was one blank she was not going to fill in.

"Not much, no." She didn't remember Dave actually using the word *perpetual*, just the fact he'd made a point of saying Ellis was never going to marry. And her earlier attempt at humor had evidently missed the mark.

"Hmm."

She unlocked her office door and motioned him in. "How is Max, anyway?"

"He's actually at the vet's office this morning—the real reason I'm here so early. He has to have the piece of his tail below the break amputated because of nerve damage and the fear that he might injure it more or get it caught somewhere."

"Oh, no! Poor guy. How's his leg?"

"He'll always have a limp—the vet says it's due to a joint fusing near where his break was. He assured me it looks more painful than it actually is, and he gets around fine. It makes him look tough."

Like his owner, although Ellis definitely didn't have a limp.

"A shorter tail will make him look even tougher." She

sat behind her desk and waited for him to find a seat, as well. "So what did you want to talk to me about?"

"I wanted to run something by you. The grant donor is having a small ceremony at his office building to officially present the hospital with a check. Jack would like each person who will benefit from it to explain their vision and how they hope it will help the people in our city."

"But, I'm not sure how that affects..." Her brain stopped for a second before restarting. "You mean the addiction-mentor program is actually getting some of the money?"

"Yes. Jack wanted it, and seeing that girl on the ground convinced me we need to help if we can."

"Alisha."

"What?"

"That's her name." She wasn't sure why it was so important that he recognize that there was a name that went with the face, but it was.

"Okay. Seeing *Alisha* convinced me."

"Sorry. I didn't mean that to come out the way it did." She paused to think through what he'd said. "What do I need to do exactly? Write up a revised proposal so Jack can read it at the ceremony?"

"No, he'd like us—as in you and me—to both be there and give a presentation."

"Can't you just roll mine into yours?" The thought of having to speak and possibly ruin the hospital's chances of getting the grant horrified her. "What if they change their minds after hearing me?"

"Not a chance. Just talk to them the way you presented it to me. You'll do great." He looked at her. "And I'll be right there, Lyric, I promise."

The way he'd said it made goose bumps roll up her

arms. Like it included more than just the presentation. But she'd better disabuse herself of that idea and fast.

"Jack really wants me to do this?"

"Yes. And so do I."

He did? Lord. First they'd revived a girl, then he'd agreed to be Alia's emergency pickup and then they'd adopted cats together. And now they were going to be giving a presentation? Together? A warning light went off in her head.

I hear those wheels turning, Ly. Do not take his words to mean more than they're meant to.

A thought hit her. "When is it? I have Alia. If it's at night…"

"It is. Tell you what, she can come with us. You can watch her during my speech, and I can watch her during yours."

"I couldn't ask that. Maybe my mom can come. How far out is the date?"

He smiled. "It's this coming Monday."

Today was Wednesday. There was no way her mom could get here by then. "What would you do if I had six children and had no one to watch them?"

"But you don't." He leaned forward. "Do you want this as much as I do?"

Another shiver went down her spine. Bigger, this time. Were they still talking about the money? She swallowed. "I do. Very much so."

"Good."

She tried to shake her thoughts free. "What is the dress code?"

"Suit and tie for men, a suit or dress for women." He smiled. "I'll be honest. I don't think anyone has ever come in and wowed Jack so quickly or completely."

Did he think she'd manipulated him? "I—I just feel strongly about it. I wasn't trying to—"

"I know. And I wasn't implying you were. I was just surprised. And yet maybe not as surprised now as I was that first day."

She had no idea what he meant and was too afraid to pick apart what he'd said, just in case she took a wrong turn and misunderstood something. "Are you sure you can't just tack my presentation onto yours?"

"I believe in giving credit where credit is due. I think you're going to be a wonderful asset to this hospital. And people in the community need to hear your passion, the way Jack did. The way I did."

He'd never said anything like that to her before and it was hard not to feel swept off her feet by it. But if she was smart, she'd keep those feet firmly planted on the ground. Where they belonged.

"Okay, I'll try. But I can't guarantee not to fall flat on my face."

"You won't. I'm sure of it."

"How about if I write up the presentation and send it to you for your thoughts? I'm sure you've done these before. I haven't." She couldn't help but think New Mercy was right where she belonged, despite her first missteps and uncertainties about being here.

"I have. I'm sure you'll do fine, but I'll be happy to look at it, if it will make you feel better."

"It definitely will, thank you. If I get it to you by Friday, will that be enough time?" She couldn't believe she was just now hearing about this. Surely it had been in the works for a while. Unless she'd just been added to the recipient list. Maybe Ellis wasn't kidding, and he'd had to be convinced before he was willing to let a cent of that grant money leave his hands. Should she be irritated…or grateful?

The latter.

Lyric's phone buzzed and she glanced at the readout. "It's the ER, wonder what they want…" She picked it up and answered. "Dr. Westphal here."

The words on the other line ran together for a second or two until one name suddenly stood out and made her blood turn to ice.

Alisha.

The patient they had just been talking about was down in the ER and her sister was asking for them.

"What happened?"

The words *coded* and *life support* stood out among the others, all given in a crisp, matter-of-fact voice by whoever was on the other end. Her heart pounded until she thought it was going to explode. She realized the staff member was still talking and that she was just sitting there frozen. Ellis took the phone from her nerveless fingers and talked to whoever was speaking. Unlike her, he asked lots of questions and listened to the responses before hanging up.

"Come on, Lyric. Alisha's sister is asking for us. Her parents are there, as well."

Somehow she got up from her desk, feeling totally numb. This couldn't be happening. She had done CPR. Ellis had administered naloxone, and they'd gotten her back. And now, a little over a week later, she was back in the hospital. But this time, she hadn't regained consciousness.

She followed Ellis to the elevator and down they went to the first floor, all thoughts of the grant and presentation wiped away. He'd explained that Alisha had hidden a small packet of heroin in her room and had tried to inject herself with a smaller dose this time, but the thought was that the drugs had been laced with fentanyl, making even that small dose more potent than her slight frame could handle. Only this time, everything had happened in private, away from the eyes and ears of people who might have helped. A late dose of naloxone had helped revive her, but her brain had been without oxygen for too long. Tests were still being done, but they suspected she could be brain-dead.

The doors opened, and Lyric stepped out of the elevator, the contents of her stomach swirling. She'd just insisted on Ellis using the girl's name, and now it seemed so ludicrous. What did that matter in the grand scheme of things? A girl was dead or possibly dying and no one had been there to help. There'd been no mentor program...no safety net to help catch a girl who'd been free-falling toward oblivion.

An ache settled in Lyric's chest that she doubted would ever go away.

She felt numb. She hugged the grieving parents, listening as they thanked her for trying to save their daughter the last time. Listened as they wished there had been some kind of help for Alisha. Listened as the words *organ donation* were mentioned in hushed tones.

She wanted to yell at them to stop. To say that maybe things would be okay, but deep down she knew they weren't going to be. Not this time. Finally she turned as someone tapped her. Alisha's sister fell into her arms with gasping sobs, a world of grief and guilt in the tears. A guilt Lyric could relate to all too well. Because she'd felt the exact same guilt after her own sister had died.

She'd tried for years to find Tessa some help—she and her parents both had—but every ounce of success had been met with a pound of failure. She and her parents had sacrificed so much in terms of time and money…and love. If only Lyric had been able to…

Suddenly she knew she was going to give that presentation to make sure neither Tessa nor Alisha were forgotten. Not by her. Not by Ellis. Not by this hospital.

"Are you okay?" Ellis slid a cup of hospital coffee into Lyric's hands, her fingers icy against his.

He was worried. He knew she'd taken Alisha's drug overdose seriously, but seeing the color drain from her face as she'd held her phone to her ear had made him realize something terrible had happened. Doctors were supposed to be objective parties, able to separate themselves from what went on with their patients. He was the master at doing that. But they all had that one patient who touched them in a way that others couldn't. There was no rhyme or reason, and this was evidently Lyric's "someone." And he was pretty sure it was because of her sister.

"No. I'm really not. God, how could this have happened? She wasn't a habitual user. She was experimenting."

"Sometimes that's all it takes."

They sat on the sofa in his office. He'd pushed back his first surgery by an hour, unable to leave Lyric like this.

"But she seemed to be interested in getting help. Her sister is still in a program, in fact."

"I know." He took a swig of his own coffee, trying to think of something to say that would help.

Lyric kicked off her shoes and curled into the corner of the couch, seeming very small and unsure. "I'm wracking my brain for a way we could have done things differently."

Her beautiful eyes were clouded with the sadness that came with their profession. It was the unfortunate reality of working in health care, but something inside of him wanted to find a way to wipe away her pain. But there was no pat answer. No magic formula. All he could do was speak the truth and hope it helped.

"We had very little time with either of those girls. The fact that Alisha's sister even remembered your name is shocking."

Although Lyric probably would have taken it even harder if they'd gotten the news secondhand. And with organ donations the way they were, there was no doubt they would have heard about Alisha eventually.

Right now they were waiting on the verdict of the latest EEG and CAT scan of her head, although things really didn't look good.

As if the universe had heard his thoughts, his phone buzzed at almost the exact same time as hers did.

She sat up, her back going ramrod-straight. "Here it comes."

Ellis looked down at the text, which had the results of both tests. They confirmed what the specialists thought. There was no brain function. The only thing keeping her alive were the machines.

Alisha would never regain consciousness. Would never hug her parents or graduate from high school.

"I'm sorry, Lyric. I wish it was better news."

"So do I. It's so hard to believe." She paused for a second before continuing. "Do they do anything to honor the donors?"

"Do anything?" He wasn't sure what she meant. "Like a memorial service?"

"No, like a walk where we can stand in the aisles to

acknowledge the decision to save others' lives through organ donation."

New Mercy had been doing that for almost a year. It was always a solemn procession with family and hospital staff alike participating. "We do. A text will be sent out with the time. As many staff participate as possible. I have a couple of patients waiting on organs. It's a strange mixture of sadness and celebration because she'll be helping others, even if we couldn't help her. But we tried, Lyric. Know that. We genuinely tried."

He wasn't sure why it was so important for her to know that, but something urged him to back up the words with a physical touch. So he slid his arm around her, feeling her scoot closer as she laid her head against his shoulder. She gave a slight sigh, which burrowed into his chest and did a number on something in there. Something that made him want to stay right there and not move. At least for a while. And that was not like him. At all.

"I'm not normally this weepy, I promise," she said. "Today was just hard."

Maybe he wasn't the only one struggling through unfamiliar territory.

"I know. But as hard as it is, Alisha will do some good beyond just organ donation. Because of her, others may have access to better services than she did. And maybe this will be the wakeup call her sister needs to get her life straight. Maybe one day, she'll be one of those mentors who helps others like her sister."

"I hope so."

His arm was still around her, but the weight of her body felt good against him. Maybe he was drawing some comfort from her, as well. Kind of like Max, the cat?

Ha! That cat had no problems forming attachments. Ellis knew he should move away, but it couldn't hurt to stay here a little longer. "Done with your coffee?"

"Yes, thanks." She handed it to him, shifting slightly as he set the cup on the glass-topped coffee table in front of him. Something about this whole thing seemed strangely...comfortable, in a way he'd not felt with other women.

He chalked it up to supporting someone he'd had a shared experience with. And not that kiss. The shared experience of losing a patient.

He'd soon forget any of this ever happened. Right?

Except no matter how many times he recited that mantra, another little voice was whispering in the background that it was all one big lie. And that if he didn't move away soon, something irrevocable was going to happen.

So he patted her shoulder. "I probably need to see about my surgical patient, but feel free to stay here as long as you want."

She sat up in a hurry, making him regret saying anything. "No, I'm fine, and I need to check on some things as well. Jacob Sellers is coming in with his parents in the morning so they can administer the first actual dose of his growth hormone, so I need to make sure I'm ready for that. And I want to work on my presentation."

"You don't have to do that right now."

"I want to. While everything is still fresh in my mind."

While what was still fresh? Certainly not this exact moment of finding themselves snuggled together on the couch like an old married couple.

No. Not a married couple. Or a couple of any kind. Despite his wandering imagination.

He stood, trying to convince himself that he hadn't done anything wrong, had merely comforted a coworker the way he would comfort anyone. Except he'd never felt the need to comfort anyone before. In fact, he normally left the scene at the first hint of tears of any kind, whether it was in his personal or professional life.

And yet, Lyric was no longer crying. And she seemed ready to get back to work, so maybe he'd done the right thing after all.

At least he hoped so. Otherwise he was going to have a mess on his hands that wouldn't be as easy to clean up as it had been to make.

CHAPTER NINE

ON THURSDAY, SHE'D just typed the final lines of her presentation when news came that Alisha York's organs were viable and would be harvested. Her lungs, liver and one of her kidneys would go to recipients in this hospital, while her heart and other tissue would be transported to other facilities. Lyric had seen Jacob Sellers this morning and had helped his parents administer the first of many shots. They'd done great, the hope of a new start to their son's life a stark contrast to what Alisha's parents and sister were now going through.

Ellis had been so kind yesterday—there hadn't been a hint of impatience at her emotionalism. It was a relief, really. He could have given her a lecture on getting too involved. But he hadn't. Instead, he'd wrapped his arm around her and murmured comforting words to her. She couldn't remember everything he'd said, but she'd felt cared for in a way that she hadn't felt in a very long time.

She had no idea where the tears had come from. She couldn't remember the last time she'd cried over a patient. But Ellis had seemed to understand.

At least until the end, when he'd suddenly seemed uncomfortable.

Had she given off some kind of weird, needy vibes

at some point? Lord, she hoped not. That was the last thing she needed.

But she was working on it. She'd almost convinced herself that what had happened in his office was an anomaly. Something that wouldn't be repeated, if she could help it.

That's all she could do, since she couldn't go back and erase the feeling of his arm around her. Nor did she want to. But that didn't mean he had to know that.

She emailed a copy of the presentation to Ellis. She'd told him she'd have it to him by Friday, but the words had poured out of her once she started writing, so she decided to go with it. She glanced at her phone just as it pinged. Staff had been invited to join in what the hospital called an Honor Walk that would start in an hour. Lyric had a short internal debate about whether she should go or not, before deciding she needed to. She not only wanted to honor Alisha's life, but also wanted to support the family in these moments of grief, even if they never knew she was there.

Should she text Ellis?

No. He would have received the same message. Whether he went or not was up to him. She was pretty sure she wouldn't turn into a waterworks on him this time. She'd pretty much cried herself out yesterday. One thing she could be glad of was that the girl's struggle was over. She wouldn't linger in some institution—hooked to machines—with no one quite sure as to what to do with her.

She finished up some loose ends on some paperwork and then went down to ICU, where other staff members were already lining up. She spotted Ellis about ten yards up the line and gave him a quick wave. He made no move to come over to where she was, so she stayed in place. Five minutes later, the doors at the end of the hallways swung open and Alisha's bed came into sight.

She swallowed as the transplant team slowly pushed the hospital bed, various cords and tubes strung over the back and snaking up poles that were attached to the bed. Behind Alisha came her parents, her sister and several people she didn't recognize but seemed to be members of the girl's family.

Staff had been through this before, but it was still a terrible and yet awesome sight to see so many people as they said goodbye to one life and placed the patient in the hands of the skilled surgeons who would have a massive undertaking to get everything completed in a timely manner.

Alisha passed by where she was standing, and Lyric had to resist the urge to touch the child's hand. Glancing over at Ellis, she caught him looking at her. Maybe wondering if she was going to lose it again? She wasn't. If anything, she felt kind of numb. She'd been honest. What had happened yesterday was a rarity. Maybe because there was no one she trusted enough with those kinds of emotions.

Not anymore.

Except she had yesterday. Did that mean she trusted Ellis? She wasn't sure. But she sensed he wasn't really the ideal person to let down her guard around. Maybe because of how controlled he seemed most of the time.

Alisha's sister walked by, sobbing softly by her mother's side. She saw Lyric and hesitated. Lyric mouthed "it's okay." And that seemed to help the girl, whose dragging feet seemed to pick up the pace. This would probably be the last time she saw this family. At least she hoped so. Not because she didn't want to see them, but because she didn't want to meet under these circumstances again. If her program proved successful, Lyric hoped the emergency room would see a reduction in patients like Alisha, and those who were physically and emotionally addicted to drugs. At least, that was her dream. What she hoped this grant money would help with.

As the procession rounded the corner and was gone from sight, staff members slowly disbursed and went back to work. She was turning to do the same when Ellis caught up with her. "Hey, I got your email. I haven't had a chance to read your presentation yet, but I will tonight, if Max lets me." He gave a quick smile.

"No hurry. I just finished it sooner than I thought I would and decided to send it on over."

"I haven't even started mine yet, so you're ahead of me."

She stopped and propped her back against the wall behind her as a thought hit her. "Will any of your patients get Alisha's organs?"

"Yes. One. The transplant team will be doing the surgery. In fact, the patient has already been prepped and they're just waiting for the signal to head to the operating room."

"I'm glad. Not about Alisha, but that she'll be able to help some other people. I'd like to think she'd be glad, too."

"I think she would. Her parents are doing a good thing." He glanced down at her, green eyes sliding over her face.

"Yes, they are."

He paused. "Did Jacob Sellers come in?"

"Yes, I'm sorry, I thought I told you he was due in today."

"You did. I just had a full surgical schedule today, so couldn't stop in. I take it he did well?"

She nodded. "He did great. So did Mom and Dad. They're not going to have any problems administering the meds."

"Good to hear."

She swallowed, feeling tongue-tied all of a sudden. Maybe because they hadn't talked about what had happened in his office yesterday. Well, they had a little, but they hadn't resolved where they stood with each other.

As far as she was concerned, they were coworkers with cases that just so happened to overlap. Laying her head on his shoulder wasn't what she should be doing with him. The sooner she remembered that, the better.

"Max still doing okay?"

"He is. Shiloh and Alia?"

"Thick as thieves and doing great. Once we get our own permanent place, we may even add another kitten so Shiloh isn't alone during the day when Alia starts kindergarten in the fall."

"I didn't realize she was almost five."

"Yes, her birthday is next month, as hard as that is to believe." Also hard to believe was the fact that her sister would be gone for seven months by then. Would Alisha's family feel the same way once that period of time passed?

Undoubtedly.

"Will your parents come out to celebrate?"

"Yes. They're excited. So is Alia."

He seemed to hesitate for a second. "Can I ask you to take a look at something?"

"Of course. Is it about a patient?"

She gave an internal eye roll. What else would he be asking her to look at?

"Not exactly."

Intrigued, she gave a nod. If it wasn't a patient, then what?

"Where is it?"

"At my house."

That made her blink. "Okay. When?"

"This afternoon, if you have time. If not it can wait until later."

"I should be able to. I'll have to pick Alia up at two so I'll have her with me if you need it to be later than that."

"Do you have any more patients today?"

She shook her head. "No, just some paperwork, but I can do it tomorrow, if need be."

Ellis was breathtaking today in black jeans and a white button-down shirt. His sleeves were rolled up, revealing tanned forearms, the muscles in them well defined. She had to harden herself to keep from staring.

"Can you follow me over?"

"Sure."

He gave her the address in case they got separated and said it was about a fifteen-minute drive from the hospital. Her curiosity was killing her. What on earth could he want her to look at? Unless it was some question on carpet color or something. If so, he was going to be horribly disappointed because she was not good at decorating. She'd always kept to whites and used throw pillows to give a punch of color. They were easy to exchange, if she wanted to, although she'd had the same set for the last five years. She and Tessa had gone shopping for her sofa and ottoman together, in fact. The pieces were getting a little worn after all this time but she couldn't bear to get rid of them. It was one of the last things the sisters had done together before Tessa's addiction had gotten really bad.

True to his word, they were at his place in no time, parking in front of his house. Like his BMW, his house was nice, but not over-the-top. The landscaping looked professionally cared for, which she could understand, since he worked so much.

She turned off the car, got out and met him at the front door. There, he said, "Feel free to say no. I won't be offended."

Lyric gulped, her mind swirling in a hundred different directions, but none of it made any sense. She was pretty sure he hadn't brought her here to have sex with her. And why would he assume she might say no to whatever it was. "Okay."

This time the word wasn't quite as sure as it had been earlier. If he did ask her something unexpected, would she turn him down?

Of course she would, one side of her brain said with a pointed look. Except the other side was a little less sure of itself and a little more eager to find out what this mysterious "something" was.

He opened the door, and waited for her to slide past him. Once inside, she glanced around. A leather sectional took up most of the space, looking long and comfortable enough to...

To nothing, Ly. No thinking along those lines.

Hadn't she just said she shouldn't trust this man with her emotions?

"It's in my shop."

His shop as in store? She glanced around, but saw no sign of anything like that, unless it was in a different part of the house. "Where is that?"

"Out back."

A meow came from behind her, making her turn. Max!

He was slowly making his way toward them, the limp from his hind leg still evident. And his tail was definitely shorter. By about three inches. She knelt in front of him. "Hi, bud. How're you doing?"

He rubbed his cheek against her hand and kept moving, until he made a complete circle around her and came back to where he started. "He looks like he's healing up well."

"He's doing great, although I will say that he's a bed hog."

She laughed, although the thought of this cat snuggling against Ellis's lanky form made her stomach tense in a way she didn't like. Before she could stop the words, she said, "He's a lucky boy."

He looked at her for a long minute. "I'd say we both are."

Leading the way into the kitchen, he stopped in front of the refrigerator, Max still on their heels. "Would you like something to drink?"

"Actually a beer, if you have one."

He glanced at her with raised eyebrows that she thought showed a hint of admiration. "I think I'll join you." Opening the door, he took out two longnecks, cradling them between his index and ring fingers, palm up. The bottles clanked together invitingly.

"I don't keep alcohol at home because of Alia, so this is a treat."

He laughed. "I never thought of beer as a treat, but I can see your point."

He opened the bottles with an opener he had hanging on the side of a cabinet. After handing her one of the bottles, he tipped his head and took a long pull at his, his throat moving in a way that caught her right below the ribs.

Stifling the urge to stare, she quickly followed his lead, letting the bitter brew linger on her tongue for a minute before she let it flow down her throat.

"Mmm, thanks." She leaned a hip against the cabinet and took another sip.

"You're welcome. The shop is just out here." He opened a sliding glass door and, using a foot to block Max from getting out, he stepped out onto a brick patio. The red herringbone fit in with the brick facade of the house's exterior.

"You have a beautiful home."

His head tilted. "Thanks. Max is making me spend more time inside it than I have in the past."

His voice sounded strange. Like he wasn't crazy about that fact. Or was it that he was so busy at the hospital, that he didn't get a chance to be here?

"Alia has done the same for me."

And she realized it was true. Her niece was quickly making her into a homebody, something she'd never seen herself as being, although she'd eventually hoped she'd have a family of her own.

She'd thought that would be with Jim, at one point. And actually, she wasn't sure why she'd ever thought that. Looking back, she could see that his focus was on his job. Most of their time together was spent in bed with very little interaction outside of that.

What had she been thinking?

A large building sat at the back of the yard, looking almost like a barn, except it couldn't be, since they were just on the outskirts of the city of Atlanta. What in the world did he need something this for?

Leading the way back to it, Ellis unlocked a side door and motioned her inside, clicking on a light. She blinked, standing there for a second, unsure at first of what she was looking at. There were several worktables that held various saws and drills, along with machines she didn't recognize. On several of the tables were pieces of wood. Some were spindles and others had curved legs.

That's right. His calluses. He said he'd gotten them from woodworking. She noticed a rocker made out of a light-colored wood sitting off to the side. It was gorgeous, and the large curved back looked like it was made from a single piece of wood. "Wow, Ellis. This is beautiful. You made this?"

"I did. Do you like it?" He moved over and gripped the back of it, pushing it slightly so that it rocked back and forth.

It was gorgeous.

"Like it? I love it. Who did you make this for, or do you sell your pieces?"

"I do sometimes, although I don't really like doing it. Dave has one of my rocking chairs. As does Jack."

The hospital administrator? Well, she'd thought they were friends, so that made sense. "Are their chairs just like this one?"

"Not exactly. I make the backs just a bit different, so that each one is unique."

She studied it. The spindles coming off the arms of the chair were like the ones she saw on another table. "How many of these have you made?"

"This is number six. I put a little stainless tag under the seat of each one listing its number." He shrugged. "I experimented with different pieces of furniture before realizing what I really like to make are rocking chairs."

"I can see why. Is this what you wanted me to look at?"

"Yes."

He wanted her to see it? Why? There was no question it was beautiful, but she was a little confused. It was like he was giving her a small peek at his life, without telling her what he expected her to do with it.

But she liked that he trusted her enough to let her see this. Especially since he'd only made six of these. Had he brought other women here?

Something she didn't need to be thinking about. Especially since she'd pictured herself taking Max's place in bed just a few minutes earlier.

And what had he meant that he wouldn't be offended if she said no? Maybe he wanted her opinion on one of his projects?

"If you want to know what I think, I would say this is a work of art. The new owner will be very lucky."

"And if I wanted Alia to have it?"

"Alia?" She frowned. "I don't understand."

"You said her birthday is next month. And I don't have anyone to give this to."

Shock dried her mouth, making it hard to speak. "Ellis, I can't accept this. Not without paying for it. Unless it costs a fortune…not that it wouldn't be worth it." Her words were tumbling out faster and faster. She was trying very hard not to read too much into his offer, although her heart was racing ahead and saying all kinds of crazy things. "I don't think you should be—"

"I'm not selling it. I want Alia to have it."

Her throat tightened. Surely he had family who would want something he made. "What about your parents? Or siblings?"

"I don't have any."

None? They hadn't talked about his relatives, but surely he had someone. Except he said that he didn't. And the way he said it—matter-of-fact, as if it was no big deal. But it was. Didn't he know that family was everything? At least to her.

The tightness in her throat grew. "I'm sorry. I didn't know."

"It's okay. My mom's been gone for a long time, and I don't have brothers or sisters."

He didn't offer any more information; evidently his dad wasn't in the picture and his grandparents were no longer alive, either, or he would have mentioned them.

"But there must be someone else you want to have it."

He gave the rocker another slight push. "I really just make these to unwind, so I'm not interested in making money off of them. I just want someone to enjoy it. Someone like Alia. She can rock Shiloh in it."

How would she feel seeing this in her house day in and day out, knowing he'd made it—that he'd wanted Alia to have it? She wasn't sure.

This would be something her niece could pass down to her own children someday. "I don't know, Ellis. And can I just say, you make me feel like a slug. The only thing I do on my off time is clean house and maybe pull a few weeds."

"You are no slug. You work hard. Alia is very fortunate to have you. More than you could ever know."

The words contained a sincerity that shook her to the core.

"Thank you. I appreciate that." She took a deep breath, suddenly knowing what she was going to do, whether it was wise or not. "I know she would love it. It'll go nicely with her bed and dresser. As long as Shiloh doesn't use it as a scratching post."

"The oak is pretty tough. I think it can withstand a scratch or two. And if not, it'll give the piece character."

Character, huh?

She motioned toward the seat. "Can I? I have to admit, I'll probably be sharing this with Alia…and Shiloh."

"Please."

Lowering herself onto the smooth wooden surface, she was surprised at how well the chair cradled her. The seat was curved in a slight *S* shape that supported her bottom and thighs—the height was perfect, as well. It was comfortable. Very comfortable. And Ellis had carved this out by hand, put it together piece by piece, sanding it, smoothing a protective finish along each curve and hollow.

It was on the tip of her tongue to ask him again if he was sure about giving this away, but she sensed he wouldn't appreciate her throwing back his offer in his face. "It's wonderful. I didn't see one in the house."

"I have one in each of the three bedrooms."

Bedrooms. Including his?

That's right. He said he'd built six of them. If he'd given ones to Jack and Dave, that left four, including this one. So this would only be the third chair he'd given away. A strange warmth went through her, sweeping from her belly up through her chest and into her face. "I'm honored."

"It's nothing. It'll be a relief not to have fifty chairs gathering dust out here."

It might be nothing to him. But it meant a lot to her. "Can you keep it here until her birthday? I'd like to sneak it into her room while she's at school and put a bow on it. I imagine she and Shiloh will get a lot of rocking time in."

"I can. If you let me know when you want it, I can bring it over."

She looked a bit dubious. "In your BMW?"

"I fit the last two in there, so, yes."

"Okay, thank you, then. Her birthday is the fifteenth, so if we could do it in the early afternoon…" She blinked, an idea coming to mind. "Actually, why don't you stay for cake afterward. I'm sure Alia would love it."

"I'll have to see what my schedule looks like that day, but if it's not too hectic, I should be able to."

He didn't sound all that thrilled, and she could have kicked herself. She was doing exactly what she'd warned herself about: making a bigger deal out of this chair than she should have. And what was she thinking inviting him? Hadn't she already lectured herself about not letting Alia get attached to him? It wouldn't take much. After all, look at her, Lyric herself was quickly becoming enamored with the pediatrician. She'd almost swooned over him gifting them a simple chair.

She'd made that same mistake with Jim, and look how that had turned out.

She couldn't exactly withdraw the invitation, though, without having to make up some kind of explanation, so she did the next best thing. "Either way is fine. And if you'd rather I pick up the chair and save you a trip, I can do that."

"It's fine. I can bring it. I just don't want to intrude on family time. I know how important that must be."

Said as if he didn't know. Or maybe he just wanted to emphasize to her that he wasn't part of their family so she didn't get any funny ideas. He needn't worry, if that was the case.

She wasn't interested in making him part of it.

She took another drink of her beer, rocking in the chair. "You wouldn't be intruding." Time to change the subject. "So you've made six chairs. How many more do you have in the works?"

"Two. It's easier to cut out multiple parts at a time, while the machines are set up for them."

Who would he be giving those chairs to? None of her business. She didn't even want to think about another woman squealing at the sight of one of these rockers.

She cleared her throat. "That makes sense."

He leaned a hip on a workbench and watched her, his own beer making a trip or two to his lips and hanging there. Her mouth watered. The man was incredible, like a ginger Adonis, there was no denying that.

"So what was Vegas like?"

The question took her by surprise, although it shouldn't have. She'd had several people at the hospital ask the same.

"Vegas is kind of hard to describe. It's glitzy like what you see in advertisements, but there are also parts of it that are kind of rough."

"Kind of like Atlanta."

"Hmm…maybe, but in a different kind of way. It can be a great place to live. But it can also be hard when the reality of day-to-day life doesn't match up with the wealthy image."

One side of his mouth hiked a bit. "I could say the same about this city. I'm sure they both have their own sets of challenges, maybe just in different areas."

"Challenges. That's a great way to put it." She leaned her head against the back of the chair. "I can't believe how comfortable this is. I'll have to be careful or I could fall asleep."

She took the last drink of her beer, then let him take

the bottle and toss it along with his into a nearby recycling can.

"Not such a bad problem, is it?"

"It is when I still have to go pick up Alia later and get her some dinner."

He tucked his hands into his back pockets. "I'd better let you go then."

Except, Lyric didn't want to go. She wanted to stay here and learn more about him, while rocking in his luscious chair. She couldn't remember a time she'd felt so relaxed.

Had to be the beer.

Or the company.

No, definitely the beer.

She got up, her fingers lingering on the arm of the chair, then trailing across it as if loath to leave it here. And really, it was true.

"I'm really glad you like it."

"I love it." The words came from a place in her heart that she hadn't opened in a while. And with it came the slightest trickle of fear. What was she doing here? Was she falling for him? Or was it just about the chair?

Right now, she didn't know and she didn't care. All she knew was it seemed like he'd given her a glimpse into what made Ellis… Ellis. He'd trusted her with that, was willing to share a piece of it with her in the form of this chair. And she wasn't sure what to do with it.

They were about five feet from each other, and Lyric couldn't stop looking at him. Was suddenly remembering the shivery sensation of being in his arms with his mouth on hers. The impossible cascade of feelings that had come along with his touch. And the memory of that was…impossible to forget.

Not good. Not smart. But there it was.

"Lyric?"

His voice was low. Soft. A husky timbre she recognized from the images that were currently dancing in her head. And the look in his eyes...

Mesmerizing.

"Yes?" She barely squeezed the word out from between suddenly dry lips.

He was going to kiss her again.

And she was going to let him.

"How soon do you have to pick up Alia?"

"Not for almost an hour." Her breathing grew heavy as his question drew up all kinds of dangerous possibilities. None of them chaste. None of them platonic. But all of them hoping he was thinking what she was thinking.

One side of his mouth kicked up. "Sixty whole minutes."

She decided to tease him just a bit, although she still wasn't sure what he was getting at. "Time enough to build another chair?"

His chuckle was low and earthy. "Not quite what I had in mind. But watching you touch that chair..." His gaze skated over her. "Come here, Lyric."

Oh, yes. He was definitely thinking what she'd hoped he was thinking. There was no way he wasn't.

"Do I have dirt on my face?" She took a step or two closer, then his fingers were at her wrist hauling her against him.

"No. No dirt. Not even a speck."

Tilting her head to look back at him, she finally allowed herself to smile, her heart feeling lighter than it had in weeks. "Well since we only have an hour, Ellis, let's not spend it in idle chitchat."

"Idle? No, what I have in mind is anything but idle."
With that, he lowered his head and slid his lips over hers.

CHAPTER TEN

HE HADN'T BROUGHT her here to kiss her, but now that he was, he saw the folly in even thinking he'd be able to bring her here and *not* kiss her.

But for some reason, he'd needed her to see that chair. And in seeing her fingers slide across the warm wood... Well, it had brought all kinds of X-rated images alive in his head. He wanted those hands on him, doing the same things to his body. He wanted it all, to hell with the consequences. They were both adults. They could handle it.

And it wasn't like he was asking her for forever or anything.

That last thought created a little glimmer of doubt— doubt that was quickly erased by the sound she made in her throat when he deepened the kiss.

Ah, that sound. Luscious and heady. Just like the woman herself.

His teeth skimmed across her lower lip. She tasted of beer and mysterious things. Things he wanted to explore in depth. And he wanted to do it here in this room, where he spent most of his off time.

He'd been honest when he said he didn't spend a whole lot of time in the house, although Max was changing that out of necessity. And he'd never invited a woman to see his workshop before, had never felt the need. He'd done all he needed to do with them in his bedroom and then had sent them on their way the next day.

So why Lyric? And why here?

Not something he wanted to thinking about right now.

His hands smoothed up her back, the silky beige blouse sliding up, leaving warm, bare skin that his palm couldn't resist.

His other hand went to the back of her head, tipping it a bit more so that his lips could find her jawline and trail down the side of her neck, relishing every inch along the way.

Lyric moaned, and like her name, it was pure music.

"I want you," he groaned against her ear. "Here. Now."

Her answer was to bring his mouth back to hers, her kisses deep and wet and capable of stealing things he might not be able to get back.

Right now, he didn't care.

His arm curved around the small of her back, pressing her tight against him. He hoped to ease the ache that was growing harder to ignore.

But, hell, he didn't want to just throw her down and rush to the finish line. He had an hour. He wanted to use it. Every second of it. If he was going to regret this later on, he was going to make sure he had plenty of reasons to do so.

He walked her slowly backward toward the door, the only safe flat surface he could think of out here other than the bare concrete floor. And when he arrived at his destination, that ache he'd been trying to ignore became a drum that beat against him.

He couldn't remember his need being this damn strong. This damn impossible to control.

He gathered her hands in one of his and slowly raised them above her head. If she touched him right now, that control would be lost in an instant. And he wanted a whole lot more than an instant. He wanted the hour. Every single minute of it.

Looking into brown eyes that had gone completely dark, he leaned over and kissed the side of her nose, her mouth, the tip of her chin, before settling back on her mouth. This time, she arched toward him with a fierceness that made him harden beyond belief. He let her hands go so that he could haul her shirt over her head, tossing it to the ground in a hurry. Her lacy pink bra played peekaboo with what was underneath and hell if he didn't need that off, as well. He reached behind her and unhooked it, letting it fall.

As if needing to reciprocate, her fingers went to the buttons of his shirt and quickly undid them, pushing the fabric off his shoulders. She watched him as he shrugged out of it.

"God, Ellis, you're beautiful," she murmured, her fingers going to his skin and sliding over it. And, damn, it was as sexy as he'd imagined it moments ago.

"Beautiful. Not sure that's the word I'd use."

Her lips touched his chest just above his left nipple. "Oh, but it's the one *I'd* use."

Right now she could call him anything she wanted as long as this moment led to the next and the one after that. He unzipped her slacks and slid them down her thighs. She helped by stepping out of them, leaving her in her very last piece of clothing. And, God, if she wasn't the most gorgeous thing he'd ever seen. Those pink hipster briefs were the same lacy material as her bra had been, cradling her hips and exposing a very sexy bellybutton. He divested himself of his own trousers, kicking them to the side before remembering something.

Reaching down, he scooped them back up and grabbed his wallet, retrieving a packet from inside as she watched him from beneath dark lashes. Then before he could say anything, her thumbs hooked in the elastic waistline of her underwear, and she pushed them down in a smooth, sexy move he never could have imitated. And then they were off and she was reaching for his briefs.

"Wait. I'll do it." He was less sure of his control than ever before, and he had no idea why. He managed to get them off and rip the condom packet open, sheathing himself.

And then he was back, kissing her, wrapping his arm beneath her buttocks and hauling her against him. And that first touch of her skin against his was almost more than he could stand. She was warm and soft, and her curves cupped him in every way possible.

His mouth went to her nipple, pulling on it like he'd done with his beer a few moments earlier, his tongue sliding around the perimeter. The gritted sounds she made drove him on as he switched from one breast to the other before the needs of his own body threatened to overwhelm him. He needed this to be soon. He moved back to her lips and kissed her deep and long, his fingers sliding down her belly and finding the juncture between her thighs.

She was warm and wet, and dipping into her was like being wrapped in the finest silk.

"Lyric." He breathed her name as a red haze slowly enveloped him, but still he stayed where he was, stroking her with light touches, letting the sway of her hips guide him as to how soft or hard he went.

She reached for his other hand, twining her fingers in his as her gyrations became more and more sure, quickening her pace as he deepened his. "Oh! Ellis, don't stop. Don't stop…"

No way, sweetheart.

Her hips pushed against him in short jerky movements, seeking what his own body was dying to find. And then it came; he felt it roll over her in a wave that he could no longer resist. He lifted her into position and thrust into her, feeling her spasm against his flesh— molten hot, squeezing him tighter than he'd dreamed possible.

Damn!

He drove into her again and again, the door behind her shuddering in protest. He found her ear, biting the lobe, whispering nonsensical phrases against it that meant nothing and yet everything. A sudden wave of heat rolled through him, scorching everything in its path. His fingers tightened on her ass as he pumped and pumped until he had nothing left to give. And still he continued, desperate not to let this moment end.

But end it did, his breath sawing in his lungs, her arms wrapped solidly around his neck as if holding on for dear life.

He knew exactly how she felt.

Exactly.

And that scared him to death.

Lowering her slowly to the ground with a groan as he slid free, he tried to wrap his head around what had just happened.

He couldn't.

One moment they'd been looking at a rocking chair and the next...

The rush of pleasure over her reaction to his work. That's what it had been. Except deep down, he knew that wasn't completely true. There'd been that other kiss. The first one. And there'd been no chair in sight that time.

Maybe it was just the combination of everything that had happened over the last little while. That girl's death and Lyric's distress over it. Her surprise over learning that her project was going to be funded by the grant. The trip to the animal shelter and watching her with her niece. All of it had just squeezed up emotion he hadn't known he'd been capable of, balling it all up inside of him until he didn't know his right from his left.

Life was a whole lot easier when he'd had trouble getting attached to things.

Except he'd gotten attached to Max a lot quicker than he'd expected to.

But Lyric wasn't a cat, and getting attached to her or her niece would be...

Impossible.

With his baggage, he wouldn't be good for anyone. Not Lyric. And especially not Alia. So he needed to back off. As fast as he could.

He gathered her clothes without a word and handed them to her, turning his back as he found his own and put them on. When he pivoted to face her, she was pulled back together. Even her hair looked like she'd somehow combed it, the choppy locks all back where they'd been before this...incident.

Incident. That was a good word for it.

He needed to try to explain. To somehow let her know that this couldn't go any further than it had.

"Lyric, listen… I—"

She shook her head. "No, don't. I'm not sure where all of this came from, but it's okay. It happened. We're both adults. We'll just handle this the way adults do."

The same thing he'd told himself a few days ago.

"And how exactly is that?"

"We were both wired from everything that happened. It was going to come out one way or another. Our emotions found the quickest, easiest place and lanced themselves."

Lanced themselves.

Somehow that was not the explanation he'd been going for. "You make it sound like an infection."

She laughed, but it lacked the quick melodic ring of the other one. "Not what I meant—maybe I should have said it was a release valve. Is that better?"

The problem was, it wasn't. But it was as good an explanation as any.

"Yes." He dragged his hand through his hair and looked at her. "So we're good?"

"We are." She paused. "Now that we know this is a problem, we need to be on guard the next time something rises up…" Her voice trailed away—maybe she realized how that sounded.

And actually, he was in danger of something rising up all over again, if he wasn't careful. "Right. We'll be on guard. And make sure this never happens again."

Funny how those words came out sounding less than certain. Probably some crazy part of his brain holding onto the possibility of having sex with her again.

Because that's all it had been. Sex. Just like every other time with every other woman. So there was nothing to be worried about. No unfamiliar emotions boiling out of some secret cavern. Things were just as they always were, except he rarely had sex with coworkers because of how complicated it could become.

But this was different. Because they were on the same page. It was a mistake that wouldn't happen again. He would make sure of it. And he was pretty sure that Lyric would be guarding against any instant replays, as well.

So, yes, they were good.

They'd be able to rebound from this with ease and wind up exactly where they'd started.

Lyric spent the weekend on edge. What should have been easy to brush off had proven a lot more difficult than she'd thought. Not only had she been mulling over what had happened constantly, but she was also thinking about avoiding him at work on Monday. Or maybe he would be avoiding her. Whichever the case, she dreaded seeing him, which now looked like it would happen the day of the presentation. Ellis hadn't written back with his thoughts, although maybe he'd just been busy and hadn't had time.

But somehow she didn't think so. And if he decided he didn't want to weigh in, she would just have to go with what she had.

Unless she'd somehow blown her chances of getting any of that grant money by sleeping with him. Would he really do that? Withdraw her funding because of a stupid mistake? No, that would be vindictive, and that wasn't like him. She hadn't used what happened against him, nor would she. She'd been just as much to blame as he was. Maybe more. She'd sure been in a hurry to strip off her underwear...and his. In fact, he'd tried to stop her, from what she remembered.

She gulped. Maybe he hadn't wanted to continue at all, and she'd forced the issue.

Her mind leapfrogged over the events leading up to that moment, and she gave a shake of her head. No, he'd wanted it. His every movement had showed just how much. He'd even said he wanted her.

She shivered as the memory of those groaned words came back to her.

So what did she do? Text him and ask him point-blank if she was still invited to the ceremony? Call him and demand to have a face-to-face meeting?

No. That was one thing she didn't want. She'd prefer they leave things exactly where they'd left them. There was no need to revisit the subject and go over the same ground.

It was a one-time event. It hadn't meant anything to either of them. They were two consenting adults who'd shared an hour of pleasure.

A kind of unearthly pleasure actually. Sex with Jim or anyone else had never been that urgent. That unchained. She was pretty sure Ellis had a bit of a naughty side that he'd reined in, although she couldn't be sure. All she knew was that she'd been willing to experiment with anything he might want to dish out. And that was not like her at all.

Was that a good thing? Or bad.

Maybe it was neither. Maybe it just meant that she'd trusted him not to hurt her, that she believed he was as interested in her pleasure as he was his own. He'd proven that.

Not that it mattered. It was not happening again.

Not. Happening.

"Auntie Lyrie! Shiloh wants a treat."

Alia appeared around the corner, interrupting her thoughts. And she was glad. This was the exact reason sex with Ellis couldn't happen again. She could not risk this little girl being hurt. She'd already been through far more than a four-year-old should ever have to endure. She was not going to put her in a position where she'd experience another loss.

At least not right now. Maybe in a year or two, Lyric would be willing to explore a relationship, and keep Alia out of it until she was very sure it wouldn't implode like it had with Jim.

Ellis is not Jim.

She knew that, but it didn't change the fact that it was too soon. And Alia was too vulnerable. To look to her own needs without thinking about what was in her niece's best interest would be beyond selfish. So she was just going to sit tight. If Ellis wanted to be stupid about this, then she would simply look for a new job and remove herself from the situation.

She'd leave the ball in his court and see what he did.

What about the rocking chair?

She'd make it clear that he didn't have to give it to Alia. In fact, maybe it would be better if he didn't.

"Okay, sweetie. Let's go to the pantry and get her a treat. And maybe we'll get one for ourselves while we're at it."

Her phone pinged just as she'd sat to watch cartoons with Alia, both of them armed with bowls of vanilla ice cream.

Her heart in her throat, she got up and retrieved the phone from its charger and sat cross-legged on the sofa. Looking down at the screen, she saw Ellis's name in bold print, with the first few words of his text visible.

Just read your...

She clicked on the button to read the rest.

Just read your presentation. All sounds good. Will see you at the ceremony. The address is Fresher Food Products, Inc. Circle 3, Fresher Boulevard. The ceremony will be on the third floor, Room 3B. Any questions, give me a yell. Oh, and bring Alia. No problems there.

She sagged against the couch. So much for not caring whether or not she got the grant money. Of course she did. But even more than that, she'd cared that their time together might have ruptured their working relationship beyond repair. Evidently it hadn't. At least his text seemed to indicate that all was well on that front.

She genuinely liked the man. Respected him. She smiled. That was far removed from her first impression of him. But it was true. And she found that it mattered what he thought of her.

But why? She didn't really care about what Dave Butler thought about her. Maybe because it wouldn't affect her in any real way. She could simply get a new Realtor. But it was a little harder when you were forced to see someone on a daily basis whether you liked them or not.

Or was it more than that?

Ugh, Ly, stop doing this. You're going to drive yourself crazy.

At that moment, Shiloh decided to take a flying leap onto Lyric's arm, knocking her phone away, before she tried to dip her paw into Lyric's bowl of ice cream. "Oh, no, you little varmint. This is mine. You've already had plenty of treats. More than plenty."

Alia was spoiling the cat, but it didn't seem to be affecting Shiloh in any negative way. She was just as sweet and affectionate as she'd been at the shelter. More so, actually. And she was finding the same with Alia. Her niece was becoming more and more loving, adapting to her preschool and home life alike. And where she'd once been fearful and afraid of things that were not familiar, she was starting to explore the world around her with a curious air that made Lyric want to grab the child and hug her tight.

Which is exactly why she didn't want to upset the apple cart. And she wouldn't. Things were back to normal—as in before-sex-with-Ellis normal—and she fully intended to keep them that way.

Monday night came before she knew it, and Lyric smoothed her palms down over her black skirt and the same cream blouse she'd worn to Ellis's house. It was one of her best shirts and worked well in a variety of settings. She wasn't wearing it for him. If anything, she'd torn apart her closet hoping to find something she liked better. But she kept coming back to this same cream top.

And now it was too late to change her mind. Grasping Alia's hand in one of hers while holding the binder with her presentation in the other, she was suddenly a bundle of nervous energy. Why was she even here?

Because a girl had died, drumming into her psyche the need for this program. And chickening out would be both selfish and cowardly.

So she moved to the front desk and signed the register. The attendant issued her a badge. "Do you know where you're going?"

"3B on the third floor, right?"

"That's the one. You have about ten minutes before they start."

She'd cut it close, but was afraid that if she got here a half hour early and had to face Ellis she might actually have some kind of meltdown. She and Alia found the elevator and made their way to the third floor.

As soon as they entered the room, her gaze met familiar green eyes and all the dread she'd pushed down burst back to the surface, where it pooled in her belly and threatened to make her go back the way she'd come. But she didn't. Instead, she moved toward him, forcing a smile that she in no way felt.

"Hi." Her fingers tightened around Alia's hand.

"I wondered if you were going to come."

Perfect. In trying to protect herself she'd put him in the not-so-nice position of having to worry about whether she would put the grant in jeopardy. Not what she'd been going for.

"I'm sorry. I would have texted you if something came up."

"When you didn't respond to my text yesterday, I couldn't help but—" His eyes tracked over her blouse for a second before coming back up to meet her gaze.

She swallowed. He remembered.

Oh, yeah. The shirt had been a mistake. A big one.

Her frozen brain tried to retrace its steps. He'd said something about her not responding. Oh, God, that's right—she hadn't. "I'm sorry. Shiloh actually knocked the phone out of my hand as I was reading your text, and I got distracted. I totally forgot. Thanks for looking the presentation over. I really appreciate it. And I'm really, really nervous, can you tell?"

"I think you're going to rock their world."

His choice of words made her falter even more. Because he'd rocked hers, as well. From the moment he'd walked into it.

He got down on his haunches and met Alia's eyes. "How is Shiloh?"

Tiny fingers squeezed hers even tighter. "Shi Shi loves me."

"Yes she certainly does." He smiled. "Max is doing well, too."

"I like Max." The fingers eased their grip. Lyric hadn't even been sure if the child would remember the other cat once they left the shelter, but she'd asked about him several times. Only there was no way she was going to take her niece to his house to visit. Because it would just bring back memories of what she'd done there.

Because she knew she was in danger of wanting to do it again. That had just been proven when his glance had swept across her shirt and she'd seen the memories parade through those green eyes. Was that why she'd worn it? Because deep down she'd wanted to see if he'd react to it?

Surely not.

God. But what if that really was the reason?

The moderator went to the podium and asked everyone to take their seats. There weren't many people here, maybe fifteen. Lyric wasn't sure if they were all employees of Fresher Foods or if there were other grant recipients besides New Mercy.

She soon had her answer when the speaker mentioned two other organizations that had been awarded matching grants. This food company must have pretty big pockets. Thankfully there weren't a hundred people here. The more intimate setting made it a little less intimidating. At least it would be until they called her name.

Ellis glanced at her and said in a low voice, "Are you okay?"

Not really, but what could she say? *I think I'm falling for you and the ramifications of that scares me to death?*

No. She was not going to confess anything.

"I'm fine. Just a little nervous." She glanced at Alia, who was happily using a blue crayon in her animal coloring book. "Are you sure you don't mind watching her when I'm up there?"

"I don't."

New Mercy would be the last to give their presentations and as she listened to the other recipients she was amazed at the great causes that were out there. Each presenter was eloquent and seemed completely at home speaking before this group; they probably did this all the time. Ellis had said he'd done this before, too.

But she hadn't.

Then it was his turn, and the moment Ellis started talking, she was captivated. This man seemed to master everything he took on with ease. He was a great doctor, was able to turn slabs of wood into gorgeous creations, cared enough for a sick and injured cat to give him a home and had made love to her with a passion that had taken her breath away.

He had. Literally. Taken her breath away.

And right now she having trouble breathing again, because she was very, very afraid that she'd done something irreversible. Something that might destroy everything she'd hoped to build here in Atlanta.

She swallowed. And swallowed again. But she couldn't rid herself of that nagging lump in her throat. The one that bobbed up and down and refused to go away.

She was in love with him.

She couldn't be. She shouldn't be. They'd only known each other a matter of weeks.

But she was. And somehow she was going to have to stop it. Before it got out of control. Before he found out the truth.

All too soon, Ellis was leaving the podium and they were calling her to speak.

Bile rolled around inside of her and threatened to make her bolt from the room. But she couldn't. Alia was here. Even worse, if she ran, he would surely come after her and demand to know what was wrong. And there was no way she wanted him to find out like that. She didn't want him to find out at all.

But he was bound to, wasn't he?

Maybe. But not right now.

She got up and waited until he took her spot next to Alia, who grinned up at him with a smile that nearly broke Lyric's heart. What had she done?

It wasn't about what she'd done. It was now about what she was *going* to do. She couldn't go back to Vegas. So she was going to have to stay here and somehow weather this. Her only saving grace was the fact that Ellis clearly didn't feel the same way about her as she did about him.

She trudged up the steps, knuckles white on her binder as she reached the podium. It was okay. It was going to be okay. She just needed to keep it together.

She opened the binder and started to speak.

CHAPTER ELEVEN

LYRIC HAD DONE an amazing job on her presentation. He couldn't remember ever feeling more proud of someone as she smiled at the right spots and leaned forward to tell Alisha's story to the board members of Fresher Foods. There was a round of applause when she finished, and several people got to their feet.

She walked calmly down the steps and made her way back to where he sat, but there was a stiffness to her that hadn't been there earlier. This was her first time doing this kind of thing, but he was pretty sure it wouldn't be her last, once Jack had heard how well she'd done.

Ellis moved over to take his original seat so she could sit next to Alia. The little girl put her hand in Lyric's and smiled up at her aunt.

He remembered when he'd thought Alia was like he'd been at her age, losing her mom to circumstances she had no control over. But she wasn't. This child was a lot more well-adjusted than he'd been at her age. He didn't remember much before his mom left, but maybe something had happened even before she'd been taken away that had caused him to be the way he was. Maddie had been a wonderful guardian and in the end her love had helped pull him back from the brink. Maybe it was what had caused him to be a useful member of society. Who knew what he would have become without her.

"You did great, Lyric. Jack and everyone else will be thrilled about the way things went."

She nodded, not quite meeting his eyes. Was she still worried about what had happened between them? She needn't be. After some soul-searching he'd come to the conclusion that it hadn't been the tragedy he'd initially thought. In fact, a tiny portion of his brain had thrown out the idea that maybe it wasn't bad at all. He'd done a lot of changing since they'd first met. Enough to have a shot at a normal life?

Who knew?

Maybe, if they took things slowly, they could see each other socially from time to time and get to know each other.

He would talk to her about it once they got out of here. Except she had Alia with her. So maybe it would be better to wait until tomorrow at work.

Except that wasn't the kind of conversation he wanted to have at the hospital, either. He could ask if he could go back with them to her place to talk. She could put Alia to bed, and he could tell her what he was thinking. But first they had to get through the rest of the ceremony.

And it wasn't quite as short as he'd hoped it would be. There were pictures to be taken. Hands to be shaken. And the board had seemed thrilled that Alia was there, several of them going out of their way to talk to her.

Another half hour went by before it was over. Then they were out of the building and on the sidewalk out front. Lyric started to say goodbye, but he smiled at her and nodded down at Alia. "I actually have something I'd like to talk to you about."

"About the presentation?"

"No. It's actually about…the other night."

She stiffened, her hand going to Alia's shoulder and pulling her close. Maybe she was afraid he was going to say something in front of the child.

"I don't understand."

Somehow he had to undo all of the stuff he'd said the other night, but he wasn't quite sure how to go about it. "I just wanted to clarify a few things, but I'd rather not do that at work if it's okay."

"Definitely okay." She seemed to relax just a bit. "Do you want to come to the house? To talk?"

Hell, hopefully she didn't think he wanted to pounce on her. He did—especially after seeing her in that silky blouse again—but that wasn't his reason for wanting to talk to her. And if he had any hope of testing the waters, he had to do it right this time. Friendship first. And then slowly move forward.

He followed her to her house and spent a half hour visiting with Alia and playing with Shiloh while the child thought of different scenarios and laughed as he acted them out. It was really the first time he'd interacted with a child outside of his office and it was a lot easier than he'd expected it to be. Lyric sat on the couch and watched without saying much, glancing at her watch periodically. Was she grading him?

Finally she got up and announced, "Time for bed, Alia. Say good-night to Ellis and Shiloh."

"But I want Shiloh to sleep with me."

Lyric smiled at her. "We talked about this, remember? If Shiloh wants to sleep with you, she will. We're not going to force her to do something she doesn't want to do."

"Okay…" The word was said with such overt disappointment that he couldn't help but smile. He'd never seen himself as wanting to be a father, but there was a hint of the tide starting to turn in a different direction.

Slowly, Ellis. Or this is not going to work.

He didn't try to insert himself into their bedtime ritual, sensing his presence might not be welcomed. Instead, he went and sat on the couch and waited for Lyric to reemerge.

He liked watching her with Alia. Liked how earnest she was and how much she adored the child, while not giving in to every little whim the little girl had. Like saying she wanted Shiloh to sleep with her.

Lyric had been smart.

If Shiloh wants to sleep with you, she will. We're not going to force her to do something she doesn't want to do.

A good thing for him to remember. This whole half-baked plan of his would only work if Lyric wanted it too. He wasn't going to try to twist her arm or talk her in to something she didn't want to do. If she wanted to explore what had happened between them, she would.

A few minutes later she came back out and glanced at him. "Drink? Sorry I don't have beer, or really anything besides tea, juice or coffee."

"No, I'm good, thanks. Any problems putting her to bed?"

"Not really, she wanted to stay out here with you, but she finally went down." She twirled an earring, and he focused on the act. She was nervous. He smiled. He was a little nervous himself. He needed to do this now, or he never would.

"And you. Do you want to stay out here with me?"

She sat. On one of the chairs, not on the couch next to him. Not a good sign. "I'm not sure what you mean."

He knew she didn't. And he wasn't exactly sure what he wanted. Only that he was willing to explore the possibilities without making any explicit promises.

"I don't think we really resolved what happened the other night. We both talked around it, and maybe even shut things down prematurely."

"Prematurely. How exactly did we do that?"

"Neither one of us expected that night to play out the way it did. I think we were both shocked by how quickly one thing led to another. And the aftermath was…maybe us being afraid to look it in the face and see it for what it was." He pulled in a deep breath. "So what I'd like to propose is that we maybe could go out periodically. Get to know one another. Become friends. And see what happens."

There was a long pause before she responded.

"Friends. You mean like friends with benefits?" The look in her eyes sent ice water shooting through his veins.

"Not exactly. We don't have to do anything more than get to know each other. At least at first."

"So where 'exactly' do you see this 'getting to know each other' going?"

There was something buzzing in the background, but he wasn't sure what it was.

"I don't have a set plan or a timetable. Maybe we'll get to know each other and then decide we have nothing in common. Or…maybe we'll decide we do."

She closed her eyes, and when they reopened, she leaned forward, her fingers gripping together. "And where will Alia be while all of this deciding is going on? All of the maybe-we-will, maybe-we-won't scenarios."

"I don't follow."

"Ellis, that little girl is my world, and she deserves

every tiny bit of happiness I can give her. And that can't happen if there is someone lurking in the background who may or may not become a permanent fixture in her life." She bit her lip. "If I said yes, and we started dating—with or without your 'set plan' in mind, and then you decide it doesn't work for you, what happens to her?"

"Nothing."

"Wrong. You saw her tonight. It would only take a hot minute for her to get attached to you. If—and probably when—this thing falls flat on its face, you won't be the one standing there watching someone she cares about walk away. It'll be Alia... She'll be absolutely devastated." Her voice wavered so much she stopped and took a couple of breaths. "And I'm not willing to put her through that."

An arrow shot straight through him, rendering him immobile for several long seconds. Isn't that what had happened with his mom when he was five years old? Hadn't she turned and walked away from him without looking back? And look how that had turned out. It had almost destroyed him.

Lyric was right. He was not going to be the guy who did that to someone else. And at this moment in time, he couldn't promise her that he wouldn't. He wasn't even sure he was capable of true, self-sacrificing love. But Lyric was. He'd seen it in the way she tried to save her sister—had done everything in her power to get help for her. He also saw it in her love for her niece. She was willing to make whatever sacrifices she needed to make sure that little girl got off to a good start in life.

Wasn't that why he went into pediatrics in the first place?

The least he could do was follow the example she'd

set and turn and walk away before it hurt that little girl. Or her aunt.

So he took a deep breath and said the words he needed to say.

"You're right, Lyric. Absolutely right. I'm sorry I didn't see it before now. As far as I'm concerned, this discussion and what we shared the other day never happened. We'll go back to work and put this behind us once and for all. And from this point forward, I think it best if we don't interact outside of the hospital. Dr. Radner can go on the rest of the research trips with you." Each word sent a burst of acid into his stomach, but it was better to do this now than risk hurt to her or Alia further down the line. "She'll be a better judge of the population segment, anyway."

"Thank you for understanding."

He understood. All too well. He only wished he'd seen it before coming over here. Because despite saying that they could go back to working together, he wasn't at all sure that was possible. And so he was going to take some time to think things through before making any kind of impulsive decisions. And he knew the perfect solution for all involved.

The next two days flew by without any sign of Ellis, for which she was profoundly glad. She'd been wracked by uncertainty over the way they'd left things. But what else could she do? To make matters worse, Jack has asked Lyric to stop by his office sometime before five o'clock. Was it about Ellis? Had he somehow found out?

The hours crawled by, and a couple of times she'd been tempted to text Ellis to see if he'd told the administrator about what had happened between them. Maybe he'd seen it as some kind of ethical dilemma.

Although she'd started a text a couple of times, she ultimately didn't want to have to interact with him unless it was absolutely necessary. It hurt too much. He'd as much as admitted that he didn't know how he felt about her. It had been a slap in the face. A reminder of how she'd misjudged Jim, thinking he would eventually want more from their relationship. But it had never happened.

This was best for all involved. Even if it felt like a hot poker being stabbed into her heart.

Finally, around four thirty, she made her way to Jack's office and sat in one of the chairs that were so similar to the ones in Ellis's office.

"I just wanted to congratulate you in person."

She blinked, not sure what he was talking about. "Is this about…?"

"About your presentation? Yes. Ellis said you did an excellent job, that everyone at Fresher Foods loved you."

"Well, I don't know about that…" He'd praised her to Jack? After their talk she was surprised that he had anything good to say about her at all. Then again, maybe he was better at separating his private life from his professional life. A skill she obviously had not developed.

"I called them. And they confirmed everything he said. I just wanted to say how glad we are that you've joined this hospital."

"Well, thank you. I like it here, as well." She hesitated before deciding to say something. "Ellis is a great department head."

"Yes, he has been. His are going to be some hard shoes to fill."

Shock left her speechless for several seconds before she managed to respond. "I don't understand. Is he leaving?"

Jack frowned. "Didn't he tell you? Ellis decided to take a teaching sabbatical. He said something personal had come up, and he needed to take a break from the hospital."

A landslide happened somewhere inside of her, rocks tumbling one over the other and piling up in her stomach until she could barely breathe. Something personal? There was no way that could be a coincidence. He'd left because of the talk they'd had, although he never even hinted that he was thinking about leaving.

"When will he be back?"

"Officially, his sabbatical is for three months, but…"

From the way the administrator's voice trailed away, he didn't think Ellis was coming back. It was there in the fingers tapping on his desk, in the tight set to his jaw.

"Did he say why?"

"Nope. Just that he needed some personal time."

So nothing about her. She should be relieved, but strangely the only thing she felt was regret. "I'm sure he has his reasons."

"I'm sure he does. I just wish he would have told me what they were."

Lyric wasn't about to admit that she was pretty sure she knew the reasons. But to leave the hospital? If anything, he should have asked her to leave instead. But she'd naively believed him when he said they could go back to the way things were.

Or had she? Wasn't that why she'd tried to avoid him for the past couple of days? Which now seemed ludicrous, since he wasn't even at the hospital.

"Where's he teaching?"

"At one of our satellite hospitals in Brunswick."

Wasn't that a long way from Atlanta? She wasn't all

that familiar with the geography of the state, but was pretty certain he wouldn't have just moved across town.

No, this was permanent. And she had herself to blame. All she could do was nod her understanding at Jack and excuse herself before she blurted out the truth. Which would help no one. As she left, she tried to tell herself this was for the best, when what she really knew was that she was going to miss him. Terribly.

CHAPTER TWELVE

HER MOM AND dad carried in Alia's birthday cake as they all sang to the child. Her mom had pulled her aside when they'd arrived yesterday and asked if anything was wrong.

Everything was wrong, but crying about it to her mom was not going to change anything. Ellis was gone. Probably for good. And true to what she'd thought, Alia had gotten over him, quickly.

Too bad Lyric hadn't been able to bounce back just as easily. She plastered on a smile and sang the final phrase of the song, clapping along with her parents as Alia blew out the candles on her cake, Shiloh keeping a close eye on the proceedings.

They cut the cake and sat at the table to eat, Lyric telling her parents about everything under the sun except for a certain pediatrician. It would be okay. Eventually. And by the time Ellis came back—*if* he decided to come back—she would be used to living life without seeing him on a daily basis. Surely that would be her new normal, and they would become just two colleagues who'd once done something so incredibly impulsive that they'd be able to laugh about it.

But right now, the last thing she felt like was laughing.

The doorbell rang, snapping her out of her stupor.

"I'll get it," her mother said, heading to the door. She opened it and stood there for a minute or two. "Honey do you have a tip?" The comment was directed at her father.

"I have some money, Mom." She wasn't exactly sure what she needed it for, since they hadn't ordered take-out, and she couldn't remember ordering anything off the internet.

Her dad beat her to the punch, as he always did. But when he came back, he wasn't empty-handed. He was carrying a chair. A familiar, beautiful chair with a wide back and a rocker at the bottom. Across the arms was a big red ribbon and a tag that said, Happy Birthday, Alia.

She stood stock-still. God. She knew that chair. Had sat in it, had slid her fingers over it in his workshop.

It was Ellis's.

Surely he knew she wouldn't expect him to give Alia that chair after all that had happened.

A huge lump formed in her throat as she took off the simple tag and studied the strong slashes that formed the letters. Ellis had written this. He'd had to have gone home to make out the card, at least. But he hadn't de-livered it in person.

He'd taken her words at face value. And she'd meant them when she said them, but...

Had she judged him unfairly because of what had happened with Jim, assuming motives where there were none?

But there was still Alia to consider. He could still hurt her without trying.

Hell, so could Lyric. She could do something stu-pid and hurt her, too. Or her mom or dad or any other human being on the planet. She'd sat there while he talked, but had she really listened, or had she heard only what she wanted to hear? What the filter of the past allowed her to hear?

"This is gorgeous, Lyric. But there's no name on the tag."

Her dad carried the chair to the center of the room. "It looks handmade."

"I know who it's from, Mom. And, yes, it's handmade." She bit her lip, trying to form her thoughts into something cohesive and failing completely. "It was actually made by a friend."

Her mom's face cleared. "A *guy* friend?"

She laughed, although it was shaky. "Yes. A *guy* friend." She turned to Alia. "This is from Ellis. It's for you. He thought you could rock Shiloh on it."

"Ellis has Max."

"Yes, he does." Had he taken the cat with him to Brunswick? Or was Max at the house by himself?

It was Saturday. Was he home for the weekend?

Suddenly she knew she had to find out. And she wanted to sit down and talk to him and let him explain what he'd meant before. This time, she would listen, not only with her mind, but also with her heart.

"I hate to ask this, but could you both watch Alia for me for about an hour? There's something I need to do."

"Right now?" her dad asked.

Her mom put her hand on his arm with a look. "It's okay, honey. Go."

So she threw a smile at both of them and gave Alia a hug before walking out the door and heading to her car.

Ellis's lathe spun with a fury born out of frustration. And regret. He probably shouldn't have sent that rocking chair to Lyric. She'd made it pretty damn clear that she didn't want a relationship with him, but that didn't mean *he* didn't want one.

Over the past month, his heart had paced in his chest, listing all the reasons they should be together. But none of that mattered, because in the end, she hadn't wanted to be with him. He understood the reasons, but after doing some soul-searching, he realized he would not have just turned and walked out on that little girl. In his heart of hearts he'd believed they should be together. He just hadn't wanted to rush in like a bull in a china shop. And the second he'd said the word *friend* her whole face had changed.

A week after he'd arrived in Brunswick the truth had hit him. He loved her. He'd wanted to take it slow to give himself a chance to adjust to that fact. To believe it was possible for him to love.

Now he knew he could, but it was too late. He carved the spindle to his newest creation, only this time it wouldn't be a rocking chair. He was done with those forever. This time he was making a headboard.

The door to his workshop cracked open a hair and at first he thought Max had somehow gotten out of the house and was trying to get in, until it opened the rest of the way and Lyric stood in the opening.

He stared for a minute before realizing his tool was still spinning, putting a huge gouge in what he'd been working on.

He shut down the machine, the space going quiet in a matter of seconds.

"Did the chair arrive okay?"

"It did. And Alia loves it, thank you." She hesitated then moved farther into the space. "I was hoping you might be home."

"Why?" He didn't move from where he sat. He

wasn't sure why she was here, but there was no way he was laying his heart on the table again.

"Because I didn't like the way we left things."

Something began spinning, but it wasn't his lathe this time. It was inside of him. "What part didn't you like?"

She came another step closer until she stood in front of his chair. "The part where you left."

"It's what you said I'd do. I figured better now than later."

"I know I said it. But I think I may have been wrong. My heart didn't want you to go, even though my head said it was for the best." She gave a tired laugh. "I found out that my head doesn't always know what it's talking about."

He sat there for a minute. "Before this goes any further, I need you to know something."

"Okay."

"I do know what it's like to have someone walk away and be the one left standing there. The one who's left devastated."

"You do?"

He shrugged. "My mom left when I was five. She gave me to a friend of hers, and I never saw her again. So, yes, I know what it's like. And when you talked about Alia being hurt, I told myself I wasn't going to be like my mom and cause someone else the pain I'd felt. It was only after I went on sabbatical that I realized I was right. I wouldn't. I would never put someone through what I'd gone through. Especially not a child."

"I think I know that now. I'm sorry, Ellis."

"Don't be. I realize I went about it the wrong way, but I needed to be sure. I had what they called an attachment disorder when I was a child—probably because of what happened—and so it's hard for me to believe in my ability to love. And I didn't want to commit until I knew for sure that I could. That I wouldn't hurt you or Alia."

"I had no idea you'd gone through that." She picked up one of his hands, her fingertips skating across his calluses. "But what if your heart didn't lose its ability to love? What if it just grew calluses to protect itself from being hurt? Like your hands did."

Calluses. He'd never thought about it that way.

She went on. "I think maybe I have calluses, too." She looked him in the eye. "But I no longer want them to stop me from loving. I need to know what you feel for me exactly. And what you hope to feel in the future."

"Why?"

"Because I love you, and I think I shut you out before you could sand those calluses away and discover was underneath them. I meant what I said about Alia. I don't want her hurt, but if you think you could come to love me…"

"I can't 'come to.'" At the stricken look on her face, he hurried to finish. "I can't, because I'm already there. I didn't know for sure the night we talked, but I do now. I'm sorry I wasn't able to express myself well enough to make you understand that I wasn't walking away. I was finally walking *to* something, even if my steps were a little tentative."

"You love me?"

"I do."

Her hand gripped his tighter. "So you're willing to give me—to give us, me *and* Alia—another chance?"

"Only if you're willing to forgive my rough start and trust me to finish well. Trust me to never walk away."

"I do."

He curled his arm around her waist and slowly reeled her in, before stopping. "Where's Alia?"

"She's at the house. My mom and dad are watching her."

"Your mom and dad. I've met your mom. I guess I should meet your dad, too."

She smiled. "Yes. But not right this second. Right now, I want you all to myself. I love you, Ellis."

"I second everything you just said." He lifted her palm and pressed his lips to it. "From now on we only grow calluses here."

"It's a deal."

This time when he kissed her it wasn't on her palm. It was on her mouth. And when they finally came up for air, Ellis gave her a smile that he hoped contained everything his heart wanted to say. Because he was ready to shed his calluses one at a time and trust that she would wait as he completed the process. Because he had no intention of going anywhere.

He was home. Finally and truly...home.

EPILOGUE

LYRIC PRESSED A protective hand to the rounded bump of her stomach as her husband slowly put his phone on the bedside table. After six months of marriage, they'd decided to add a baby to their little family. She'd also decided to take a leave of absence from her job at the hospital to work on her drug-prevention program, which—while still in its infancy—showed a lot of promise.

"Ellis? What's wrong?"

He lowered himself into the rocker and shook his head. "That was someone from the FBI."

"What?" A spike of fear went through her.

"My mom…"

Ellis had told her the full story about how his mom had been taken away when he was five. She'd been devastated for him, unable to imagine what he must have gone through. At least Lyric knew what had happened to her sister, not that it made it any easier. "Did they find out what happened to her?"

Max came into the room and jumped in Ellis's lap as if he also knew something was wrong. The two cats had both become beloved family members, though it was clear Max loved Ellis the most.

Her husband stroked the cat's fur as Lyric sat across from him on the bed.

His eyes came up and she could swear she saw moisture in those gorgeous green depths. "I think she's alive, Lyric. My mom's alive."

She reached across and gripped one of his hands. "How? Where?"

She wasn't sure whether to be ecstatic or furious with the woman who'd abandoned her own child, leaving him to face a wealth of pain. Alone.

"My father was evidently a mobster. She testified against him. But before she did, she hid me with Maddie and made her FBI handler promise to give me a new identity, along with Maddie and herself."

"And they're just now telling you this?"

"She was convinced my father would try to find me, even from prison, and thought the only way to keep me safe was to leave me behind." He gave a visible swallow. "She sacrificed herself so that I could grow up far away from that life."

Lyric's free hand went to her chest. "That's what I wanted to do for Alia. Get her away from anything that could link her back to my sister and that way of life."

"Exactly."

"Wow, it's so hard to fathom… Where is she?"

"California. My dad died in prison a week ago. So the danger to her is evidently over. She asked her handler to contact me and ask if I wanted to see her."

"You do, don't you?"

"I don't know, Lyric. I really don't."

Her fingers traced the area just below his fingers with a smile. "Calluses, Ellis. Calluses."

One side of his mouth quirked in that crooked smile she loved so much.

"Point taken. I'm not sure I want her in our lives, though. We're just getting started. And she—"

"She loves you, Ellis. Can you imagine how hard it must have been to leave behind your child, possibly for the rest of your life? To protect him the only way you knew how?"

"I think somewhere along the way, I realized that. On some level. It was the only way I could allow myself the freedom to love you like I do. And I do love you. And Alia and now Sarah."

"I know you do." They'd decided to name the baby after Lyric's maternal grandmother.

"So, you think we should meet her?"

"I do. But if you need some time to process it, it's okay."

He reached up and slid his hand behind her nape, pressing his forehead to hers, even as Max abandoned his post and stalked from the room. "What did I ever do to deserve you?"

"The same thing I did to deserve you. We're two people in love. And it looks like we may be growing our family in more ways than just this baby."

He pulled back to look at her. "Will you go with me? To meet her, I mean."

"I will if you want me to." She put her finger to his lips. "But as far as names go, you will always be Ellis Rohal to me, no matter what your birth name may have been."

"What if it's something really cool, like Brad or Johnny?"

"I think Ellis is pretty darned cool. And it suits you."

He kissed her. "God, I love you."

"I love you, too."

With that he stood and reached a hand out to help

her up. Then they turned and headed out to the living room, where Lyric's mom and dad were playing with Alia and trying to keep Shiloh from chasing Max. Their household was pure chaos, but that was okay, because it was *their* chaos.

And no matter how things turned out with Ellis's mom, they would face it together.

Because that was what love did.

* * * * *

COMING SOON!

We really hope you enjoyed reading this book. If you're looking for more romance, be sure to head to the shops when new books are available on

Thursday 20th August

To see which titles are coming soon, please visit

millsandboon.co.uk/nextmonth

MILLS & BOON

Coming next month

THE VET'S SECRET SON
Annie O'Neil

Lucas threw Ellie a confused look and caught a flare of guilt lance through her green eyes. She looked pale, her hands shaking as she feebly tried to wave away her white lie. He looked back at the little boy, registered his hair colour, his eye colour, the way they sloped a bit, like his mother's...and his. Almond shaped, he called them. Sleepy sexy, Ellie had called them. He had the strangest feeling of déjà vu. As if he was looking at a photo of himself from when he had been a little boy.

He tried to estimate the little boy's age and then, with the power of a lightning strike, he got it.

Maverick was his son.

His heart crashed against his ribcage with a ferocity he wouldn't have believed possible.

One look at Ellie, eyes bright with a sheen of tears, and he knew he was right.

Trying his best not to frighten the boy, who quite clearly did not know Lucas was his father, he knelt down in front of him, took the paper and signed it, drawing in his signature pawprint at the end of the 's' in Williams.

This was not the way he'd expected to meet his son. Not even close.

He felt Ellie's eye boring into him throughout the short interlude.

When he looked up at her, she was shaking her head, No, no, no—don't you dare tell him.

So what was he meant to do? Leave?

Not a chance.

Emotions assaulted him like knife wounds. Elation. Pride. Loss at having missed so many precious moments. His birth. His first word. His first tooth. Disbelief that Ellie had kept Maverick a secret all these years.

He knew things hadn't ended with any sort of grace between them but hiding a child? His child? What the hell had she been thinking? This gorgeous little boy was his flesh and blood. More than any of their shared hopes and dreams, Ellie knew he'd wanted a family of his own. With her! But life had ripped that possibility away from him.

And now, thanks to her, he'd missed the first five years of his son's life.

He forced his raging thoughts into a cage as he reminded himself, thanks to Ellie, he had a son. A beautiful, healthy, happy little boy. But at this moment? The gratitude ended there. She should have told him.

He rose and looked her straight in the eye. 'You and I need to talk.'

Continue reading
THE VET'S SECRET SON
Annie O'Neil

Available next month
www.millsandboon.co.uk

WE'RE LOOKING FOR NEW AUTHORS FOR THE MILLS & BOON MEDICAL SERIES!

Whether you're a published author or an aspiring one, our editors would love to read your story.

You can submit the synopsis and first three chapters of your novel online, and find out more about the series, at **harlequin.submittable.com/submit**

We read all submissions and you do not need to have an agent to submit.

IF YOU'RE INTERESTED, WHY NOT HAVE A GO?

Submit your story at:
harlequin.submittable.com/submit

MILLS & BOON